Alexander Thom und Co.

Return of judicial rents fixed

Notified to Irish Land Commission, December 1883

Alexander Thom und Co.

Return of judicial rents fixed
Notified to Irish Land Commission, December 1883

ISBN/EAN: 9783742805942

Manufactured in Europe, USA, Canada, Australia, Japa

Cover: Foto ©Andreas Hilbeck / pixelio.de

Manufactured and distributed by brebook publishing software
(www.brebook.com)

Alexander Thom und Co.

Return of judicial rents fixed

Irish Land Commission.

The Land Law (Ireland) Act, 1881, 44 & 45 Victoria, ch. 49

RETURN

ACCORDING TO PROVINCES AND COUNTIES

OF

JUDICIAL RENTS

FIXED BY

SUB-COMMISSIONS

AND

CIVIL BILL COURTS,

AS NOTIFIED TO THE IRISH LAND COMMISSION DURING THE MONTH OF

DECEMBER, 1883,

SPECIFYING DATES AND AMOUNTS RESPECTIVELY OF THE LAST INCREASES OF RENT WHERE ASCERTAINED;

ALSO

RENTS FIXED UPON THE REPORTS OF VALUERS APPOINTED BY THE IRISH LAND COMMISSION ON THE JOINT APPLICATIONS OF LANDLORDS AND TENANTS.

Presented to both Houses of Parliament by Command of Her Majesty.

DUBLIN:
PRINTED BY ALEX. THOM & CO. (LIMITED), 87, 88, & 89, ABBEY-STREET,
THE QUEEN'S PRINTING OFFICE.

To be purchased, either directly or through any Bookseller, from any of the following Agents, viz.:
Messrs. HANSARD, 13, Great Queen-street, W.C., and 32, Abingdon-street, Westminster;
Messrs. EYRE and SPOTTISWOODE, East Harding-street, Fleet-street, and Sale Office, House of Lords;
Messrs. ADAM and CHARLES BLACK, of Edinburgh;
Messrs. ALEXANDER THOM and Co. (Limited), or Messrs. HODGES, FIGGIS, and Co., of Dublin.

1884.

INDEX.

COUNTY.

ANTRIM, ...

ARMAGH, ...

CARLOW, ...

CAVAN, ...

CLARE, ...

CORK, ...

DONEGAL, ...

DOWN, ...

FERMANAGH, ...

GALWAY, ...

KERRY, ...

KILDARE, ...

KILKENNY, ...

KING'S, ...

LEITRIM, ...

LIMERICK, ...

LONDONDERRY, ...

LONGFORD, ...

MAYO, ...

MEATH, ...

MONAGHAN, ...

QUEEN'S, ...

ROSCOMMON, ...

SLIGO, ...

TIPPERARY, ...

TYRONE, ...

WATERFORD, ...

SUMMARY.

Showing, according to Counties and Provinces, the Number of Cases in which Judicial Rents have been Fixed by Sub-Commissions during the Month of December, 1889; and also the Acreage, Tenement Valuation, Former Rents, and Judicial Rents of the Holdings.

	Number of Cases in which Judicial Rents have been fixed.	Acreage.	Tenement Valuation.	Former Rent.	Judicial Rent.
		Statute Acres. A. R. P.	£ s. d.	£ s. d.	£ s. d.
ULSTER—					
Antrim, ...	359	7,304 0 1	4,606 18 1	5,768 11 7	4,612 16 2
Armagh, ...	390	3,972 0 39	3,835 6 0	4,109 6 8½	3,171 5 3
Cavan, ...	84	1,612 0 33	1,079 19 9	1,339 9 2	1,084 0 11
Donegal, ...	716	6,366 0 16	1,889 13 6	2,370 17 9	1,860 4 1
Down, ...	13	690 2 13	518 15 0	535 13 6	724 10 3
Fermanagh, ...	101	2,946 1 35	1,831 16 0	1,587 1 5	1,345 6 6
Londonderry, ...	6	153 0 32	76 0 0	93 16 0	65 6 0
Monaghan, ...	65	1,478 0 38	1,065 3 0	1,209 8 0½	966 0 6
Tyrone, ...	816	6,505 0 14	3,169 18 0	3,768 1 8	3,018 9 3
Total, ...	1,530	30,137 0 13	17,693 7 7	21,122 8 3	16,618 5 0
LEINSTER—					
Carlow, ...	5	69 3 35	29 16 0	63 13 8	39 1 6
Kildare, ...	1	11 3 8	11 16 0	19 0 0	19 0 0
King's, ...	45	2,205 0 25	1,139 11 0	1,447 16 1	1,156 5 8
Longford, ...	43	1,065 3 26	600 13 0	960 19 0	730 18 6
Meath, ...	1	9 2 37	6 5 0	7 16 2	6 6 0
Queen's, ...	55	2,618 3 3	1,358 11 8	2,001 12 7	1,615 19 0
Total, ...	148	5,987 0 9	3,146 13 8	4,593 17 6	3,577 7 8
CONNAUGHT—					
Galway, ...	311	3,509 2 16½	1,169 11 6	2,377 8 6½	1,738 1 3
Leitrim, ...	116	2,663 2 20	943 19 6	1,320 11 0	1,080 15 7
Mayo, ...	130	8,713 1 22½	2,302 14 0	3,300 3 3	3,162 18 11½
Roscommon, ...	10	223 1 2	96 3 0	135 10 4	105 16 0
Sligo, ...	116	2,678 0 11½	1,065 17 0	1,366 17 0	1,119 0 0
Total, ...	686	17,903 3 31½	6,463 5 0	6,900 9 0½	7,162 10 9½
MUNSTER—					
Clare, ...	179	6,058 0 34	3,670 19 9	5,009 11 9½	4,155 7 3
Cork, ...	194	8,967 1 15	3,974 14 3	5,791 0 0	5,101 11 7
Kerry, ...	57	4,030 1 29	1,194 10 6	2,118 5 5	1,911 16 8
Limerick, ...	11	567 3 23	947 15 0	353 11 0	315 4 8
Tipperary, ...	97	3,824 0 2	2,816 12 0	2,931 2 6	2,483 12 7
Waterford, ...	66	1,263 0 19	1,010 3 0	1,456 1 10	1,379 3 3
Total, ...	554	24,279 3 31	10,714 14 5	18,894 18 6½	13,567 14 8

IRELAND.

ULSTER, ...	1,530	30,137 0 13	17,693 7 7	21,122 8 3	16,618 5 0
LEINSTER, ...	148	5,987 0 9	3,146 13 8	4,593 17 6	3,577 7 8
CONNAUGHT, ...	686	17,903 3 34½	6,463 5 0	6,900 9 0½	7,162 10 9½
MUNSTER, ...	554	24,279 3 31	10,714 14 5	18,694 18 6½	13,567 14 8
TOTAL, ...	2,918	78,308 0 7½	38,147 0 6	50,521 7 4	40,045 18 1½

D

PROVINCE OF

COUNTY OF

Names of Assistant Commissioners by whom Cases were decided.	No.	Name of Tenant.	Name of Landlord.	Townland.
Assistant Commissioners—				
E. Greer (Legal). J. B. Hamilton. G. A. Pringle. John Love. James M. Ross.	3405	Mary B. Saunderson, ...	James Moore, ...	Charlesbury, ...
	3406	Adam Adams, ...	James S. Moore, ...	Fruorn, ...
	3407	Joseph Linton, ...	do.	do. ...
	3408	Andrew Linton, ...	do.	do. ...
	3409	Samuel Linton, ...	do.	do. ...
	3410	Adam Patton, ...	do.	do. ...
	3411	John Adams, ...	do.	do. ...
	3412	Hugh Kyle, ...	do.	do. ...
	3413	James Millar, ...	James Moore, ...	Ravarnagh, ...
	3414	Robert C. Price, ...	Hugh Price, ...	Ballinlea, Lower,
	3415	Pat McConaghey, ...	Alexander O. Fullerton, ...	Magheraroddy, ...
	3416	Archibald McAllister, ...	Abraham Kidd, ...	Coolkeeny, ...
	3417	James Hill, ...	do.	Toberdally, ...
	3418	James Finlay, ...	Austin Cornwall and another,	Carnagh, ...
	3419	Margaret Darragh and another,	do.	Carnacmoran, ...
	3420	Sarah McCormick, ...	do.	Carngall, ...
	3421	Robert Kilough, ...	Captain R. J. Montgomery, ...	Carnagorough, ...
	3422	William Armour & anor.	James G. Irvine, ...	Altavradan, ...
	3423	Robert Dunlop, ...	F. A. St. M. Shiel, ...	Gillistown, ...
	3424	Samuel Hilton, ...	do.	Ardseglan, ...
	3425	Michael Hamill, ...	do.	do. ...
	3426	Andrew McFall, ...	Andrew McIlwraith, ...	Dunguman, ...
	3427	J. McLean, ...	Thomas H. Purdon, ...	Ardnaglass, ...
	3428	J. Mulholland, ...	do.	do. ...
	3429	Arthur Murphy, ...	Samuel Thompson, ...	Taylorstown, ...
	3430	Thomas Waters, ...	Joseph B. Black, ...	Gillistown, ...
	3431	William Dunseath, ...	do.	do. ...
	3432	Patrick McCann, ...	J. Kilpatrick, ...	Lisheenduby, ...
	3433	Andrew McKee, ...	John Young, ...	Galgorm Park, ...
	3434	John Dysart, ...	R. J. Alexander, ...	Mullanabeagh, ...

TABLE OF JUDICIAL RENTS.

Former Rent.			Judicial Rent.			Observations.
£	s.	d.	£	s.	d.	
25	0	0	18	0	0	By consent.
80	10	0	65	0	0	do.
38	0	0	30	16	3	do.
13	0	0	10	0	0	do.
13	0	0	10	0	0	do.
8	15	0	7	10	0	do.
46	0	0	36	0	0	do.
18	0	0	13	10	0	do.
13	6	0	10	5	0	do.
13	0	0	8	0	0	
24	0	0	23	0	0	
24	6	0	20	10	0	
14	10	0	13	0	0	Rent changed in 1864 from £ 18 s. 1 d. 8
10	10	0	8	0	0	
16	19	10	14	7	0	
16	15	0	13	10	0	
20	0	0	17	10	0	
70	0	0	70	0	0	
10	16	6	9	0	0	
15	1	7	13	10	0	
13	0	9	11	15	0	
9	0	0	6	15	0	
15	18	0	16	18	0	
12	18	3	10	6	0	
7	10	10	6	12	0	
6	18	0	4	0	0	By consent.
5	0	0	3	5	0	
10	0	0	7	10	0	
66	0	0	58	0	0	
18	0	0	10	0	0	

2439	William Walker, ...	William Miller and Agnes Fry, his Guardian.	Glgad, ...
2440	Martin M'Clelland, ...	Edward Mercer, ...	Glenbank, ...
2441	Alexander M'Master, ...	William Elder, ...	Dunaryvaine, ...
2442	James Curry (otherwise Dickey).	F. S. Henderson and William Henderson, his guardian.	Ranvan, ...
2443	John Orr and another,	John Potter, ...	Ballynamaddy, ...
2444	James Shaw, ...	Henry Boyd, ...	Killyboga, ...
2445	David Ellison, ...	Jane Higginson, ...	Drumakelly, ...
2446	James Carson, ...	William Kerr, ...	Ballybrean, ...
2447	William Templeton, ...	Rev. Robert Campbell, ...	Ballylaughan, ...
2448	Mary Jane Barkley, ...	Victor Coates, ...	[illegible],
2449	Campbell Munce, ...	James Mathews, ...	Craigs, ...
2450	John Martin, ...	John Armstrong, ...	Carnaygallagh,
2451	William Abernethy, ...	Captain A. Murray, ...	Eglish ...
2452	John A. Mulvenna, ...	John Carath, ...	Killyree, ...
2453	Thomas Houston, ...	do.	do. ...
2454	Robert M'Nalney, ...	James Orr and another, Trustees of William Orr, deceased.	Ballygilly, ...
2455	William Martin, ...	Rev. J. H. Smythe, ...	Ballyrough, ...
2456	James Orr, ...	do.	do. ...
2457	Margaret Spiers, ...	do.	do. ...
2458	Robert M'Clure, ...	Captain Pottinger, ...	Ballyealon, ...
2459	Mary Adams, ...	Dr. John Adams, ...	Kernyhill, ...
2460	Archibald Stevenson, ...	George Cumming, ...	Broughdone, ...
2461	Patrick Murray, ...	Julius Casement, ...	Aughnacloy, ...
2462	Patrick Nugent, ...	do	do. ...
2463	Douglas Kenny, ...	Lord Waveney, ...	Ballygarvey, ...
2464	Robert Kenny, ...	do.	do. ...
2465	Arthur Wightman, ...	do.	Dolaun, ...
2466	Robert M'Dowell, ...	Joseph B. Black, ...	Gilbstown,
2467	James Brown, ...	do.	Aughnasiary ...
2468	Alexander Park, ...	David O. Adams, ...	Kilcreen, ...
2469	Robert Curry, ...	do.	do. ...

ANTRIM—*continued.*

Extent of Holding—Statute	Poor Law Valuation	Former Rent	Judicial Rent	Observations	Value of Tenancy
A. R. P.	£ s. d.	£ s. d.	£ s. d.		£ s. d.
18 1 17	11 10 0	17 10 0	11 10 0		
27 0 0	10 15 0	17 10 0	13 10 0		
18 2 14	18 5 0	17 7 8	15 0 0		
1 0 8	—	7 0 0	4 14 0		
9 3 10	8 10 0	9 0 0	6 11 0		
26 3 10	10 10 0	14 0 0	9 9 0		
7 2 28	5 9 0	11 0 0	11 0 0		
11 0 6	7 10 0	10 15 0	7 7 0		
24 1 5	23 6 0	27 18 4	31 10 0		
11 0 32	—	18 0 0	7 0 0		
23 1 25	13 0 0	22 0 0	16 10 0		
9 2 35	—	17 0 0	15 0 0		
6 1 22	10 0 0	16 12 0	12 10 0		
71 0 7	11 10 0	35 0 0	20 0 0		
20 0 10	—	20 0 0	18 0 0		
6 0 10	—	7 0 0	5 10 0		
16 3 13	13 10 0	13 14 0	12 0 0		
8 1 20	5 10 0	10 10 0	7 0 0		
24 1 6	17 10 0	23 5 0	22 0 0		
18 0 20	16 15 0	25 0 0	22 0 0		
13 1 18	13 0 0	18 1 8	13 10 0		
17 3 38	14 0 0	19 0 4	18 0 0		
35 2 23	18 6 0	21 0 10	17 10 0		
4 3 31	4 16 0	7 10 0	4 5 0	By consent.	
8 2 0	4 0 0	6 0 0	4 5 0	do.	
60 2 20	29 0 0	62 16 10	22 17 0	do.	
10 2 8	9 16 0	11 8 0	9 0 0	do.	
18 1 6	13 10 0	15 9 0	18 0 0	do.	
23 3 25	—	15 9 0	13 0 0	do.	
23 3 28	—	18 18 4	14 0 0	do.	
10 0 35	18 10 0	16 0 0	13 0 0	do.	
5 0 0	3 0 0	7 1 3	4 18 6	do.	
4 3 0	1 18 0	8 0 0	1 0 0	do.	
67 3 15	23 0 0	40 0 0	29 0 0	do.	
33 0 39	23 0 0	28 10 0	29 5 0	do.	

Names of Assistant Commissioners by whom Cases were decided.	No.	Name of Tenant.	Name of Landlord.	Townland.
Assistant Commissioners—				
[illegible] (Legal).	2470	Archibald Elliott, ...	John Woods, ...	Drumdarragh,
J. R. [illegible]	2471	John Redmond, ...	Sarah Dowds, ...	Carnmore,
C. A. [illegible]	2472	David Johnston & anor.,	John Colwell and another, ...	Dunloughy,
John Love.	2473	Thomas Moorehead, ...	Jane M'Kee, ...	Rosevan,
James M. Ross.	2474	John Stevenson, ...	do.	do.
	2475	Robert Shaw, ...	James Orr and others, Trustees of Wm. Orr, deceased	Ballygilly,
	2476	James Reid, ...	do.	do.
	2477	James M'Master, ...	do.	do.
	2478	Samuel M'Master, ...	Richard K. Boyd, ...	Rosevan,
	2479	Wm. Anderson & anor.,	do.	do.
	2480	Elizabeth Clarke, ...	David Morrow and another,	do.
	2481	Alexander Kennedy, ...	Alexander M'Master, ...	Ballygilly,
	2482	Thomas Mark, ...	James Adams, ...	Loughhill,
	2483	Thomas Kennedy, ...	Alexander M'Master, ...	Ballygilly,
	2484	James Curry, ...	Archibald Boyd, ...	Rosevan,
	2485	Archibald M'Kendry, ...	Thomas Dickey, ...	Ballyclose,
	2486	John Surgenor, ...	do.	do.
	2487	William Dunn, ...	John Patrick, ...	Drumnaleering,
	2488	Hugh Nevin, ...	do.	do.
	2489	John Forbes, ...	do.	do.
	2490	John Forbes, ...	do.	do.
	2491	William Morrison, ...	do.	Cape Castle,
	2492	John Clarke, ...	do.	Drumnaleering,
	2493	James Davison, ...	do.	do.
	2494	Joseph Clarke, ...	do.	do.
	2495	William M Graham, ...	John Armstrong, ...	Finnaygallough or Kinnaygallough
	2496	William Crawford, ...	Daniel H. S. M'Kay. ...	Ballyportagh, ...
	2497	William Alexander, ...	do.	do.
	2498	James Armstrong, ...	John White, ...	Upper Carrow,
	2499	James M'Bride, ...	do.	do.
	2500	John Agnew, ...	John K. Smith and others, Reps. of late John Smith,	Appleton,
	2501	Henry Boyd, ...	do.	do.
	2502	William Agnew, ...	do.	Crowdly Valley.
	2503	Newton Cussack, ...	do.	Appleton,
	2504	Alexander Cussack, ...	do.	Crowdly Valley.

ANTRIM—*continued.*

Extent of Holding, Statute.	Poor Law Valuation.	Former Rent.	Judicial Rent.	Observations.
A. R. P.	£ s. d.	£ s. d.	£ s. d.	
9 0 0	6 10 0	11 11 0	8 0 0	By consent.
23 0 35	16 5 0	27 0 0	22 0 0	do.
16 0 0	11 5 6	14 19 10	10 10 0	do.
26 0 23	9 0 0	15 0 0	11 5 0	
32 1 33	19 0 0	26 10 0	24 0 0	do.
14 2 5	11 16 0	11 10 0	9 10 0	do.
17 2 15	36 10 0	31 0 0	30 0 0	do.
15 2 35	11 10 0	13 13 6	11 10 0	do.
33 3 0	21 10 0	27 0 4	17 0 0	do.
33 3 25	31 15 0	30 16 1	20 0 0	do.
28 0 5	17 10 0	19 0 0	17 5 0	do.
20 1 37	18 15 0	22 10 0	13 17 6	do.
19 1 30	15 0 0	25 0 0	16 0 0	
7 2 5	1 15 0	7 10 0	1 12 6	do.
9 3 37	7 0 0	10 0 0	8 0 0	do.
5 0 32	1 15 0	6 6 8	5 7 6	do.
8 3 28	7 5 0	9 4 11	7 0 0	do.
53 2 20	27 18 0	34 1 11	25 18 9	do.
9 3 6	4 10 0	7 5 0	6 5 0	do.
10 0 0	8 10 0	9 10 0	7 15 0	do.
15 2 22	—	8 10 0	7 10 0	do.
45 2 0	22 5 0	34 9 4	22 9 8	
16 3 1	11 0 0	13 10 0	11 0 6	do.
40 0 9	21 10 0	29 8 6	24 10 0	do.
13 3 34	10 0 0	12 0 0	10 0 0	do.

Names of Assistant Commissioners by whom Cases were decided.	No.	Name of Tenant.	Name of Landlord.	Townland.
Assistant Commissioners— E. Greer (Legal). J. S. Heard. G. A. Pringle. John Lowe. James M. Ross.				
	2505	John Hume, ...	John K. Smith and others, Reps. of late John Smith,	Crevilly Valley,
	2506	Peter M'Erlean (Red Peter),	Kenneth Jones, ...	Aghavarry, ...
	2507	Horace Nelson, ...	do.	Ardnaglass, ...
	2508	Henry M'Caw, ...	do	Mullinsallagh, ...
	2509	John Logan, ...	do.	Garvaghey, ...
	2510	Hugh Logan, ...	K. H. Jones, ...	Aghavarry, ...
	2511	Archibald M'Gowan, ...	Edward Murray, ...	Glenbank, ...
	2512	William Kenny, ...	Edmund M'Neill, ...	Craigs, ...
	2513	Mary Harper, ...	H. H. M'Neill, ...	Dunmaney, ...
	2514	John Selfridge, ...	do.	Craigs, ...
	2515	Robert M'Loughlin, ...	Earl of Antrim, ...	West Torr, ...
	2516	Anne M'Caughan, ...	do.	Broughanore, ...
	2517	Dan M'Mullan, ...	do.	Tenaghs, ...
	2518	Esther M'Cormick, ...	do.	Gruigan, ...
	2519	Samuel Devlin, ...	do.	Ballypatrick, ...
	2520	Thomas White, ...	Alexander Dunlop, ...	Carvally, ...
	2521	Daniel Gowdy, ...	do.	Dundale, ...
	2522	Bernard Keenan, ...	do.	Clare Mountain,
	2523	Bernard Keenan, ...	do	Kilrobert,
	2524	Patrick Gowdy, ...	do.	Ardagh & Dundale,
	2525	William James Reid, ...	James S. Moore, ...	Glenside, ...
	2526	John Craig, ...	do.	Tullykittagh, ...
	2527	Joseph Brown, ...	do.	Lower Tullykittagh
	2528	John H. Conaghy, ...	do	do ...
	2529	William M'Burney, ...	do.	do. ...
	2530	Susan M'Grath, ...	Samuel D. Crommelin, ...	Scotch Omerbane,
	2531	Daniel M'Watters, Rep. of John M'Watters,	do.	do ...
	2532	William Marshall, ...	do	Skerry, West, ...
	2533	Sarah Jane M'Killop,	do.	Scotch Omerbane,
	2534	Francis Adams, ...	do.	Skerry, West, ...
	2535	Catherine Delargy, ...	do.	Skerry, East, ...
	2536	John Bird, ...	do.	do. ...
	2537	John Reid, ...	do	Skerry, West, ...
	2538	W. Simpson, ...	do	do. ...

Names of Assistant Commissioners by whom Cases were decided.	No.	Name of Tenant.	Name of Landlord.	Townland
Assistant Commissioners—				
E. Greer (Legal). J. R. [illegible]. C. A. [illegible]. John Love. James M. Ross.	2540	William Johnston, ...	Samuel D. Crommelin, ...	Skerry, West, ...
	2541	James Paul, ...	James Gray & anor., Trustees of Major Gray, deceased.	Moylarg, ...
	2542	Do.	do.	do. ...
	2543	John Gamble, Rep. of James Gamble, decd.	do.	Killycowan, ...
	2544	David Kernohan, ...	do.	Broughshane, ...
	2545	John Stevenson, ...	do.	Kells, ...
	2546	Thomas Sherrard, ...	do.	Kellystown, ...
	2547	James McGookin, ...	do.	Glenbuck, ...
	2548	Samuel Foster, ...	do.	Cromkill, ...
	2549	Francis Dinsmore, ...	do.	Kells, ...
	2550	Do.	do.	do. ...
	2551	John Cathcart, ...	do.	do. ...
	2552	James Devinney and Rev. Samuel Devinney,	do.	do. ...
	2553	Samuel Barr, ...	do.	Cromkill,
	2554	J. Boyd, ...	J. McMartin, ...	Millquarter, ...
	2555	W. Fawcett, ...	do.	do. ...
	2556	David Duncan, ...	D. D. Casement & anor., Trustees of Thos. Casement, decd.	Gallybracks, ...
	2557	William Atkinson, ...	do.	do. ...
	2558	James Hinkley, ...	do.	Ballylurgan, ...
	2559	Patrick Brogan, ...	Rev. Adam Cappage, ...	Glenbuck, ...
	2560	J. McGookin, ...	do.	do. ...
	2561	Patrick McAleenan, ...	do.	do. ...
	2562	Isaac Adams, ...	do.	do. ...
	2563	John Morgan, ...	do.	do. ...
	2564	Paul Dixon, ...	do.	do. ...
	2565	J. O'Neill, ...	do.	do. ...
	2566	Richard Carey, ...	do.	do. ...
	2567	James McKay, ...	Henry Dawson, ...	Little Ballymena,
	2568	Gordon McKay, ...	do.	do. ...
	2569	William McTurk, ...	do.	do. ...
	2570	David McKay, ...	do.	do. ...
	2571	John Maxwell, ...	Richard Dyott, ...	Ballyhemmin, ...
	2572	John Holmes, ...	do.	Tullynamullan, ...
	2573	Ellen McCaughey, ...	do.	Killycarrigan, ...
	2574	Hugh Law, ...	do.	Gortfad, ...

Former Rent.	Judicial Rent.	Observations.	Value of Tenancy.
£ s. d.	£ s. d.		£ s. d.
7 6 6	6 0 0		
25 0 0	22 10 0		
13 11 8	13 12 0		
37 6 5	22 10 0		
24 0 0	23 0 0		
5 3 0	3 18 0		
47 16 0	42 0 0		
13 1 0	9 0 0		
4 10 0	3 10 0		
3 0 0	2 0 0		
13 0 0	13 0 0		
8 0 0	6 10 0		
16 0 0	12 10 0		
6 13 0	6 13 0		
18 3 1	8 5 0		
6 10 11	4 4 0		
38 16 6	28 10 0		
6 5 11	4 17 0		
11 0 0	9 0 0		
14 0 0	9 0 0		
10 6 8	7 10 0		
7 15 0	6 0 0		
24 0 0	18 15 0		
8 3 4	6 0 0		
64 17 10	29 0 0		
13 16 0	10 0 0		
11 8 0	8 0 0		
29 8 4	24 0 0		
36 5 0	36 6 0		
6 10 0	4 15 0		
15 0 0	11 0 0		
25 0 0	23 3 8	By contract.	
25 0 0	18 8 0	do.	
9 0 0	7 12 6	do.	
8 0 0	7 5 0	do.	

...	do. ...
...	do. ...
...	do. ...
...	do. ...
...	Hugh W. Montgomery,
...	James Montgomery,
...	E. J. C. H James,
...	do. ...

[AN]TRIM—*continued.*

[Ext]ent of Holding. Statute.	Poor Law Valuation.	Former Rent.	Judicial Rent.	Observations.	Value of Tenancy.
A. R. P.	£ s. d.	£ s. d.	£ s. d.		£ s. d.
37 1 36	31 0 0	34 0 0	14 0 0	By consent.	
51 0 0	45 10 0	40 0 0	32 0 0	do.	
30 0 0	22 15 0	29 0 0	25 0 0	do.	
61 3 35	29 10 0	37 0 0	28 10 0		
30 0 32	24 10 0	36 0 0	21 0 0		
10 3 38	8 10 0	9 6 8	6 15 0		
17 2 0	18 0 0	20 0 0	14 0 0		
20 0 39	18 15 0	17 5 5	12 10 0	do.	
17 3 10	17 5 0	19 8 2	16 0 0	do.	
7 1 5	5 5 0	6 17 0	5 0 0	do.	
17 1 29	6 0 0	11 10 0	8 0 0	do.	
22 0 0	10 10 0	12 0 0	9 10 0	do.	
29 3 31	28 15 0	28 0 0	21 0 0		
13 3 23	8 0 0	11 0 0	8 0 0		
30 0 0	21 0 0	30 0 0	24 0 0		
26 0 23	20 5 0	25 0 0	19 5 0		
34 0 20	25 10 0	20 0 0	17 10 0		
58 0 6	47 10 0	12 0 0	34 0 0		
16 0 10	12 13 0	14 18 9	10 0 0		
10 3 10	9 5 0	10 12 6	7 0 0		
11 1 16	11 10 0	18 0 0	18 0 0		
80 1 32	58 5 0	84 0 0	61 0 0		
13 1 0	14 0 0	17 1 8	11 0 0		
73 0 18	67 0 0	121 2 4	98 10 0		
4 3 26	—	14 15 0	10 0 0		
11 1 9	15 5 0	18 0 0	14 5 0		
17 1 27	—	23 7 8	20 0 0		
11 1 0	12 15 0	15 0 0	11 0 0		
36 3 39	30 5 0	31 13 6	28 10 0		
10 0 2	18 15 0	23 0 0	16 0 0		
4 0 7	9 10 0	11 0 0	9 9 0		
6 8 0	9 10 0	11 0 0	8 15 0		
25 1 17	24 15 0	30 0 0	27 10 0		
26 2 35	—	23 10 0	18 0 0		
9 3 5	—	13 10 0	9 15 0		

Names of Assistant Commissioners by whom Cases were decided.	No.	Name of Tenant.	Name of Landlord.	Townland.
Assistant Commissioners— E. Greer (Legal). J. B. Heasman. G. A. Fanning. John Lowe. James M. Ross.	2610	Mary E. Thompson, ...	Barbara Snyley, ...	Ladyhill, ...
	2611	Allen Barkley, ...	Rev. Francis M'Cammon, ...	Walkmill, ...
	2612	John White, ...	Arthur H. Pakenham, ...	Ballyrobin, ...
	2613	Joseph Connelly, ...	Gen. Visct. Bridport and anor. Trus. of late Lord Downshire.	Clonmorehill, ...
	2614	William McMinn, ...	do.	Dairyland, ...
	2615	William Baird, ...	do.	Clonmorehill, ...
	2616	William Hall, ...	do.	Straidland, ...
	2617	James Kerr, ...	do.	Dairyland, ...
	2618	James McKeen, ...	do.	do. ...
	2619	William Hugh Crow, ...	do.	do. ...
	2620	Mary Kirk, Sarah Kirk, and Jane Eliza Kirk.	do.	Clonmorehill, ...
	2621	Samuel Kirk, ...	do.	do. ...
	2622	Samuel Kennedy. ...	do.	do. ...
	2623	Robert Connelly, ...	do.	do. ...
	2624	George Wilson, ...	do.	Middle Division, Carrickfergus.
	2625	Hugh McKendry, ...	Thomas Thompson, ...	Killyree, ...
	2626	James Nesbitt, ...	Samuel Thompson, ...	Taylorstown, ...
	2627	William Dawson, ...	James S. Moore, ...	Upper Tullykittagh.
	2628	James McBurney, ...	do.	Lower Tullykittagh.
	2629	George Bunby, ...	W. D. D. Wilson, ...	Eden, ...
	2630	David Boyd, ...	John Martin, ...	Kelmaing, ...
	2631	Samuel Agnew, ...	C. R. Dobbs, ...	Kilbreet, ...
	2632	James Armstrong, ...	George McAnliffe, ...	North-west Ballyvarry.
	2633	Samuel McKee, ...	do.	South-west Ballyvarry.
	2634	James McDowell, ...	Lord Arthur Edward Hill Trevor,	Ballyvallough, ...
	2635	Robert Smyth, ...	James McBride, Executor of late John McFerran.	Altilevelly, ...
	2636	Thomas Rainey, ...	Sir Edward Coey, ...	Ballyhome and Antsville.
	2637	William Campbell, ...	James Chaine, ...	Lomley, South [illegible]
	2638	Daniel Crawford, ...	do.	do. ...
	2639	Robert Hunter, ...	do.	do. ...
	2640	Robert Smith, ...	[illegible]	[illegible], ...
	2641	Alexander McCarte, ...	Duke of Marlborough and Marquis of Londonderry, Trus. of Lord H. L. Vane-Tempest.	Fallowen, ...
	2642	John McGinnis, ...	do.	do. ...
	2643	Richard Given, ...	Marquis of Londonderry, Trustee of late Marchioness of Londonderry.	Carrowreagh, ...

ANTRIM—*continued.*

Extent of Holding in acres.	Poor Law Valuation.	Former Rent.	Judicial Rent.	Observations.	Value of Tenancy.
a. r. p.	£ s. d.	£ s. d.	£ s. d.		£ s. d.
17 1 35	18 5 0	21 0 0	16 18 0	By consent.	
45 1 0	45 15 0	50 18 0	49 0 0	do.	
27 1 7	21 10 0	25 6 0	16 0 0	do.	
27 0 16	21 15 0	23 18 0	22 12 0		
27 3 6	14 10 0	17 6 0	17 6 0		
33 1 22	29 10 0	30 5 0	30 8 0		
6 1 20	9 10 0	6 13 0	8 13 0		
15 3 0	13 10 0	18 10 0	18 0 0		
20 0 15	13 0 0	18 0 0	18 0 0		
50 3 28	29 8 0	33 0 0	33 0 0		
17 2 30	13 15 0	15 17 0	14 0 0		
23 2 22	31 0 0	30 7 0	25 16 0		
31 3 16	31 10 0	23 11 0	25 0 0		
16 3 5	15 5 0	16 18 6	14 16 0		
90 1 29	85 0 0	36 0 0	36 0 0		
22 3 5	11 10 0	23 0 0	17 0 0		
7 3 3	5 10 0	7 10 0	5 10 0		
3 0 17	3 10 0	3 15 0	4 0 0		
29 0 0	13 5 0	20 0 0	18 10 0		
11 3 0	20 0 0	27 0 0	20 0 0		
16 0 31	3 10 0	5 13 0	5 0 0		
34 3 10	54 5 0	67 17 3	60 0 0		
30 1 25	13 0 0	19 7 0	18 0 0		
5 0 19	9 0 0	9 0 0	8 0 0		
37 1 37	17 0 0	18 18 0	17 0 0		
9 1 0	9 0 0	10 0 0	6 10 0		
85 0 12	62 10 0	51 16 0	51 14 0		
40 2 25	10 7 0	11 14 6	12 0 0		
19 2 10	16 4 0	10 9 9	14 10 0		
73 0 22	42 10 0	40 18 9	43 0		
16 2 23	17 10 0	19 18 4	14 10 0		
16 0 22	13 0 0	12 8 10	12 8 10		
29 0 0	19 15 0	17 0 10	19 0 10		
28 3 10	25 10 6	19 16 8	16 10 0		

COUNTY OF

Names of Assistant Commissioners by whom Cases were decided.	No.	Name of Tenant.	Name of Landlord.	Townland.
Assistant Commissioners—				
E. Greer (Legal). J. R. Heapock. C. A. Prentice. John Love. James M. Ross.	2644	James Brown, ...	Captain Thomas Slingsby, ...	Granshaw, ...
	2645	Jane M'Ilgorm, ...	do.	Cortamlet, ...
	2646	John M'Gladdery, ...	do.	Granshaw, ...
	2647	John Verner, ...	do.	Ballyvernon Mon.,
	2648	Alex. Ross, ...	do.	do. ...
	2649	Do.	do.	Ballydown, ...
	2650	James Holmes, ...	do.	Ballyvernon Beg.
	2651	Do.	do.	Ballyvernon Mon.,
	2652	Henry Alexander, ...	do.	Ballyvernon Beg.
	2653	Margaret Houston, ...	do.	Castletown, ...
	2654	Daniel M'Nally, ...	Philip Gibbons, ...	Carnalough, South,
	2655	William Crawford, ...	Major G. S. White, ...	Loughtown, ...
	2656	John Lavery, ...	G. R. Dobbs and G. W. Cuppage, Trs. of late Alexr. Cuppage.	Bay Lodge, ...
	2657	James Hunter, ...	The Earl of Antrim, ...	Ballygown, ...
	2658	Alexander M'Curdy, ...	do.	Carnanerphy, ...
	2659	John M'Ginnis, ...	do.	do. ...
	2660	John O'Neill, ...	do.	do. ...
	2661	Patrick Gillan, ...	do.	do.
	2662	Thomas M'Kee, ...	John M'Auley, ...	Red Hall,
	2663	Samuel Alexander, ...	do.	do. ...
	2664	William Weatherup, ...	William D. D. Wilson, ...	West Division,
	2665	Patrick Gamble, ...	do.	do. ...

ANTRIM—*continued.*

Extent of Holding. Statute.			Poor Law Valuation.			Former Rent.			Judicial Rent.			Observations.	Value of Tenancy.
A.	R.	P.	£	s.	d.	£	s.	d.	£	s.	d.		£ s. d.
10	3	35	37	0	0	30	17	6	33	0	0		
13	3	35	15	15	0	11	3	4	13	0	0		
17	0	28	16	15	0	16	0	0	12	0	0		
7	3	0	7	5	0	6	6	1	6	6	0		
30	3	30	29	10	0	31	6	6	25	10	0		
9	3	10	9	5	0	10	7	6	8	6	0		
137	6	25	119	0	0	141	0	0	118	0	0		
33	0	30	33	0	0	30	0	0	25	0	0		
11	0	30	10	0	0	48	0	0	33	0	0		
11	1	10	13	10	0	11	18	0	8	0	0		
34	3	5	28	0	0	37	10	0	34	0	0		
41	1	5	55	10	0	40	18	5	30	0	0		
1	0	15	1	10	0	4	10	0	1	10	0		
33	1	16	21	12	0	20	4	0	17	5	0		
17	3	0	16	10	0	18	4	0	15	0	0		
7	3	0	7	5	0	7	19	0	6	10	0		
14	1	35	—			11	0	0	9	0	0		
11	3	8	—			11	5	6	6	10	0		
51	2	18	53	10	0	71	6	10	58	10	6	By consent.	

COUNTY OF

Names of Assistant Commissioners by whom Cases were decided.	No.	Name of Tenant.	Name of Landlord.	Townland
Assistant Commissioners— F. O. [illegible] (Legal). J. M. Weir. J. F. [illegible]. J. [illegible]. [illegible].	3536	Mary Robb, ...	William de S. Filgate and another, Trustees of Count de Salis.	Lisnagat and another,
	3537	James Horner, junr., ...	do.	Ballykeel,
	3538	Mary Hughes, ...	Ralph S. Obre, ...	Tartlogue,
	3539	George Vennard, ...	do.	Derrycaw,
	3540	David Kilpatrick, ...	do.	Balligary,
	3541	James Boyce, ...	John Richardson, ...	Boraghra,
	3542	William H. Stevenson, ...	Lavington Thompson, ...	Derrycorr,
	3543	Jane Morris, ...	Lord Lurgan, ...	Knocknashane,
	3544	Richard Mallomb, ...	do.	Derryadd,
	3545	James McCann, ...	do.	Ballinary,
	3546	John Corner, ...	do.	Derrytrasna and another,
	3547	Hugh Thompson, ...	Col. Donald H. Stewart, ...	Ballynaweed,
	3548	William Crawford, ...	Mrs. Ann Grimason, ...	Kilmoriarty,
	3549	Henry Cousin, ...	John Finnegan, ...	Mullantine,
	3550	William Calmshaw, ...	Robert Hart, ...	Kilmoriarty,
	3551	Thomas Porter, ...	Baroness Von Stieglitz, ...	Ballinagone,
	3552	William Hamilton, ...	Francis F. Meade, ...	Silverwood,
	3553	William Forsythe, ...	Mrs. Anna O. Craig, ...	Foybeg,
	3554	John Hamilton, ...	do.	do.
	3555	John McNally, ...	Thomas A. Woodhouse, ...	Derritraw,
	3556	George Mallowes, ...	John B. Atkinson, ...	Balliney,
	3557	Hamilton Hamilton, ...	John Lenoy, ...	Drumgaskilly,
	3558	Elizabeth Henderson, ...	Robert Todd, ...	Upper Breagh,
	3559	John Benson, ...	Rev. Thomas F. Blash, ...	Ballinagone,
	3560	William Bowers, ...	William Charley, ...	Ballynakeagh,
	3561	Isaac Morrow, ...	Alexander D. Kelly, ...	Ballynacahan,
	3562	James Garthen, ...	Mrs Ellen Stevenson, ...	Derryadd,
	3563	Richard Mathews, ...	Mrs. Agnes Reed, ...	Muckery,
	3564	John Walsh, ...	Rev. Thomas F. Blash, ...	Ballinagone,
	3565	James Wolsey, ...	Julia F. Molyneux, ...	Markyconnor,
	3566	George Wright, Rep. of James Wright,	Mrs Anna Craig, ...	Foybeg,
	3567	John Trevors, ...	Baroness Von Stieglitz, ...	Ballinagone,
	3568	William Boyce, ...	Canon O. Woodhouse, ...	Breagh, Upper,
	3569	Margaret Henry, ...	Mrs. Catherine Henry, ...	Araragh,
	3570	John Lewis, ...	Arthur McCann, ...	Loughery,

ARMAGH.

Extent of Holding. Statute	Poor Law Valuation	Former Rent	Judicial Rent	Observations	Value of Tenancy
A. R. P.	£ s. d.	£ s. d.	£ s. d.		£ s. d.
13 2 37	16 0 0	16 13 8	13 10 0		
11 3 24	20 0 0	21 19 3	18 0 0		
11 2 23	10 6 0	12 5 4	8 10 0		
8 0 5	3 5 0	5 5 0	3 10 0		
5 2 37	—	8 11 5	6 0 0		
21 3 20	35 10 0	63 6 11	36 0 0		
8 3 0	5 5 0	6 6 0	4 15 0	By consent.	
70 0 20	34 0 0	19 0 0	16 0 0	do.	
18 0 27	12 6 0	13 0 0	9 10 0	do.	
6 3 0	8 0 0	8 10 0	5 17 6	do.	
3 2 31	1 10 0	5 0 0	3 5 0	Rent changed in 1858 from . . . £ s. d. 4 5 0	
21 1 0	17 5 0	33 6 9	29 10 0		
8 0 15	3 15 0	7 10 0	5 0 0		
1 1 0	3 5 0	5 5 0	3 10 0		
18 3 18	19 0 0	20 18 0	18 10 0		
5 2 0	6 10 0	7 8 0	5 10 0	1860 8 8 1	
6 1 36	16 5 0	12 11 9	10 10 0		
15 1 33	18 10 0	18 6 0	16 0 0		
7 2 15	8 10 0	9 10 7	8 0 0		
1 3 23	—	1 0 0	3 0 0		
0 2 3	0 10 0	3 0 0	2 0 0		
9 0 34	21 10 0	21 5 0	19 0 0		
1 0 0	2 15 0	5 5 0	3 15 0		
8 1 25	15 5 0	16 16 0	10 10 0		
9 0 0	11 10 0	18 0 0	18 0 0		
25 2 2	29 0 0	31 13 4	27 10 0		
1 2 0	2 10 0	4 10 0	5 10 0		
26 1 16	22 10 0	31 17 1	20 0 0		
9 0 0	11 0 0	16 17 3	10 5 0		
10 3 30	12 5 0	15 0 0	18 10 0		
12 2 16	17 10 0	22 10 6	15 0 0		
15 1 0	17 5 0	20 11 0	14 0 0	1856 18 11 10	
5 2 35	9 5 0	7 15 7	6 10 0		
2 0	—	2 16 8	2 2 6		
1 0	7 5 0	6 3 0	6 3 0		

Names of Assistant Commissioners by whom Cases were decided.	No.	Name of Tenant.	Name of Landlord.	Townland.
Assistant Commissioners—				
P. G. Hobson (Legal). J. M. Weir. J. F. Benson. J. Cunningham. Andrew Sproule.	3571	Daniel Mulholland,	Jacob Hutton,	Armagh,
	3572	Benjamin Pardo,	John Wright,	Artabrackagh,
	3573	Richard M'Cann,	Rev. Edward Hardy and anor.,	Derrymacash,
	3574	Thomas Blair,	do.	do.
	3575	Samuel Carson,	John Robinson,	Derrinraw,
	3576	Thomas England,	Rev. W. Richmond, Trustee of William Richmond.	Knocknamuckly,
	3577	Thomas Leckie,	William B. Swift,	Ballyworkan,
	3578	Do.	do.	do.
	3579	Thomas Wright,	do.	do.
	3580	William Pentland,	do.	Drumnakelly,
	3581	Samuel Wright,	do.	do.
	3582	John Pentland,	do.	do.
	3583	Alexander Cole,	Charles Stanley,	Derrinraw,
	3584	Margaret M'Adam,	do.	do.
	3585	William M'Fadden,	do.	do.
	3586	James Neville,	do.	do.
	3587	David Kilpatrick,	do.	Ballinary,
	3588	Sarah Jackson,	do.	Derrinraw,
	3589	Thomas Hewitt,	Sir Francis E. Macnaghten, Bart.	Artabrackagh,
	3590	Daniel Fearon,	do.	do.
	3591	William Conn	do.	Ballyhannon,
	3592	John Gribben,	do.	Artabrackagh,
	3593	Richard Thompson,	do.	do.
	3594	Jonathan Hewitt,	do.	do.
	3595	William Robinson,	do.	Artabrackagh and others.
	3596	Francis Gribben,	do.	Artabrackagh,
	3597	Fanny Murphy,	do.	do.
	3598	Benjamin Matchett,	do.	Ballyhannon,
	3599	Charles Hall,	do.	Artabrackagh,
	3600	John M'Fadden,	do.	do.
	3601	Hugh Marley,	do.	Ballyhannon,
	3602	James Wright,	do.	Artabrackagh,
	3603	Thomas Alexander,	do.	do.
	3604	William Wright,	do.	do.
	3605	John Cumming,	Lord A. E. H. Trevor,	Drumgask,

ARMAGH—*continued.*

Extent of Holding. Statute.	Poor Law Valuation.	Former Rent.	Judicial Rent.	Observations.	Value of Tenancy.
A. R. P.	£ s. d.	£ s. d.	£ s. d.		£ s. d.
1 2 26	—	7 10 0	4 10 0		
1 3 20	—	7 15 0	6 15 0	By consent.	
61 0 20	63 5 0	69 9 5	48 0 0	do.	
11 3 0	10 10 0	15 6 5	10 0 0	do.	
1 2 0	—	6 0 0	3 15 0	do.	
1 0 30	5 10 0	5 5 0	5 5 0	do.	
22 1 35	21 10 0	27 6 10	21 0 0		
30 2 10	27 5 0	29 18 1	31 0 0		
6 2 32	—	10 11 10	8 0 0		
16 2 30	21 10 0	28 16 0	20 10 0		
20 0 0	24 15 0	27 13 9	23 5 0		
9 2 0	13 0 0	18 6 6	10 10 0		
6 1 8	6 0 0	8 6 0	5 10 0		
20 2 22	—	23 11 0	16 0 0		
3 1 15	1 10 0	8 19 0	2 0 0		
4 0 5	5 0 0	6 0 0	4 15 0	£ s. d.	
5 0 0	—	5 16 0	3 0 0	Rent changed in 1874 from . . . 2 16 6	
2 0 10	0 15 0	3 16 0	1 10 0		
11 3 15	12 0 0	18 0 0	10 10 0	1875 11 5 7	
3 2 0	1 15 0	4 15 0	3 15 0		
11 0 6	23 10 0	20 5 0	16 0 0		
20 3 10	29 10 0	27 10 0	24 10 0		
5 3 25	8 10 0	8 10 0	6 0 0		
6 0 20	10 10 0	10 15 0	8 0 0	do. 9 15 9	
37 2 31	34 15 0	17 0 2½	35 0 0		
9 3 25	11 15 0	11 16 0	11 15 0		
0 3 27	2 10 0	2 10 0	1 5 0	do. 2 0 0	
8 3 34	15 15 0	20 0 0	16 0 0		
6 3 14	18 5 0	11 10 0	9 15 0	do. 11 0 0	
7 1 25	11 10 0	10 15 0	8 5 0		
3 1 0	5 10 0	7 10 0	5 10 0	do. 6 11 5	
6 1 24	13 0 0	12 15 0	10 0 0	do. 11 12 0	
9 2 5	12 15 0	12 5 0	10 5 0	do. 11 8 7	
11 1 10	16 0 0	16 0 0	13 10 0	do. 16 13 8½	
13 3 10	74 0 0	50 0 0	15 0 0	1880 24 3 1	

COUNTY OF

Names of Assistant Commissioners by whom Cases were decided.	No.	Name of Tenant.	Name of Landlord.	Townland.
Assistant Commissioners—				
F. G. Hodgson (Legal). J. M. Weir. J. F. Bomford. J. Greenhalgh. Andrew Sproule.	3606	William Carter, ...	Lord A. E. H. Trevor, ...	Drumgesh, ...
	3607	Robert Sullivan, ...	E. T. Wakefield, ...	Clonmore, ...
	3608	Mathew McAnuffy, ...	do.	Derrymeaw, ...
	3609	Henry McAdam, ...	do.	Clonmore, ...
	3610	William H. McAdam, Rep. of Jas. McAdam,	do.	do. ...
	3611	Daniel Cullen, ...	do.	Derrymeaw and another,
	3612	Patrick Connolly, ...	do.	do. ...
	3613	Christopher Magee, ...	do.	do. ...
	3614	John Connolly, ...	James Forde, ...	Derryadd, ...
	3615	James Reilly, ...	do.	do. ...
	3616	James Finn, ...	Wm. de S. Filgate & another, Trustees of Count de Salis	Carnmacnile, ...
	3617	John Gillespie, ...	do.	Lisnagore, ...
	3618	John Kane, ...	do.	do. ...
	3619	Mrs. Jane Harper, ...	do.	do. ...
	3620	Nathaniel Glass, ...	do.	do. ...
	3621	William Conn, ...	do.	Tamnavalley and another,
	3622	James Turner, ...	do.	do. ...
	3623	Lawrence Dermott, ...	do.	Brackagh, ...
	3624	Dickey Dickson, ...	Duke of Manchester, ...	Lismiskey, ...
	3625	William Lawson, ...	do.	Mullantine, ...
	3626	Thomas Madden, ...	do.	Cargans, ...
	3627	Edward Hale, ...	do.	Aughlish, ...
	3628	Henry Grimshaw, ...	Robert Hart, ...	Kilmoriarty, ...
	3629	Joseph Forde, ...	do.	do. ...
	3630	James Forde, ...	do.	do. ...
	3631	Mary Carr, ...	Nathaniel Bridges & another, Trustees of T. W. Heath.	Derryvore, ...
	3632	James O'Neill, ...	do.	do. ...
	3633	Robert Holland and another,	do.	do. ...
	3634	John Neill, ...	do.	do. ...
	3635	John Forsythe, ...	do.	do. ...
	3636	John Sweeney, junior, ...	Sir John F. B. Douglas & anor., Trustees of Stewart Blacker.	Seagoe, Lower, ...
	3637	Samuel Guy, ...	Nathaniel Bridges & another, Trustees of T. W. Heath.	Derryvore, ...
	3638	Charles Twinam, ...	do.	do. ...
	3639	William McCaughley, ...	do.	do. ...
	3640	David Porter, ...	Sir John F. B. Douglas & anor.,	Seagoe, Lower, ...

ARMAGH—*continued.*

Extent of Holding (Statute).			Poor Law Valuation.			Former Rent.			Judicial Rent.			Observations.			
A.	R.	P.	£	s.	d.	£	s.	d.	£	s.	d.		£	s.	d.
19	1	16	21	10	0	19	4	0	16	10	0				
8	1	22	7	0	0	10	17	1	6	15	0				
7	0	0	3	0	0	8	15	6	4	0	0				
6	2	30	6	0	0	7	1	7	4	5	0	Rent changed in 1877 from . . .	6	18	7
12	3	0	18	15	0	14	19	2	10	5	0				
23	3	0	24	0	0	31	6	7	20	10	0				
27	2	15	19	10	0	27	5	0	18	0	0				
5	1	0	4	15	0	5	18	3	4	0	0	1861	5	10	0
3	0	7	—			6	6	0	3	10	0				
8	0	12	7	5	0	11	3	10	8	3	0				
8	1	7	8	10	0	10	15	0	7	10	0				
14	0	16	17	5	0	17	5	6	13	10	0				
4	0	14	6	5	0	5	17	3	4	0	0				
9	1	16	10	16	0	11	16	3	9	0	0				
8	0	14	10	15	0	11	16	3	9	0	0				
31	0	13	30	0	0	26	16	7	23	0	0				
9	1	7	11	5	0	11	15	6	9	10	0				
35	3	13	27	5	0	35	8	0	28	0	0				
5	0	16	7	13	0	5	13	0	5	5	0				
38	0	0	53	15	0	68	1	8	43	0	0	1876	45	1	8
33	1	25	53	10	0	63	0	0	43	0	0				
11	0	28	12	5	0	11	6	0	9	0	0				
17	3	0	24	10	0	27	11	0	21	0	0				
5	3	0	6	15	0	6	18	0	4	12	6	1858	5	9	10
17	0	30	23	10	0	27	1	0	23	0	0				
27	0	27	31	0	0	30	3	4	24	10	0	1859	27	0	3
10	2	15	11	18	0	11	19	0	8	0	0				
11	2	0	13	10	0	12	15	0	8	15	0	do.	7	13	9
3	3	0	4	10	0	4	0	0	3	5	0				
11	1	16	11	10	0	12	8	6	9	0	0	do.	9	0	0
14	1	0	17	10	0	20	0	0	14	0	0	1869	18	0	0
8	1	20	7	5	0	8	11	3	6	0	0	1855	5	11	3
33	3	30	30	0	0	30	10	6	23	10	0	1859	23	18	11
18	1	30	21	5	0	21	14	3	16	10	0	do.	16	13	6
14	3	20	18	0	0	20	14	0	15	0	0	1868	18	14	0

Names of Assistant Commissioners by whom Cases were decided.	No.	Name of Tenant.	Name of Landlord.	Townland.
Assistant Commissioners—				
F. G. Hamilton (Legal). J. M. Weir. J. F Bingham. J. Cunningham. Andrew Sproule.	3641	George Porter, ...	St. John F. B. Douglas & anor., Trustees of Stewart Blacker.	Bengie, Lower, ...
	3642	John Sweeny, senior, ...	do.	do. ...
	3643	David Moore, ...	do.	Loughry, ...
	3644	Ellen Robinson, ...	do.	Bengie, Lower, ...
	3645	William Henry Patterson,	Wm. de Salis Filgate & anor., Trustees of late Count de Salis.	Corcreevy, ...
	3646	John Campbell, ...	Sir Francis E. Macnaghten, Bart.	Maghon, ...
J. O. Wylie (Legal). J. Smith. G. G. Kenny. William Davidson. A. Ferguson.	3647	James Edgar, junior, ...	Michael G. O. Burke, ...	Ballinderry,
	3648	Samuel McClelland, Rep. of John McClelland.	Robert W. Peebles, ...	Lenaler, ...
	3649	David McConnell, ...	R. D. Sinclair, ...	Mullabrack, ...
	3650	Thomas Scott, ...	H. B. Armstrong, ...	Derryhaw, ...
	3651	Mrs. Jane Warren, ...	do.	Corparsion, ...
	3652	Thomas Johnston, ...	W. M. Kirk, Trustee of Mrs. Homer's Settlement.	Killymaddy, ...
	3653	Ellen Burke, ...	W. M. Kirk & another, Trustees of John Kirk, deceased,	Rathcarbery, ...
	3654	John Mitchell, ...	do.	Tullygeeeh, ...
	3655	Alexander Johnston, ...	Hugh Harris, ...	Gavenagh, ...
	3656	Alexander Lyons, ...	do.	do. ...
	3657	Francis Todd and others, Reps. of Anne Todd,	do.	do. ...
	3658	Martin Buchanan.	Duke of Manchester, ...	Tullyheppy, ...
	3659	Hugh Hawthorne, ...	do.	do. ...
	3660	William Buchanan, ...	do.	do. ...
	3661	Patrick McKeown, ...	J. W. E. Macartney, ...	Leish, ...
	3662	John Quinn, ...	do.	do. ...
	3663	Francis McCabe, ...	James Haggerty, ...	Glenhouse, ...
	3664	John Donaghey, ...	do.	do. ...
	3665	James Daly, ...	do.	Loughross, ...
	3666	Michael Mallon, ...	do.	do. ...
	3667	Owen Lafferty, ...	H. N. Thorp and another, ...	Crieveloonan, ...
	3668	James Grant, ...	do.	Castles, ...
	3669	Patt McNulty, ...	do.	Crieveloonan, ...
	3670	Patrick Wade, ...	do.	Ulker, ...
	3671	Mary McElroy, ...	do.	Drumbybe, ...
	3672	Patrick McCaule, ...	do.	do. ...
	3673	John McCaule, ...	do.	do. ...

ARMAGH—*continued.*

Extent of Holding. Statute.	Poor Law Valuation.	Former Rent.	Judicial Rent.	Observations.	Value of Tenancy.
A. R. P.	£ s. d.	£ s. d.	£ s. d.	£ s. d.	£ s. d.
10 2 25	13 15 0	15 15 0	13 0 0	Rent changed in 1868 from . . . 14 17 0	
7 3 15	10 5 0	10 10 0	7 10 0	1867 10 0 0	
5 1 21	8 0 0	6 12 6	7 15 0		
31 3 0	26 0 0	34 16 0	31 10 0	1866 31 11 0	
8 0 34	8 5 0	10 12 11	7 10 0		
21 1 20	25 0 0	34 0 0	27 0 0		
36 2 2	52 10 0	60 13 9	50 13 6		
21 3 0	21 15 0	28 0 0	18 0 0		
4 0 0	5 15 0	5 11 11	4 8 0		
34 3 0	27 10 0	30 13 1	24 0 0		
30 1 17	85 10 0	80 0 0	60 0 0		
16 2 25	21 0 0	19 10 0	15 0 0		
10 0 20	8 10 0	10 7 0	8 5 0		
10 1 0	11 0 0	12 3 6	8 15 0		
27 1 20	29 10 0	32 8 4	25 0 0		
57 2 31	71 10 0	65 16 8	64 0 0		
20 2 20	27 0 0	29 10 10½	23 10 0		
20 2 0	13 10 0	22 5 6	18 0 0		
23 1 15	33 5 0	28 19 4	23 5 0		
7 0 20	6 0 0	8 10 8	7 0 0		
12 0 10	12 5 0	13 1 0	10 12 6		
38 2 16	40 16 0	41 17 8	33 10 0		
19 2 15	18 0 8	18 5 4	16 5 0		
6 3 30	5 10 0	5 17 6	4 0 0		
16 2 4	11 10 0	10 13 0	10 0 0		
31 1 0	34 0 0	28 2 6	26 0 0		
13 1 15	9 10 0	10 6 0	7 15 0	Rent changed in 1841 from . . . 6 0 0	
14 2 0	10 5 0	15 2 0	8 10 0		
37 0 20	26 15 0	27 10 0	25 10 0		
11 3 0	9 10 0	7 10 0	5 17 6		
33 2 5	31 5 0	20 0 0	18 0 0		
18 0 30	14 0 0	11 10 0	10 12 6		
14 1 21	11 10 6	10 12 0	8 15 0		

COUNTY OF

Names of Assistant Commissioners by whom Cases were decided.	No.	Name of Tenant.	Name of Landlord.	Townland.
Assistant Commissioners—				
J. O. Wylie (Legal). J. Smith. G. C. Kenny. William Davidson. A. Ferguson.	3674	Bryan McNulty, ...	H. N. Thorp and another, ...	Drumloghier, ...
	3675	Felix McConey, ...	do.	do. ...
	3676	Bernard O'Hare, Rep. of Peter O'Hare.	do.	do. ...
	3677	Edward McShane, ...	do.	do. ...
	3678	Catherine Campbell, ...	do.	do. ...
	3679	Anne Ward, ...	do.	do. ...
	3680	George Herron ...	Rev. A. Crawford, ...	Tullyrallo, ...
	3681	Margaret McCorry, ...	Kendrick Jones, Rep. of T. H. Jones, deceased.	Faughilletra, ...
	3682	Joseph Donaldson, ...	J. F. Erskine and another, ...	Cloghoge, ...
	3683	Bryan McNulty, ...	do.	Greenhill, ...
	3684	Alexander Hill, ...	Ralph C. Jordan, ...	Freuderk, ...
	3685	John Hoey, ...	do.	do. ...
	3686	Rose Conlin, Rep. of Michael Conlin.	A. H. Synge, ...	Tullimurvil, ...
	3687	Pat McCreesh, ...	do.	do. ...
	3688	Mary Donnelly, ...	do.	do. ...
	3689	John McGill, ...	do.	do. ...
	3690	Peter Hughes, ...	do.	do. ...
	3691	Pat Rooney (Peter), ...	do.	do. ...
	3692	Joseph Mackin, ...	do.	do. ...
	3693	Patrick Quinn, ...	do.	do. ...
	3694	Bryan Grant, ...	do.	do. ...
	3695	Mary Mackin, ...	do.	do. ...
	3696	Anne Toner, ...	do.	do. ...
	3697	Mary Donnelly, Rep. of John Donnelly.	do.	do. ...
	3698	Owen Rooney, Rep. of Patt Rooney.	do.	do. ...
	3699	Patrick Donnelly, ...	do.	do. ...
	3700	Bernard Heenan, ...	do.	do. ...
	3701	Arthur Donnelly, ...	do.	do. ...
	3702	Barbara Mackin, ...	do.	do. ...
	3703	John Gaffney, ...	do.	do. ...
	3704	Thaddeus Brannigan, ...	do.	do. ...
	3705	John Loy, ...	do.	do. ...
	3706	Peter Loy, ...	do.	do. ...
	3707	Felix Mackin & Patt Reel, Reps. Bryt. Mackin, decd.	do.	do. ...
	3708	Patrick Mackin (Bevn),	do.	do. ...

ARMAGH—*continued.*

Extent of Holding Stated—	Poor Law Valuation.	Former Rent.	Judicial Rent.	Observations.		Value of Tenancy.
A. R. P.	£ s. d.	£ s. d.	£ s. d.		£ s. d.	£ s. d.
15 1 0	8 0 0	7 15 0	6 10 0			
10 3 1	5 15 0	7 0 0	6 10 0			
7 0 0	1 15 0	4 7 0	3 17 6			
9 3 20	7 0 0	7 6 0	5 15 6			
6 1 30	6 10 0	1 14 0	3 17 6			
5 1 20	5 0 0	4 0 0	3 12 6			
13 3 9	9 10 0	15 10 0	9 10 0			
6 2 25	—	8 18 3	6 10 0			
10 1 26	32 0 0	31 9 10	22 0 0			
6 3 5	3 5 0	4 0 0	3 0 0			
18 0 25	47 15 0	33 10 0	25 0 0	Rent changed in 1858 from . .	26 5 11	
6 2 0	6 0 0	5 10 9	4 5 0	do.	5 6 0	
6 0 15	5 5 0	4 3 0	2 12 6			
5 2 25	3 10 0	2 7 0	3 0 0			
21 3 0	20 0 0	14 14 0	13 0 0			
4 0 35	3 0 0	2 15 6	2 5 0			
11 3 33	9 5 0	7 13 6	7 2 6			
8 3 35	7 5 0	5 18 0	5 2 6			
22 3 20	16 5 0	15 5 0	13 0 0	1858	18 3 5	
6 1 6	6 5 0	5 1 0	4 5 0			
8 2 10	5 15 0	5 9 0	4 10 0			
9 1 35	5 10 0	6 0 0	5 0 0	1856	5 0 6	
7 3 25	5 5 0	4 1 3	3 10 0	1855	3 9 4	
11 3 10	8 10 0	7 4 5	6 0 0			
14 1 5	10 5 0	5 15 0	8 5 0			
11 0 5	5 10 0	5 6 0	5 15 0			
7 2 5	4 15 0	4 2 0	3 5 0			
19 2 10	13 0 0	23 4 0	19 5 0	1853	18 0 0	
8 2 15	7 15 0	5 13 0	4 17 6			
10 3 15	8 5 0	6 15 0	5 15 0			
11 2 25	7 10 0	7 0 0	6 0 0			
9 2 30	6 5 0	5 11 0	4 15 0			
16 0 20	12 5 0	10 0 0	7 0 0	1855	8 11 4	
15 1 28	11 15 0	9 8 0	6 15 0			
11 3 8	9 5 0	8 0 0	7 8 6	1870	7 16 0	

Names of Assistant Commissioners by whom Cases were decided.	No.	Name of Tenant.
Assistant Commissioners—		
J. O. Wylie (Legal). J. Reeves. G. C. Kenny. William Davison. A. Ferguson.	3709	Patrick McAneff,
	3710	John Holywood,
	3711	Bernard McQuade,
	3712	John Holywood,
	3713	Patrick McManus,
	3714	Thomas Mullan & ors Reps. of Pat Mullan
	3715	Elizabeth Kane,
	3716	Hugh McGivern,
	3717	Thomas McAneny,
	3718	Laurence Murphy,
	3719	John Devey,
	3720	Bernard McKeown,
	3721	Pat Thompson,
	3722	Bridget McQuade,
	3723	Owen McShane
	3724	Peter McConniskey,
	3725	Frank McConniskey,
	3726	Esther Harvey,
	3727	James Harvey,
	3728	James McGuill,
	3729	Rose Callaghan,
	3730	Joseph Garriston,
	3731	Patrick Martin, Rep. Mary White,
	3732	John McShane,
	3733	Joseph Green,
	3734	Thomas Hanna,
	3735	James Flanagan.

ARMAGH—*continued.*

Extent of Holding, Statute.	Poor Law Valuation.	Former Rent.	Judicial Rent.	Observations.	Value of Tenancy
A. R. P.	£ s. d.	£ s. d.	£ s. d.		£ s. d.
7 1 35	5 10 0	4 13 8	4 10 0	By consent.	
5 2 0	3 8 0	4 8 0	3 0 8	do.	
5 1 30	8 10 0	4 3 6	3 0 0		
8 8 0	7 15 0	7 1 1	1 18 6		
21 1 33	10 0 0	8 10 0	8 0 0		
6 2 20	5 15 0	6 18 0	1 5 0		
12 2 0	9 10 0	10 18 0	7 5 0	Rent changed in 1863 from £15 0 0	
5 0 35	4 5 0	8 8 6	2 17 6		
7 0 7	4 5 0	6 17 6	5 16 0		
4 1 14	4 5 0	5 0 0	4 0 0		
3 3 27	2 10 0	3 14 8	1 17 8		
7 0 23	5 15 0	8 3 8	4 5 0		
13 0 28	8 0 0	11 3 6	7 10 0		
2 1 10	2 15 0	3 9 6	3 9 8		
3 8 1	3 15 0	4 13 9	3 15 6	By consent.	
8 1 20	8 15 0	8 8 8	6 15 0		
8 0 20	8 10 0	8 19 7	4 15 0	Rent changed in 1843 from 4 18 0	
4 1 30	4 5 0	5 6 3	3 0 0	1858 3 7 11	
8 3 15	2 0 0	3 0 0	1 2 6	1857 1 7 3	
15 3 10	7 5 0	9 16 10	6 10 0	1878 2 8 3	
11 0 31	4 15 0	7 8 9	4 15 0		
11 0 8	8 0 0	11 5 0	7 15 0	1873 9 3 9	
3 8 16	8 15 0	4 18 0	3 12 6	do. 2 17 3	
8 3 25	6 15 0	8 8 8	8 8 0	do. 6 3 6	
18 3 0	10 0 0	13 6 4	8 0 0	do. 10 11 0	
8 0 30	8 5 0	7 16 3	8 0 0	do. 6 1 2	
8 2 0	8 15 0	10 18 9	7 10 0	do. 8 8 5	
3 2 20	2 10 0	3 8 11	3 5 0	By consent.	
5 0 20	2 10 0	3 6 9	2 0 0	do	
6 0 0	7 5 0	5 19 4	5 10 0		
10 2 5	8 10 0	9 10 0	8 0 0		
21 3 25	27 0 0	28 3 0	21 0 0		
11 1 28	11 6 0	12 0 0	6 0 0		
25 0 34	9 0 0	8 5 0	8 6 0	Rent changed in 1853 from . . . 3 10 0	
40 1 20	31 8 0	29 15 0	22 15 0		

COUNTY OF

Names of Assistant Commissioners by whom Cases were decided.	No.	Name of Tenant.	Name of Landlord.	Townland.
Assistant Commissioners— J. O. Wylie (Legal). J. Shaw. G. C. Kenny. William Davidson. A. Ferguson.	3744	Mary Todd, ...	Mark S. Synnott, ...	Cavanakill,
	3745	Edward Haughian, ...	do.	Ballynagh,
	3746	Michael Flanagan, ...	do.	Knockavanny,
	3747	Francis Simpson, ...	do.	Ballinderry,
	3748	Hugh Pyper, ...	Earl of Caledon, ...	Cortynan,
	3749	Samuel E. Kane, ...	do.	do.
	3750	Robert M'Whirter, ...	do.	do.
	3751	Thomas Bryars, ...	do.	do.
	3752	James Armstrong, ...	do.	do.
	3753	Robert Ewart, ...	do.	do.
	3754	William Henderson, ...	do.	do.
	3755	David Gibson, ...	do.	do.
	3756	Robert Orr, ...	The Commissioners of Education in Ireland.	Ballyvalley,
	3757	Robert Girvan, ...	do.	Killean,
	3758	James McQuade, ...	do.	Mullaghnure,
	3759	Joseph O'Hagan, ...	M. C. Close, ...	Drumlanagher,
	3760	Do.	do.	Lisnamaw,
	3761	Do.	do.	do.
	3762	John Todd, ...	Joseph Wilson, ...	Liddian,
	3763	Andrew Barron, ...	do.	Dernagh,
	3764	John Donnelly, ...	do.	Liddian,
	3765	Peter Fearon, ...	Rev. J. W. Ball, ...	Ballinahinch,
	3766	Patrick O'Hare, ...	do.	do.
	3767	Thomas Humphreys, ...	G. H. J. Alexander, ...	Bunnoe Quarter,
	3768	Patrick Murphy, ...	do.	do.
	3769	James Marvin, ...	do.	Levallyrome,
	3770	John Hannaway, ...	do.	do.
	3771	Michael Maginnis, ...	do.	do.
	3772	John M'Cleade & another,	do.	do.
	3773	Patrick Bennett, ...	do.	Levalmore,
	3774	Peter Murphy, ...	do.	Clarkhill,
	3775	Joseph Murphy, ...	do.	do.
	3776	Patrick Maginnis, ...	do.	Levalleane,
	3777	Ross Hannaway, ...	do.	Shevagallen,
	3778	Patrick O'Neill, ...	do.	Levallymore,

ARMAGH—*continued.*

Extent of Holding (Statute).	Poor Law Valuation.	Former Rent.	Judicial Rent.	Observations.	
A. R. P.	£ s. d.	£ s. d.	£ s. d.		£ s.
11 3 30	8 0 0	6 0 0	6 0 0		
41 3 31	29 5 0	26 15 0	24 0 0		
14 0 20	10 0 0	7 10 0	7 10 0	Rent changed in 1869 from - - -	5 0
10 3 38	8 0 0	7 3 0	6 10 0		
18 0 4	—	16 5 4	13 10 0		
33 0 31	35 10 0	35 4 0	29 15 0	1877	29 16
9 0 30	6 15 0	5 0 0	4 0 0		
22 3 31	25 0 0	27 15 0	23 0 0		
30 3 33	30 15 0	31 15 3	24 0 0		
22 0 15	28 16 0	26 11 0	20 10 0		
41 0 0	43 10 0	39 11 0	35 0 0		
7 3 15	8 15 0	8 0 0	8 0 0		
38 0 [illegible]	33 10 0	20 13 7	17 15 0		
12 1 6	70 0 0	65 17 7	37 10 0		
4 1 11	4 10 0	5 3 0	3 7 6		
8 2 0	9 0 0	10 0 0	8 7 6		
23 2 5	27 10 0	33 16 6	31 0 0		
17 0 20	23 0 0	17 13 6	15 0 0		
16 2 5	—	16 3 0	13 4 0		
7 1 35	7 0 0	4 16 8	3 16 0		
14 3 0	10 0 0	16 19 8	11 7 6		
6 3 18	4 3 0	4 8 0	5 0 0	1856	4 17
6 1 30	4 5 0	5 6 0	3 15 0		
11 1 33	8 0 0	5 15 9	5 0 0	1853	5 15
21 3 23	14 0 0	10 1 8	8 0 0	do.	6 15
20 3 8	0 10 0	8 13 10	6 5 0		
11 0 23	3 0 0	4 3 4	3 0 0		

COUNTY

Names of Assistant Commissioners by whom Cases were decided.	No.	Name of Tenant.	Name of Landlord.	Townland
Assistant Commissioners—				
J. O. Wylie (Legal). J. Smith. G. G. Kenny. William Davidson. A. Ferguson.	3779	John O'Hare, ...	G. H. J. Alexander, ...	Ballyhoel,
	3780	Cormack McNally, ...	Miss Alicia Bell and others,	Ballinalea,
	3781	Cormack McAnally, ...	do.	do.
	3782	James Murphy, ...	do.	do.
	3783	James Pond, ...	J. W. E. Macartney, M.P., and another.	Ballydugherty
	3784	David Stuart, ...	do.	do.
	3785	David Shields, ...	do.	do.
	3786	Terence Carty, ...	do.	do.
	3787	Michael Mallarkey, ...	James L. Bell, Reps. of Anne and James Bell.	Drumully.
	3788	John Maginnity, ...	Miss Alicia Bell and others,	Ballinalea,
	3789	Mary Crossey, ...	do.	do.
	3790	John McAnally, ...	do.	do.
	3791	Owen Carr, ...	do.	do.
	3792	Betty Hardy, Rep. of Anne Lonergan.	do.	do.
	3793	Pat Fearon, ...	do.	do.
	3794	Hugh McCann, ...	G. J. C. Henry & ors., Trustees of Thos. G. Henry, deceased.	Seafin,
	3795	Thomas Malone, ...	do.	do.
	3796	Catherine Taggart, ...	do.	do.
	3797	Michael Byrne, ...	do.	do.
	3798	John Lonergan, ...	do.	do.
	3799	John Fearon, ...	do.	do.
	3800	Denis Teal, ...	do.	do.
	3801	Do., ...	do.	do.
	3802	Sarah Hanlon (widow), ...	do.	do.
	3803	Patrick McNally, ...	do.	do.
	3804	Bridget McTaggart, ...	do.	do.
	3805	Anne McElheny, ...	do.	do.
	3806	Michael Callaghan, ...	do.	do.
	3807	Owen Larkin, ...	do.	do.
	3808	Christopher Callaghan, ...	do.	do.
	3809	Dominick McNally, ...	do.	do.
	3810	Thomas Henry, ...	do.	do.
	3811	John Henry, ...	do.	do.
	3812	James Gunn, ...	do.	do.
	3813	Bernard Larkin, ...	do.	do.

ARMAGH—*continued.*

Extent of Holding, Statute.	Poor Law Valuation.	Former Rent.	Judicial Rent.	Observations.	Value of Tenancy.
A. R. P.	£ s. d.	£ s. d.	£ s. d.	£ s. d.	£ s. d.
6 1 10	7 10 0	10 0 0	6 0 0		
4 1 30	4 10 0	4 8 9	3 3 4		
1 2 18	3 5 0	2 19 0	2 0 0		
7 0 10	5 18 0	6 7 0	4 5 0		
14 0 10	16 10 0	18 10 3	13 12 6		
65 2 12	52 15 0	84 16 7	63 10 0		
60 2 15	40 15 0	35 10 5	33 10 0		
27 3 0	28 16 0	32 4 8	25 5 0		
7 2 16	5 15 0	6 11 9½	3 13 6		
5 2 17	1 0 0	1 6 1	3 0 0		
6 0 23	4 10 0	5 12 0	3 17 6		
4 2 20	5 5 0	4 3 7	3 5 0		
4 0 23	3 10 0	3 17 6	2 5 0		
6 3 30	6 0 0	6 16 0	4 3 6		
5 0 3	4 15 0	4 18 0	3 12 6	Rent charged in 1848 from . . . 5 10 0	
6 2 10	3 15 0	4 3 4	2 17 6		
12 0 5	9 10 0	13 2 0	8 0 0		
7 3 3	6 10 0	7 0 6	4 10 0		
8 2 21	7 0 0	7 10 3	5 0 0		
3 0 10	3 10 0	5 14 6	2 10 0		
5 2 24	5 15 0	4 11 6	3 5 0		
3 2 20	2 5 6	3 10 6	1 17 6		
9 1 0	8 10 0	6 18 9	6 5 0		
9 3 12	7 10 0	10 1 6	6 10 0		
8 1 0	3 5 0	7 2 4	1 5 0		
14 0 10	11 0 0	15 6 3	8 10 0		
19 1 0	6 0 0	8 11 6	5 10 0		
9 3 0	4 18 6	5 16 3	3 13 4		
5 1 30	6 10 6	7 8 6	4 15 6		
6 0 7	5 0 0	6 3 3	4 0 0		
14 3 0	12 10 0	15 4 0	9 10 0		

Names of Assistant Commissioners by whom Cases were decided.	No.	Name of Tenant.		Name of Landlord.			Townland.	
Assistant Commissioners—								
J. O. Wylie (Legal). J. Smith. G. C. Kenny. William Davidson. A. Ferguson	3814	David Lockhart,	...	Earl of Kilmorey,		...	Lisdrumliska,	...
	3815	John Fox, ...	...	do.	...	...	do.	...
	3816	James McConnell,	...	do.	...	...	do.	...
	3817	William Hendren,	...	do.	...	...	do.	...
	3818	Nathaniel Shaw,	...	do.	...	...	do.	...
	3819	James McConnell,	...	do.	...	...	Drumalane,	...
	3820	Josiah McConnell,	...	do.	...	...	do.	...
	3821	David Lockhart,	...	do.	...	...	Altnaveigh,	...
	3822	Robert Little,	...	do.	...	...	Lisdrumliska,	...
	3823	John McKeown,	...	do.	...	...	Altnaveigh,	...
	3824	John Farrell,	...	do.	...	...	Drumalane,	...
	3825	John McKnight,	...	do.	...	...	Cloghoge,	...
	3826	James Hendren,	...	do.	...	...	Drumalane,	...
	3827	William Trimble,	...	do.	...	...	do.	
	3828	William Fox,	...	do.	...	...	do.	...
	3829	Hugh McAvoy,	...	do.	...	...	Cloghoge,	...
	3830	Henry Magill,	...	do.	...	...	Drumalane,	...
	3831	Bernard Conlon,	...	W. B. Brown(?),	...	...	Aughanteraghan and Federnagh(?),	
	3832	William Baird,	...	do.	...	...	do.	...
	3833	George Kerr,	...	Earl of Kilmorey,		...	Lisdrumliska,	...
	3834	Bernard O'Hare,	...	Kendrick Jones, ...		...	Drumalane,	...
							Total,	...

ARMAGH—*continued.*

Extent of Holding. Statute.	Poor Law Valuation.	Former Rent.	Judicial Rent.	Observations.		Value of Tenancy.
A. R. P.	£ s. d.	£ s. d.	£ s. d.		£ s. d.	£ s. d.
8 3 8	9 13 0	9 9 0	7 12 6	Rent changed in 1840 from . . .	12 0 0	
6 3 30	8 0 0	7 13 4	5 7 6			
3 0 30	—	1 18 9	8 8 0	1835	5 8 0	
7 3 19	10 5 0	8 3 8	8 10 0	1853	11 0 0	
1 3 27	—	3 8 0	2 8 0			
8 1 29	14 10 0	13 9 10	9 16 0			
10 2 21	7 10 0	10 7 0	7 15 0			
5 1 0	3 15 0	4 8 2	3 7 6	1850	5 0 6	
7 2 16	10 0 0	11 1 6	9 0 0	1849	11 11 6	
7 2 30	—	7 9 0	7 9 0	1853	10 1 0	
3 2 8	5 10 0	6 6 0	1 5 0			
4 0 18	—	4 6 6	3 10 0			
3 3 1	4 15 0	8 15 0	4 5 0			
4 1 21	5 10 0	6 1 6	5 5 0			
4 0 1	8 5 0	7 4 10	6 3 0			
6 3 15	8 10 0	8 12 0	6 5 0			
8 0 35	8 10 0	7 0 8	8 0 0			
9 0 20	8 5 0	16 0 0	9 0 0			
7 1 25	6 0 0	15 10 0	9 10 0	1875	12 0 0	
14 1 8	20 5 0	22 18 4	19 10 0			
13 0 5	3 15 0	8 5 8	5 15 0	By consent.		
4,772 0 32	3,835 5 0	4,108 8 3½	3,171 5 2			

CAVAN.

Names of Assistant Commissioners by whom Cases were decided.	No.	Name of Tenant.	Name of Landlord.	Townland.
Assistant Commissioners— L. Doyle (Legal). J. Hoolan. J. J. Gunn. J. T. Davys. Hugh Johnston.	1347	Ellen Hicks, ...	Bernard O. Shaw, ...	Raleighan,
	1348	Lawrence Connell, ...	do.	Drumkeen,
	1349	Elizabeth Connell ...	do.	do.
	1350	Patrick Morris, ...	Isabella Smith and another, Trustees of Edward Smith, deceased.	Killyvaghan,
	1351	Charles Jameson, ...	do.	do.
	1352	Ellen Maguire, ...	do.	do.
	1353	Edward Kearns, ...	do.	Carolina,
	1354	Thomas Sullivan, ...	do.	Lisnavaddin,
	1355	Robert Foster, ...	do.	Killyvaghan,
	1356	Anne McCabe, ...	Thomas Atkinson, ...	Barraghy,
	1357	John Mullen, ...	do.	do.
	1358	Patrick Mathews, ...	do.	do.
	1359	Rose Mathews, ...	do.	do.
	1360	Edward Mathews, ...	do.	do.
	1361	John Armstrong, ...	William M. Leslie, ...	Latary,
	1362	William Auld, ...	do.	Coronary,
	1363	John Gamble, ...	do.	Knocknalosset,
	1364	William Morrow, ...	do.	Pottle,
	1365	Philip Brady, ...	Isabella Smith and another, Exors. of Edward Smith.	Crus,
	1366	Bernard McQuillan, ...	do.	Pottlereagh,
	1367	Hugh Duffy, ...	do.	Mayo,
	1368	Andrew McBrien, ...	do.	Corfad,
	1369	Robert Stewart, ...	do.	Corclare,
	1370	Robert Stewart, Admor. of Archibald Stewart.	do.	do.
	1371	Francis McNeely, Admor. of Alex. McNeely.	do.	Drumcrumhill,
	1372	Patrick Nicholl, Admor. of George Nicholl.	do.	Killyvaghan,
	1373	Rebecca Whitten, Rep. of Joseph Whitten.	do.	do.
	1374	Anne Hiles, ...	do.	Corclare,
	1375	Owen Carroll, ...	do.	Killyvaghan,
	1376	James Dempsey, ...	do.	do.
	1377	John Smith, senr., ...	do.	Corfad,
	1378	Bridget Smith, ...	do.	Killyvaghan,
	1379	Catherine Lynch, ...	Henry Kelly, ...	Lisnaderragh,
	1380	James Sheridan, ...	Henry Simmonds, ...	Cornahill,
	1381	William Fox, ...	Elizabeth Clarke, ...	Latnaviff,

CAVAN—*continued.*

Extent of Holding. Statute.	Poor Law Valuation.	Former Rent.	Judicial Rent.	Observations.	Value of Tenancy.
A. R. P.	£ s. d.	£ s. d.	£ s. d.	£ s. d.	£ s. d.
20 0 24	19 17 0	13 18 6	11 7 6		
24 3 13	16 0 0	16 8 1	14 5 0		
15 1 29	8 0 0	18 5 6	10 13 6	Rent changed in 1846 from . . . 11 5 0	
18 0 3	9 6 0	9 17 6	6 10 0		
8 1 10	8 0 0	7 5 4	5 7 6		
6 0 11	5 16 0	7 9 4	5 12 6		
11 3 30	7 0 0	10 1 0	7 15 0		
18 2 10	13 15 0	13 0 0	11 7 6		
30 2 31	20 0 0	34 18 0	16 19 6		
47 0 37	26 15 0	37 4 6	26 17 6		
6 0 10	4 15 0	6 0 0	5 0 0		
4 2 8	3 5 0	1 3 10	3 5 0		
0 3 30	1 0 0	1 10 0	1 0 0		
16 0 13	7 0 0	10 1 10	8 0 0		
37 3 25	17 0 0	17 13 1	16 17 6		
10 1 28	6 7 6	9 0 0	6 17 6		
50 1 6	35 5 0	41 3 6	26 12 6		
29 0 17	20 10 0	23 10 10	20 4 0		
24 0 39	4 15 0	7 15 6	6 10 0		
9 2 33	1 5 0	8 15 6	4 15 0		
14 2 0	5 6 0	6 9 8	5 19 6		
17 2 19	6 16 0	11 10 11	7 0 0		
20 2 14	15 10 0	16 13 4	11 16 0		
8 2 10	6 15 0	7 12 1	5 5 0		
31 3 16	20 10 0	37 0 1	23 4 0		
32 1 36	14 10 0	19 3 6	14 10 0	1866 16 1 10	
10 3 8	7 0 0	10 6 3	7 17 6		
9 3 37	6 10 0	9 3 6	6 15 0		
16 1 26	19 0 0	11 2 10	10 10 0		
6 0 1	4 5 0	5 5 9	3 7 6		
10 0 32	5 10 0	7 5 0	6 7 6		
12 1 2	8 15 0	10 11 8	6 5 0	1856 5 18 6	
0 2 0	—	8 0 0	2 0 0	By consent.	
8 0 37	2 0 0	5 0 0	1 16 0		
23 2 10	14 0 0	16 6 6	16 3 6		

Names of Assistant Commissioners by whom Cases were decided.	No.	Name of Tenant.	Name of Landlord.	Townland.
Assistant Commissioners—				
L. Doyle (Legal). J. Howley. J. J. Gorey. J. T. Davis. Hugh Johnston.	1382	John Gordon, ...	Elizabeth Clarke, ...	Drummanmuck,
	1383	Charles O'Reilly, ...	Joseph Pratt, ...	College,
	1384	Patrick McEnaney, ...	S. H. Adams, ...	Cornahan,
	1385	Terence Brady, ...	Robert Doughty and another,	Killinure,
	1386	Rose Doughey, ...	do.	do.
	1387	Anne Keating, ...	Marcus Beresford and others,	Callan,
	1388	Andrew McCabe, ...	do.	do.
	1389	Mary Reilly, ...	Patrick Reilly, ...	Smita,
	1390	Mathew Smith, ...	J. H. Orpen, ...	Carrickgarran,
	1391	John Nickson, ...	Henry S. Seakey, ...	Drummullagh,
	1392	James Clarke, ...	Elliott Armstrong, ...	Corigarine,
	1393	Do.	do.	Carnaklark,
	1394	Mary McMahon, ...	Edward M. Davies, ...	Corraworden,
	1395	Terence Reilly, ...	do.	do.
	1396	Michael Tully, ...	Sherne H. Miller, ...	Laurim,
	1397	Patrick Farrelly, ...	do.	Lower Leitrim,
	1398	John Clarke, ...	Lady Lisgar and another, ...	Carkish,
	1399	Thomas Clarke, ...	do.	do.
	1400	Phil Reilly, ...	Bridget McKenney, ...	Edenagully,
	1401	Andrew Clarke, ...	do.	do.
	1402	Peter Gough, ...	Rev. B. H. Blacker, ...	Ballinamantry,
	1403	Owen Tully, ...	do.	do.
	1404	James Reilly, Admor. of Michael Reilly,	do.	do.
	1405	Samuel Nugh, ...	Dean Warburton, ...	Begliff,
	1406	Patrick Farrell, ...	do.	Kilmorum,
	1407	Thomas Leddy, ...	do.	Begliff,
	1408	Thomas Carolan, ...	do.	do.
	1409	Anne McGuire, ...	do.	Kilnacrum,
	1410	Maria Scott, Rep of Robert Scott,	do.	do.
	1411	George Wilson, ...	do.	Begliff,
	1412	Samuel Thistle, ...	Thomas Boyle and another, Exors. of Dr. McFadden,	Croaghkeagh,
	1413	Anthony Daly, ...	do.	do.
	1414	John Thistle, ...	do.	do.
	1415	William Rusk, ...	do.	do.
	1416	Edward Hartley, ...	do.	do.

TABLE OF JUDICIAL RENTS.

Former Rent.	Judicial Rent.	Observations.	
£ s. d.	£ s. d.		£ s. d.
5 0 0	3 13 0		
5 7 9	3 7 8		
11 10 2	11 10 0		
18 19 0	8 10 0		
18 8 10	9 2 6		
17 18 6	16 10 0		
16 15 0	15 0 0		
8 0 9	4 15 0		
5 1 4	4 5 0		
17 11 0	15 7 6	Rent changed in 1864 from . . .	18 0 0
20 0 0	22 5 0	By consent.	
38 0 0	37 16 3	do.	
57 6 3	61 0 0		
19 8 0	16 10 0		
6 0 0	4 17 6		
9 17 0	7 7 6		
15 5 0	12 13 6		
16 10 10	14 17 6		
23 10 3	18 0 0		
14 12 0	11 7 6		
11 0 0	9 0 0		
9 1 0	8 0 0		
11 18 0	9 17 6		
10 3 9	8 2 6		
17 3 2	11 10 0	By consent.	
7 17 6	7 0 0	do.	
6 0 0	5 5 6	do.	
10 19 4	8 1 0	do.	
14 19 8	11 0 0	do.	
8 1 0	7 3 3	do.	
20 13 0	15 0 0		
14 9 6	10 18 0		
25 16 1	18 0 0		
11 18 0	9 15 0		
18 2 6	16 0 0		

do.

ph Porter,

y Sinclair and

ton Irwin,

do,

do,

CAVAN—*continued.*

Extent of Holding. Statute.	Poor Law Valuation.	Former Rent.	Judicial Rent.	Observations.	Value of Tenancy.
A. R. P.	£ s. d.	£ s. d.	£ s. d.		£ s. d.
37 2 26	17 10 0	20 5 0	16 5 0		
9 2 12	4 5 0	6 15 0	5 6 0		
7 0 0	1 10 0	8 0 0	6 0 0		
7 2 11	5 5 0	5 0 10	1 2 8		
20 1 20	16 0 0	18 0 0	14 10 0		
15 2 36	8 10 0	10 0 0	8 0 0		
1,818 0 13	1,029 19 8	1,339 8 8	1,051 0 11		

DONEGAL.

Extent of Holding. Statute.	Poor Law Valuation.	Former Rent.	Judicial Rent.	Observations.	Value of Tenancy.
91 3 7	21 0 0	23 11 0	19 0 0	Rent changed in 1865 from . . £ s. d. 16 2 9	
10 0 0	7 5 0	7 18 1	6 15 0		
75 0 0	22 0 0	29 0 0	33 10 0		
2 3 4	10 10 0	12 0 0	8 0 0	By consent.	
31 3 20	11 10 0	20 0 0	11 0 0	Rent changed in 1848 from . . 13 0 0	
43 0 25	12 5 0	11 4 0	9 5 0		
47 3 20	10 5 0	12 0 0	7 0 0		
33 2 16	8 15 0	8 11 10	7 0 0		
16 0 10	4 10 0	6 1 5	4 0 0		
14 0 0	10 5 0	15 0 0	13 0 0		
6 3 0	8 5 0	9 0 0	7 10 0		
26 1 14	18 0 0	29 17 0	19 0 0		
21 3 17	18 5 6	19 12 4	16 15 0	1878 16 15 6	
13 3 5	13 10 0	14 0 0	13 0 0		
44 2 20	7 5 0	8 8 0	8 10 0	1824 6 18 0	
37 1 22	7 10 0	8 7 4	6 0 0	do. 7 18 0	
11 3 9	6 10 0	6 18 0	5 0 0		
8 3 7	5 5 0	7 10 0	5 10 0		
13 3 10	6 5 0	7 10 0	5 10 0	1881 6 0 0	
30 0 0	9 0 0	11 11 0	6 15 0		
15 1 26	5 10 0	6 14 0	5 0 0		
69 1 25	15 0 0	17 5 0	16 0 0		
33 2 0	16 10 0	22 10 0	19 0 0		

Names of Assistant Commissioners by whom Cases were decided	No.	Name of Tenant	Name of Landlord	Townland
Assistant Commissioners—				
Ulick Bourke (Legal). R. Sproule. William Gray. Thomas Mears. R. R. Cowen.	3433	Bridget McGrath, Admin. of Thomas McIlrath.	Rupert F. Cullen, ...	Greenanridge, ...
	3434	Daniel McNulty, ...	Rebecca Jones and another,	Croaknelly, ...
	3435	Do.	George Barnard, Exec. of Ebenezer Barnard.	Ballyshannon, ...
	3436	Hugh Strong, ...	Thomas Dickson, ...	Glenkeeragh, ...
	3437	Bernard Reynolds, ...	John Trelcastick, ...	Carter, ...
	3438	James Mulhern, ...	James W. S. Murray, ...	Lisnakelly, ...
	3439	John Munday, ...	John Sharpe, ...	Magheramay, ...
	3440	John McGinty, ...	Lord Arran, ...	Birchill,
	3441	John Stevenson, ...	do.	Keeldrum, ...
	3442	Jane Stewart (widow),	Marquis of Conyngham, ...	Dromgorman, ...
	3443	William McBrearty, ...	Thomas Brooke, ...	Lough Fad Drum[illegible]
	3444	Ellen Tunny, Rep. of Edward Tunny.	do.	Greenans, ...
	3445	Michael McLoughlin, ...	Samuel Thompson, ...	Mountyderragh, ...
	3446	Mary Kelly, ...	do.	do. ...
	3447	Ann McGonigle & anor.,	do.	do. ...
	3448	Michael McLoughlin, ...	do.	do. ...
	3449	Patrick Collins, ...	Hon. E. Cochrane and another,	Carrickmagregory,
	3450	Henry Doherty, ...	Hon. Ernest E. L. Cochrane,	Altnadua, ...
	3451	Owen Barr, ...	do.	Granshe, ...
	3452	Charles McLoughlin, ...	do.	do. ...
	3453	Hugh Scott, ...	Earl of Leitrim, ...	Ballyharran, ...
	3454	Anne McAteer, ...	do.	Doughbeg, ...
	3455	James Hunter, ...	do.	Carnamoy, ...
	3456	Samuel Culbertson, ...	do.	Ballymonie, Up.,
	3457	Bryan Mulhern, ...	Elizabeth Barrett, ...	Tully, ...
	3458	Edward Boyle, ...	do.	do. ...
	3459	Michael Slavin, ...	Rev. John Hamilton, ...	Cooling, ...
	3460	John Daly, ...	do.	do. ...
	3461	Patrick McGahern, ...	do.	Lighmary, ...
	3462	Samuel McNeely, ...	do.	do. ...
	3463	Patrick O'Hara, ...	do.	Meenadrean, ...
	3464	James Ingram, ...	do.	Drumnaskey, ...
	3465	John Mallin, ...	do.	Drumnaleet, ...
	3466	Rev. Andrew Lowry, ...	Mrs. Rebecca Jones, ...	Croaknelly, ...
	3467	Bryan Brady, ...	do.	do. ...

DONEGAL—*continued.*

Extent of Holding, Statute.	Poor Law Valuation.	Former Rent.	Judicial Rent.	Observations.		Value of Tenancy.
A. R. P.	£ s. d.	£ s. d.	£ s. d.		£ s. d.	£ s. d.
23 2 4	6 10 0	5 6 8	7 0 0			
4 2 0	5 10 0	6 18 8	6 18 8			
4 2 0	5 0 0	6 16 0	6 14 0			
74 2 11	5 15 0	9 10 0	8 10 0	Rent changed in 1866 from . . .	7 0 0	
11 2 0	6 15 0	6 18 8	5 0 0			
14 2 20	18 10 0	27 0 0	18 0 0			
4 3 0	5 0 0	9 0 0	7 0 0			
15 3 10	7 0 0	10 8 6	7 10 0	1862	5 5 0	
23 2 18	30 0 0	21 15 6	19 10 0	1863	23 10 6	
28 2 0	12 0 0	12 0 0	10 0 0			
21 1 10	8 0 0	10 0 0	8 5 0			
148 3 30	13 10 0	13 0 0	13 10 0			
10 1 15	3 8 0	1 14 0	3 11 0	By consent.		
25 0 16	5 13 0	8 14 4	6 13 0			
67 0 0	14 5 0	19 15 10	15 5 0	Rent changed in 1874 from . . .	14 16 0	
36 2 0	18 0 0	21 9 0	17 15 0	do.	19 10 0	
12 1 35	8 5 0	8 0 0	6 5 0			
12 1 4	7 10 0	7 1 7	6 0 0			
23 2 0	6 15 0	9 10 0	7 10 0			
34 3 31	18 0 0	31 0 5	17 10 0			
30 2 0	19 13 0	24 10 0	19 0 0			
7 1 0	3 0 0	4 0 0	3 0 0	1858	3 13 6	
15 2 0	3 10 0	5 14 0	3 15 0			
22 2 28	13 0 0	11 0 0	13 0 0	do.	11 10 7	
5 1 10	4 0 0	6 10 0	5 10 0			
24 1 19	20 0 0	18 0 0	23 10 0			
29 0 5	20 4 0	25 0 0	16 0 0			
27 2 34	18 10 0	30 0 0	17 0 0			
59 2 0	5 18 0	4 0 0	3 5 0			
81 0 27	9 5 0	11 0 0	9 5 0			
85 0 6	6 5 0	8 0 0	7 0 0			
10 0 25	3 15 0	5 14 0	4 6 0	1860	4 5 0	
7 3 30	6 8 0	5 6 8	6 5 0			
17 2 21	15 0 0	21 18 4	15 10 0			
9 3 25	6 10 0	6 8 5	5 3 0			

Assistant Commissioners—	No.	Tenant	Landlord
Ulick Bourke (Legal). R. Stubbs. William Gray. Thomas Meik. R. R. Crozier.	3468	Patrick McColgan and another,	Robert G. Young,
	3469	Margaret McDaid, ...	do. ...
	3470	Michael Quigley, ...	do. ...
	3471	Daniel M'Gonagle, ...	do. ...
	3472	Edward Doherty, ...	do. ...
	3473	Owen Harkins, ...	do. ...
	3474	Denis McKenny, ...	do. ...
	3475	Patrick M. Doherty, ...	do. ...
	3476	Patrick McConagle, ...	do. ...
	3477	James McGonagle, ...	do. ...
	3478	Thomas McLaughlin, ...	do. ...
	3479	John McLaughlin, ...	do. ...
	3480	John Smith, ...	G. M. Harvey, ...
	3481	James McLaughlin, ...	do. ...
	3482	Bridget McLaughlin, ...	do. ...
	3483	Daniel McLaughlin, ...	do. ...
	3484	James Lafferty, ...	Bartholomew McCorkell another.
	3485	Elizabeth Lafferty, ...	do. ...
	3486	John Anderson, ...	do. ...
	3487	Daniel McNulty, ...	Rev. Joseph W. Dic Exor. of John R. Dic
	3488	Patrick Sweeny, ...	do. ...
	3489	Joseph McNutter, ...	do. ...
	3490	William Ward, ...	do. ...
	3491	James Gavigan, ...	do. ...
	3492	James Black and another,	do. ...
	3493	Robert McBride, ...	do. ...
	3494	John Gavigan, ...	do. ...
	3495	William Doherty, ...	Leslie Alexander, ...

a.	r.	p.	£	s.	d.	£	s.	d.
20	0	0	6	10	0	9	0	0
17	0	0	7	15	0	11	10	0
25	2	0	9	15	0	12	0	0
5	3	0	3	15	0	7	0	0
45	0	15	18	10	0	21	0	0
6	2	0	3	10	0	6	10	0
7	2	0	3	15	0	7	10	0
3	1	5	3	12	6	6	0	0
1	0	0	2	0	0	5	0	0
33	1	25	6	5	0	9	10	0
3	2	20	3	0	0	3	0	0
6	3	20	2	15	0	4	0	0
34	0	21	18	15	0	16	5	0
105	0	0	19	18	0	24	16	5
13	2	0	5	10	0	8	16	6
10	2	0	4	15	0	5	1	8
10	3	25	5	10	0	5	0	0
64	1	10	15	10	0	18	10	0
13	2	25	8	0	0	9	10	0
50	3	35	16	6	0	16	0	0
35	3	30	10	10	0	11	5	0
19	2	34	13	10	0	13	0	0
9	2	10	1	0	0	4	15	0
14	0	7	19	0	0	52	18	0
32	2	35	19	0	0	87	16	11
22	0	20	6	15	0	10	10	0
67	2	33	32	10	0	57	9	2
137	2	30	5	15	0	6	14	10
5	1	22	4	0	0	6	6	0
87	0	21	2	10	0	7	15	0
4	2	0	3	5	0	5	4	0
83	0	0	3	0	0	8	10	0
55	1	26	14	0	0	28	6	8
93	2	10	9	18	0	15	0	0
93	3	10	3	15	6	6	6	0

Ulick Bourke (Legal).
R. Spencer.
William Gray.
Thomas Meek.
R. R. Church.

3503	Philip Coyle,	...	Leslie Alexander,	
3504	Neal Bradley,	...	do.	...
3505	James M'Callion,	...	do.	...
3506	William M'Laughlin,	...	do.	...
3507	Hugh Doherty,	...	do.	...
3508	John Doherty,	...	do.	...
3509	Thomas Baldrick,	...	Sir Robert B. Harvey,	
3510	Ellen Carolan,	...	do.	...
3511	George Baldrick,	...	do.	...
3512	James M'Callion,	...	do.	...
3513	James Kelly,	...	do.	...
3514	John M'Guigan & anor.,		David Gilliland,	...
3515	John Doherty,	...	do.	...
3516	William Parven,	...	George M. Harvey,	
3517	Betty Molloy,	...	do.	...
3518	John Nelson,	...	do.	...
3519	Cecilia Parven,	...	do.	...
3520	Patrick Doherty,	...	do.	...
3521	Hugh M'Cafferty,	...	Sir John Leslie, Bart.,	
3522	James Britton,	...	do.	...
3523	William Britton,	...	do.	...
3524	Felix Monaghan, Rep. of Terence Monaghan,		do.	...
3525	Bernard M'Garrigle,	...	do.	...
3526	James Mulreine, Rep. of Owen Mulreine,		do.	...
3527	Thomas Monaghan,	...	do.	...
3528	John Gallagher,	...	do.	...
3529	Hugh M'Goldrick,	...	do.	...
3530	James M'Grath,	...	do.	...
3531	Do. ...	...	do.	...
3532	Patk. M'Grath (Teague),		do.	...
3533	Owen M'Grath,	...	do.	...
3534	Patrick M'Cafferty,	...	do.	...

TABLE OF JUDICIAL RENTS.

DONEGAL—*continued.*

Extent of Holding. Statute.	Poor Law Valuation.	Former Rent.	Judicial Rent.	Observations.
A. R. P.	£ s. d.	£ s. d.	£ s. d.	
63 3 14	8 8 0	6 13 8	5 15 0	
19 2 6	9 0 0	14 8 0	8 10 0	
9 3 16	3 10 0	7 15 8	4 0 0	
21 0 18	4 0 0	7 18 4	5 0 0	
343 3 16	8 5 0	16 11 10	10 10 0	
6 3 4	5 10 0	6 8 4	9 17 6	
13 3 25	23 10 0	21 18 6	23 10 0	
1 3 17	9 15 0	4 16 0	8 17 6	
11 1 18	27 0 0	34 10 4	23 10 0	Provision has been made in this case as regards a labourer.
183 0 5	4 15 0	6 17 8	4 5 0	
68 3 34	8 5 0	3 0 0	8 12 0	
41 1 20	15 10 0	19 0 0	14 5 0	
45 3 8	11 15 0	15 14 4	10 10 0	
11 0 0	4 5 0	6 0 0	4 12 0	
12 0 0	4 15 0	6 5 8	4 15 0	Rent changed in 1851 from . . . £6 7s. 0d.
8 2 0	3 0 0	4 9 0	3 15 0	
30 0 0	11 15 0	18 14 6	11 10 0	do. 13 15 0
36 0 0	16 15 0	19 1 4	17 0 0	do. 18 0 0
17 3 0	9 15 0	5 0 0	8 10 0	
108 0 30	20 5 0	35 5 8	27 0 0	
120 1 20	18 8 0	21 17 4	16 0 0	
16 0 0	7 17 0	9 10 0	6 0 0	
31 0 0	6 5 0	7 15 0	6 10 0	
62 0 0	8 15 0	11 0 0	7 15 0	
20 0 30	1 10 0	3 0 0	1 13 6	
15 3 20	3 5 0	4 8 5	8 10 0	
10 2 20	4 10 0	6 17 0	6 0 0	
66 0 10	4 6 0	6 10 0	4 7 6	
140 0 0	10 15 0	12 8 8	9 10 0	
8 3 30	3 5 0	4 10 8	3 15 0	
85 0 0	8 15 0	13 4 6	7 10 0	
18 2 20	3 7 0	5 0 0	4 0 0	
7 2 12	3 5 0	1 6 0	3 10 0	
7 1 3	3 10 0	1 0 0	2 17 6	
344 1 20	5 15 0	0 9 0	7 10 0	1856 4 15 0

3556	John Maxwell,
3557	Richard Graham,
3558	Catherine Gallagher,
3559	Robert Scott,
3560	Sally Gallagher,
3561	Edward Gillespie,
3562	Susan Walsh, Admi: Catherine Walsh.
3563	Michael Gallagher.
3564	Edward Carr,
3565	George Orswurd,
3566	Bridget Devlin,
3567	Bryan McGullion,
3568	Mary Walsh,
3569	Charles Gildea,
3570	Thomas Ross, Rep. Ann Brown,
3571	Alexander Scott,
3572	Margaret Slavin,

DONEGAL—*continued.*

Extent of Holdings. Statute.	Poor Law Valuation.	Former Rent.	Judicial Rent.	Observations.
A. R. P.	£ s. d.	£ s. d.	£ s. d.	
65 1 33	3 5 0	5 10 0	3 15 0	Rent changed in 1858 from . . .
115 0 0	3 8 0	7 0 0	4 5 8	
80 0 0	2 10 0	3 18 0	8 0 0	
16 1 5	6 5 0	7 15 0	6 0 0	do.
13 0 0	3 10 0	5 10 6	3 15 0	do.
5 3 37	4 0 0	6 10 0	4 15 0	1853
8 0 23	6 0 0	6 6 0	5 5 0	1857
3 8 20	2 15 0	6 10 0	3 10 0	1859
14 3 25	10 5 0	13 0 0	9 0 0	
23 3 6	18 15 6	23 0 0	11 15 0	1856
30 3 35	5 18 0	12 15 0	9 5 0	1858
17 1 3	8 0 0	11 0 0	5 5 0	1866
19 3 0	10 0 0	16 0 0	10 15 0	1867
4 3 7	3 0 0	4 0 0	2 15 0	
19 1 10	11 0 0	15 11 6	10 10 0	
15 3 3	11 15 8	15 0 0	10 5 0	1856
30 1 0	11 0 0	16 0 0	11 10 0	
11 1 0	5 15 0	9 6 0	8 0 0	
13 2 20	6 10 0	9 10 0	8 10 0	1864
21 0 0	18 10 0	15 12 0	13 10 0	do.
5 1 20	—	4 0 0	3 6 8	
6 3 15	1 18 0	4 14 0	3 15 0	1865
7 3 29	3 5 0	6 10 0	3 15 0	
16 2 18	6 10 0	11 0 0	6 0 0	
2 2 0	1 0 0	2 0 0	1 5 0	
3 0 10	2 10 0	3 10 0	2 10 0	1858
6 2 4	3 0 0	3 10 0	3 0 0	
1 0 25	3 10 0	3 11 10	3 2 6	1860
16 3 15	6 5 0	11 5 0	6 0 0	1864
4 2 9	5 0 0	3 18 6	2 15 0	1867
3 0 20	1 10 0	3 16 0	1 15 0	do.
13 2 0	7 5 0	8 15 3	6 15 0	
7 1 10	6 0 0	7 18 0	5 10 0	do.
12 0 0	4 10 0	6 0 0	1 12 0	
13 1 15	— ..	10 0 0	6 0 0	By consent.

Names of Assistant Commissioners by whom Cases were decided.	No.	Name of Tenant.	Name of Landlord.	Townland.
Assistant Commissioners—				
Ulick Bourke (Legal). R. Sproule. William Gray. Thomas Meek. R. B. Cauvin.	3573	Francis Kennedy, ...	Thomas Colquhoun, ...	Drumore, ...
	3574	James Sent and another,	do.	do. ...
	3575	James Wilson, ...	do.	do. ...
	3576	John Wilson, ...	do.	do. ...
	3577	William Syms, ...	do.	do. ...
	3578	Andrew Magee, ...	Charles Johnston, ...	Rossmore, ...
	3579	Anne Gilder, ...	do.	Whitehill, ...
	3580	Thomas Stewart, ...	do.	Ardnaguade, ...
	3581	Joseph Rea, ...	do.	do. ...
	3582	Do.	do.	Tonalough, ...
	3583	Hugh Hammond (Irish),	do.	Drumany, Long,
	3584	Charles Moran, ...	do.	Drumnacarry, ...
	3585	James McNight, ...	do.	Rossmore, ...
	3586	Lucy Miller, ...	do.	Tullyearl, ...
	3587	Alexander Crawford, ...	do.	do. ...
	3588	Richard Graham, ...	do.	Rossmore, ...
	3589	Francis McCadden, ...	do.	Tullyearl, ...
	3590	John Wray, ...	do.	Tonagh & another,
	3591	David Graham, ...	do.	Rossmore & another,
	3592	John Graham, ...	do.	Tullyearl, ...
	3593	James Harron, ...	do.	Tullykeeragh, ...
	3594	Edward Graham, ...	do.	Tullyearl, ...
	3595	William Graham, ...	do.	do. ...
	3596	Gilbert Rea, ...	do.	Ardnaguade, ...
	3597	Patrick Mahon, ...	Henry Bruen and others, Trustees of Thos. Conolly, decd.	Ballymagrorty, ...
	3598	John Langan, ...	do.	Rockhill, ...
	3599	Thomas Barrett, ...	do.	do. ...
	3600	Owen Carney, ...	do.	Cow Park, ...
	3601	Do.	do.	Abbey, ...
	3602	Thomas Kelly, ...	do.	Abbeylands and another.
	3603	George Patton, ...	do.	Kinahey, ...
	3604	Michael Tourry, ...	do.	Tullymore, ...
	3605	Philip Kennedy, ...	do.	do. ...
	3606	Patrick McNeely, ...	do.	Tullypark, ...
	3607	Francis Gallagher, ...	do.	Tullymoan, ...

Extent of Holding. Statute.	Poor Law Valuation.	Former Rent.	Judicial Rent.	Observations.		Value of Tenancy.
A. R. P.	£ s. d.	£ s. d.	£ s. d.		£ s. d.	£ s. d.
17 3 6	4 5 0	6 0 0	4 15 0	By consent.		
11 2 5	3 5 0	4 18 10	4 0 0	do.		
14 1 20	5 5 0	8 18 0	5 10 0	do.		
7 0 25	2 0 0	4 1 0	3 0 0	do.		
11 2 5	3 5 0	5 7 3	4 10 0	do.		
10 3 35	7 5 0	9 10 10	7 3 0	Rent changed in 1868 from	6 8 0	
11 2 1	6 15 0	7 14 8	6 0 0	do.	5 18 0	
16 0 25	6 0 0	7 16 5	6 0 0	do.	6 17 9	
7 2 35	3 10 0	5 13 4	4 18 0			
13 1 30	5 0 0	6 4 8	5 10 0	do.	5 3 0	
21 0 10	12 0 0	14 8 4	11 0 0			
5 0 1	2 15 0	4 0 0	2 15 0	do.	2 0 0	
2 1 0	3 0 0	3 14 8	2 0 0			
12 0 10	7 5 0	11 4 10	7 10 0	do.	8 15 0	
8 0 15	7 10 0	9 19 10	7 10 0	do.	8 11 8	
13 1 10	10 15 0	11 16 0	8 0 0			
12 2 30	10 5 0	11 19 0	9 0 0			
10 0 35	6 15 0	7 14 8	5 15 0	do.	6 10 0	
15 3 27	10 0 0	11 3 5	9 0 0			
16 0 29	8 0 0	11 5 5	8 10 0	do.	9 18 0	
4 2 5	3 15 0	3 18 0	3 0 0			
5 3 0	2 5 0	3 4 5	2 18 0	do.	2 16 0	
16 1 30	10 5 0	12 11 0	10 0 0			
8 0 37	3 5 0	5 15 4	4 9 0	do.	5 0 0	
[illegible] 3 12	5 10 0	7 4 7	7 6 7			
10 2 25	8 10 0	12 18 11	10 0 0			
60 2 25	29 0 0	29 10 11	25 10 0			
6 2 0	5 0 0	4 10 10	4 0 0			
7 0 35	11 0 0	16 0 0	10 10 0			
11 1 30	14 5 0	14 18 0	13 0 0			
5 3 0	7 10 0	8 13 4	7 10 0			
27 3 35	10 0 0	9 14 0	8 10 0			
10 2 0	7 15 0	7 16 4	7 0 0			
25 2 5	13 5 0	12 15 0	11 10 0			
17 3 20	5 10 0	7 8 0	6 10 0			

P. O. [illegible] (Legal).
J. M. W[illegible].
J. [illegible].
J. F. [illegible].
A. [illegible].

DONEGAL—*continued.*

Extent of Holding. Statute.	Poor Law Valuation.	Former Rent.	Judicial Rent.	Observations.	Value of Tenancy.
A. R. P.	£ s. d.	£ s. d.	£ s. d.		£ s. d.
17 2 20	9 10 0	9 0 0	7 15 0		
15 1 20	8 10 0	8 14 0	8 14 0		
23 2 16	18 10 0	12 8 10	9 10 0		
36 3 25	15 0 0	16 17 6	14 10 0		
22 0 30	18 10 0	12 8 10	11 0 0		
34 2 16	11 0 0	18 0 0	13 0 0		
41 1 10	17 0 0	18 14 4	15 10 0		
29 1 27	14 0 0	17 11 0	14 10 0		
15 3 35	11 10 0	12 13 0	10 15 0		
4 0 35	5 16 0	9 0 0	9 0 0		
8 3 20	10 5 0	10 4 0	10 4 0		
3 3 10	4 5 0	6 10 0	1 5 0		
17 0 6	8 15 0	9 10 0	8 6 0		
15 3 25	16 16 0	19 0 0	15 0 0		
28 0 6	16 10 0	15 16 0	14 0 0		
23 3 0	—	9 0 0	7 5 0		
11 3 15	4 10 0	8 10 0	4 15 0		
13 3 20	14 0 0	16 0 0	15 0 0		
4,394 0 16	1,889 13 6	2,870 17 9	1,860 6 4		

DOWN.

Extent of Holding. Statute.	Poor Law Valuation.	Former Rent.	Judicial Rent.	Observations.	Value of Tenancy.
18 0 20	15 15 0	19 0 0	15 0 0		
34 0 6	33 0 0	36 13 0	31 16 0		
31 1 30	30 10 0	31 18 2	29 0 0		
62 0 0	55 0 0	61 0 4	45 0 0		
3 1 30	6 0 0	9 0 0	7 0 0		
17 2 20	18 5 0	20 16 0	15 15 0		
94 0 25	26 0 0	30 7 8	26 0 0	By consent.	
10 3 10	9 0 0	11 5 0	5 16 0		
11 2 22	8 12 6	11 18 8	7 10 0		
10 0 10	7 15 0	10 7 0	7 10 0		
14 3 0	9 10 0	12 16 1	9 5 0		

COUNTY OF

Names of Assistant Commissioners by whom Cases were decided.	No.	Name of Tenant.	Name of Landlord.	Townland.
Assistant Commissioners—				
F. G. Hosmer (Legal). J. M. Ware. J. Cuttingham. J. F. Hobson. A. Stewart.	3655	Edward O'Hara, ...	Pierce Francis John Newell, a Minor.	Lower Ballo, ...
	3656	Patrick McAvoy, ...	do.	do. ...
	3657	Samuel Stoop, ...	do.	do. ...
	3658	Charles Keenan, ...	do.	do. ...
	3659	Thomas Stoop, ...	do.	do. ...
	3660	James Keenan, ...	do.	do. ...
	3661	Felix Morris, ...	do.	do. ...
	3662	Patrick Mulcunville, ...	do.	do. ...
	3663	William Morrow, ...	Visct. Bridport & anor., Trustees of Marquis of Downshire.	Cronan, ...
	3664	William Davidson, ...	Colonel Donald H. Stewart, ...	Ballyrawood and Ballywalter.
	3665	Alexander Marchant, ...	Andrew Cowan, ...	Carnbane, ...
	3666	William Hospital, ...	William A. Gilbert, ...	Seagoe, Upper, ...
	3667	Robert McCaw, ...	Lord Lurgan, ...	Taghnevan, ...
	3668	William Pickering, ...	do.	Monbrief, ...
	3669	Richard Stevenson, ...	do.	do. ...
	3670	Do., ...	do.	do. ...
	3671	James Hagan, ...	James W. Pepper, ...	Ballyworkan, ...
	3672	Bleaker McGowan, ...	Rose A. Crookie and another, Exors. of Thomas Crookie.	do. ...
	3673	Sarah Pentland, Admix. of Mary Pentland.	do.	do. ...
	3674	James Fitzvelle, ...	John J. Banniston, ...	do. ...
	3675	John McCracken (The Hill).	George Allen, ...	Donover, ...
	3676	Robert Dilworth, ...	Duke of Manchester, ...	Lisnisky, ...
	3677	John Walker, ...	do.	Upper Seagoe, ...
	3678	William Metcalf, ...	do.	Tarson, ...
	3679	Andrew Hall, ...	do.	Lisnisky, ...
	3680	Thomas Reddell, ...	do.	Lisnisky and another.
	3681	Robert Baxter, ...	do.	Tullyhugh, ...
	3682	Thomas McGuinness, ...	do.	Ballymore, ...
	3683	Samuel McCullen, ...	do.	Tullyhugh and another.
	3684	Mary McGuinness, ...	do.	Ballymore, ...
	3685	Thomas Mathers, ...	do.	do. ...
				Total, ...

1371	Hugh Coulter,
1372	Neal Keon, ...
1373	Catherine Keown,
1374	Francis McManus,
1375	Michael McDonagh,
1376	William Crawford,
1377	William Burton,
1378	James Monaghan,
1379	John Bird, ...
1380	Jane Brandon,
1381	Charles Dogherty,
1382	Francis Carroll,
1383	James Moore,
1384	Francis Dornan,
1385	Margaret Wilson,
1386	Patrick Leonard,
1387	William Stephenson,
1388	Henry Woods,
1389	John Gallagher,
1390	James Monaghan,
1391	Edward McCree,
1392	Michael Barnes,
1393	John Simpson,
1394	William Thompson,
1395	Patrick McCormick,
1396	Henry Nixon,
1397	Edward Corrigan,
1398	William H. Keys,
1399	Rev. James McQuade,

FERMANAGH.

Extent of Holding (Statute).	Poor Law Valuation.	Former Rent.	Judicial Rent.	Observations.	Value of Tenancy.
A. R. P.	£ s. d.	£ s. d.	£ s. d.	£ s. d.	£ s. d.
46 2 0	21 10 0	27 0 0	20 5 0		
21 1 4	11 0 0	10 0 0	8 1 0		
17 1 23	14 0 0	11 0 0	11 10 0		
24 2 8	20 0 0	27 0 0	22 10 0		
11 2 10	7 0 0	7 0 0	6 0 0		
16 1 35	7 10 0	10 0 0	6 5 0	Rent changed in 1881 from . . 8 0 0	
20 0 35	8 13 0	9 16 0	8 10 0		
21 3 15	10 5 0	13 0 0	10 0 0		
11 3 30	6 5 0	8 8 0	7 0 0		
10 3 23	5 15 0	6 16 0	4 15 0		
6 1 25	6 15 0	6 0 0	5 0 0		
31 1 10	14 0 0	18 0 0	14 10 0	do. 16 0 0	
45 3 20	13 10 0	13 0 0	10 0 0		
18 1 15	4 15 0	4 16 0	1 0 0		
74 3 5	20 15 0	31 0 0	27 10 0		
20 2 23	8 15 0	10 10 0	8 15 0		
21 3 5	8 10 0	11 0 0	8 10 0		
15 1 10	7 13 0	10 12 0	6 0 0		
37 1 24	14 5 0	31 0 0	17 10 0		

Names of Assistant Commissioners by whom Cases were decided.	No.	Name of Tenant.	Name of Landlord.	Townland.
Assistant Commissioners:—				
M. T. Crean (Legal). S. Mowbray. J. H. McIntyre. J. A. O'Kelly. J. Blood-Smyth.	1400	Andrew McCaskar, ...	Earl of Belmore, ...	Aleaga, ...
	1401	Robert Philips, ...	Henry L. St. George, ...	Drumcolure, ...
	1402	John Porter, ...	H. de F. Montgomery, ...	Drummond, ...
	1403	Francis Hamilton, ...	Lord Rathdonnell, ...	Knockaninskea,
	1404	Roger Maguire, ...	do.	do. ...
	1405	Ashman Fitzpatrick (Blank).	Captain Edward Barton, ...	Clonmell & anr.,
	1406	Do.	do.	Aghabahana, ...
	1407	Alexander Armstrong, ...	H. W. Hamilton, ...	Rossghlry, ...
	1408	Johnston Wilson, ...	Mrs. E. J. Johnston & others, Odes of James C. Johnston	Kilmacormaund,
	1409	John Elliott, ...	Irvine Elliott, ...	Crieve, ...
	1410	Rachel Ward, ...	George Fowler & anr., Exors. of George Fowler & another,	Rathkerine, ...
	1411	Bartly McGrath, ...	John Anderson and another,	Dring, ...
	1412	Thomas Flanagan, ...	Louisa H. Dowling, ...	Drumcullion, ...
	1413	William McSherry, ...	Christopher Buchanan, ...	Kellytaggart, ...
	1414	Patrick Magirr, ...	Acheson H. Irvine, ...	[illegible], ...
	1415	Thomas Bibbit, ...	Elizabeth Brudden, ...	Aghameen, North,
	1416	Thomas Gilroy, ...	Philip Percival, ...	Knocknahenska,
	1417	Hugh Curry, ...	Very Rev J. M. Beresford, ...	Gortmullin, ...
	1418	Peter Curry, ...	do.	do. ...
	1419	Pat Boshill, ...	do.	Clonmully, ...
	1420	Bernard Reilly, Rep. of Hugh Reilly, deceased,	do.	do. ...
	1421	James McGovern, ...	do.	Gortmullin, ...
	1422	Edward Dunnion, ...	do.	do. ...
	1423	Andrew Kerr, ...	Rev. William Hall & another,	Dungaughey, ...
	1424	Thomas Busby, ...	do.	do. ...
	1425	Thomas McCaffrey, ...	Colonel J. G. Irvine, ...	Drumgowna, ...
	1426	Mary Johnston, ...	do.	Creeva, ...
	1427	Philip McGuinness, ...	do.	Drumcunn, ...
	1428	James Crozier, ...	do.	Drumlone, ...
	1429	Catherine Maguire, ...	do.	Leggy, ...
	1430	William Surphlis, ...	Earl of Erne, ...	Carrowcastle, ...
	1431	Thomas Mortimer, ...	do.	Cleenishmeen & anr.,
	1432	Owen Cassidy, ...	do.	Tubrada, ...
	1433	John Keenan, ...	do.	do. ...
	1434	Patrick Morris, ...	do.	Kilegarrow, ...

FERMANAGH—*continued.*

Extent of Holding. Statute.	Poor Law Valuation.	Former Rent.	Judicial Rent.	Observations.	Value of Tenancy.
A. R. P.	£ s. d.	£ s. d.	£ s. d.		£ s. d.
21 3 32	13 0 0	15 10 0	18 10 0		
46 3 20	21 10 0	45 5 0	35 0 0		
79 2 3	31 0 0	31 10 0	24 10 0		
18 0 0	—	30 0 0	30 0 0		
25 0 0	14 10 0	11 17 0	21 10 0		
11 0 4	5 10 0	6 17 6	6 17 6		
35 2 15	18 10 0	19 1 10	15 15 6		
16 0 15	9 0 0	15 0 0	11 0 0		
8 0 25	3 15 0	4 14 0	3 18 0		
24 0 27	16 5 0	18 15 0	15 10 0		
11 2 30	9 5 0	10 10 0	8 0 0		
14 0 0	14 10 0	14 0 0	18 0 0	By consent.	
83 1 0	18 15 0	16 17 6	12 15 0		
8 2 5	6 5 0	8 6 6	6 10 0		
36 3 14	—	28 11 0	19 0 0	Rent changed in 1840 from . . £ s. d. 23 16 0	
37 2 35	19 5 0	26 12 4	20 0 0		
143 3 25	21 10 0	15 0 0	15 0 0		
24 0 30	8 10 0	8 7 11	5 15 0		
31 2 10	6 5 0	7 17 11	5 10 0		
1 3 35	1 15 0	1 8 0	1 8 0		
11 1 0	7 0 0	8 16 4	8 16 4		
28 3 37	10 0 0	11 16 0	9 0 0		
11 2 30	—	4 5 5	3 0 0		
15 2 38	13 10 0	17 0 0	10 0 0		
34 3 20	20 0 0	24 0 0	18 10 0		
7 3 20	2 10 0	3 14 0	3 15 0		
28 0 14	17 0 0	18 6 8	13 0 0		
27 0 21	17 10 0	21 18 6	15 10 0		
18 1 20	12 10 0	14 0 0	11 10 0	1870 11 10 0	
23 0 15	8 10 0	6 10 8	4 15 0		
48 0 35	20 0 0	19 15 0	16 0 0		
24 3 15	11 5 0	11 0 0	7 0 0		
20 1 5	8 10 0	10 9 11	6 0 0		
9 1 8	5 5 0	3 18 8	2 10 8		
13 2 30	5 0 0	8 0 0	4 10 0	1865 5 15 5	

Names of Assistant Commissioners by whom Cases were decided.	No.	Name of Tenant.	Name of Landlord.	Townland.
Assistant Commissioners— M. T. Crean (Legal). S. Mowbray. J. H. McIntyre. J. A. O'Kelly. J. Bagod-Smyth.	1435	John McManus,	Earl of Erne,	Derryhalla and another.
	1436	Patrick Clarke,	do.	Stonepark,
	1437	Thomas Maguire,	do.	do.
	1438	James Clarke,	do.	[illegible],
	1439	Richard Neill,	do.	Stonepark,
	1440	Rev. James O'Reilly,	do.	Derrylin,
	1441	Thomas Magee,	W. Darcy Irvine,	Rossmore,
	1442	Do.	do.	Drogan,
	1443	Do.	do.	Moynaghan,
	1444	Elizabeth Guttridge,	Earl of Enniskillen,	Drumm,
	1445	Robert Dunn,	do.	Derryhillagh,
	1446	William Wilson,	do.	do.
	1447	Farrell Reilly,	Thomas G. Collins and others, Minors, by Eleanor Collins.	Aughyoule,
	1448	Susan Costello, Rep. of James Costello,	do.	do.
	1449	James Willis,	do.	Derryart,
	1450	Anne McCaffrey,	do.	Gortalowrtich,
	1451	Edward McGarr,	George Hurst,	Lergy,
	1452	Thomas Logan,	do.	do.
	1453	Sarah Cox,	do.	do.
	1454	Margaret Gallagher, Rep. of Edward Gallagher.	Christopher Lestrange,	Aghamore,
	1455	John Reid,	do.	do.
	1456	Thomas Scott,	do.	Mossen,
	1457	William Sproule,	Captain Mervyn Archdale,	Drumbulkin,
	1458	James McAnally,	do.	Gortgarron,
	1459	Denis Reid,	do.	Doonan,
	1460	Patrick Brady,	Francis J. Graham,	Kilmore,
	1461	Edward Phair,	do.	do.
	1462	Tobias McElroy,	Sir Victor Brooke, Bart.,	[illegible],
	1463	John McMillan,	do.	Aghavea,
	1464	George Betty,	do.	Clonn,
	1465	James Drohan,	do.	Altawark,
				Total,

FERMANAGH—*continued*.

Extent of Holding (Statute).	Poor Law Valuation.	Former Rent.	Judicial Rent.	Observations.	Value of Tenancy.
A. R. P.	£ s. d.	£ s. d.	£ s. d.		£ s. d.
67 1 33	32 10 0	30 5 6	31 10 0		
16 1 25	7 10 0	6 13 0	4 10 0		
18 1 20	8 5 0	10 13 4	7 10 0		
23 1 8	18 10 0	10 1 0	9 0 0		
29 1 36	18 0 0	11 18 0	8 15 0		
33 0 15	25 0 0	20 0 0	19 0 0		
1 0 31	—	8 5 0	5 0 0	By consent.	
15 3 25	16 5 0	16 16 7	14 10 0		
8 3 26	7 0 0	7 17 8	6 0 0		
18 1 5	13 5 0	13 0 0	11 5 0	Rent changed in 1875 from . . £11 8s. 0d.	
63 0 30	27 10 0	29 0 0	24 0 0		
41 3 18	34 5 0	38 0 0	30 0 0		
13 2 15	6 0 0	8 5 0	6 0 0		
16 0 0	6 16 0	8 10 0	5 5 0	1870 7 4 0	
28 0 25	15 0 0	21 10 0	18 0 0		
27 3 5	9 1 0	18 10 0	8 10 0		
53 3 10	19 10 0	24 0 0	23 0 0		
22 3 30	7 10 0	9 0 0	9 0 0		
28 3 0	10 10 0	18 0 0	12 0 0		
17 0 1	5 0 0	7 0 0	6 0 0		
31 2 10	7 10 0	18 0 0	14 10 0		
37 1 25	31 10 0	81 5 0	24 0 0		
38 0 0	24 5 0	21 0 0	14 10 0	1857 10 0 0	
71 3 10	18 15 0	12 0 0	11 10 0		
6 1 0	6 0 0	10 0 0	7 5 0		
37 3 0	18 0 0	26 0 0	23 0 0	1863 25 0 0	
33 1 0	13 15 0	20 0 0	14 0 0	1860 16 0 0	
40 0 30	13 10 0	11 1 10	10 10 0		
61 0 8	62 0 0	57 5 0	47 0 0		
66 1 0	21 0 0	23 7 10	20 0 0		
64 7 20	8 0 0	10 5 0	8 5 0		
2,016 1 33	3,331 15 0	3,587 1 3	3,243 5 6		

Name of Assistant Commissioners by whom Case was decided	No.	Name of Tenant.	Name of Landlord.	Townland.
Assistant Commissioners—				
R. Greer (Legal). J. B. H[illegible]. C. A. Pringle. John Love. James M. Ross.	1641	William Hanna, ...	R. T. O'Neill, ...	Derrynoyd,
	1642	Philip Henry, ...	do.	do.
	1643	James McNeill (Rodger),	do.	do.
	1644	James McNeil (Edward),	do.	do.
	1645	Bridget Connor, ...	do.	do.
	1646	Bella McEldowney, ...	do.	do.
	1647	Bernard McOsk[illegible], ...	do.	do.
	1648	Patrick Doyle, ...	do.	do.
				Total, ...

Name of Assistant Commissioners by whom Case was decided	No.	Name of Tenant.	Name of Landlord.	Townland.
Assistant Commissioners—	1526	Sarah McGorman, Admin. of Owen McGorman,	William S. Brunker, ...	Curravaskin, ...
L. Doyle (Legal). J. Howlin. J. J. Gerety. J. T. Davys. Hugh Johnston.	1527	Sarah Winslow, Admin. of James Winslow,	do.	Corragary, ...
	1528	Elizabeth Donahoe, ..	do.	do. ...
	1529	Robert Brown, ...	The Earl of Dartrey, ...	Tonnaskeady and another,
	1530	Patrick Growman, ...	Lord Plunket, Bishop of Meath,	Lisarraney, ..
	1531	Thomas Brady, ...	Henry Crawford, Rep. of Henry Rowley,	Bakam, .
	1532	William Clarke, ...	Miss Watt, ...	Drollagh & anr.,
	1533	David Clarke, ...	Sir William T. Power, ...	Knockrow, ...
	1534	William C. Elliott, ...	Thomas R. H. Moorehead, ...	Faltagh, ..
	1535	William Hanavan, ...	Mary E. Braddell and others, Reps. of Captain Brien,	Rovalt, ...
	1536	Hugh Magill, ...	do.	do. ...
	1537	Bernard Mulligan, ...	do.	do. ...
	1538	James Lang, ...	do.	do. ...
	1539	Archibald Stewart, ...	Marshall Moore, ...	Tonaghanny, .
	1540	William Ritchie, ...	Madam Le Clair, ...	Aughnamullen, ...
	1541	James McMurray, ...	do.	do. ...
	1542	Patrick McMahon, ...	do.	Tonlan, .
	1543	James Ritchie, ...	do.	Annaghanullen,
	1544	Edward Potts, ...	Thomas Atkinson, ...	Lisnalong, ...
	1545	John Gillespie, ...	do.	Corragarry, ...
	1546	Jane Whiteside, Extrix. of Rev. John Whiteside,	do.	do. ..

LONDONDERRY.

Extent of Holding, Statute.	Poor Law Valuation.	Former Rent.	Judicial Rent.	Observations.	Value of Tenancy.
A. R. P.	£ s. d.	£ s. d.	£ s. d.	£ s. d.	£ s. d.
20 0 30	15 15 0	15 0 0	10 0 0		
22 2 28	17 10 0	16 8 0	11 14 0		
11 0 30	7 0 0	9 4 0	6 10 0		
18 0 5	9 5 0	11 14 0	8 0 0		
19 0 13	10 5 0	12 0 0	9 15 0		
16 3 30	8 15 0	12 8 0	8 0 0		
13 2 25	7 5 0	8 14 0	6 0 0		
14 1 33	7 5 0	9 10 0	5 7 0		
131 0 21	78 0 0	93 18 0	65 8 0		

MONAGHAN.

Extent of Holding, Statute.	Poor Law Valuation.	Former Rent.	Judicial Rent.	Observations.	Value of Tenancy.
21 2 11	16 0 0	19 19 0	15 15 0		
11 2 13	8 0 0	11 10 8	8 8 0		
1 0 0	— ..	1 5 0	1 0 0	Rent charged in 1865 from - - 0 5 0 1882 20 0 0	
22 0 0	16 15 0	19 0 0	16 0 0		
11 0 23	9 0 0	11 7 9	8 15 0		
25 3 26	20 0 0	23 18 6	17 0 0		
23 0 28	14 10 0	22 0 0	15 5 0		
30 3 30	17 10 0	28 10 0	18 15 0		
23 0 19	18 5 0	15 8 0	17 0 0		
12 1 16	9 0 0	10 0 0	7 16 0		
17 0 1	12 0 0	15 14 0	11 15 0		
16 2 28	12 5 0	15 10 0	11 0 0		
34 0 6	22 0 0	25 0 0	19 0 0		
60 2 0	33 0 0	51 16 10	31 0 0		
23 3 34	13 6 0	16 15 0	18 0 0		
13 2 33	6 6 0	9 1 3	7 0 0		
10 0 15	6 0 0	8 12 3	5 7 8		
9 3 30	5 0 0	6 7 6	5 3 6		
24 2 10	22 15 0	31 0 0	23 0 0		
25 3 18	18 10 0	20 18 8	17 5 0		
31 3 4	41 15 0	46 15 9	45 16 9		

Names of Assistant Commissioners by whom Cases were decided.	No.	Name of Tenant.	Name of Landlord.	Townland.
Assistant Commissioners—				
L. Doyle (Legal). J. Howlin, J. J. Guiry, J. T. Davys, Hugh Johnston.	1547	John Graham, ...	Mrs. Coote, ...	Fough, ...
	1548	Patt McKenna & anor.,	do.	Aghalog, ...
	1549	Henry Grimes, ...	do.	Cordoo, ...
	1550	Thomas McCabe, ...	do.	Fough, ...
	1551	William Gordon, ...	do.	Cavanlea, ...
	1552	William Kells, ...	John Madden, ...	Clerrans, ...
	1553	Francis Connolly, ...	do.	Tullyglaister, ...
	1554	James Brawley, ...	do.	Drumscraher, ...
	1555	George Fawcett, ...	do.	Dromgoose, ...
	1556	Do.	do.	Drumscraher, ...
	1557	James Pritchard, ...	do.	Largnalary and another,
	1558	Thomas Hawthorn, ...	do.	Derries, ...
	1559	Robert Weir, ...	do.	Drumgrane, ...
	1560	Alexander Moffit, ...	do.	Drumgrain, ...
	1561	Alexander Hawthorn, ...	do.	Clerrans, ...
	1562	Joseph Balfe, ...	do.	Killymeagh, ...
	1563	John Armstrong, ...	do.	Garvaghey, ...
	1564	William Rogers, ...	do.	Clerrans, ...
	1565	William Rowley, ...	do.	Garrymaly, ...
	1566	John Maguire, ...	do.	do. ...
	1567	Owen McCusk, ...	do.	Largnalary and another,
	1568	John Burke, ...	do.	Balakmagh, ...
	1569	Samuel Gillespie, ...	do.	Drumgrain, ...
	1570	Andrew Brawley, ...	do.	Carramary, ...
	1571	James Franney, ...	do.	Largnalary, ...
	1572	John Lawson, ...	do.	Clerrans, ...
	1573	John Bradshaw, ...	do.	Derrans, ...
	1574	John Atwell, ...	do.	Drumgoose, ...
	1575	Owen McCluskey, ...	do.	Carramary, ...
	1576	Thomas Kelly, ...	do.	Drumcrumagh, ...
	1577	Robert Hawthorn, ...	do.	Clerrans, ...
	1578	John Gillespie, ...	do.	Magheraskeagh,
	1579	George Armstrong, ...	do.	Garrymaly, ...
	1580	William Lawson, ...	do.	Largnalary and another,
	1581	John Burke, ...	do.	Clervat, ...

MONAGHAN—*continued.*

Extent of Holding. Statute.	Poor Law Valuation.	Former Rent.	Judicial Rent.	Observations.	Value of Tenancy.
A. R. P.	£ s. d.	£ s. d.	£ s. d.	£ s. d.	£ s. d.
9 1 8	6 10 0	8 13 6	6 7 6		
19 1 0	11 0 0	31 15 0	15 18 0		
9 1 0	5 15 0	7 6 10	6 5 0		
21 1 8	18 0 0	24 12 0	16 0 0		
39 3 0	29 15 0	33 13 4	27 5 0		
52 3 15	36 0 0	39 10 5	30 10 0		
21 0 25	13 0 0	14 8 8	11 15 0		
24 0 0	17 10 0	14 8 1	14 8 1		
28 1 0	18 0 0	18 15 6	14 15 0		
16 3 30	10 10 0	9 16 3	8 16 3		
43 0 17	27 5 0	31 13 4	26 0 0		
18 3 35	15 10 0	14 15 6	11 17 6		
20 3 29	15 10 0	17 10 11	14 0 0		
21 3 38	24 0 0	25 1 5	22 12 8		
13 3 9	9 18 0	10 15 3	8 5 0		
21 0 14	16 0 0	15 17 9	13 17 6		
27 2 0	15 17 0	17 13 7	11 17 6		
25 1 16	16 0 0	18 18 11	14 12 6		
19 3 29	14 15 0	18 0 0	16 6 0		
19 2 16	13 15 0	16 5 5	12 18 0		
16 3 23	12 18 0	15 4 7	11 17 6		
44 1 25	29 15 0	34 17 6	26 0 0		
42 0 17	26 5 0	31 0 0	25 8 6		
20 0 29	17 5 0	18 5 6	13 18 6		
45 3 35	31 0 0	37 3 4	28 15 0		
13 0 11	9 5 0	10 17 5	8 2 6		
34 0 20	25 0 0	25 14 6	20 18 6		
7 2 27	6 5 0	6 0 0	4 18 6		
17 1 8	12 5 0	13 4 10	11 17 6		
14 1 8	8 5 0	11 15 7	9 12 6	Rent changed in 1867 from . . 10 10 7	
12 3 38	9 10 0	10 14 5	6 3 6		
19 2 27	15 8 0	15 8 0	13 15 0		
33 3 9	21 12 0	28 8 5	23 0 0		
33 2 33	20 0 0	23 12 11	18 10 0		
50 1 23	36 15 0	48 13 3½	33 0 0		

D K

COUNTY OF

Names of Assistant Commissioners by whom Cases were decided.	No.	Name of Tenant.	Name of Landlord.	Townland.
Assistant Commissioners—				
L. Doyle (Legal). J. Howard. J. J. Gerty. J. T. Davys. Hugh Jefferys.	1582	John Gillespie, ...	John Madden, ...	Drumgrone, ...
	1583	Hugh Lawson, ...	do.	Lurganboy and another,
	1584	Mary West, ...	do.	Cravan, ...
	1585	James Williamson, ...	do.	Drumnavahey, ...
	1586	Pat Casey, ...	do.	Magheranaglory,
	1587	Do., ...	do.	Killyneeragh, ...
	1588	Alexander Magill, ...	do.	Drumgoine, ...
				Total, ...

COUNTY OF

Names of Assistant Commissioners by whom Cases were decided.	No.	Name of Tenant.	Name of Landlord.	Townland.
Assistant Commissioners—	3730	David Dunbar, ...	Rev. William H. Oakley, ...	Lurganboy, ...
B. Foley, Q.C. (Legal). A. Ellis. S. Byrne. A. Montgomery. H. Stevens.	3731	Peter Early, ...	Alexander O. S. McClintock,	Cloghfin, ...
	3732	Charles Kerr, ...	do.	Drumnakelly, ...
	3733	Owen McCrory, ...	do.	Fernagh, ...
	3734	John Daly (Felix), ...	do.	Drumnakelly, ...
	3735	John Daly (Leahy), ...	do.	do. ...
	3736	Margaret Rafferty, ...	do.	Fernagh, ...
	3737	Patrick McAleer, ...	do.	Drumnakelly, ...
	3738	Owen McAleer, ...	do.	do. ...
	3739	Peter Early, ...	do.	Cloghfin, ...
	3740	John Kyle, ...	do.	Drumnakelly, ...
	3741	James Kelly, Admor. of Anne Kelly.	do.	Cloghfin, ...
	3742	James Kerr, ...	do.	do. ...
	3743	James McAleer, ...	do.	Drumnakelly, ...
	3744	Patrick Hare, ...	do.	do. ...
	3745	Sarah McSwiggan, ...	do.	do. ...
	3746	John Conway, ...	do.	do. ...
	3747	Margaret Daly, ...	do.	do. ...
	3748	Owen McCann, ...	do.	do. ...
	3749	Peter Conway, ...	do.	do. ...
	3750	John Daly (Foundry), ...	do.	do. ...
	3751	Do., ...	do.	do. ...

MONAGHAN—*continued.*

Extent of Holding Statute.			Poor Law Valuation.			Former Rent.			Judicial Rent.		
A.	R.	P.	£	s.	d.	£	s.	d.	£	s.	d.
[illegible]	3	27	16	5	0	16	8	9	13	5	0
[illegible]	2	3	14	15	0	16	10	7	13	15	0
21	3	16	18	0	0	20	18	10	15	0	0
23	1	16	20	0	0	16	11	8	13	17	6
18	2	10	11	15	0	16	2	8	12	5	0
[illegible]	2	30	18	0	0	18	9	8	15	8	6
16	0	38	13	0	0	16	0	0	11	8	0
1,473	0	38	1,003	3	0	1,279	3	0½	956	0	6

TYRONE.

A.	R.	P.	£	s.	d.	£	s.	d.	£	s.	d.
41	2	30	23	10	0	21	2	0	20	0	0
[illegible]	0	25	7	10	0	10	16	0	7	5	0
33	1	14	10	0	0	15	19	0	9	5	0
63	1	[illegible]	10	10	0	18	0	0	10	0	0
13	0	27	3	15	0	6	11	0	4	10	0
49	1	30	10	10	0	13	15	0	10	0	0
58	0	0	17	0	0	21	0	0	15	0	0
47	2	0	15	0	0	21	6	0	16	0	0
11	1	0	5	5	6	7	6	6	5	0	0
17	0	21	6	5	0	9	15	0	6	15	6
23	2	17	12	15	0	14	18	6	11	10	0
17	1	0	8	10	0	13	18	0	9	10	0
87	0	25	17	5	0	23	0	0	15	0	0
[illegible]	2	11	9	10	0	14	0	0	9	0	0

Assistant Commissioners—

R. F[illegible], Q.C. (Legal).
A. Ellis.
S. Byrne.
A. Montgomery.
H. Stephen.

3752	Patrick Rafferty,	...	Alexander O. S. McClean	
3753	John Daly (Hugh),	...	do.	...
3754	George McFarland,	...	do.	...
3755	John Kerr, ...	...	do.	...
3756	George Bell, ...	...	do.	...
3757	Felix McAleer,	...	do.	...
3758	Samuel Campbell (Big),		do.	...
3759	Eliza Blythe,	...	do.	...
3760	Andrew Campbell,	...	do.	...
3761	John Haynes,	...	do.	...
3762	Samuel Campbell, junior,		do.	...
3763	James Campbell, junior,		do.	...
3764	John Kerr, ...	...	do.	...
3765	Andrew McFarland,	...	do.	...
3766	James McCrory,	...	do.	...
3767	Do. ...	...	do.	...
3768	James McSwiggan,	...	do.	...
3769	Hugh Harvey,	...	do.	...
3770	Charles McSwiggan,	...	do.	...
3771	Patrick Daly,	...	do.	...
3772	Charles Rafferty,	...	do.	...
3773	Michael Higgins,	...	do.	...
3774	Bernard McSwiggan, Rep. of James McSwiggan.		do.	...
3775	Owen McAleer,	...	do.	...
3776	John A. Bell,	...	do.	...
3777	Samuel Lyons,	...	do.	...
3778	John Frame, ...	...	Thomas de D. Godfrey another.	
3779	Peter Early, ...	...	Alexander O. S. McClean	
3780	Owen McAleer, Admor. of Susan McAleer.		do.	...
3781	Mary Kelly, ...	...	do.	...
3782	Denis Quinn,	...	Oliver Sproule and other	
3783	Ellen Carney, Admix. of Felix Carney.		William Douglas and ot Trustees of C. W. L. C	
3784	James Houston,	...	Rose Kealy and another,	
3785	Patrick McNamee,	...	do.	...
3786	John McCusker,	...	do.	...

TYRONE—*continued.*

Extent of Holding. Statute.	Poor Law Valuation.	Tenant Rent.	Judicial Rent.	Observations.	
A. R. P.	£ s. d.	£ s. d.	£ s. d.		£ s. d.
63 1 0	10 0 0	19 19 0	7 10 0	Rent changed in 1862 from	6 0 0
29 1 30	11 0 0	14 16 0	9 10 0		
22 0 0	4 15 0	8 0 0	4 0 0	1830	5 3 0
18 1 33	9 15 0	13 1 6	8 10 0	1862	11 18 0
33 0 0	11 0 0	16 0 0	12 10 0		
29 0 35	9 0 0	12 8 0	6 15 0	do.	8 0 0
18 2 30	8 5 0	10 18 0	7 10 0	1830	2 0 0
21 0 0	12 5 0	16 0 0	12 0 0	1862	14 8 3
23 0 15	9 10 0	15 10 0	10 10 0	1870	14 18 0
31 1 29	15 0 0	19 14 0	13 0 0	1862	17 14 0
21 0 0	8 0 0	13 0 0	8 0 0		
18 0 38	7 15 0	13 0 0	8 0 0	do.	8 10 4
45 0 17	11 15 0	15 11 6	11 0 0		
25 2 8	10 5 0	15 0 0	11 0 0		
13 1 38	3 0 0	5 18 0	[illegible] 10 0		
18 2 0	6 13 0	13 5 0	9 0 0		
23 0 0	9 2 0	13 2 0	8 10 0	do.	9 17 6
30 1 0	18 15 0	25 11 0	18 10 0	1835	15 6 8
17 0 0	15 10 0	18 3 0	18 15 0		
43 3 17	16 10 0	21 0 0	17 10 0	1810	7 10 0
29 2 20	9 10 0	11 18 0	9 0 0		
16 0 0	7 10 0	9 12 0	8 0 0	do.	5 15 0
15 1 20	5 8 0	12 5 0	8 5 0		
31 2 15	10 0 0	14 0 0	8 10 0		
18 0 20	9 6 0	14 11 6	10 0 0	1863	10 0 0
64 3 30	34 5 0	39 13 0	23 0 0	1818	25 15 8
66 3 25	21 5 0	29 0 0	18 0 0	1857	19 11 0
23 0 0	9 10 0	13 14 0	10 15 0	do.	10 3 2
11 1 0	5 0 0	8 0 0	5 5 0	1862	5 0 0
20 3 0	5 5 0	7 7 0	4 10 0	1861	1 0 0
15 1 20	5 6 0	8 10 0	6 10 0	1850	8 0 0
27 3 20	8 15 0	10 13 6	7 0 0		
53 3 24	27 5 0	45 0 0	35 0 0	1876	30 7 0
7 1 14	4 5 0	9 0 0	5 10 0		
8 3 35	5 15 0	7 0 0	5 5 0		

COUNTY OF

Names of Assistant Commissioners by whom Cases were decided.

Assistant Commissioners—

R. Foley, Q.C. (Legal).
A. Barr.
S. Byrne.
A. Montgomery.
H. Sexton.

No.	Name of Tenant.	Name of Landlord.	Townland.
3787	Francis McCauley, ...	Ross Keely and another, ...	Rathfragan, ...
3788	Francis McKenny, ...	James B. Graham and others,	Mountjoy, West
3789	Hugh O'Neill, ...	Lord Lifford, ...	Aughan, ...
3790	Peter Maguire, ...	James Young and another, ...	Drumnakilly, ...
3791	Mary Wilkie, ...	Hamilton Stewart, ...	Cavanalee, ...
3792	John Coulter, ...	John H. Buchanan, ...	Barnagh, ...
3793	John Daly (Patrick), ...	A. O. S. McCausland, ...	Drumnakilly, ...
3794	James Musgrove, ...	Col. George P. McClintock,	Tullyvalley, ...
3795	John Scott, ...	do.	Seskinore, ...
3796	Patrick McMackin, ...	do.	Fernaghandrum, ...
3797	Mary McAlinney and another, Admors. of Harriett Fox.	do.	do. ...
3798	George O'Hara, ...	do.	Kilgort, ...
3799	David Crawford, ...	do.	do. ...
3800	Mary A. Crawford, ...	do.	do. ...
3801	William Sloan, ...	do.	Fernaghandrum, ...
3802	Joseph Sloan, ...	do.	do. ...
3803	Robert Cunningham, ...	do.	do. ...
3804	William McFarland, ...	A. O. S. McCausland, ...	Killyscarragh, ...
3805	John Monteith, ...	do.	Ballynagilly, ...
3806	Joseph Armstrong, ...	do.	do. ...
3807	David Johnston, Admor. of William Johnston.	do.	do. ...
3808	Joseph Mitchell, ...	do.	Remigo, ...
3809	Peter McIlwiggan, ...	do.	Ballynagilly, ...
3810	James Colhoun, ...	do.	do. ...
3811	Henry Donnelly, ...	Sir James H. Stronge, Bart.,	Aghlane, ...
3812	John Doherty, ...	do.	Cashlereagh and another.
3813	William Graham, ...	do.	Drumgarve, ...
3814	William Jas. McIlwrath,	Robert Harvey, ...	Tattymoyle, ...
3815	Thomas Cunningham, ...	do.	do. ...
3816	William Baxter, ...	do.	Tully, ...
3817	Andrew Fulton, ...	do.	do. ...
3818	William Fife, ...	do.	do. ...
3819	John Fife, ...	do.	do. ...
3820	Patrick McGowan, Admor. of Francis McGowan.	do.	do. ...
3821	Ellen Martin, ...	do.	do. ...

TYRONE—*continued.*

Extent of Holding, Statute.	Poor Law Valuation.	Former Rent.	Judicial Rent.	Observations.
A. R. P.	£ s. d.	£ s. d.	£ s. d.	
13 3 35	10 0 0	13 3 4	9 0 0	
16 0 15	7 5 0	10 10 0	9 0 0	
7 2 17	5 15 0	9 10 0	5 0 0	
21 0 25	9 5 0	10 0 0	9 0 0	
26 0 28	11 5 0	16 12 4	10 15 0	By consent.
—	8 10 0	14 0 0	10 0 0	do.
17 0 0	5 5 0	5 0 0	6 0 0	Rent changed in 1880 from . . . £ s. d. 8 0 0
13 1 10	10 15 0	11 5 0	9 0 0	
25 1 0	17 0 0	19 1 0	16 10 0	
14 0 0	11 0 0	10 13 0	10 13 0	
14 0 0	13 0 0	21 8 0	21 2 0	
17 3 0	13 10 0	19 9 0	11 10 0	
51 0 0	35 0 0	38 1 0	34 0 0	
30 0 0	26 10 0	23 12 0	27 8 6	
15 2 0	—	10 7 9	10 7 9	
74 2 5	20 10 0	18 17 0	17 0 0	
13 0 0	10 0 0	8 0 0	8 0 0	
43 0 0	8 5 0	10 10 0	7 12 11	By consent.
9 3 0	8 10 0	5 5 0	6 0 0	
13 0 0	14 15 0	14 10 0	11 5 0	
4 1 28	5 0 0	5 0 0	5 10 0	
46 2 20	16 15 0	23 0 0	20 0 0	
34 3 19	21 0 0	18 5 0	9 0 0	
19 1 35	13 15 0	14 10 0	11 0 0	
38 1 0	18 0 0	25 0 0	18 10 0	Rent changed in 1879 from . . . 22 0 0 1880 18 15 0 1881 11 16 0
94 2 20	30 10 0	22 4 0	17 0 0	
23 0 0	18 5 0	13 2 9	9 18 0	
51 2 27	39 10 0	37 9 4	35 10 0	
16 3 3	11 3 0	8 19 6	5 0 0	
29 2 10	16 10 0	17 18 3	13 10 0	
15 0 0	6 15 0	7 0 0	5 10 0	
31 3 20	25 15 0	23 0 0	23 16 0	
64 1 0	56 10 0	46 18 6	44 0 0	

Names of Assistant Commissioners by whom Cases were decided.	No.	Name of Tenant.	Name of Landlord.	Townland.
Assistant Commissioners—				
E. Falkiner, Q.C. (Legal). A. Baird. S. Dykes. A. Montgomery. H. Stevens.	3822	Thomas Buchanan, ...	Robert Harvey, ...	Tully, ...
	3823	John Rennie, ...	do.	do. ...
G. H. Gartlan (Legal.) E. B. Bayly. Richard Garland. F. O'Callaghan. G. H. Mitchell.	3824	James Milne, ...	William W. Harris, ...	Derrywhinny, ...
	3825	John McClea, ...	Henry B. Kelly, ...	Aghakinnigh,
	3826	John McVey, ...	do.	do. ...
	3827	Edward Conlon, ...	do.	do. ...
	3828	James Kane, ...	do.	Aghakinnigh and another.
	3829	Patrick Donnelly, ...	do.	do. ...
	3830	Terence Quin, ...	do.	do. ...
	3831	Robert Murray, ...	Trustees of late Mary Campbell,	Glenkeen, ...
	3832	George Joyce, ...	do.	do. ...
	3833	Richard Marshall, ...	do.	do. ...
	3834	Thomas Murray, ...	do.	do. ...
	3835	John Hagan, ...	do.	do. ...
	3836	Isabella Harvey & anor.,	do.	do. ...
	3837	Robert Wilson, ...	do.	do. ...
	3838	James Murray, ...	do.	do. ...
	3839	Thomas Clarke, ...	do.	do. ...
	3840	William Fleming, ...	do.	do. ...
	3841	Do.	do.	do. ...
	3842	Catherine Hughes, ...	Joseph Mayne, ...	Glenderonald,
	3843	Timothy Hughes, ...	do.	do. ...
	3844	Hugh Muldoon, ...	do.	do. ...
	3845	John Johnston, ...	Andrew W. McCreight, ...	Grilly, ...
	3846	James McNeely, ...	Mrs. Jane E. Rankin and anor.	Glandarragh, ...
	3847	Peter McGlone, ...	James Irwin, ...	Aughnamurry, ...
	3848	Do.	Isabella Irwin, Executrix of Wm. Irwin.	do. ...
	3849	Daniel McClean, ...	Col. James G. Lowry, ...	Knall, ...
	3850	William Howard, ...	do.	Tullyanran, ...
	3851	Charles McMullan, Admor. of Patrick McMullan.	Rev. James H. Smith & others, Reps. of Mrs. Isabella Smith.	Gortaclarragh ...
	3852	Mary Quin, ...	do.	do. ...

TYRONE—*continued*.

Extent of Holding. Statute.	Poor Law Valuation.	Former Rent.	Judicial Rent.	Observations.	Value of Tenancy.
A. R. P.	£ s. d.	£ s. d.	£ s. d.	£ s. d.	£ s. d.
30 2 30	10 10 0	11 18 3	10 5 0		
18 3 10	9 10 0	7 10 9	6 10 0		
13 3 0	15 3 0	14 10 0	13 0 0		
10 0 25	8 15 0	10 0 0	8 10 0		
7 1 13	7 5 0	7 14 0	8 0 0		
12 1 7	11 10 0	11 16 8	8 0 0		
11 2 8	8 10 0	10 5 10	6 0 0		
4 0 15	4 0 0	3 19 8	3 19 6		
8 3 15	7 5 0	5 17 0	6 0 0		
11 1 19	10 0 0	10 19 0	8 10 0		
15 1 25	15 0 0	18 18 0	11 5 0		
14 2 10	15 5 0	16 0 0	11 10 0		
21 3 1	23 10 0	24 15 0	17 0 0		
19 0 7	18 5 0	18 12 6	11 0 0		
19 2 29	17 10 0	18 0 1	18 15 0		
19 3 37	14 0 0	13 0 0	11 5 0		
18 1 20	—	18 17 6	10 10 0		
17 2 19	13 0 0	13 18 3	9 0 0		
25 0 25	18 0 0	12 0 0	10 10 0		
13 1 35	9 10 0	9 0 0	7 0 0		
18 0 6	8 18 0	8 0 0	6 10 0		
18 2 15	8 18 0	10 0 0	6 12 0		
6 2 0	3 10 0	4 10 0	8 18 0		
14 0 10	13 10 0	13 0 0	9 8 0		
14 1 25	9 15 0	13 0 0	6 0 0		
7 0 7		12 2 3	8 15 0		
8 2 1	—	7 10 1	4 0 0		
16 3 2	12 5 0	15 10 0	10 15 0	Rent changed in 1875 from . . . 11 3 1	
19 0 10	14 5 0	18 18 10	12 10 0		
18 0 25	8 10 0	13 18 4	7 17 6		
7 3 15	6 0 0	8 0 0	5 5 0		
17 1 30	1 0 0	5 0 0	2 0 0	1875 1 10 0	
11 2 24	5 10 0	5 17 6	3 0 0		

Names of Assistant Commissioners by whom Cases were decided.	No.	Name of Tenant.	Name of Landlord.	Townland.
Assistant Commissioners—				
C. H. Gartlan (Legal). E. B. Bayly. Richard Garland. F. O'Callaghan. G. H. Mitchell.	3655	John McKane, ...	Capt. Livingstone Thompson,	Clonavaddy, ...
	3656	Mary Morrow, ...	Joseph Mayne, ...	Glenadrummond,
	3657	Henry Donaghey, ...	Trustees of late Mary Campbell,	Glenlarn, ...
	3658	Robert Murray, ...	do.	do. ...
	3659	James Donaghy, ...	do.	do. ...
	3660	Margaret Oakman, ...	Miss C. Cochrane, ...	Legane, ...
	3661	Francis McCullagh, ...	General William Irwin, ...	Aghavea, ...
	3662	Patrick Clarke, ...	Francis Mansfield, ...	Largylea, ...
	3663	Patrick McGuirk, ...	Mrs. Margaret K. Hamilton,	Ballylurey, ...
	3664	Owen Loughran, ...	do.	do. ...
	3665	Bernard Kennedy, ...	Mrs. Letitia Kilpatrick, ...	Dungannon, ...
	3666	Allen Campbell and anor.,	The Irish Land Commission,	Killary Glebe, ...
	3667	Robert Watt, ...	Margaret McDonagh & others,	Tulnagall, ...
	3668	Joseph Montgomery, ...	do.	do. ...
	3669	William Ross, ...	William Fleming, ...	Glenone, ...
	3670	Catherine Hackett, ...	Miss Lilly McKelvey and another,	Lisnamaghery, ...
	3671	William Caldwell, ...	do.	Mullaghtinny, ...
	3672	Stewart Thompson, ...	Mrs. Gall, ...	Derrycreevy, ...
	3673	Thomas Martin, ...	Edward Roper, ...	do. ...
	3674	John Liggett, ...	do.	do. ...
	3675	Mary Henderson, Admx. of Alex. Henderson,	Mrs. Jane McFarlane, ...	Plaister, ...
	3676	William Hurst, ...	Charles H. James and another, Assignees of Andw. M. Miller.	Glenaul, ...
	3677	James Robinson, ...	Averill Lloyd, ...	Tamlaghtmore, ...
	3678	Charles A. Pringle, ...	Earl of Caledon, ...	Tullanaglare, ...
	3679	Do.	do.	Killeenan, ...
	3680	John Hale, ...	do.	Ards, ...
	3681	James Mullan, ...	R. S. Moore and another, Exors. of James H. Moore.	Mulnabura, ...
	3682	Joseph Abraham, ...	do.	Drumnamore, ...
	3683	Patrick Burns, ...	James Bruce, ...	Rosa, ...
	3684	Patrick Bloomer, ...	do.	Lisgobbin, ...
	3685	Patrick Kelly, ...	do.	Mossmore, ...
	3686	John McCurry, ...	do.	Lisbanclenaghy, ...
	3687	Sarah Daly and another,	do.	Lysaria, ...
	3688	James W. Reid, ...	do.	Ballymacilchrieff,
	3689	James Cardwell, ...	do.	Cabragh, ...

TYRONE—*continued.*

Extent of Holding Statute.	Poor Law Valuation.	Former Rent.	Judicial Rent.	Observations.		Value of Tenancy.
A. R. P.	£ s. d.	£ s. d.	£ s. d.		£ s. d.	£ s. d.
5 3 0	5 0 0	6 17 0	1 10 0			
21 3 0	17 10 0	16 0 0	10 10 0			
21 3 30	16 15 0	18 8 0	18 10 0			
30 3 23	38 15 0	37 13 6	27 0 0			
14 1 6	10 0 0	11 18 6	8 10 0			
25 2 15	13 15 0	15 1 1	10 10 0			
8 3 10	7 7 0	8 10 8	6 10 0			
3 3 23	—	3 6 8	1 6 0	Rent changed in 1845 from . . .	1 18 8	
8 3 35	1 15 0	8 13 1	4 10 0			
6 3 0	8 15 0	10 10 4	7 15 0			
0 2 30	1 5 0	2 0 0	2 0 0			
11 1 0	6 15 0	8 0 0	6 15 0			
16 3 30	15 10 0	18 17 0	15 16 8	By consent.		
13 3 35	13 5 0	13 16 0	11 13 6	do.		
1 0 0	—	2 10 0	1 15 0	do.		
3 0 6	3 15 0	5 0 0	3 10 0			
46 1 11	51 10 6	53 10 0	52 10 0			
14 1 0	10 5 0	9 18 2½	8 10 0			
15 0 31	10 5 0	10 11 0	8 15 0			
17 1 0	13 5 0	18 0 0	11 10 0			
18 3 35	14 0 0	15 0 0	11 5 0			
16 0 0	12 10 0	17 0 0	18 0 0			
10 0 0	4 10 0	7 10 0	5 0 0	Rent changed in 1880 from . . .	5 0 0	
71 1 08	67 15 0	73 9 10	53 10 0			
77 1 03	78 10 0	71 5 10	59 10 0			
95 0 4	87 0 0	118 18 4	90 0 0			
23 2 18	23 16 0	27 0 0	20 10 0			
15 3 0	12 0 0	16 0 0	13 0 0			
23 3 18	31 0 0	23 0 0	23 0 0			
7 0 0	1 15 0	7 0 0	5 15 0	1875	6 17	
13 1 25	9 5 0	11 3 8	8 5 0			
6 3 10	5 10 0	6 5 8	5 10 0			
15 2 20	11 0 0	13 18 3	13 10 0	do.	14 10 0	
3 3 5	6 5 0	5 10 0	7 0 0			
31 2 28	31 0 0	24 10 0	19 5 0			

b

3899	Ann McCaughey, ...	do. ...
3900	Patrick Keenan, ...	Sir John Stewart, Bart.,
3901	Francis Dowgan, ...	do. ...
3902	James McAlpin, ...	A. A. M. Moore and a
3903	Eliza Wilson, ...	do. ...
3904	Sarah Murray, ...	do. ...
3905	James Miller, ...	do. ...
3906	Ellen Bailey, ...	do. ...
3907	James Hughes, ...	do. ...
3908	Isabella Robinson, ...	do. ...
3909	William McAlpin, ...	do. ...
3910	William Armstrong, ...	James M. Cochrane,
3911	John Mullan, ...	do. ...
3912	Mary McWilliam, ...	do. ...
3913	Mary A. Corbett, ...	do. ...
3914	John McKeown, ...	William Scott, ...
3915	Thomas Wright, ...	do. ...
3916	John McCaughey, ...	do. ...
3917	John Hamilton, ...	do. ...
3918	Charles Thompson, ...	do. ...
3919	Hugh McF. Simpson, ...	Rev. John J. Montray,
3920	Bernard McCusker, ...	do. ...
3921	Owen Hamill, ...	do. ...
3922	Patrick Flood, ...	do. ...
3923	James McElhoned, ...	do. ...
3924	James McKenna, ...	do. ...

TYRONE—*continued.*

Extent of Holding. Statute.	Poor Law Valuation.	Former Rent.	Judicial Rent.	Observations.		Value of Tenancy.
A. R. P.	£ s. d.	£ s. d.	£ s. d.		£ s. d.	£ s. d.
19 3 13	9 0 0	10 1 8	8 14 0			
19 1 25	10 0 0	18 9 0	15 5 0			
20 1 6	18 10 0	17 0 0	13 0 0			
33 0 20	35 5 0	34 10 0	28 10 0	Rent changed in 1878 from . . .	29 10 0	
31 1 5	24 0 0	30 17 8	23 10 0			
21 2 29	28 10 0	34 0 0	21 5 0			
13 0 10	—	12 17 0	9 7 0			
7 0 8	8 0 0	7 7 0	5 6 0			
30 3 23	30 0 0	29 3 0	25 5 0			
19 0 20	9 10 0	10 5 0	8 15 0	1875	7 16 0	
6 0 39	8 8 0	9 13 6	8 10 0			
5 2 10	6 10 0	8 10 0	8 10 0			
7 3 0	4 15 0	5 0 0	1 7 0			
15 1 0	15 5 8	13 4 4	13 4 4			
15 2 23	17 0 0	22 10 0	16 10 0			
18 1 70	17 16 0	20 0 0	16 10 0			
8 0 25	3 10 0	5 3 0	3 15 0			
22 3 0	13 5 0	15 0 0	11 5 0			
10 2 18	9 10 0	11 0 0	9 0 0			
28 1 0	31 10 0	20 0 0	17 0 0			
10 2 4	6 10 0	8 7 0	6 0 0			
12 0 0	6 10 0	9 18 8	7 10 0			
16 2 24	10 10 0	13 18 9	10 10 0			
14 2 15	10 10 0	11 18 10	10 0 0			
12 2 25	9 0 0	10 8 0	8 0 0			
29 2 0	38 0 0	29 10 0	26 0 0			
34 3 23	75 5 0	25 10 8	22 10 0			
35 0 0	33 10 0	40 19 0	32 10 0			
10 2 36	7 10 0	8 6 2	6 5 0			
37 0 0	87 10 0	51 11 11½	44 10 0			
31 1 5	15 5 0	19 8 5	10 15 0			
8 1 6	5 0 0	6 8 11½	5 8 0			
11 0 10	4 15 0	5 14 0	4 1 0			
23 2 16	4 0 0	8 0 0	6 0 0			
18 1 10	5 10 0	6 18 0	4 0 0			

Assistant Commissioners—

G. H. Cawley (Legal).
E. R. Bayly.
Richard Garland.
F. O'Callaghan.
C. H. Mitchell.

3925	Dennis Dawson,	H. S. Moore and another,	Drumara,
3926	James Early,	Rev. William Montray,	Cabinhove,
3927	Elizabeth Thompson,	do.	do.
3928	William Giles,	do.	do.
3929	Charles McGirr,	do.	do.
3930	John Campbell,	do.	do
3931	Andrew Trimble,	Major Harvey K. Brown,	Girlaw,
3932	Charles Keys,	do.	Rowlies,
3933	Thomas Morgan,	do.	Mountstewart,
3934	John Morgan,	do.	do.
3935	James McDermott,	do.	Bolies,
3936	Peter Colhoun,	do.	Mountstewart,
3937	James Corbett,	H. S. Moore and another,	Drumara,
3938	William Johnston,	do.	Mulnabore,
3939	Joseph Fraser,	do.	Drumara,
3940	Samuel McGowan,	do.	Mulnabore,
3941	Thomas Martin,	Miss Charlotte Carter,	Derrycreevy.
3942	Samuel Ferguson,	do.	do.
3943	Robert Burton,	do.	do.
3944	Owen Garthand,	The Commissioners of Education in Ireland.	Derrytreak and another.
3945	Bernard Donaghey,	do.	Derrytreak,
3946	Patrick O'Neill,	do.	Derrytreak and another.
3947	Do.	do.	Derrytreak,
3948	Edward Hagan,	do.	do.
3949	James Johnston,	do.	do.
3950	John Connor,	do.	do.
3951	James Garthany,	do.	do.
3952	Laurence Garthand,	do.	do.
3953	Sarah J. Campbell,	do.	do.
3954	Hugh O'Neill,	do.	do.
3955	Felix Hagan,	do.	do.
3956	James Garthany,	do.	do.
3957	John McGrath,	do.	do.
3958	Catherine Fitzgerald,	do.	Derrytreak and another.
3959	Peter McGrath,	do.	do.

TYRONE—*continued.*

Extent of Holding. Statute.	Poor Law Valuation.	Former Rent.	Judicial Rent.	Observations.
A. R. P.	£ s. d.	£ s. d.	£ s. d.	
11 2 0	18 10 0	13 0 0	10 10 0	
18 3 0	16 0 0	17 0 11	13 0 0	
5 1 15	5 0 0	6 0 6	4 10 0	
37 2 11	17 5 0	21 12 3½	19 10 0	
19 2 10	11 10 0	14 8 1	10 0 0	
27 1 10	8 10 0	11 4 5	7 10 0	
19 0 15	10 13 0	11 5 0	10 0 0	
30 1 19	11 5 0	18 0 0	15 0 0	
21 1 20	8 10 0	10 0 0	9 0 0	
29 1 30	14 5 0	13 17 0	11 15 0	
47 1 5	33 15 0	35 0 0	29 10 0	
45 2 30	20 10 0	24 0 0	19 0 0	
33 0 0	11 0 0	21 1 10	16 16 0	
15 0 30	11 15 0	18 10 0	11 0 0	
65 0 0	26 5 0	35 0 0	27 0 0	
13 3 0	10 16 0	12 3 8	10 0 0	
11 0 0	8 6 0	8 0 0	7 3 0	
9 0 25	5 5 0	5 8 0	4 15 0	
18 1 0	9 10 0	10 4 0	8 10 0	
15 2 15	12 8 0	14 8 6	10 10 0	
7 0 0	6 15 0	7 7 4	5 8 0	
19 1 37	10 17 0	11 10 4	9 0 0	
23 1 25	—	14 14 8	11 0 0	
15 1 28	7 15 0	10 8 4	8 5 0	
9 1 0	—	3 17 7	3 17 7	
21 1 14	7 5 0	8 18 8	7 10 0	By consent.
9 1 0	7 0 0	9 13 8	7 15 0	do.
11 1 9	9 0 0	9 15 3	7 10 0	do.
4 3 20	7 10 0	6 3 7	5 10 0	do.
7 3 10	1 13 0	5 12 4	5 0 0	do.
15 3 25	13 0 0	12 8 6	10 0 0	do.
22 0 30	10 16 0	14 3 1	10 15 0	do.
8 1 15	8 0 0	7 6 9	5 5 0	do.
20 1 20	8 9 0	10 5 4	8 5 0	do.
13 3 26	8 1 0	10 9 6	9 0 0	do.

Michael Donaghy,

Richard Connelly,

Felix Donnelly,

Francis Donaghey,

Hugh Donaghy,

William Beatty,

James Brackenridge,

James McNiece,

John Johnston,

Thomas Brush, Adr
of Samuel Brush.

William Adams,

Hugh Thompson,

David Falls,

Samuel McCleery,

William Murphy,

TYRONE—*continued.*

Extent of Holding. Statute.	Poor Law Valuation.	Former Rent.	Judicial Rent.	Observations.	Value of Tenancy.
A. R. P.	£ s. d.	£ s. d.	£ s. d.		£ s. d.
14 0 26	10 15 0	12 17 9	10 0 0	By consent.	
20 1 30	18 11 0	15 0 8	15 10 0	do.	
24 2 5	20 4 8	27 0 0	21 0 0	do.	
15 1 30	6 15 0	8 6 4	7 0 0	do.	
6 0 0	5 0 0	6 18 9	5 15 0	do.	
20 0 5	11 10 0	14 5 6	11 5 0	do.	
14 3 1	8 7 0	9 13 1	7 15 0	do.	
7 0 11	—	5 15 3	5 0 0		
29 1 35	—	20 0 0	15 15 0		
11 3 5	7 10 0	11 0 0	7 10 0		
25 2 5	18 5 0	29 9 8	18 10 0		
17 1 20	13 10 0	16 0 0	13 10 0		
6 3 5	6 10 0	8 8 5	7 3 0		
13 2 20	10 0 0	11 5 0	8 10 0		
6 3 10	5 5 0	6 15 0	5 10 0		
5 3 0	3 5 0	5 0 0	3 5 0		
5 2 10	2 15 0	3 10 0	2 15 0		
16 1 29	11 5 0	13 0 0	8 15 0		
4,500 0 11	3,152 18 9	3,766 1 8	2,918 9 3		

PROVINCE OF

COUNTY OF [CARLOW]

Names of Assistant Commissioners by whom Cases were decided.	No.	Name of Tenant.	Name of Landlord.	Townland.
Assistant Commissioners—				
R. R. Kane (Legal). Thomas Roche. J. G. Barry. J. H. Dunne. P. Moran.	331	Benjamin Hopkins, ...	Patrick Byrne, ...	Eaglehill, ...
	332	James Roache, ...	do.	do. ...
	333	William Byrne, ...	do.	do. ...
	334	Julia Brophy, ...	G. O. Newton, ...	Ballinaquilty, ...
	335	James Byrne, ...	Edward Keogh, ...	Mountkelly, ...
				Total, ...

COUNTY OF [KILKENNY]

Names of Assistant Commissioners by whom Cases were decided.	No.	Name of Tenant.	Name of Landlord.	Townland.
Assistant Commissioners—				
R. R. Kane (Legal). Thomas Roche. J. G. Barry. J. H. Dunne. P. Moran.	[illegible]	Mathew Minch, ...	Jane Peppard, ...	Bennett's Bridge,

KING'S

Names of Assistant Commissioners by whom Cases were decided.	No.	Name of Tenant.	Name of Landlord.	Townland.
Assistant Commissioners—	586	Michael Minnock, ...	James Rosenbecker & anor.,	Cloonkearny, ...
R. R. Kane (Legal). Thomas Roche. J. G. Barry. J. H. Dunne. P. Moran.	587	Owen Egan, ...	Earl of Rosse, ...	Cloghan, ...
	588	Kieran Murray, ...	Robert J. E. Mooney, ...	Loughill, ...
	589	George Bruce, ...	William Harding, ...	Mossfield, ...
	590	Andrew Hutchinson, ...	Major C. F. Rolleston, ...	Frankfort, ...
	591	John Houlan, ...	do.	do. ...
	592	Michael Kennedy, ...	J. R. Fraser, M.D., ...	Lockaboy, ...
	593	Keiran Gaffy, ...	Captain R. W. Williams, ...	Clonmore, ...
	594	George Rourke, ...	Captain Howard Bury & anor.,	Muchlagh, ...
	595	Thomas Ross, ...	do.	Grutt, ...
	596	Patrick Bolton, ...	Bridget Daly, ...	Newtown, ...
	597	Edward J. Odlum, ...	Lord Digby, ...	Cappincur, ...
	598	Mathew Dempsey, ...	Mrs. E. J. Milliken, ...	Ardra, ...

LEINSTER.

CARLOW.

Extent of Holding. Statute.	Poor Law Valuation.	Former Rent.	Judicial Rent.	Observations.	Value of Tenancy.
a. r. p.	£ s. d.	£ s. d.	£ s. d.		£ s. d.
19 1 10	5 0 0	11 0 0	7 10 0	By consent.	
20 3 23	8 15 6	13 0 0	9 5 0	do.	
8 3 0	8 10 0	10 0 0	6 0 0	do.	
15 1 27	10 6 0	24 0 0	13 0 0	do.	
5 2 16	2 5 0	5 13 8	8 6 8	do.	
69 3 35	33 15 0	63 13 8	39 1 4		

KILDARE.

11 2 5	11 16 0	19 0 0	19 0 0		

COUNTY.

13 2 25	9 16 0	14 0 0	10 5 0	By consent.	
43 3 5	16 0 0	19 0 0	16 5 0	Rent changed in 1851 from . . . £16 11s. 4d.	
23 0 39	12 15 0	17 0 0	13 0 0		
104 0 0	21 0 0	30 0 0	24 0 0		
134 1 21	17 13 0	40 0 0	33 0 0		
134 1 31	18 3 0	40 0 0	38 0 0		
55 0 0	36 5 0	45 17 10	42 0 0		
18 2 20	4 5 0	4 10 0	3 3 0		
810 2 12	127 10 0	182 0 0	165 0 0		
38 3 18	20 0 0	30 0 0	24 0 0		
2 1 10	8 0 0	4 8 0	4 0 0		
830 2 38	135 0 0	381 10 0	179 0 0		
27 0 30	18 10 0	21 10 0	21 10 0	1816 24 0 0	

KING'S

Names of Assistant Commissioners by whom Cases were decided.	No.	Name of Tenant.	Name of Landlord.	Townland.
Assistant Commissioners—				
R. R. Kane (Legal). Thomas Roche. J. G. Barry. J. H. Dunne. F. Moran.	599	Mathew Dempsey, ...	James Gatchell, ...	Derrymore, ...
	600	Patrick Quinn, ...	Henry L. Peirse, ...	Derrycoffey, ...
	601	Patrick Colclough, ...	Viscount Ashbrook, ...	Clonever, ...
	602	William Johnston, ...	do.	Woodbank, ...
	603	Owen Dooley, ...	do.	Lisnaliskey, ...
	604	Daniel Tierney, ...	do.	Killaphort, ...
	605	Mary Egan, ...	do.	Garrymore & an.,
	606	Patrick Daly, ...	do.	do. ...
	607	Hannah Daly, ...	do.	Lamrow, ...
	608	Michael Burns, ...	do.	Woodbank, ...
	609	Michael Daly, ...	do.	Charlestown, ...
	610	James Daly, ...	do.	Garrymore, ...
	611	Michael Dowery, ...	do.	Lamrow, ...
	612	John Rigney, ...	do.	Cloghbrennan, ...
	613	James Hill, ...	do.	Deerpark, ...
	614	Catherine Farrell, ...	do.	Cloghbrennan, ...
	615	Anne Burns, ...	do.	do. ...
	616	Martin Flynn, ...	do.	do. ...
	617	Anne Flynn, ...	do.	do. ...
	618	Patrick Kenny, ...	do.	Deerpark and an.,
	619	James Daly, ...	do.	Cloghbrennan, ...
	620	Kieran Kenny, ...	do.	Garrymore, ...
	621	Thomas Sheridan, ...	do.	Clonever, ...
	622	Michael Connolly, ...	do.	Annaghmore, ...
	623	Anne Lyons, ...	do.	Garrymore, Lamrow.
	624	John Kenny and another,	do.	Garrymore, ...
	625	Patrick Flynn, ...	do.	Cloghbrennan, ...
	626	Michael Temple, ...	do.	do. ...
	627	John Feeny, ...	do.	Cloghbrennan and Gileste.
	628	Daniel Tierney, ...	do.	Deerpark. ...
				Total, ...

COUNTY—*continued.*

Extent of Holding. Statute.			Poor Law Valuation.			Former Rent.			Judicial Rent.		
A.	R.	P.	£	s.	d.	£	s.	d.	£	s.	d.
114	0	2	43	5	0	56	0	0	45	0	0
17	0	8	1	0	0	3	11	0	3	0	0
71	3	28	56	10	0	47	1	8	35	10	0
108	0	18	73	5	0	90	6	3	71	0	0
13	1	5	8	15	0	7	18	4	8	10	0
5	1	0	3	18	0	8	0	0	3	15	0
94	0	13	50	0	0	62	19	4	54	0	0
42	0	18	25	10	0	34	1	6	23	0	0
31	0	23	17	10	0	18	3	9	14	0	0
51	1	27	23	10	0	26	17	6	20	10	0
18	0	31	9	0	0	11	16	0	8	0	0
34	0	35	19	10	0	23	11	6	18	0	0
13	1	0	4	15	0	7	0	0	4	15	0
20	0	8	13	5	0	16	0	0	11	10	0
47	3	8	26	0	0	28	5	0	24	10	0
14	3	16	11	10	0	13	6	0	10	10	0
17	3	23	11	10	0	14	7	6	10	13	0
20	0	0	10	0	0	11	12	9	10	5	0
18	0	0	10	5	0	11	12	9	10	7	6
76	1	0	33	5	0	30	1	2	29	1	2
40	0	0	19	0	0	23	15	0	14	10	0
35	2	18	16	5	0	19	7	6	15	0	0
15	1	0	7	5	0	9	1	5	6	0	0
4	0	25	4	0	0	5	0	0	3	0	0
34	2	19	20	15	0	24	7	4	17	10	0
30	0	19	19	0	0	18	7	6	17	0	0
30	1	32	14	15	0	16	15	0	12	12	0
18	0	0	11	10	0	14	4	0	13	10	0
67	2	0	28	10	0	33	1	3	30	0	0
94	0	0	59	15	0	46	12	0	45	13	0
1,308	0	25	1,129	11	0	1,447	14	1	1,186	5	8

Names of Assistant Commissioners by whom Cases were decided.	No.	Name of Tenant.	Name of Landlord.	Townland.
Assistant Commissioners—				
R. R. Kane (Legal). Thomas Rochfort. J. G. Barry. J. H. Dunne. P. Moran.	554	Michael Gannon, senr., ...	Francis V. Mackey, ...	Killinalagh,
	555	William Dinnegan, ...	Algernon W. B. Greville, ...	Cloontern, ...
	556	Mary Dinnegan, ...	do.	Ballyminion and another,
	557	James Baxter, ...	Georgina A. Whitney, by F. R. Walsh, her guardian,	Lismagan—, ...
	558	Edward Donnellan, ...	James Barry and another, ...	Cloonmaghield, ...
	559	Dominick Irwin, ...	George W. W. Slator, ...	Killeen, ...
	560	Bridget Ward, ...	Henry B. Armstrong, ...	Bawn Mountain,
	561	John McKenna, ...	Anthony Lefroy, ...	Derryhenian, ...
	562	Michael Clarke, ...	Earl of Granard, ...	Rayhage, ...
	563	Anne Evers, ...	do. ...	do. ...
	564	James Chibby, ...	Charles McGarl and another,	Aughantemple, ..
	565	Catherine Gormley, ...	John S. Ireland, ...	Hebar, South, ...
	566	William Garraghan, ...	Lord Annaly, ...	Kenagh, ...
	567	Catherine Lennon, ...	John B. Galbraith, ...	Drumbad, ...
	568	John Conway, ...	do.	Dooloon, ...
	569	Thomas Farrell, ...	William Allen, ...	Cruffagan, ...
	570	Michael Corcoran, ...	do.	do. ...
	571	William Glennon, Rep. of Michael Glennon,	do.	do. ...
	572	Maria Coleman, Rep. of Pat Coleman,	do.	do. ...
	573	Michael Coleman, ...	do.	do. ...
	574	Charles Farrell, ...	do.	do. ...
	575	John Reilly, ...	Col. E. R. King-Harman, ...	Toneagh, ...
	576	Felix Gormley, ...	do.	Shanmullagh, ...
	577	Catherine Lennon, ...	do.	Cloonlaghta, ...
	578	William Mourhead, ...	do.	do. ...
	579	Edward McCappin, ...	A. W. B. Greville, ...	Cloontown, .
	580	Thomas Denison, ...	Col. E. R. King-Harman, ...	Derrygeel, ...
	581	James Gillan, ...	Ambrose Bain, ...	Moyne, ...
	582	Peter Farrell, ...	do.	do.
	583	Edward Egan, ...	do.	Carnaboy, ...
	584	John Farrell, ...	do.	do. ...
	585	John Dowd, ...	do.	do. ...
	586	Catherine Crabe, ...	do.	Castlerea, ...
	587	Edward Flanan, ...	A. W. B. Greville, ...	Cartangcurragh,
	588	Mary Harvey, ...	do.	Cloonsanny, ...

LONGFORD.

Extent of Holding in acres.	Poor Law Valuation.	Former Rent.	Judicial Rent.	Observations.	
A. R. P.	£ s. d.	£ s. d.	£ s. d.		£ s. d.
11 0 27	6 10 0	9 15 0	7 0 0	Rent changed in 1859 from . . .	5 15 0
18 1 35	7 18 0	23 0 0	19 17 6		
19 1 17	6 15 0	55 10 0	37 5 0		
26 0 30	23 0 0	30 17 4	28 10 0		
30 1 8	16 15 0	28 9 4	16 0 0		
29 0 9	18 10 0	22 10 0	19 0 0		
36 1 37	25 0 0	36 0 0	27 4 0	1870	38 0 0
33 3 30	13 0 0	18 4 10	13 12 0		
16 0 31	6 13 0	8 6 8	5 18 0		
18 2 0	7 18 0	11 16 0	9 0 0		
3 1 31	1 10 0	8 0 0	2 5 0		
40 3 19	23 18 0	29 14 6	27 0 0		
20 0 25	16 15 0	21 0 0	16 0 0		
37 3 30	9 0 0	14 10 0	13 0 0		
28 0 8	19 0 0	34 0 0	18 16 0	1867	23 0 0
30 0 17	18 8 0	21 8 4	18 8 0	1876	18 7 0
17 0 8	13 0 0	19 2 5	16 12 0	do.	16 7 8
9 0 15	8 5 0	9 18 2	8 18 6	do.	8 8 6
18 3 5	10 10 0	15 9 0	13 8 6		
6 3 0	5 15 0	9 13 8	8 14 0	do.	8 8 8
11 1 6	8 10 0	11 14 9	10 0 0	do.	10 1 0
14 0 0	14 10 0	20 0 0	14 10 0		
37 0 37	16 0 0	18 0 0	15 0 0		
15 3 0	5 15 0	6 4 0	5 15 0		
20 1 25	16 0 0	20 0 0	16 17 0	1868	15 0 0
37 0 14	18 15 0	26 12 6	22 0 0		
35 0 12	2 10 0	12 0 0	9 3 0	1851	7 7 0
33 0 35	22 15 0	35 15 8	30 3 0	1869	30 0 0
53 1 6	63 5 0	25 10 0	35 5 0	do.	30 10 0
17 3 37	18 5 0	20 1 6	15 7 6	1857	16 10 0
14 2 16	13 10 0	17 8 1	16 0 0	1868	15 16 4
35 1 37	21 5 0	29 8 10	23 7 6	do.	23 1 1
37 3 1	27 0 0	38 9 10	37 0 0	do.	30 12 6
12 1 21	7 5 0	8 18 0	7 8 0		
34 1 6	12 5 0	23 3 2	16 10 0		

Names of Assistant Commissioners by whom Cases were decided.	No.	Name of Tenant.	Name of Landlord.
Assistant Commissioners—			
R. R. Kane (Legal). Thomas Roche. J. G. Barry. J. H. Dunne. P. Moran.	589	John Farrell, ...	A. W. B. Greville,
	590	James Davis, Admor. of Bridget Davis.	do. ...
	591	Martha Murphy, ...	do. ...
	592	James McLoughlin, ...	do. ...
	593	John Dunnigan and anor.	do. ...
	594	Edward Dunnigan, ...	do. ...
	595	Eliza Bermingham, ...	do. ...
	596	Edward Gaffney, ...	do. ...

Names of Assistant Commissioners by whom Cases were decided.	No.	Name of Tenant.	Name of Landlord.
Assistant Commissioners—			
R. R. Kane (Legal). Thomas Roche. J. G. Barry. J. H. Dunne. P. Moran.	556	Peter Reynolds, ...	Earl of Darnley, ...

Names of Assistant Commissioners by whom Cases were decided.	No.	Name of Tenant.	Name of Landlord.
Assistant Commissioners—			
R. R. Kane (Legal). Thomas Roche. J. G. Barry. J. H. Dunne. P. Moran.	484	William Doole, ...	William Mercier, ...
	485	John Doody, ...	Richard Colbeck, ...
	486	Joshua Glynn, ...	Robert Watson, ...
	487	Edward Richardson, ...	Rev. William Lyster,
	488	William Kay, ...	do. ...
	489	James Delany, ...	do. ...
	490	Michael Whelan, ...	Rev. Richard Fitzgerald,
	491	Matilda Pratt, ...	Sir A. J. Walsh, Bart.,
	492	Elizabeth Lukes, ...	Walter Hackett, ...
	493	Denis Keeffe, Admor. of Mary Keeffe,	do. ...
	494	Thomas Breen, ...	do. ...

LONGFORD—*continued.*

Extent of Holding. Statute.	Poor Law Valuation.	Former Rent.	Judicial Rent.	Observations.	Value of Tenancy.
A. R. P.	£ s. d.	£ s. d.	£ s. d.		£ s. d.
34 0 2	31 0 0	20 13 7	13 0 0		
41 1 29	18 10 0	27 6 6	18 10 0		
25 0 37	14 15 0	45 0 0	30 0 0		
35 0 0	21 0 0	28 18 8	29 0 0		
25 0 15	19 10 0	27 9 6	18 0 0		
3 2 6	1 10 0	11 0 0	7 0 0		
50 2 22	21 10 0	32 0 0	25 0 0		
16 2 0	5 10 0	35 17 6	17 5 0		
1,048 3 25	600 13 0	960 13 0	710 15 6		

MEATH.

Extent of Holding. Statute.	Poor Law Valuation.	Former Rent.	Judicial Rent.	Observations.	Value of Tenancy.
9 2 37	6 5 0	7 16 2	6 5 0	Rent changed in 1868 from . . . £ s. d. 4 14 6	

COUNTY.

Extent of Holding. Statute.	Poor Law Valuation.	Former Rent.	Judicial Rent.	Observations.	Value of Tenancy.
3 0 28	2 10 0	3 10 0	2 10 0		
44 0 0	34 10 0	41 1 6	35 0 0	By consent	
77 2 23	26 0 0	54 18 0	43 16 0	do.	
33 2 1	19 0 0	53 0 0	34 0 9	do.	
9 3 7	5 0 0	11 1 3	7 0 0	do.	
5 2 23	6 10 0	5 0 0	6 0 0	do.	
13 1 21	4 5 0	6 7 9	5 18 0	do.	
94 2 0	61 10 0	77 0 0	67 0 0	do.	
153 0 31	70 5 0	120 9 8	93 0 0		
101 2 38	44 5 0	63 10 0	45 0 0		
133 0 20	53 13 0	65 0 0	59 0 0		
64 0 0	26 18 0	48 0 0	30 0 0		
6 1 24	3 15 0	5 10 0	4 0 0		
1 2 13	6 13 0	7 10 0	6 15 0		
25 0 6	16 15 8	24 10 0	21 15 0		

QUEEN'S

Names of Assistant Commissioners by whom Cases were decided.	No.	Name of Tenant.	Name of Landlord.	Townland.
Assistant Commissioners— R. R. Kane (Legal). Thomas Roche. J. G. Barry. J. H. Dunne. P. Moran.	499	Bridget Dunne, Admin. of Timothy Dunne.	John Ross, ...	Parkahoughill, ...
	500	John Kavanagh, ...	Robert G. Cosby, ...	[illegible],
	501	Bridget Ryan, ...	do.	do. ...
	502	Edmond Lynch, ...	Lieut.-Col. H. H. Pratt, ...	Cloonagh, ...
	503	Joseph Meredith, ...	do.	South Field, ...
	504	Richard Knowles, ...	do.	Cranagh, ...
	505	Patrick Byrne, ...	Mrs. Pauline G. Bellew, ...	Vicarstown Cosby,
	506	Patrick Conroy, ...	John W. Dunne, ...	Ballycarroll,
	507	Michael Fitzpatrick, ...	Lord Castletown, ...	Rathmoyle, ...
	508	Peter Delaney, ...	do.	Moany, ...
	509	James Carey, ...	Rev. William R. Trench, ...	Ballinakill, ...
	510	Catherine Dunne, ...	do.	Ballintubbert, ...
	511	Edward Delaney, ...	Marquis of Lansdowne, ...	Garrough, ...
	512	Thomas Moore, ...	do.	Monamanry, ...
	513	Denis Dunne, ...	do.	Luggacurren, ...
	514	Jeremiah Brennan, ...	do.	do. ...
	515	Patrick Lawlor, Admor. of Michael Lawlor.	do.	Coolglass, ...
	516	Laurence Byrne, ...	do.	Fallowbeg, Middle,
	517	Michael Dunne, ...	do.	Luggacurren, ...
	518	Do.	do.	do. ...
	519	Do.	do.	do. ...
	520	Denis Dunne, Rep. of William Dunne.	do.	do. ...
	521	John Johnston, ...	do.	do. ...
	522	Margaret Troy, ...	do.	do. ...
	523	Do.	do.	Garrough, ...
	524	Edward Kelly, ...	do.	Luggacurren, ...
	525	James Moore, ...	do.	do. ...
	526	Bryan Coffey, ...	do.	do. ...
	527	John Brennan, ...	do.	Coolglass, ...
	528	Jeremiah Murphy, ...	do.	Luggacurren and another.
	529	Do.	do.	Coolglass, ...
	530	Julia McGrath, ...	do.	Brennan's Hill and another.
	531	Do.	do.	Coolglass, ...
	532	Andrew Murphy, ...	do.	do. ...
	533	Denis Brennan, ...	do.	Fallowbeg, Lower,

COUNTY—*continued.*

Extent of Holding. Statute.	Poor Law Valuation.	Former Rent.	Judicial Rent.	Observations.	Value of Tenancy.
A. R. P.	£ s. d.	£ s. d.	£ s. d.		£ s. d.
14 3 8	8 0 0	11 4 8	9 15 0		
22 3 4	31 0 0	30 0 0	30 0 0	Provision has been made in this case as regards a labourer.	
15 3 18	19 10 0	18 10 0	13 0 0		
147 1 14	93 10 0	105 0 0	86 0 0	Rent changed in 1866 from £70 10s. Provision has been made in this case as regards a labourer.	
69 1 7	61 0 0	67 10 0	64 0 0		
51 2 23	67 10 0	41 0 0	64 10 0		
86 2 22	50 0 0	60 10 0	58 0 0		
17 3 0	19 0 0	22 13 8	15 0 0		
55 1 22	35 0 0	42 0 0	43 0 0	Rent changed in 1867 from . . £19 3 11	
34 3 29	18 15 0	23 6 0	20 0 0		
100 1 16	98 10 0	67 0 0	11 0 0	1877 65 0 0	
31 2 36	29 0 0	30 0 0	28 0 0		
60 3 8	53 15 0	55 13 7	64 10 0		
16 0 13	16 0 0	28 5 6	20 10 0		
84 1 26	10 15 0	30 0 0	18 10 0		
47 0 9	30 0 0	33 16 4	27 10 0		
71 1 35	27 5 0	49 14 0	11 0 0		
93 3 23	53 5 0	47 0 0	41 0 0	1859 43 0 0	
26 1 18	13 10 0	31 16 9	15 0 9		
29 2 10	33 10 0	29 15 6	25 10 0		
7 1 4	5 0 0	6 0 0	7 0 0		
61 0 0	13 5 0	25 7 2	19 0 6		
40 3 10	17 15 0	30 9 3	22 10 0		
14 3 26	5 15 0	14 18 0	10 10 0	1875 18 0 0	
38 0 7	17 5 0	22 8 6	23 8 0		
28 0 20	19 15 0	14 18 4	14 5 0		
41 0 13	16 15 0	23 5 4	29 10 0	1831 11 0 0	
16 0 10	11 0 0	16 0 0	14 10 0	1873 20 14 0	
33 1 36	19 10 0	25 8 0	18 0 0		
11 0 18	5 15 0	7 15 0	5 5 0	1869 4 12 0	
26 3 26	9 5 0	17 3 0	13 10 0	do. 12 10 0	

Names of Assistant Commissioners by whom Cases were decided	No.	Name of Tenant.	Name of Landlord.	Townland.
Assistant Commissioners—				
E. R. Kane (Legal). Thomas Roche. J. G. Barry. J. H. Dwyer. P. Moran.	534	James Brehany, ...	Marquis of Lansdowne, ...	Shragaraun, ...
	535	James Mahon, ...	do.	Threegan, ...
	536	Pat Kelly, ...	do.	Lugganarrive, ...
	537	Michael Kelly, ...	do.	do. ...
	539	John Dunne, ...	do.	do. ...
				Total, ...

PROVINCE OF

COUNTY OF

Names of Assistant Commissioners by whom Cases were decided	No.	Name of Tenant.	Name of Landlord.	Townland.
Assistant Commissioners—				
T. P. Lynch (Legal). P. Taaffe. R. L. Henry. E. J. Kiernan. P. Gibbons.	2610	Thomas Ward, ...	Martin G. Ffrench, ...	Cloonkeen and another.
	2611	Mary Lohan, ...	do.	Cloonkeen, ...
	2612	Owen Connolly, ...	do.	Cloonkeen and another.
	2613	Cecily Lohan, ...	do.	Cloonkeen, ...
	2614	Luke Lohan (Larry), ...	do.	do. ...
	2615	Patrick Brown, ...	do.	do. ...
	2616	Thomas Mannion, ...	do.	Cloonkeen and another.
	2617	Edward Fallon, ...	do.	do. ...
	2618	Catherine Coffey, ...	do.	Cloonkeen, French,
	2619	Michael Kerrane, ...	do.	do. ...
	2620	Augustine Quinn, ...	do.	Cloonkeen and another.
	2621	John Noone, ...	do.	Lisnatreaghy, ...
	2622	John Naven, ...	do.	do. ...
	2623	Patrick Lynch, ...	do.	do. ...
	2624	Patrick Lohan, ...	do.	do. ...
	2625	Mary Quinn, ...	do.	do. ...
	2626	Laurence Carroll and Mary Carroll,	do.	do. ...
	2627	Mark Lohan, ...	do.	do. ...
	2628	Andrew McCormick, ...	do.	do. ...
	2629	Mathew Hession, ...	do.	do. ...
	2630	Honor Hession, ...	do.	do. ...
	2631	James Hussey, ...	Michael O'Kelly, ...	Mountsilk, ...
	2632	William Dempsey, ...	do.	Moyleaghbeg, ...
	2633	John Loughnan, ...	do.	do. ...

COUNTY—*continued.*

Extent of Holding, Statute.	Poor Law Valuation.	Former Rent.	Judicial Rent.	Observations.	Value of Tenancy.
A. R. P.	£ s. d.	£ s. d.	£ s. d.		£ s. d.
80 1 8	15 0 0	18 0 0	16 10 0		
158 3 18	132 0 0	205 11 6	160 0 0	Provision has been made in this case as regards a labourer.	
80 0 23	53 9 0	56 3 0	47 0 0		
83 3 8	13 15 0	18 8 0	15 5 0		
38 3 15	16 5 0	29 8 0	25 10 0		
1,618 3 3	1,356 11 8	2,004 13 7	1,815 19 0		

CONNAUGHT.

GALWAY.

Extent of Holding, Statute.	Poor Law Valuation.	Former Rent.	Judicial Rent.	Observations.	Value of Tenancy.
11 3 6	4 15 0	7 17 10	5 16 0		40 0 0
10 3 33	8 10 0	6 11 0	3 15 0		25 0 0
9 0 34	3 10 0	5 11 6	3 3 0		20 0 0
11 1 25	6 0 0	8 6 0	5 8 0		30 0 0
10 0 21	3 10 0	6 10 3	3 16 0		25 0 0
5 1 26	1 5 0	3 5 2	1 10 0		12 0 0
12 1 3	4 10 0	6 1 2	5 0 0	Rent changed in 1878 from . . £7 16 0	30 0 0
12 2 12	4 0 0	8 0 9	4 18 0	1854 £5 13 0	30 0 0
10 0 36	3 6 0	6 17 6	2 13 0		25 0 0
9 3 38	3 0 0	6 17 6	4 10 0		28 0 0
13 0 33	6 0 0	8 17 6	6 5 0		30 0 0
8 3 35	3 10 0	4 6 0	4 0 0		31 0 0
9 2 22	3 10 0	7 4 8	4 0 0		34 0 0
9 1 18	3 10 0	7 1 1	3 18 0		34 0 0
9 3 24	3 10 0	7 1 10	3 10 0		36 0 0
9 1 15	3 16 0	7 3 11	4 0 0		36 0 0
11 1 6	5 10 0	11 0 4	4 5 0		24 0 0
9 1 8	3 15 0	7 7 0	4 1 0		25 0 0
9 3 11	3 0 0	6 8 0	3 18 0		25 0 0
2 1 31	1 5 0	2 3 0	1 5 0		10 0 0
7 1 12	3 15 0	5 3 9	3 0 0		20 0 0
6 3 15	2 15 0	4 0 0	3 0 0	By consent.	
13 3 3	6 2 0	8 8 8	6 5 0	do.	
25 1 6	9 15 0	13 2 10	10 2 3	do.	

Names of Assistant Commissioners by whom Cases were decided.	No.	Name of Tenant.	Name of Landlord.
Assistant Commissioners—			
T. P. Lynch (Legal). P. Taaffe. E. L. Hunt. E. J. H[illegible]. P. G[illegible].	2634	Thomas Boyle, ...	Michael O'Kelly, ...
	2635	Thaddeus Fleming, ...	do. ...
	2636	John Greany, ...	do. ...
	2637	Martin Dempsey, ...	do. ...
	2638	Thomas McLoughlin, ...	do. ...
	2639	John Dempsey, ...	do. ...
	2640	Michael Naughton, ...	do. ...
	2641	Patrick Devly, ...	do. ...
	2642	John Lohan (Terry), ...	Martin G. [illegible],
	2643	William Furey, ...	do. ...
	2644	Ferdinand Lohan, ...	do. ...
	2645	Martin Conneely and another,	do. ...
	2646	Michael Nolan, ...	do. ...
	2647	John Dowd, ...	do. ...
	2648	Mary Heavey, ...	do. ...
	2649	Michael Downey, ...	do. ...
	2650	Thomas Lahey, ...	do. ...
	2651	Michael Higgins, ...	do. ...
	2652	John Higgins, ...	do. ...
	2653	Martin Conn, ...	do. ...
	2654	Mary Hannon, ...	do. ...
	2655	John Nolan, ...	do. ...
	2656	Martin Nolan, ...	do. ...
	2657	Mary Conneely, ...	do. ...
	2658	Michael Ward, ...	do. ...
	2659	James Lohan, ...	do. ...
	2660	Thomas Killelea, ...	do. ...
	2661	John Hannon, ...	do. ...
	2662	John Carroll, ...	do. ...
	2663	Mary McHugh, ...	do. ...
	2664	Thomas McDermott, ...	do. ...
	2665	Catherine Hannon, ...	do. ...
	2666	Thomas Kelly, ...	do. ...
	2667	Eliza Kelly, ...	do. ...
	2668	Michael Cryhan, ...	do. ...

GALWAY—*continued.*

Extent of Holding. Statute.	Poor Law Valuation.	Former Rent.	Judicial Rent.	Observations.	Value of Tenancy.
A. R. P.	£ s. d.	£ s. d.	£ s. d.		£ s. d.
16 0 38	6 15 0	10 0 0	4 17 8	By consent.	
6 1 17	3 11 0	3 9 8	3 13 3	do.	
11 1 14	4 18 0	6 5 0	4 13 10	do.	
1 3 17	1 11 0	3 0 0	2 5 0	do.	
18 0 11	8 5 0	8 0 0	8 0 0	do.	
4 3 17	1 10 0	3 0 0	2 8 6	do.	
6 2 23	2 10 0	3 13 0	3 11 8	do.	
4 3 17	3 4 0	3 10 9½	1 18 0	do	
11 2 34	3 15 0	7 10 0	4 16 0		
6 1 23	3 10 0	4 10 7	3 0 0		
23 1 7	8 10 0	17 0 0	8 18 6		
16 3 39	7 5 0	14 14 0	7 12 6		
13 0 28	5 0 0	9 18 0	5 3 0		
19 3 6	7 5 0	14 18 0	5 8 0		
11 0 2	5 10 0	10 15 4	5 15 0		
7 0 33	3 10 0	4 13 11	3 15 0		
6 3 34	3 13 0	4 8 0	3 0 0		
6 1 28	3 10 0	5 0 0	2 16 0		
6 1 38	3 13 0	5 0 0	3 18 0		
10 2 8	5 0 0	8 2 6	4 18 0		
11 0 14	6 10 0	10 15 11	6 10 0		
9 3 33	4 13 0	7 18 1	4 10 0		
13 2 38	4 5 0	8 10 8	5 10 0		
13 0 16	6 0 0	10 3 0	5 16 0		
10 1 32	4 0 0	7 11 5	1 7 8		
3 3 34	3 18 0	7 3 6	1 7 6		
6 1 21	2 15 0	5 8 0	3 3 0		
8 3 1	3 16 0	7 6 0	3 13 6		
8 0 33	3 15 0	7 10 0	1 12 6		
11 1 38	6 0 0	8 0 0	5 0 0		
9 2 31	3 15 0	8 6 3	4 17 8	Rent changed in 1878 from £7 15 0 / 1876 £3 13 9	
10 2 12	3 5 0	6 0 0	8 15 0		
10 0 19	3 10 0	6 11 0	3 16 0		
12 0 23	6 10 0	9 12 0	6 0 0		
18 1 20	6 13 0	9 11 0	3 13 6		

Names of Assistant Commissioners by whom Cases were decided.	No.	Name of Tenant.	Name of Landlord.	Townland.
Assistant Commissioners—				
T. P. Lynch (Legal). P. Taaffe. R. L. Hunt. R. J. Kiernan. P. Grehan.	2669	Luke Cunningham, ...	Martin O. Ffrench, ...	Ballynamona, ...
	2670	Mary Lehan, ...	do.	Lisnavraggy, ...
	2671	John Graham, ...	do.	Ballyneenare, ...
	2672	Luke McLoughlin, ...	do.	do. ...
	2673	Owney Nome, ...	do.	do. ...
	2674	Margaret Creaghan, ...	do.	do. ...
	2675	Patrick Pansey, ...	do.	do. ...
	2676	Luke McDermott, ...	do.	Lisnavraggy, ...
	2677	Dominick McDonnell, ...	Thomas Carrowell, ...	Buggaun Carrowell,
	2678	Pat Lyons, sen., ...	do.	do.
	2679	Michael Hannan, ...	do.	do.
	2680	Bridget Lally, ...	do.	do. ...
	2681	Darby Dowd, ...	do.	do. ...
	2682	John Dowd, ...	do.	do. ...
	2683	Michael Dillon, ...	do.	do.
	2684	Mary Lally, ...	do.	do. ...
	2685	Michael Fenneran, ...	do.	do. ...
	2686	Thomas Loughan, ...	do.	do. ...
	2687	Patrick Finneran, ...	Joseph A. Holmes and another, Trustees of late G. N. Bagot.	Kilmore, ...
	2688	James Naughton, ...	do.	Clooncalyon,
	2689	Michael Delany, ...	do.	Drynane, ...
	2690	Redmond Fitzmaurice, ...	do.	do. ...
	2691	Thomas Fitzmaurice, ...	do.	Kilmore,
	2692	Bryan Martin, ...	do.	Drynane, ...
	2693	Patrick Mannion, ...	do.	do. ...
	2694	John Downey, ...	do.	do. ...
	2695	John Keeffe, ...	do.	do.
	2696	Thomas Kelly, ...	do.	do. ...
	2697	Martin Nolan, ...	do.	do. ...
	2698	Patrick Flynn, ...	do.	Mucklough, ...
	2699	Patrick Nolan, ...	do.	do. ...
	2700	Patrick Martin, ...	do.	Cartron, ...
	2701	Margaret Murry, ...	do.	Hermitage and another,
	2702	Patrick Kelly, ...	do.	Mucklough, ...
	2703	Michael Farrell, ...	do.	do. ...

GALWAY—*continued.*

Extent of Holding. (Statute)	Poor Law Valuation.	Former Rent.	Judicial Rent.	Observations.		Value of Tenancy.
A. R. P.	£ s. d.	£ s. d.	£ s. d.		£ s. d.	£ s. d.
13 3 28	8 16 0	11 3 0	6 5 0			
10 0 2	3 16 0	8 0 4	4 16 0			
13 0 7	7 5 0	8 18 4	6 3 0	Rent changed in 1866 from . . .	6 15 0	
13 2 28	8 15 0	9 16 9	5 15 0			
11 1 14	8 15 0	7 0 0	4 8 8	1867	8 5 0	
14 3 35	3 10 0	5 10 0	3 17 8			
8 2 16	2 0 0	3 10 0	2 0 0			
9 1 7	5 16 0	7 10 0	4 5 0			
15 1 15	3 15 0	6 0 0	4 10 0			
15 0 35	3 10 0	5 0 0	5 10 0			
14 0 37	3 5 0	5 16 4	4 10 0			
18 2 17	3 0 0	5 0 0	3 15 0			
11 3 31	6 0 0	10 0 0	8 2 6			
10 0 23	8 0 0	17 0 0	13 15 0			
18 0 5	4 5 0	7 5 0	5 5 0			
14 1 38	3 0 0	5 17 6	4 13 0			
18 2 32	4 10 0	8 0 0	8 0 0			
16 0 3	3 15 0	6 0 0	4 15 0			
35 1 36	14 18 0	15 16 11	14 5 0			
64 0 7	24 0 0	34 0 0	26 0 0			280 0 0
13 3 18	6 0 0	8 18 0	7 10 0			
20 3 9	17 5 0	23 16 0	19 7 0			
16 2 15	5 10 0	6 13 6	4 10 0			
19 3 32	10 10 0	14 12 6	11 0 0			
10 3 20	6 0 0	8 15 8	7 0 0			
4 1 25	1 5 0	2 4 0	1 18 0			
6 1 0	5 0 0	6 5 0	4 15 0			
12 3 35	4 18 0	7 15 0	8 10 0			
11 1 14	7 0 0	8 10 0	7 0 0			
18 0 10	11 3 0	15 5 9	13 0 0			
18 1 4	11 5 0	18 4 0	11 10 0			
21 3 26	5 5 0	13 0 6	10 5 0			50 0 0
20 0 10	8 0 0	11 4 0	8 10 0			
15 3 34	5 5 0	9 9 0	7 10 0			
11 1 28	7 5 0	8 7 6	6 12 0			

Names of Assistant Commissioners by whom Cases were decided.	No.	Name of Tenant.	Name of Landlord.	Townland.
Assistant Commissioners— T. P. Lynch (Legal). P. Taaffe. R. L. Hunt. E. J. Keenan. F. G[illegible].	9704	Mary Farrell, ...	Joseph A. Holmes and another, Trustees of late C. N. Bagot.	Moorhaugh, ...
	9705	Thomas Hennie, senior,	do.	do. ...
	9706	John Mallee, ...	George E. Deering, ...	Ballymurray, Nth.,
	9707	Michael Mallee, ...	Thomas Higgins, ...	Carrowpadden, East,
	9708	Bryan Kenny, senior, ...	do.	do. ...
	9709	Thomas McHugh, ...	Miss Anastasia Nolan, ...	Ballybanaghan, ...
	9710	Denis McHugh, ...	do.	do. ...
	9711	Michael Cunniffe, ...	Thomas Cunniffe, ...	Carrowntober, ...
	9712	Martin Mannion, ...	Michael O'Kelly, ...	Moyloughbeg, ...
	9713	Thomas Donohue, ...	D. O'C. Donnellan, ...	Woodquay, ...
	9714	John Kane, ...	do.	Pollnamorris, ...
	9715	Francis Lohan, ...	do.	Sylane, ...
	9716	Pat Daly, ...	George G. Lynch, ...	Dugarva, ...
	9717	James Mealy, ...	do.	Ballyboy, ...
	9718	John Rafferty, ...	do.	Mullagh, ...
	9719	Michael Treacy, ...	do.	Dugarva, ...
	9720	Thomas Burke, ...	Hugh Henry, ...	Cumbrough, ...
	9721	John Dunkerry, ...	do.	do. ...
	9722	James Ward, ...	do.	do. ...
	9723	Thomas Stephens, ...	do.	do. ...
	9724	James Hughes, ...	do.	do. ...
	9725	John Nolan, ...	do.	do. ...
	9726	Thomas Kelly, ...	do.	do. ...
	9727	Thomas Rafferty, ...	do.	do. ...
	9728	William Donohoe, ...	Sir Henry G. Bellew, Bart.,	do. ...
	9729	Patrick Gavin, ...	do.	Clonmelliga, ...
	9730	John Lyons, ...	John Joyce, ...	Oenigue Coltra, ...
	9731	Catherine Thornton, ...	Robert J. Martin, ...	Drumnakeen, ...
	9732	Michael Cunningham, ...	Richard A. Clarke, ...	Gelden Park, ...
	9733	Andrew Turley, ...	Martin O. Ffrench, ...	Creevaun, ...
	9734	Patrick Darcy, ...	do.	Lissavruggy,
	9735	Michael Quinn, ...	do.	Creevaun, ...
	9736	Michael Clarke, ...	Mrs. Julia Browne, ...	Carrowmoyle, ...
	9737	Patrick Geraghty, ...	do.	Killimore, ...
	9738	Ellen Griffin, ...	do.	Carranurragy, West,

GALWAY—*continued.*

Extent of Holding—Statute.	Poor Law Valuation.	Former Rent.	Judicial Rent.	Observations.	Value of Tenancy.
A. R. P.	£ s. d.	£ s. d.	£ s. d.		£ s. d.
16 1 17	6 9 0	7 16 6	7 7 8		
13 3 14	9 13 0	11 2 6	9 0 0		
1 3 38	7 13 0	7 3 0	8 10 0		
17 0 1	10 5 0	13 4 4	8 15 0		
19 3 2	11 16 0	15 5 4	11 5 0		
11 2 30	6 10 0	13 7 0	8 10 0		
21 2 0	10 5 0	23 7 11	19 0 0		
13 3 33	7 0 0	7 6 5	7 3 8	By consent.	
11 2 30	3 15 0	10 0 0	7 10 0	do.	
14 3 38	6 10 0	13 0 0	8 13 0	do.	
15 0 0	6 17 0	10 18 8	8 18 1	do.	
11 2 36	4 10 0	7 0 8	5 10 0	do.	
6 3 20	3 10 0	5 10 8	3 10 8		40 0 0
5 3 28	2 10 0	5 0 0	4 10 0		
14 0 30	6 10 0	13 0 0	11 10 0		55 0 0
6 1 23	3 10 0	5 10 8	3 10 8		
40 1 25	18 8 0	27 0 0	20 0 0		
15 0 19	6 5 0	11 16 0	8 0 0		
21 3 11	9 10 0	14 0 0	10 5 0		
10 1 6	4 11 0	6 13 0	4 15 0		
15 0 19	6 10 0	10 10 0	8 0 0		
14 0 19	5 0 0	6 15 0	4 10 0		
17 0 19	8 10 0	9 0 0	7 0 0		
8 3 12	3 5 0	4 10 0	2 5 0		
18 2 4	7 0 0	10 9 5	6 15 0		
19 0 18	10 5 0	14 14 0	14 14 0		
20 0 5	9 5 0	15 13 0	14 0 0		
30 1 8	15 5 0	20 0 0	14 0 0		
120 1 15	66 15 0	110 0 0	120 0 0		
17 2 3	7 0 0	8 16 0	6 5 0	Rent changed in 1877 from . . . £ s. d. 6 15 4	36 0 0
6 3 8	2 10 0	4 16 8	2 13 8		20 0 0
17 1 8	5 0 0	8 6 0	5 0 0	1875 7 0 0	35 0 0
13 0 15	5 0 0	8 7 5	6 10 0		
10 3 35	7 5 0	18 0 0	10 5 0		
16 2 14	8 10 0	10 0 0	10 0 0		

COUNTY OF

Names of Assistant Commissioners by whom Cases were decided.	No.	Name of Tenant.	Name of Landlord.	Townland.
Assistant Commissioners—				
T. P. Lynch (Legal). P. Taaffe. E. L. Hunt. E. J. [illegible]. P. [illegible].	2739	Thomas Higgins, ...	Sir William Lawson and others,	Craiguecullen, ...
	2740	Thomas Treacy, ...	do.	Bunkram, ...
	2741	Patrick Rourke, ...	do.	Graiguecullane, ...
	2742	John Treacy, ...	do.	[illegible],
F. G. Holmes (Legal). J. M. Weir. J. F. Bamford. J. Cunningham. Aubrey Spencer.	2743	Michael Higgins, ...	William S. Waithman, ...	[illegible], ...
	2744	Patrick Comber, ...	Theobald Blake, ...	Carrowgross, ...
	2745	Thomas Molloy, ...	Rev. Henry Ede, ...	Tumbrocky, ...
	2746	[illegible] Kilkenny, ...	do.	do. ...
	2747	Katherine Folan, ...	do.	do. ...
	2748	Henry Connell, ...	Marquis of Clanricarde, ...	Castlegar, ...
	2749	Patrick Rowan, ...	do.	do. ...
	2750	Luke Ryan, ...	do.	do. ...
	2751	Michael Rowan, ...	do.	do. ...
	2752	Thomas Morris, ...	do.	do. ...
	2753	Francis Coleman, ...	do.	do. ...
	2754	James Rowan, ...	do.	do. ...
	2755	John Murphy, ...	do.	do. ...
	2756	Michael Toohey, ...	do.	do. ...
	2757	Mary Rowan, ...	do.	do. ...
	2758	Catherine Kyne, ...	John A. O'Flaherty, ...	Drumaloughane, ...
	2759	Patrick Gragan, ...	do.	Carrowmanagh, ...
	2760	John Burnside, ...	do.	Drumaloughane, ...
	2761	Martin Hanley, ...	Nicholas Blake, ...	Shela, ...
	2762	Walter Cunningham, ...	do.	do. ...
	2763	Patrick Cunningham, ...	do.	do. ...
	2764	Martin Melville, ...	George C. Davenport, ...	Rosshill, ...
	2765	Bartholomew Walsh, ...	Marcus F. O'Flaherty, ...	Gortatleva, ...
	2766	James Sheridan, ...	do.	Tawnagh, ...
	2767	Patrick Murphy, ...	do.	Lisnavilla, ...
	2768	James Redkin, ...	do.	Gortalnia, ...
	2769	Mary Murphy, ...	do.	Lisnavilla, ...
	2770	James Grealy, ...	Lord Wallscourt, ...	Prospect, ...
	2771	Patrick Brady, ...	do.	Lower Carraun, ...

TABLE OF JUDICIAL RENTS.

GALWAY—*continued.*

Extent of Holding. Statute.	Poor Law Valuation.	Former Rent.	Judicial Rent.	Observations.	
A. R. P.	£ s. d.	£ s. d.	£ s. d.		£ s.
5 0 27	6 8 0	7 5 0	4 10 0		
29 1 17	12 10 0	14 11 6	10 5 0		
18 0 0	12 10 0	16 4 6	10 0 0		
16 1 15	10 5 0	12 6 0	11 0 0		
33 2 30	18 10 0	27 0 0	21 0 0	Rent changed in 1873 from . .	19 13
30 2 18	10 15 0	19 0 0	18 0 0		
6 1 8	2 0 0	4 2 8	3 10 0		
23 0 35	4 0 0	7 13 9	5 10 0		
11 0 11	5 16 0	8 17 9	4 16 0		
28 0 29	10 17 6	12 17 6	10 15 0	1865	6 5
16 3 30	6 15 6	7 7 6	6 10 0	do.	6 10
13 0 1	3 6 6	5 5 0	4 12 6	do.	3 6
11 3 14	6 2 0	7 17 5	7 0 0	do.	4 16
37 3 18	19 1 0	20 9 4	17 15 0	do.	13 15
17 1 26	7 11 0	8 0 0	7 5 0	do.	5 5
10 2 5	5 16 0	6 1 0	5 10 0	do.	4 10
18 2 17	7 5 0	7 6 0	6 18 0	do.	4 10
20 2 1	11 15 0	12 10 0	10 15 0	do.	8 5
21 3 18	8 2 0	9 11 0	8 0 0	do.	6 10
9 3 20	3 6 0	5 8 4	4 2 6		
5 0 0	4 16 0	6 5 0	4 17 0	By consent.	
11 0 10	3 14 0	5 15 7	4 10 6		
13 3 37	4 0 0	6 7 0	4 7 0	do.	
64 0 17	11 0 0	23 15 0	13 4 0	do.	
64 0 17	17 5 0	27 4 0	16 15 0	do.	
5 1 0	8 5 0	14 16 1	11 10 0	do.	
30 2 1	5 15 0	9 6 8	8 0 0		
16 3 5	1 0 0	5 12 6	6 0 0		
25 0 20	7 11 0	14 0 0	18 10 0		
12 2 23	3 6 0	4 0 0	3 0 0		
7 1 22	2 19 0	4 15 6	3 13 6		
11 2 0	16 10 6	13 18 9	9 0 6		
25 0 24	20 0 0	24 7 6	18 0 0		

Assistant Commissioners—

F. G. [illegible] (Legal).
J. M. Weir.
J. F. [illegible].
J. [illegible].
Andrew [illegible].

2772	John Darcy, ...	Mrs. Catherine Browne
2773	James Hersfield, ...	do. ...
2774	Tady Kyne, ...	do. ...
2775	Patrick Gavin, ...	do. ...
2776	Tady Kyne, ...	do. ...
2777	Ulick Kenedy, ...	do. ...
2778	Martin Walsh, ...	do. ...
2779	Tady Kyne, ...	do. ...
2780	Do.	do. ...
2781	Do.	do. ...
2782	Stephen Reane & ancr.,	C. Dennis O'Rorke,
2783	Bryan O'Neill, ...	do. ...
2784	Margaret Fox, Admix. of John Fox.	Richard A. H. Kirwan,
2785	Maurice Duggan, ...	do. ...
2786	Martin Healy, ...	do. ...
2787	Patrick Walsh, ...	do. ...
2788	Thomas Mealia, ...	do. ...
2789	Martin Sherrett, ...	do. ...
2790	Mary Redington, Admix. of James Redington.	do. ...
2791	Martin Lawless, ...	do. ...
2792	John Ford, ...	do. ...
2793	Patrick Ford, ...	do. ...
2794	Walter Walsh, ...	do. ...
2795	William Joyce, ...	do. ...
2796	John Murphy, ...	do. ...
2797	Miles Walsh, ...	do. ...
2798	Thomas Horwood, ...	Major Thomas Lambert,
2799	Thomas Hughes, ...	do. ...
2800	Patrick Keane, ...	do. ...
2801	Michael Sherrett, ...	do. ...
2802	John Connell, ...	do. ...
2803	Mary Lee, Admix. of Michael Lee.	do. ...
2804	Malachy Cunnane, ...	do. ...
2805	Patrick Lenahan, ...	do. ...
2806	John Fahey, ...	do. ...

GALWAY—*continued.*

Extent of Holding. Statute.			Poor Law Valuation.			Former Rent.			Judicial Rent.			Observations.
A.	R.	P.	£	s.	d.	£	s.	d.	£	s.	d.	
7	2	4	5	15	0	8	0	0	7	0	0	
4	1	16	3	0	0	4	10	0	3	15	0	
6	0	23	6	6	0	9	0	0	7	5	0	
6	1	16	6	10	0	10	0	0	8	0	0	
13	3	34	10	0	0	20	0	0	16	15	0	
11	1	10	6	15	0	7	10	0	6	0	0	
6	1	16	3	0	0	4	10	0	3	15	0	
6	1	30	5	0	0	6	5	0	6	7	6	
6	2	25	6	0	0	9	0	0	8	3	6	
6	0	17	5	0	0	10	0	0	8	17	0	
66	2	6	13	0	0	31	4	0	23	0	0	
40	2	0	9	1	0	23	2	3	14	10	0	
34	1	15	8	10	0	12	16	0	11	10	0	
30	0	25	3	10	0	10	19	6	7	10	0	
16	3	33	2	15	0	10	18	0	6	10	0	
9	3	7	3	0	0	9	3	6	5	10	0	
8	3	35	6	5	0	10	0	0	8	0	0	
28	2	31	11	0	0	19	18	0	17	0	0	
14	3	5	3	0	0	7	8	0	3	15	0	
17	3	25	2	10	0	6	10	0	4	3	4	
63	1	36	10	15	0	35	11	0	19	0	0	
16	3	38	0	16	0	6	1	0	4	0	0	
10	2	16	3	10	0	7	11	6	5	15	0	
14	2	37	5	10	0	9	0	6	7	15	0	
28	2	37	—			11	0	0	10	0	0	
33	0	29	5	0	0	14	11	0	11	0	0	
25	0	20	8	15	0	18	14	10	13	14	10	
29	0	6	11	0	0	18	18	5	13	10	0	
30	0	30	7	15	0	11	17	0	11	0	0	
13	1	15	4	10	0	6	13	0	6	18	0	
30	0	20	8	15	0	13	6	4	12	8	1	
24	1	8	8	5	0	9	15	0	9	15	0	
16	3	28	5	10	0	8	0	0	6	10	0	
16	2	26	5	10	0	8	0	0	6	10	0	
16	2	25	5	10	0	7	17	3	6	10	0	

Assistant Commissioners—	No.				
F. G. Hodder (Legal). J. M. Weir. J. F. Bedford. J. Cunningham. Andrew Spencer.	2907	Patrick Hession, Rep. of John Cunningham.	Major Thomas Lambert, ...	Gortnaloe,	—
	2908	John Glynn, ...	do.	Gortaloe and another,	
	2909	Darby Grealy, ...	do.	do.	
	2910	John Cain, ...	do.	Mullaneen,	—
	2911	Michael Heffernan and another,	Bernard Mullins, ...	Upper Dungan,	
	2912	Thomas Lenihan, ...	do.	do.	
	2913	William Malley, ...	do.	do.	
	2914	Bridget Commons, Admx. of Patrick Commons,	James French, ...	Clone,	—
	2915	Thomas Kelly, ...	do.	do.	—
	2916	John Moran, ...	do.	do.	—
	2917	Bridget Flesk, ...	do.	do.	—
	2918	Martin Wynne, ...	James Blake, ...	Ballaghan,	—
	2919	John Scully, ...	do.	Castlequarter,	—
	2920	Martin Carr, ...	do.	do.	—
	2921	John Meyhan, ...	do.	Cloonboo,	—
	2922	John Small, ...	do.	Castlequarter,	—
	2923	James Carr, ...	do.	do.	—
				Total,	-

COUNTY OF

Assistant Commissioners—	No.				
Cecil Roche (Legal). M. P. Lynch. H. B. Mossmore. R. B. Heygate. Redmond Roche.	1193	Michael Reynolds, ...	Francis O'Beirne, a Minor, by Ellen O'Beirne.	Feerglass,	.
	1194	Cath. Fitzpatrick, Rep. of Michael Fitzpatrick.	William C. B. Bathven, ...	Aughavoghan,	—
	1195	James Wynne (Francis),	do.	Drumbarlum,	—
	1196	James Wynne (James),	do.	do.	—
	1197	Farrell Cafferty, ...	Francis O'Beirne, a Minor, Rep. of Hugh O'Beirne.	Strawkingford,	—
	1198	John McCann, Rep. of Peter McCann.	John Madden, ...	Bannaghbing,	-
	1199	Anne Lynch, Rep. of Pat Lynch.	Rev. Henry Stepney, ...	Gortinure,	—
	1200	John Gilhooly, ...	Thomas R. Palmer, ...	Derrinavona,	...
	1201	Miles Gilhooly, ...	do.	do.	—
	1202	Mick Hodden, ...	do.	do.	—
	1203	Peter Gilhooly, ...	James Tate and others, Reps. of Thomas Palmer.	Shevdill,	
	1204	Patrick Keany (John),	Lord Massey, ...	Cabmattersday,	
	1205	Patrick Keany, ...	do.	do.	—
	1206	Michael McLoughlin, ...	do.	do.	—

GALWAY—*continued.*

Extent of Holding. Statute.	Poor Law Valuation.	Former Rent.	Judicial Rent.	Observations.		Value of Tenancy.
a. r. p.	£ s. d.	£ s. d.	£ s. d.		£ s. d.	£ s. d.
16 2 26	5 10 0.	7 17 3	6 10 0			
19 3 34	7 0 0	10 8 11	9 10 0			
16 3 28	5 10 0	8 0 0	6 5 0			
20 0 30	7 15 0	11 17 0	11 0 0			
33 0 25	15 0 0	27 10 0	20 10 0			
19 1 30	23 10 0	40 0 0	33 0 0			
97 1 27	6 10 0	16 7 8	10 17 6	Rent changed in 1845 from	9 0 0	
11 3 13	5 0 0	7 18 10	6 10 0			45 0 0
8 0 0	4 0 0	4 11 6	5 10 0			40 0 0
18 0 18	5 15 0	9 10 0	8 5 0			55 0 0
30 2 0	11 15 0	17 4 0	16 5 0			180 0 0
15 0 6	20 0 0	33 12 8	30 0 0			
10 3 29	4 5 0	8 0 0	6 0 0	By consent.		
9 1 9	3 6 0	8 0 0	5 0 0	do.		
13 2 37½	6 15 0	10 0 0	7 10 0	do.		
10 3 4	4 0 0	8 0. 0	6 0 0	do.		
9 1 8	3 19 0	8 0 0	5 0 0	do.		
3,599 3 18½	1,429 11 6	2,277 6 6½	1,735 3			

LEITRIM.

Extent of Holding. Statute.	Poor Law Valuation.	Former Rent.	Judicial Rent.	Observations.		Value of Tenancy.
18 0 35	6 10 0	12 18 0	6 10 0			
55 2 20	29 10 0	30 11 0	26 0 0	Rent changed in 1858 from	25 0 0	
16 3 11	8 0 0	12 0 0	10 0 0			
85 3 31	18 0 0	23 10 0	19 10 0			
19 0 21	6 0 0	8 9 6	6 15 0	1857	3 10 10	
9 3 15	13 13 0	5 6 0	4 5 0			
19 1 5	7 0 0	9 0 0	6 10 0	By consent.		
14 3 30	7 15 0	13 6 0	9 1 6	do.		
18 1 38	9 15 0	15 5 0	11 5 0	do.		
6 1 7	2 5 0	3 4 0	3 15 0			
10 0 23	4 16 0	3 10 0	5 15 0			
35 1 17	7 0 0	8 2 0	8 2 0			
165 0 13	20 0 0	23 0 0	19 10 0			
17 2 28	3 10 0	5 5 0	5 10 0	do.		

COUNTY OF

Names of Assistant Commissioners by whom Cases were decided.	No.	Name of Tenant.	Name of Landlord.	Townland.
Assistant Commissioners—				
Cecil Roche (Legal). M. F. Lynch. H. B. Morrison. E. B. Heuston. Reginald Bagot.	1207	William Kenny, ...	Lord Massy, ...	[illegible],
	1208	William Flynn, Rep. of Mary Flynn,	Colonel R. Phibbs, ...	[illegible], ...
	1209	John Flynn, ...	do.	do. ...
	1210	Bryan McTiernan, ...	do.	[illegible]
	1211	John McDermott, ...	Henry L. Montgomery, ...	[illegible], ...
	1212	Pat McAniff, Rep. of Michael McAniff.	do.	[illegible],
	1213	James Carroll, ...	do.	[illegible], ...
	1214	William Gilmor, ...	George L. Fox, ...	Fawn, ...
	1215	Terence Clancy, ...	do.	Derrybrick, ...
	1216	William Gilmor, ...	do.	[illegible], ...
	1217	Do.	do.	[illegible], ...
	1218	Do.	do.	do. ...
	1219	Bridget Flynn, Rep. of James Flynn.	Charles G. B. White, ...	[illegible], ...
	1220	Owen Banks, ...	do.	Gortnagarvan and another.
	1221	Charles Mahon, ...	Arthur L. Tottenham, ...	Loughros, ...
	1222	Michael Flynn, ...	do.	Loughros & anr.
	1223	Miles McFadden, ...	John Palmer, ...	Garvagh, ...
	1224	John Ford, Rep. of Ellen Ford.	do.	Garvagh Glebe, ...
	1225	Michael McMorrow, jun.	do.	Garvagh, ...
	1226	Hugh Rooney, senior, ...	do.	do. ...
	1227	James McSharry, ...	do.	do. ...
	1228	Michael McMorrow, sen.,	do.	[illegible] Glebe
	1229	Patrick McPadden, ...	do.	Garvagh Glebe, ...
	1230	Mathew Kilkenny, ...	do.	do. ...
	1231	Patrick Carney, ...	Simon Armstrong, ...	Friarstown, ...
	1232	Peter Gallagher, ...	do.	[illegible], ...
	1233	John Gallagher, ...	do.	do. ...
	1234	Hannah Keegan, ...	do.	do. ...
	1235	Catherine Hopper, Admix. of Francis Hopper.	do.	do. ...
	1236	John Flynn, ...	do.	do. ...
	1237	James McSharry, ...	do.	do. ...
	1238	Patrick Clancy, ...	Miss Ada C. Ray, ...	[illegible], ...
	1239	Mary Gilmartin, Rep. of William Gilmartin.	do.	do. ...
	1240	John Boland, ...	do.	do. ...
	1241	Michael McGowan, ...	do.	do. ...

LEITRIM—*continued.*

Extent of Holding, Statute.	Poor Law Valuation.	Former Rent.	Judicial Rent.	Observations.	Value of Tenancy.
A. R. P.	£ s. d.	£ s. d.	£ s. d.		£ s. d.
17 2 35	3 10 0	4 5 0	4 5 0	By consent.	
15 0 2	4 0 0	4 5 0	3 16 0	do.	
35 2 16	7 10 0	8 0 0	6 18 0	do.	
15 3 8	5 10 0	8 0 0	5 0 0	do.	
18 0 28	3 15 0	6 15 0	4 8 0	do.	
37 3 35	5 10 0	11 5 2	6 8 6	do.	
30 2 7	7 5 0	12 0 0	8 0 0	do.	
15 3 0	10 10 0	13 10 0	9 10 0	do.	
66 2 2	49 10 0	61 0 0	61 0 0	do.	
40 0 0	21 10 0	39 13 6	25 10 0	do.	
17 3 10	13 0 0	16 0 0	16 0 0	do.	
21 2 9	13 15 0	11 16 0	16 0 0	do.	
52 2 25	18 10 0	22 0 0	17 10 0	Rent changed in 1877 from . . . £31 0 0	
23 2 4	11 0 0	19 12 0	13 0 0		
15 1 23	4 5 0	8 18 0	5 0 0		
11 3 37	7 10 0	15 15 0	11 10 0		
50 0 0	5 5 0	6 0 0	4 0 0		
40 2 14	5 0 0	10 10 0	7 0 0		
14 0 0	8 0 0	12 0 0	9 5 0		
39 0 25	4 2 8	6 0 0	1 5 0		
4 3 9	1 15 0	3 0 0	2 0 0		
14 0 0	5 2 8	13 0 0	9 0 0		
7 2 30	2 2 8	4 0 0	2 15 0		
19 1 12	3 12 0	8 0 0	4 10 0		
12 3 33	7 10 0	14 0 0	11 0 0		
17 1 0	11 0 0	12 15 0	11 0 0		
11 1 27	6 10 0	11 5 0	8 0 0		
10 1 16	18 5 0	10 0 0	14 0 0		
29 0 11	13 0 0	21 8 0	16 0 0		
17 2 28	11 5 0	18 0 0	15 0 0		
27 3 23	17 10 0	35 0 0	22 0 0		
23 3 25	7 5 0	11 0 0	8 10 0		
11 3 35	4 5 0	8 0 0	5 2 0		
35 3 23	6 0 0	9 10 0	6 10 0		
80 3 2	27 10 0	16 8 0	33 10 0		

COUNTY OF

Names of Assistant Commissioners by whom Cases were decided.	No.	Name of Tenant.	Name of Landlord.	Townland.
Assistant Commissioners—				
Cecil Roche (Legal). M. P. Lynch. H. B. Moorhead. R. B. Harvey. Edmund Rogers.	1242	Bridget M'Loughlin, ...	Lieut.-Col. H. T. Clements, ...	Ross, ...
	1243	Denis Magowan, ...	do.	do. ...
	1244	Patrick Mitchell, ...	do.	Carrowcrumaragh,
	1245	John Clancy, ...	do.	do. ...
	1246	John M'Hugh, ...	John M. Clements, ...	Gortnasillagh, ...
	1247	Michael M'Morrow, ...	do.	Ardvarney, ...
	1248	Bridget Clancy, ...	Captain Hugh M'Tiernan, ...	Killavoggy, ...
	1249	Bridget Fallon, ...	do.	do. ...
	1250	Francis M'Morrow, ...	do.	do. ...
	1251	Lacky M'Morrow, ...	do.	do. ...
	1252	Owen Rourke, ...	do.	do. ...
	1253	Hugh M'Goldrick, Admor. of John M'Goldrick.	do.	do. ...
	1254	Joseph Flynn, ...	do.	do. ...
	1255	Patrick M'Cann, ...	do.	do. ...
	1256	Robert Mossell, ...	William Fry and others, Trustees of Mrs. Weir, deceased.	Gortnatorlagh, ...
	1257	Thomas Devany, ...	do.	do. ...
	1258	Anne Mason, ...	do.	do. ...
	1259	James Reilly, ...	do.	do. ...
	1260	Hugh Hannon, junior, ...	John Palmer, ...	Garvagh Glebe,
	1261	Thomas Hannon, ...	do.	do. ...
	1262	Patrick M'Gowan, ...	do.	Garvagh, ...
	1263	Thomas Hannon, ...	do.	Garvagh Glebe, ...
	1264	Miles M'Padden, ...	do.	do. ...
	1265	Patrick Morrow, ...	do.	Carrickysoure Glebe
	1266	Ralph M'Goldrick, ...	Elliott A. White, ...	Rossaugh, ...
	1267	John Harrison, ...	do.	do. ...
	1268	John Harrison, junior, ...	do.	do. ...
	1269	James Kelly, ...	do.	do. ...
	1270	Allen Mitchell, ...	do.	Drummany, ...
	1271	Miles M'Padden, ...	do.	Rossaugh, ...
	1272	John Gallagher, ...	do.	do. ...
	1273	James White, ...	do.	do. ...
	1274	Thomas M'Tiernan, ...	do.	do.
	1275	James Cosgrove, ...	do.	do. ...
	1276	Michael M'Tiernan, ...	do.	do. ...

LEITRIM—*continued.*

Extent of Holdings. Statute.	Poor Law Valuation.	Former Rent.	Judicial Rent.	Observations.
A. R. P.	£ s. d.	£ s. d.	£ s. d.	
11 3 31	8 10 0	12 17 6	9 0 0	
12 1 16	7 0 0	13 0 0	9 0 0	
16 3 34	8 0 0	12 0 0	9 5 0	
26 1 5	14 10 0	23 0 0	16 0 0	
18 0 20	4 0 0	4 1 1	4 1 1	
25 3 35	13 0 0	13 0 0	13 0 0	
24 0 1	12 5 0	16 0 0	13 10 0	By consent.
16 1 30	6 10 0	8 0 0	6 10 0	do.
18 0 35	8 15 0	11 0 0	8 0 0	do.
17 2 20	6 5 0	10 0 0	7 15 0	
17 2 12	6 15 0	10 0 0	7 5 0	
15 2 17	3 10 0	6 0 0	4 0 0	
17 3 10	8 5 0	12 0 0	9 10 0	
12 3 20	1 15 0	4 0 0	3 0 0	
14 0 0	12 0 0	14 10 0	12 0 0	do.
5 3 28	3 11 0	4 0 0	3 10 0	do.
10 3 8	6 0 0	6 10 0	6 10 0	do.
12 0 0	10 10 0	12 0 0	9 0 0	do.
21 2 23	3 5 0	3 5 0	3 10 0	
30 3 1	15 10 0	20 10 0	15 0 0	
5 1 0	2 0 0	4 10 0	3 10 0	
35 2 6	6 10 0	12 16 0	8 15 0	
67 0 0	4 10 0	7 10 0	6 0 0	
9 2 0	4 18 0	9 0 0	6 15 0	
18 2 4	2 0 0	2 10 0	2 5 0	do.
10 3 6	3 0 0	3 7 6	3 3 9	do.
16 1 4	3 6 0	3 6 0	3 5 0	do.
9 1 23	2 10 0	4 5 0	3 5 0	
16 0 32	7 5 0	10 0 0	7 15 0	
16 2 12	6 5 0	3 5 0	2 15 0	
11 1 16	2 10 0	3 10 0	3 0 0	
22 0 0	4 15 0	6 0 0	5 0 0	
11 1 14	2 10 0	3 10 0	3 0 0	
84 0 31	1 10 0	7 8 6	6 0 0	
19 2 26	5 0 0	5 5 0	1 0 0	

1288	Francis McMorrow, ...	do.
1289	Michael McMorrow, ...	do.
1290	John Rooney, ..	do.
1291	Hugh McMorrow, ...	do.
1292	James Clancy, ...	do.
1293	Owen O'Hara, ...	do.
1294	Thomas Loughlin and another,	do.
1295	Barclay McMorrow, ...	do.
1296	Patrick McMorrow, ...	do.
1297	Michael McMorrow, ...	do.
1298	Thomas Keany, ...	G. G. B. White,
1299	John McLoughlin, ...	do.
1300	Michael Diamond, ...	do.
1301	Catherine Diamond, ...	do.
1302	John McElhatty, senior,	Roger Parke
1303	Mary Harte, ...	do.
1304	Terence McDermott, ...	do.
1305	Dora McElharry, Admix. of Patrick McElharry.	do.
1306	Bridget O'Connor, Admix. of Pat O'Connor.	do.
1307	James Burke, ...	do.
1308	Michael O'Connor, ...	do.

LEITRIM—*continued*

Extent of Holdings. Statute.	Poor Law Valuation.	Former Rent.	Judicial Rent.	Observations
A. R. P.	£ s. d.	£ s. d.	£ s. d.	
18 3 83	4 10 0	0 17 0	4 15 0	
16 0 23	8 8 0	11 11 6	8 15 0	
10 1 39	3 6 0	6 3 0	4 15 0	By consent.
13 0 10	8 0 0	8 8 11	5 13 0	do.
23 1 13	9 5 0	13 5 8	11 15 0	do.
10 2 9	3 0 0	8 8 8	4 0 0	do.
9 0 0	5 5 0	5 10 0	4 17 6	do.
5 0 0	1 10 0	1 16 8	1 5 0	do.
11 3 30	7 0 0	8 0 0	6 3 0	do.
21 3 13	10 6 0	13 0 4	10 5 0	do.
18 2 35	6 15 0	5 15 6	6 5 0	do.
6 0 0	3 0 0	2 18 6	2 13 6	do.
39 2 36	18 0 0	23 10 0	21 0 0	do.
6 0 30	4 15 0	6 0 0	6 0 0	
35 0 27	8 5 0	8 7 0	6 7 0	
18 2 8	4 13 0	6 15 0	5 15 8	
19 3 23	2 10 0	3 10 0	3 0 0	
43 1 35	18 0 0	20 0 0	17 10 0	
23 3 11	8 0 0	9 3 6	7 10 0	
20 0 21	4 0 0	9 6 0	6 0 0	
47 1 6	10 0 0	18 13 4	11 0 0	
34 1 0	13 5 0	17 15 0	14 15 0	do.
31 1 35	13 0 0	15 4 0	13 0 0	do.
13 2 35	4 5 0	7 10 0	7 0 0	do.
15 2 26	4 5 0	7 10 0	7 0 0	do.
41 1 27	9 0 0	11 15 0	9 15 0	do.
10 0 0	5 5 0	6 0 0	5 0 0	
8 5 5	3 0 0	7 0 0	5 10 0	
45 3 14	11 10 0	20 0 0	14 0 0	
52 2 8	19 5 0	36 0 0	31 0 0	

Assistant Commissioners—

William Rowan (Legal).
A. R. Nolan.
E. O'Kelly.
H. G. Gaussen.
P. Fitzpatrick.

4964	John Calpin, ...	Edward Wingfield,
4965	John Loftus, ...	do. ...
4966	James Loftus, ...	do. ...
4967	John Igoe, ...	do. ...
4968	Mary Igoe, ...	do. ...
4969	John Broderick, ...	do. ...
4970	William Loftus, ...	do. ...
4971	Michael Higgins, ...	do. ...
4972	James Glennelly, ...	do. ...
4973	John Loftus, ...	do. ...
4974	Bridget Igoe, ...	do. ...
4975	Anthony Igoe, ...	do. ...
4976	Patrick McGuinness, ...	do. ...
4977	Anthony Melvin, ...	do. ...
4978	John Diamond, ...	do. ...
4979	John Magee, ...	Sir Roger W. H. Palmer
4980	Patrick Kilroy, ...	Mathew O'R. Dease,
4981	Charles Geoghegan, ...	George T. S. Carter,
4982	James Kelly, ...	Uttred A. Knox, ...
4983	Thomas Kelly, ...	do. ...
4984	John McHale, ...	do. ...
4985	John McHale and others,	do. ...
4986	Anthony Brogan, ...	E. H. Pery, ...
4987	John McLean, ...	do. ...
4988	Catherine Durkan, ...	Thomas H. Thompson
4989	Michael Sarsfield, ...	do. ...
4990	John Moran, ...	do. ...

MAYO.

Extent of Holding (Statute).	Poor Law Valuation.	Former Rent.	Judicial Rent.	Observations.	Value of Tenancy.
A. R. P.	£ s. d.	£ s. d.	£ s. d.		£ s. d.
13 0 0	8 8 0	8 6 0	8 0 0	By consent.	
15 0 8	1 15 0	6 17 0	8 6 8	do.	
7 8 0	7 7 0	6 10 0	5 16 6	do.	
8 0 0	5 12 4	4 0 8	4 8 0	do.	
3 0 0	2 4 8	1 13 0	1 18 0	do.	
3 0 0	1 10 0	1 7 6	1 7 6	do.	
18 3 18	7 17 0	7 0 0	6 0 0	do.	
5 0 0	3 16 6	8 4 0	8 16 0	do.	
3 0 0	2 4 6	1 13 0	1 13 0	do.	
8 0 0	6 17 0	6 15 0	6 15 0	do.	
3 0 0	2 4 8	1 13 0	1 18 0	do.	
8 0 0	5 13 6	4 0 0	4 0 0	do.	
10 0 0	6 3 0	4 15 0	4 16 0	do.	
13 0 0	8 18 0	8 5 0	7 0 8	do.	
7 0 0	7 0 0	5 4 0	4 18 0	do.	
23 0 14	8 15 0	11 0 0	10 0 0		
310 3 25	2 10 0	8 0 0	8 0 0		
30 0 0	7 5 0	8 8 0	8 8 0		
12 0 27	6 10 0	9 18 0	8 0 0	do.	
14 1 20	7 10 0	10 13 3	8 10 0	do.	
11 3 23	6 15 0	10 2 6	8 0 0	do.	
21 1 23	5 18 0	8 16 6	7 5 0	do.	
10 0 16	4 0 0	5 0 0	3 15 0	do.	
53 1 21	47 5 0	62 15 0	60 0 0	do.	
3 0 0	1 0 0	0 11 6	0 14 4	do.	
7 1 0	2 18 0	4 13 2	3 13 2	do.	
8 0 0	3 8 0	2 14 0	2 14 0	do.	
4 0 0	3 13 0	3 7 0	2 10 0	do.	
7 0 0	4 10 0	4 18 0	4 10 0	do.	
6 3 1	3 10 0	4 16 0	4 0 0	do.	
9 2 20	2 15 0	3 10 0	3 0 0	do.	
8 0 30	8 5 0	5 10 0	4 18 6	do.	
18 3 1	6 8 0	6 14 0	5 0 0	do.	
27 2 0	11 16 8	18 0 0	16 10 0	do.	
19 2 0	10 15 8	18 0 0	9 18 0	do.	

Names of Assistant Commissioners by whom Cases were decided.	No.	Name of Tenant.	Name of Landlord.	Townland.	
Assistant Commissioners—					
William Rogers (Legal). A. B. Nolan. E. O'Kelly. H. C. Greenhow. P. Fitzpatrick.	4999	Michael Rafter, ...	John T. Kirkwood, ...	Rathmore, ...	
	5000	Patrick Geraty, ...	do.	Kilgarvan, ...	
	5001	John Boland, ...	do.	Rathmore, ...	
	5002	John Cassidy, ...	Earl of Arran, ...	Derreen, ...	
	5003	Mary Flynn, ...	do.	Grange, ...	
	5004	Dominick Hope, ...	do.	Wherren, ...	
	5005	Anne O'Boyle, ...	do.	do. ...	
	5006	Michael Hamilton, ...	do.	Carrowgarden, ...	
	5007	Anthony Ruane, ...	do.	Oranbay, ...	
	5008	John Congrave, ...	do.	Wherren, ...	
	5009	John O'Boyle, ...	do.	Carrowgarra Sth.,	
	5010	John Munnelly, ...	do.	Ballymacharles,	
	5011	Thomas Mayock, ...	do.	do. ...	
	5012	Bridget Higgins, ...	do.	Wherren, ...	
	5013	Thomas Mortland, ...	do.	Carrowcarde, ...	
	5014	Edward Hope, ...	do.	Wherren, ...	
	5015	John Hope, ...	do.	do. ...	
	5016	John Jordan, ...	do.	Gressane, ...	
	5017	Patrick Keane, ...	do.	Slievangark, ...	
	5018	Patrick Egan, ...	do.	Crofton Park, ...	
	5019	Daniel O'Hara, ...	do.	do. ...	
	5020	Patrick Egan and anor.,	do.	do. ...	
	5021	Mathew Durkan, ...	do.	do. ...	
	5022	Anthony Hobin, ...	do.	Slievangark, ...	
	5023	Thomas Clarke, ...	do	Cloonglassny, ...	
	5024	James Barrett, ...	do.	do. ...	
	5025	Michael Hobin, ...	do.	Slievangark, ...	
	5026	John Moran, ...	do.	do. ...	
	5027	Patrick Sweeney, ...	do.	Cloonglassny, ...	
	5028	Michael Barrett, ...	do.	do. ...	
	5029	Peter Wynne, ...	do.	Slievangark, ...	
	5030	Bryan Ruane, ...	do.	Rathglass, ...	
	5031	Henry McKenna, ...	do.	Derreen, ...	

MAYO—*continued*.

Extent of Holding Statute.	Poor Law Valuation.	Former Rent.	Judicial Rent.	Observations.	Value of Tenancy.
A. R. P.	£ s. d.	£ s. d.	£ s. d.		£ s. d.
22 3 0	9 0 0	14 0 0	11 0 0	By consent.	
19 0 0	4 0 0	5 0 0	3 15 0	do.	
17 3 0	8 6 0	8 0 0	6 8 0	do.	
11 0 6	5 0 6	6 5 6	5 5 0	do.	
19 2 0	9 10 0	10 6 0	9 0 0	do.	
10 2 38	7 15 0	9 19 6	8 10 0	do.	
13 0 34	7 0 0	7 5 0	6 0 0	do.	
25 0 7	5 0 0	6 9 6	5 5 0	do.	
31 0 0	11 16 0	12 0 0	10 10 0	do.	
11 3 24	8 0 0	10 16 0	8 8 0	do.	
23 1 4	11 0 0	13 18 6	11 0 0	do.	
16 2 23	5 10 0	6 8 0	5 10 0	do.	
23 0 12	9 0 0	9 0 0	8 10 0	do.	
14 3 14	8 0 0	9 9 0	8 5 0	do.	
77 1 4	41 0 0	46 12 0	41 0 0	do.	
16 3 9	10 15 0	13 5 9	10 18 0	do.	
10 1 35	7 15 0	8 6 0	7 15 0	do.	
11 0 29	5 16 0	5 12 6	5 0 0	do.	
24 0 4	11 15 0	13 0 6	11 10 0	do.	
24 0 7	10 15 0	16 10 6	13 0 0	do.	
19 3 30	8 0 0	9 2 0	8 0 0	do.	
8 1 30	4 0 0	6 6 6	6 0 0	do.	
6 2 0	3 16 0	4 6 0	3 0 0	do.	
27 1 27	11 15 0	14 3 6	12 0 0	do.	
14 0 12	6 6 0	6 1 6	5 10 0	do.	
21 3 31	11 0 0	12 4 0	11 0 0	do.	
19 0 29	8 15 0	10 3 0	8 10 0	do.	
9 2 35	4 13 0	5 2 6	4 15 0	do.	
6 1 25	4 10 0	6 15 6	4 10 0	do.	
5 2 27	4 15 0	6 14 6	4 10 0	do.	
14 3 6	6 15 0	6 5 0	6 5 0	do.	
25 3 8	15 10 0	16 18 6	15 10 0	do.	
9 1 15	6 10 0	7 3 6	5 10 0	do.	
23 0 0	9 15 0	11 10 6	10 0 0	do.	
14 2 20	10 15 0	11 7 0	10 10 0	do.	

Names of Assistant Commissioners by whom Cases were decided	No.	Name of Tenant	Name of Landlord	Townland
Assistant Commissioners—				
WILLIAM ROWAN (Legal). A. B. NOLAN. E. O'KELLY. H. C. GRENFELL. P. FITZPATRICK.	5034	Martin Hosick, ...	The Earl of Arran, ...	Derrens, ...
	5035	Patrick Brennan, ...	do.	do. ...
	5036	James Walsh, ...	do.	do. ...
	5037	Anthony Henehan, ...	do.	do. ...
	5038	William Carson, ...	do.	Ballinrana, ...
	5039	Honor Conroy, Widow, Rep. of Michl. Conroy,	do.	Grafton Park, ...
	5040	Patrick McAndrew, ...	do.	do. ...
	5041	Winifred McAndrew, ...	do.	do. ...
	5042	Michael Clarke, ...	do.	Cloonaghmore, ...
	5043	John Munnelly, ...	do.	do. ...
	5044	Patrick Gordon, ...	do.	Lenarrow, ...
	5045	John Patterson, ...	do.	Carrowkelly, ...
	5046	Arthur Gardiner, ...	do.	Newtown White,
	5047	Bryan Kinnie, ...	do.	Knockbrough, ...
	5048	Ellen McAndrew, ...	Sir Charles K. Gore, Bart., ...	Ballyghadalla,
	5049	Judith Regan, ...	do.	Rathrowen, ...
	5050	Bridget Brennan, ...	do.	Rosmark, ...
	5051	Bartly Maughan, ...	do.	Ballyteskary, ...
	5052	Honoria O'Dowd, ...	do.	Carrowkerribly, ...
	5053	Patrick Quinn, ...	do.	Mullahowney, ...
	5054	Martin Geraghty, ...	do.	Carrowkerribly, ...
	5055	Edward Sweeney, ...	do.	do. ...
	5056	Patrick Killbride, ...	do.	Mullahowney, ...
	5057	Thomas Sweeney, ...	do.	Rathrowen, ...
	5058	Patrick Flynn, ...	do.	Ballyghadalla, ...
	5059	Thomas Gillespie, ...	do.	Cloonaleigh, ...
	5060	Martin Rattleigh, ...	do.	do. ...
	5061	Bryan Connell (Neal), ...	do.	Carrowkerribly, ...
	5062	Anne Brown, ...	do.	do. ...
	5063	John Hughes, ...	do.	do. ...
	5064	Peter Brown, ...	do.	do. ...
	5065	Do. ...	do.	do. ...
	5066	James Dowd, ...	do.	do.
	5067	John McGuff, ...	do.	do. ...
	5068	Mary Fergus, ...	Sir Roger W. H. Palmer, Bart.,	Shraghmoragher,

MAYO—*continued.*

Extent of Holding Statute.	Poor Law Valuation.	Former Rent.	Judicial Rent.	Observations.
A. R. P.	£ s. d.	£ s. d.	£ s. d.	
19 1 20	8 10 0	10 7 6	9 0 0	By consent.
26 0 0	15 5 0	21 11 0	16 15 0	do.
14 1 25	9 0 0	9 15 0	9 0 0	do.
17 3 30	8 15 0	10 18 0	9 10 0	do.
10 0 23	10 0 0	11 17 6	11 0 0	do.
63 5 0	16 10 0	20 4 6	16 10 0	do.
16 1 20	8 0 0	9 10 0	8 0 0	do.
8 3 15	5 15 0	6 10 0	5 15 0	do.
14 0 23	10 15 0	16 1 0	12 10 0	do.
25 1 26	5 15 0	7 14 6	6 8 0	do.
34 1 30	19 10 0	22 9 0	21 0 0	do.
35 0 0	23 15 0	24 7 0	20 15 0	do.
43 0 0	15 16 0	18 12 0	14 0 0	do.
33 2 19	16 10 0	20 18 0	16 10 0	do.
28 0 18	7 0 0	9 0 0	6 10 0	Rent changed in 1887 from . . .
18 3 22	9 15 0	11 0 0	10 0 0	
23 3 10	7 15 0	10 8 0	9 0 0	
18 3 23	6 5 0	9 1 8	7 10 0	
28 3 0	10 10 0	11 0 0	9 10 0	
11 1 6	3 8 0	5 0 0	8 6 0	
15 0 0	6 5 0	8 0 0	6 10 0	
9 1 0	5 0 0	6 5 0	4 10 0	
28 1 15	5 15 0	10 15 0	10 0 0	
23 0 16	13 0 0	17 5 0	17 8 0	
30 3 4	21 5 0	24 0 0	26 0 0	
16 2 0	7 0 0	10 10 0	8 0 0	
32 0 8	13 0 0	17 10 0	15 10 0	
81 2 0	8 0 0	9 10 0	8 0 0	
9 1 70	6 5 0	7 0 0	6 4 0	
10 0 0	4 7 0	5 3 10	4 0 0	
14 0 20	6 5 0	9 0 0	7 0 0	
23 2 0	10 15 0	13 5 9	12 0 0	
30 0 10	6 15 0	10 8 4	6 8 0	
33 3 36	11 10 0	13 14 0	10 10 0	
9 8 19	3 4 0	6 0 0	5 15 0	

COUNTY OF

Names of Assistant Commissioners by whom Cases were decided.	No.	Name of Tenant.	Name of Landlord.	Townland.
Assistant Commissioners—				
William Rowan (Legal). A. B. Nolan. E. O'Kelly. H. C. Gregory. P. Fitzpatrick.	5069	John Hughes, ...	Sir Roger W. H. Palmer, Bart.,	Shraghmoeigan,
	5070	Patrick M'Hugh, ...	do.	do. ...
	5071	James Cavanagh, ...	do.	Knockmoyle,
	5072	William Brennan, ...	do.	Knockduff,
	5073	Bridget Padden, ...	do.	Shraghmoeigan,
	5074	Patrick M'Namara, ...	do.	do. ...
	5075	John M'Dermott, ...	do.	do. ...
	5076	Bridget Moyles, ...	do.	do. ...
	5077	Mark M'Donnell, ...	do.	do. ...
	5078	John Lynn, ...	do.	do.
	5079	Patrick Joyce, ...	do.	Derryhallagh, ...
	5080	Patrick Judge, ...	do.	do. ...
	5081	William Judge, ...	do.	do. ...
	5082	Dominick Corcoran, ...	do.	do. ...
	5083	John Barrett, ...	do.	do. ...
	5084	Patrick Barrett, ...	do.	do. ...
	5085	Thomas Judge, ...	do.	Derrahallagh, ...
	5086	Thomas Naughton, ...	do.	Derryhallagh, ...
	5087	John Geraghty, ...	do.	do.
	5088	Edward Murphy, ...	do.	do. ...
	5089	Thomas Padden, ...	do.	Shraghmoeigan,
	5090	Michael Clark, ...	do.	do. ...
	5091	John Duffy, ...	do.	Rinmore, ...
	5092	John Lynn, ...	do.	Shangvolahan, ...
	5093	Michael Brennan, ...	do.	do. ...
	5094	Patrick Hopkins, ...	do.	Doolagreenan,
	5095	Patrick Lynn, ...	do.	do.
	5096	Martin Durkan, ...	do.	Cloonaghmore,
	5097	Anthony Cavanagh, ...	do.	Knockmore, ...
	5098	Francis Carolan, ...	do.	Derryhillagh, ...
	5099	Bridget Price, ...	do.	do. ...
	5100	Patrick Jordan, ...	do.	Derrahillagh, ...
	5101	Catherine Holmes, ...	do.	Doolagreenan, ...
	5102	Owen Fergus, ...	do.	do. ...
	5103	Bridget Duffy, ...	do.	Rinmore, ...

MAYO—*continued.*

Extent of Holding Statute	Poor Law Valuation	Former Rent	Judicial Rent	Observations	Value of Tenancy
a. r. p.	£ s. d.	£ s. d.	£ s. d.		£ s. d.
31 3 28	2 0 0	8 0 0	3 0 0		
17 2 16	4 5 0	6 15 0	4 15 0		
16 1 27	10 0 0	11 0 0	10 0 0		
[illegible] 1 31	13 10 0	23 15 0	12 0 0		
[illegible] 3 34	3 5 0	5 5 0	3 15 0		
79 0 0	3 10 0	6 0 0	1 18 0		
16 2 10	3 10 0	6 0 0	1 10 0		
27 2 31	3 0 0	5 0 0	3 12 0		
3 8 8	3 15 0	4 10 0	3 10 0		
[illegible] 0 0	4 5 0	7 0 0	6 17 0		
[illegible] 0 11	5 0 0	7 0 0	5 5 0		
48 3 19	12 10 0	16 5 0	11 0 0		
13 0 20	3 11 0	5 0 0	3 10 0		
15 2 15	5 6 0	6 6 0	5 12 0		
25 3 0	5 6 0	8 6 0	5 0 0		
19 3 16	4 8 0	7 5 0	6 5 0		
[illegible] 2 15	7 19 0	12 0 0	8 12 0		
19 0 3	7 8 0	8 15 0	7 8 0		
40 0 16	6 8 0	9 5 0	8 12 0		
10 0 35	3 1 0	8 7 0	3 0 0		
14 1 3	3 5 0	5 10 0	3 0 0		
16 0 20	3 5 0	5 10 0	4 0 0		
25 0 10	6 10 0	11 10 0	9 10 0		
148 3 9	9 15 0	13 10 0	10 10 0		
61 0 0	2 5 0	2 10 0	3 10 0		
63 3 22	6 15 0	9 0 0	7 0 0		
71 0 0	4 15 0	6 0 0	5 5 0		
10 3 31	4 5 0	4 5 0	3 10 0		
16 0 11	11 5 0	11 0 0	10 0 0		
34 3 0	5 0 0	7 0 0	5 5 0		
17 0 0	8 2 0	2 10 0	3 10 0		
19 0 13	5 17 0	8 17 0	6 0 0		
61 0 0	6 15 0	8 0 0	7 10 0		
31 1 20	5 15 0	7 10 0	6 0 0		
18 3 30	6 15 0	11 10 0	9 0 0		

William Bayne (Legal). A. R. Nolan. R. O'Kelly. H. C. Gernon. F. Fitzpatrick.	5104	Honor Hegarty,	...	Sir Roger W. H. Palmer, Bart.,
	5105	Bryan Hegarty,	...	do. ...
	5106	Anne Cafferky,	...	Mervyn Pratt, ...
	5107	Patrick Leonard,	...	do. ... ...
	5108	Robert Gill, ...	...	do. ... ...
	5109	Thomas Murphy,	...	do. ... ...
	5110	Michael Murphy,	...	do. ... ...
	5111	Hugh Gallagher,	...	do. ... ...
	5112	James Cafferky,	...	do. ... ...
	5113	Hugh Loftus,	...	do. ... ...
	5114	John Walsh,	...	do. ... ...
	5115	Michael Moran,	...	do. ... ...
	5116	John McGoff,	...	do. ... ...
	5117	Richard Gillespie,	...	do. ... ...
	5118	Michael McDonagh,	...	do. ... ...
	5119	James Loden,	...	do. ... ...
	5120	Patrick Donnelly,	...	do. ... ...
	5121	Mary O'Donnell,	...	do. ... ...
	5122	Michael Leonard,	...	do. ... ...
	5123	Patrick Tierney,	...	do. ... ...
	5124	John McGoff,	...	do. ... ...
	5125	Anthony O'Boyle,	...	do. ... ...
	5126	Patrick Brogan,	...	do. ... ...
	5127	John O'Boyle,	...	do. ... ...
	5128	Patrick Gallen, senior,	...	do. ... ...
	5129	Daniel Kearns,	...	do. ... ...
	5130	Patrick Lynn,	...	do. ... ...
	5131	James Kearns,	...	do. ...
	5132	Mathew Kearns,	...	do. ... ...
	5133	Patrick Melvin,	...	Henry H. Jones and others,
	5134	Ellen Jordan,	...	do. ... ...
	5135	Mary Robinson,	...	do. ... ...
	5136	Thomas Timlin,	...	do.
	5137	Thomas Clarke,	...	do. ...
	5138	William Mallale,	...	do. ... ...

MAYO—*continued.*

Extent of Holding Statute.	Poor Law Valuation.	Former Rent.	Judicial Rent.	Observations.	Value of Tenancy.
A. R. P.	£ s. d.	£ s. d.	£ s. d.		£ s. d.
18 1 30	3 15 0	5 10 0	4 18 0		
14 2 35*	4 5 0	4 16 6	4 16 6		
84 1 18	11 9 0	12 0 0	10 10 0		
90 0 16	10 18 0	11 0 0	8 10 0		
95 1 33	13 18 0	14 14 0	13 0 0		
57 0 12	12 0 0	18 0 0	15 0 0		
37 1 8	8 8 0	10 10 0	10 10 0		
19 2 20	8 0 0	10 10 0	9 5 0		
63 0 22	16 5 0	19 10 0	19 10 0		
15 1 30	4 1 0	1 6 0	1 6 0		
64 3 3	12 5 0	13 0 0	15 0 0		
46 3 2	10 16 0	12 6 0	10 13 0		
25 0 0	6 15 0	5 0 0	5 0 0		
67 1 27	15 10 0	17 5 0	16 10 0		
41 3 30	9 15 0	10 0 0	10 0 0		
125 1 9	8 0 0	10 10 0	10 10 0		
37 1 8	8 17 0	10 0 0	8 15 0		
24 0 1	2 15 0	2 16 0	2 18 0		
23 0 0	6 11 0	6 18 0	6 0 0		
136 2 36	5 15 0	6 0 0	5 8 0		
84 3 21	8 5 0	8 10 0	9 10 0		
23 2 37	7 0 0	6 6 0	6 6 0		
20 3 30	6 0 0	6 0 0	6 0 0		
17 0 31	3 19 0	4 10 0	4 0 0		
64 0 7	8 16 0	9 0 0	8 0 0		
54 3 23	12 10 0	13 10 0	13 10 0		
26 1 36	6 5 0	5 10 0	3 12 0		
31 2 21	8 10 0	5 10 0	5 10 0		
17 1 7	5 10 0	6 15 0	5 10 0		
17 3 29	5 9 0	5 6 0	5 6 0		
9 3 27	5 10 0	5 10 0	3 16 0		

Names of Assistant Commissioners by whom Cases were decided.	No.	Name of Tenant.	Name of Landlord.	Townland.
Assistant Commissioners—				
William Bewer (Legal). A. B. Nolan. B. O'Reilly. H. C. Ormsby. P. Fitzpatrick.	5139	Bridget Flaherty, ...	Henry H. Jones and others,	Ballagarragh, ...
	5140	John McAndrew, ...	The Earl of Arran, ...	Ballymachola, ...
	5141	Mary Lynch, ...	do.	do. ...
	5142	James Gandy, ...	do.	Ballymahorry, ...
	5143	James Diamond, ...	do.	Knockeragan, ...
	5144	Catherine Murphy, ...	do.	Cloonaghmanny, ...
	5145	Michael Melody (John),	Mrs. R. Nicholson, and the Rev. J. Nicholson,	Carrick, ...
	5146	Thomas and Martin Hennigan,	do.	do. ...
	5147	Patrick Walsh, ...	do.	do. ...
	5148	Michael and John Melody,	do.	do. ...
	5149	Patrick Langan and John Melody,	do.	do.
	5150	Patrick Finnerty, ...	Very Rev. William Jackson,	Ballyhag, ...
	5151	Michael Corcoran, ...	do.	do. ...
	5152	Thomas Lyons, ...	John Rooney, ...	Carrowcastle, ...
	5153	Michael O'Hara, ...	do.	do. ...
	5154	Anthony Hurst, ...	George A. Moore, ...	Kilgellia, ...
	5155	James Loftus, ...	do.	do. ...
	5156	Francis Murray, ...	do.	Ballymore, ...
	5157	Michael Murray, ...	do.	do. ...
	5158	Thomas Ferguson, ...	do.	do. ...
	5159	Patrick Murray, ...	do.	do. ...
	5160	Anthony Kearney, ...	R. H. Perry, ...	Knockmore, ...
	5161	John Orchan, ...	do.	Carrowcanan, ...
	5162	James McDonnell, ...	do.	Cordagrenan, ...
	5163	Patrick Gaughan (Mars),	do.	Lisduvaun, West,
	5164	Thomas Jordan, Rep. of Mary Moyles,	do.	Rathduff, ...
	5165	Michael Brown (Tom), ...	do.	Newtown, ...
	5166	James Geraghty, ...	do.	Derryjohnston, ...
	5167	Mary McKenna, ...	do.	do. ...
	5168	Michael Redington, ...	do.	Newtown, ...
	5169	Seldon McHale, ...	Ussed A. Knox, ...	Ballymacrehand,
	5170	Patrick Reap, ...	do.	do. ...
	5171	Anthony Hanily, ...	do.	do. ...
	5172	Patrick Reap (Jack), ...	do.	do.
	5173	Anthony Ferguson, ...	do.	Rathkeeran, ...

MAYO—*continued.*

Extent of Holding Statute.	Poor Law Valuation.	Former Rent.	Judicial Rent.	Observations.	Value of Tenancy.
A. R. P.	£ s. d.	£ s. d.	£ s. d.		£ s. d.
10 1 28	6 10 0	7 5 0	7 0 0		
51 0 22	13 13 0	17 6 0	15 10 0	By consent.	
30 3 1	14 0 0	17 0 0	14 10 0	do.	
25 1 27	5 10 0	5 14 0	5 0 0	do.	
16 0 24	20 10 0	20 11 6	19 0 0		
49 3 0	25 10 9	24 14 6	24 14 6		
10 0 0	4 5 0	7 1 0	5 7 0		
13 1 25	5 15 0	7 0 0	4 10 0		
16 2 0	4 5 0	6 5 6	5 7 6		
18 1 20	6 10 0	12 19 8	8 0 0		
20 1 30	8 12 0	11 8 10	8 0 0		
1 2 0	—	1 5 0	0 18 0		
23 1 27	10 0 0	12 0 0	10 15 0		
4 1 24	3 2 0	3 17 9	3 0 0		
17 0 2	7 5 0	10 0 0	6 10 0		
11 0 5	5 0 0	6 0 0	6 0 0		
20 1 6	4 5 0	4 8 2	4 0 0		
10 3 18	8 16 0	8 11 4	8 11 4		
5 1 27	1 18 0	1 15 7½	1 15 7½		
15 0 22	8 15 0	5 12 0	4 0 0		
5 1 27	1 18 0	1 16 0	1 16 0	£ s. d.	
18 2 30	3 8 0	5 0 0	4 0 0	Rent changed in 1873 from . . . 4 0 0	
9 3 20	4 15 0	8 5 0	7 0 0	1868 7 10 0	
65 3 25	8 0 0	18 10 0	9 0 0		
9 1 0	8 15 0	5 10 0	4 0 0	1867 4 15 0	
6 3 20	5 10 0	4 16 0	3 16 0		
14 2 0	10 18 6	18 0 0	11 0 0		
7 0 0	2 15 0	4 0 0	2 18 0		
11 2 10	3 15 0	7 0 0	5 0 0		
18 1 35	9 5 0	14 0 0	11 0 0		
6 2 25	2 10 0	4 17 0	6 5 0		
16 0 18	8 0 0	10 18 0	7 10 0		
5 3 20	2 5 0	4 0 0	3 0 0		
11 0 25	6 0 0	7 0 0	5 8 0		
20 0 10	12 0 0	14 0 0	12 0 0		

COUNTY OF

Judges of Assistant Commission by whom Cases were decided.	No.	Name of Tenant.	Name of Landlord.	Townland.
Assistant Commissioners—				
William Roper (Legal). A. B. Nolan. E. O'Kelly. H. C. [illegible]. P. Fitzpatrick.	5174	Francis Rodgers, ...	Ulred A. Knox, ...	[illegible], ...
	5175	Henry O'Hara, ...	Francis Knox, ...	Carrowreagh, ...
	5176	Michael Muldowney, junr.,	Margaret Knox, ...	do. ...
	5177	Michael Muldowney, senr.,	do.	do. ...
	5178	John McHale, ...	Capt. Annesley Knox, ...	Rathglass, West
	5179	John Langan, ...	William F. Black, ...	Callows, ...
	5180	Anthony Cullen, ...	William R. Orme, ...	Gortnaher, ...
	5181	Michael Gallagher, ...	E. H. Perry, ...	Carrowcastle, ...
Charles [illegible] (Legal). J. Rice. A. Coote. E. Reilly. W. C. [illegible].	5182	Anne Walsh (widow), ...	Sir Roger Palmer, Bart., ...	Loughanmachree
	5183	Thomas Mulroy, junr., ...	do.	do.
	5184	Thady McGowan, ...	do.	Ballinacallan, ...
	5185	Thomas Mulroy, ...	do.	Loughanmachree
	5186	James Ryan, ...	do.	Ballyglass, ...
	5187	William Jeffers, ...	do.	Loughanmachree
	5188	Pat Conway, ...	do.	do. ...
	5189	Edward McGowan, ...	do.	do.
	5190	James Mulroy, ...	do.	do. ...
	5191	Peter McGowan, ...	do.	Ballyglass, ...
	5192	Patrick Conway, ...	do.	Knox, ...
	5193	Patrick Mullen, ...	do.	do. ...
	5194	Hugh McGowan, ...	do.	Loughanmachree
	5195	James Ryan, ...	do.	Aughaward, ...
	5196	William McAndrew, ...	do.	Lisduff, ...
	5197	Bridget Connolly, ...	do.	Aughaward, ...
	5198	Dennis Dunney, ...	do.	Lisduff, ...
	5199	James Harry, ...	do.	do. ...
	5200	Martin Ruddy, ...	do.	Knox, ...
	5201	Michael King, ...	Henry Lyons, ...	Tawnaney, ...
	5202	Terence McDonnell, ...	do.	do. ...
	5203	James Gallagher, ...	do.	do. ...
	5204	Bridget McNulty (widow),	do.	do. ...
	5205	Patrick Durkan, ...	do.	do. ...
	5206	James Durkan, ...	do.	Magheraboy, ...

MAYO—continued.

Extent of Holding. (Statute).	Poor Law Valuation.	Former Rent.	Judicial Rent.	Observations.	Value of Tenancy.
a. r. p.	£ s. d.	£ s. d.	£ s. d.		£ s. d.
34 0 8	8 5 0	9 0 0	7 10 0		
4 1 1	4 15 0	6 0 0	5 3 0		
14 0 0	6 15 0	9 0 0	7 0 0		
8 0 17	6 0 0	8 10 0	7 5 0		
22 3 3	14 0 0	16 9 0	16 0 0		
20 1 26	10 0 0	10 16 0	9 6 0		
6 3 28	3 15 0	4 10 0	5 18 0		
8 0 0	5 10 0	7 0 0	5 18 0		
13 2 18	5 0 0	6 5 0	6 5 0		
13 1 26	5 10 0	7 0 0	5 17 6		
79 0 3	61 5 0	30 5 0	38 0 0		
25 0 10	9 15 0	12 10 0	12 10 0		
11 0 38	5 6 0	6 0 0	6 0 0		
17 2 10	6 5 0	7 15 0	6 10 0		
23 0 11	11 10 0	15 10 0	13 10 0		
17 2 2	6 10 0	8 5 0	7 5 0		
36 3 10	14 18 0	19 0 0	18 5 0		
23 2 0	5 10 0	6 5 0	5 15 0		
13 0 7	5 10 0	6 17 6	5 10 0		
49 1 5	7 13 0	10 0 0	8 0 0		
6 1 0	5 5 6	4 10 6	6 5 0		
22 0 17	13 0 0	14 10 0	14 10 0		
5 3 35	4 0 0	5 0 0	5 0 0		
5 0 0	5 10 0	6 0 0	6 0 0		
6 0 0	3 10 0	4 5 0	4 5 0		
4 0 0	3 5 0	4 0 0	4 0 0		
32 0 0	18 15 0	15 5 8	18 5 0		
18 3 0	3 10 0	5 16 0	4 12 0	By consent.	
7 0 0	3 0 0	6 0 0	5 0 0	do.	
7 1 0	3 3 0	5 4 0	5 5 0	do.	
14 0 0	5 16 0	5 13 0	4 13 0	do.	
11 1 0	3 10 6	5 17 0	4 15 0	do.	
10 0 34	5 5 0	6 15 0	4 0 0	do.	

Names of Assistant Commissioners by whom Cases were decided.	No.	Name of Tenant.	Name of Landlord.	Townland.	
Assistant Commissioners—					
Charles Hamilton (Legal). J. Rice. A. Cowie. E. Kelly. W. C. Cochrane.	5207	Martin McDonnell, ...	Henry Lyons, ...	Tawnary,	–
	5208	Michael Durkan, Rep. of Brian Durkan.	Roger McHarrick, ...	Culleen,	–
	5209	James McAndrew, ...	do.	do.	–
	5210	John Noon, Rep. of Thomas Noon.	do.	do.	–
	5211	Winifred Gallagher, ...	do.	Culleen, Sranbane.	
	5212	Martin Durkan, ...	do.	Rubble,	–
	5213	Catherine Toole, ...	do.	do.	–
	5214	Patrick Malloy (Anthony),	do.	do.	–
	5215	William Malloy, ...	do.	do.	–
	5216	Richard McNicholas, ...	do.	do.	.
	5217	Thomas Durkan, ...	do.	do.	–
	5218	Pat Durkan, ...	do.	do.	–
	5219	Bridget McCann (widow),	do.	do.	–
	5220	James Durkan, ...	do.	do.	–
	5221	Michael Ratchford, ...	do.	do.	–
	5222	Pat Garvan, ...	Captain John Brabazon, ...	Tonlegee,	–
	5223	Pat Devine, ...	do.	do.	–
	5224	Pat Foley, ...	do.	do.	–
	5225	Honoria Gallagher, ...	do. ...	do.	.
	5226	Thomas Lyndsey, ...	do.	Rathscanlan,	–
	5227	John Greally (John), ...	do.	Tonlegee,	–
	5228	Francis Campbell, ...	do.	do.	–
	5229	Michael Garvan, ...	do.	do.	
	5230	Thomas Costello, ...	do.	Barnagurry,	
	5231	Michael Costello, ...	do.	...	
	5232	Peter Reilly, ...	do.	Tonlegee,	–
	5233	Mary Brennan, Rep. of James Brennan, decd.	do.	do.	
	5234	Thomas Moore (Peter), ...	do.	Newpark and Kilbride.	
	5235	Michael Greally, ...	do.	Tonlegee,	–
	5236	Bridget Golden, ..	do.	do.	–
	5237	Charles McMann, ...	do.	Newpark,	–
	5238	Anne Gallagher, Rep. of Thomas Gallagher.	do.	Rathscanlan,	–
	5239	Anthony McNicholas, ...	George A. Moore, ...	Lissaniska,	–
	5240	Martin McNicholas, Rep. of Honor McNicholas	do.	Carrowcastle,	–
	5241	Anthony Higgins, ...	do.	do.	–

MAYO—*continued.*

Extent of Holding. Statute.	Poor Law Valuation.	Former Rent.	Judicial Rent.	Observations.	Value of Tenancy.
A. R. P.	£ s. d.	£ s. d.	£ s. d.		£ s. d.
7 0 0	8 5 0	8 8 0	4 8 0	By consent.	
8 3 0	8 15 0	9 7 0	7 10 0	do.	
6 2 6	4 12 0	7 8 9	5 12 6	do.	
3 3 0	3 15 0	6 8 6	5 5 0	do.	
12 1 0	8 0 0	10 18 7	8 0 0	do.	
11 2 9	4 5 0	6 10 0	6 5 0	do.	
5 0 9	1 10 0	8 10 0	1 15 0	do.	
15 1 29	5 10 0	9 15 0	7 0 0	do.	
15 1 29	5 10 0	9 15 0	7 0 0	do.	
29 1 18	8 10 0	16 0 0	10 15 0	do.	
5 3 10	2 15 0	4 0 0	3 0 0	do.	
9 1 0	3 0 0	6 5 0	4 5 0	do.	
5 3 16	2 16 0	4 15 0	3 12 6	do.	
10 0 31	6 10 0	9 10 0	7 0 0	do.	
13 0 28	4 0 0	7 10 0	5 10 0	do.	
9 2 26	5 0 0	7 8 9	6 5 0	do.	
8 2 0	5 0 0	6 1 0	4 15 0	do.	
8 1 6	3 11 0	6 15 10	4 12 6	do.	
13 3 2	5 5 0	5 17 5	5 5 0		
5 0 34	0 15 0	2 15 8	3 10 0		
7 3 18	3 12 0	4 16 0	4 0 0		
11 0 1	4 18 0	8 13 10	5 0 0		
7 0 33	5 19 0	6 13 10	4 5 0		
11 0 7	5 15 0	6 1 3	5 0 0		
16 0 7	5 5 6	8 11 2	6 10 0		
8 1 29	4 3 0	5 16 11	4 0 0		
7 0 37	5 19 0	9 7 3	6 5 0		
13 2 25	5 0 0	10 1 4	5 15 0		
9 3 26	5 1 0	8 5 0	5 10 0		
8 3 28	4 16 0	7 3 10	5 0 0		
30 2 12	14 0 0	37 10 0	19 10 0		
5 0 37	3 10 0	5 0 0	4 0 0		
13 1 16	7 7 0	8 15 0	7 10 0		
9 0 8	4 18 0	6 12 10	5 7 6		
11 3 32	7 5 0	9 11 4	8 0 0		

Names of Assistant Commissioners by whom Cases were decided.	No.	Name of Tenant.	Name of Landlord.	Townland.
Assistant Commissioners— Charles H[illegible] (Legal). J. [illegible]. A. [illegible]. R. [illegible]. W. C. [illegible].	5242	Thomas McNicholas, ...	George A. Moore, ...	[illegible],
	5243	Phelim Campbell, ...	do.	do.
	5244	Thomas Moran, ...	do.	[illegible],
	5245	Patrick J. McNicholas,	do.	[illegible],
	5246	Michael McNicholas, ...	do.	do.
	5247	William and Ellen McNicholas, Reps. of Martin McNicholas.	do.	[illegible],
	5248	Patrick McNicholas, ...	do.	[illegible],
	5249	Anthony L. McDonagh,	do.	[illegible],
	5250	John Murphy, ...	do.	[illegible],
	5251	James McGeever, ...	Myles Jordan, ...	[illegible],
	5252	Patrick McGeever, ...	do.	[illegible],
	5253	Margaret Durkan ...	do.	—
	5254	Martin Deacy, ...	Nicholas Lynch, ...	[illegible],
	5255	Martin Collins, ...	do.	do.
	5256	John McGlein, ...	do.	do.
	5257	Patt McDonnell, jun., ...	Jonathan [illegible], ...	[illegible],
	5258	Patt Durkan, ...	do.	do.
	5259	John Durkan, ...	do.	do.
	5260	Owen McCoy, ...	do.	Kilgariff,
	5261	James McGeever, ...	do.	[illegible],
	5262	John Finn, ...	do.	do.
	5263	Patt Phillips (Pat), ...	do.	[illegible],
	5264	Charles Phillips, ...	do.	do.
	5265	Catherine McDonnell, ...	do.	[illegible],
	5266	James Phillips, ...	do.	[illegible],
	5267	Patt Phillips (Peter), ...	do.	do.
	5268	John [illegible], sen., ...	do.	[illegible],
	5269	Martin Owens, ...	do.	do.
	5270	Patt Kenny, ...	do.	do.
	5271	James McCormack, ...	Col. A. Gun Bell-Martin, ...	[illegible],
	5272	Mark Healy & Dominick Jordan.	do.	[illegible],
	5273	John Mullarky, ...	do.	[illegible],
	5274	James Coleman, sen., ...	do.	do.
	5275	John Sweeny, ...	do.	do.
	5276	Henry Prendergast, ...	do.	do.

MAYO—*continued.*

Extent of Holding, statute.	Poor Law Valuation.	Former Rent.	Judicial Rent.	Observations.	Value of Tenancy.
A. R. P.	£ s. d.	£ s. d.	£ s. d.		£ s. d.
13 3 33½	8 16 0	14 0 10	11 10 0		
21 0 36	9 10 0	14 0 9	11 10 0		
14 1 30	8 5 0	8 13 5	8 0 0		
13 0 9	7 10 0	9 15 8	6 18 6		
12 0 0	5 0 0	6 17 6	5 18 0	By consent.	
13 0 9	7 18 0	9 3 0	8 7 6	do.	
172 3 10	86 5 0	108 0 0	100 0 0	do.	
9 2 0	4 0 0	5 6 8	1 13 6	do.	
6 1 13	3 10 0	4 13 0	3 17 6	do.	
9 0 0	4 10 0	7 0 0	4 10 0	do.	
4 1 0	3 5 0	3 10 0	2 9 1	do.	
21 0 0	6 15 0	10 0 0	7 8 6	do.	
13 1 10	3 18 0	5 10 0	4 0 0		
10 2 0	3 10 0	6 6 6	4 10 0		
13 0 0	3 15 0	4 0 0	4 0 0		
39 3 35	15 10 0	21 0 0	18 10 0		
16 0 0	6 5 0	6 5 0	6 10 0		
20 2 0	6 2 0	6 5 0	6 10 0		
17 3 38	8 15 0	9 10 0	7 0 0		
27 3 10	6 0 0	11 0 0	9 0 0		
20 3 0	6 5 0	8 5 0	6 10 0		
34 3 31	8 10 0	13 10 0	9 10 0		
24 0 0	4 18 0	6 10 0	5 5 0		
21 0 1	7 5 0	9 15 0	7 17 6		
13 3 26	6 0 0	6 5 0	3 10 0		
21 0 15	6 10 0	9 13 0	7 0 0		
—	5 13 0	5 15 0	5 0 0		
—	3 8 0	3 15 0	3 7 6		
8 3 0	9 11 0	3 0 0	3 7 6		
10 0 0	4 0 0	5 6 0	4 5 0	do	
30 0 0	8 18 0	11 0 0	8 16 0	do.	
6 1 25	3 18 0	8 0 0	3 18 0		
6 3 31	4 5 0	5 8 0	4 0 0		
6 2 39	2 4 0	3 15 10	3 0 0		
17 2 17	5 10 0	8 10 0	6 15 0		

Names of Assistant Commissioners by whom Cases were decided.	No.	Name of Tenant.	Name of Landlord.
Assistant Commissioners—			
Charles Hamilton (Legal). J. Rice. A. Gaffe. E. Kelly. W. C. Cornwall.	5277	Mary Dunleavy (Widow),	Luke Horkan, ...
	5278	Michael Moran, ...	do. ...
	5279	Michael Houghagan, ...	do. ...
	5280	Thomas Houghagan, ...	do. ...
	5281	Anne Houghagan (Wid.),	do. ...
	5282	John Healy, ...	do. ...
	5283	Ellen Durkan (Widow),	do. ...
	5284	Owen Moran, ...	do. ...
	5285	Dominick Mannion, ...	do. ...
	5286	John Bedington, ...	George Horkan, ...
	5287	Michael Tom Doyle, ...	do. ...
	5288	Sabina Mannion (Wid.),	do. ...
	5289	Dominick Phillips, ...	do. ...
	5290	Anthony McVealy, ...	do. ...
	5291	Owen Gallagher, ...	Peter Horkan, ...
	5292	Anthony Gallagher, senr.,	do. ...
	5293	Patrick Lundy, ...	do. ...
	5294	Mary Gallagher (Pat), Widow.	do. ...
	5295	James Gallagher, ...	do. ...
	5296	Andrew Murray, ...	do. ...
	5297	James Conwell, ...	do. ...
	5298	Martin Doughan, ...	do. ...
	5299	Pat Hughes, ...	Mary Durkan, ...
	5300	Thomas, Martin, and Patrick Dunne.	Lord Lucan, ...
	5301	Michael Reilly, ...	do. ...
	5302	Andrew Gurney, ...	do. ...
	5303	Anthony Bland, ...	Reps. Henry Joynt,
	5304	John Kilgallen. ...	do. ...
	5305	Pat Burke, ...	do. ...
	5306	Robert Moran, ...	do. ...
	5307	Thady Loftus, ...	do. ...
	5308	John Conwell, ...	do. ...
	5309	Reps. of James Hughes,	do. ...
	5310	Pat McNulty, ...	do. ...
	5311	John Forkan, ...	Thomas Leetch, ...

MAYO—*continued.*

Extent of Holding. Statute.	Poor Law Valuation.	Former Rent.	Judicial Rent.	Observations.	Value of Tenancy.
A. R. P.	£ s. d.	£ s. d.	£ s. d.		£ s. d.
7 0 0	3 15 0	4 16 0	4 0 0		
5 0 0	3 15 0	3 13 6	3 0 0		
9 2 35	4 10 0	6 0 0	5 0 0		
7 0 0	3 15 0	4 16 0	4 0 0		
7 0 0	3 16 0	4 16 0	4 0 0		
5 0 0	2 18 0	3 13 0	3 0 0		
10 0 0	5 5 0	7 3 9	5 10 0		
7 0 0	3 15 0	4 16 0	4 0 0		
5 0 0	2 15 0	3 12 0	3 0 0		
5 2 0	3 7 0	4 11 3	3 13 6		
7 0 0	3 15 0	3 4 7	1 5 0		
5 2 0	3 4 0	4 11 3	3 18 6		
5 0 0	2 10 0	3 16 8	3 0 0		
6 2 0	3 16 0	5 4 3	4 0 0		
11 0 0	6 5 0	10 18 6	7 10 0		
10 0 0	6 13 0	6 0 7	7 5 0		
13 0 0	6 14 0	11 0 8	7 12 6		
7 0 0	3 10 0	4 0 5½	3 10 0		
7 3 0	6 5 0	10 0 0	7 0 0		
9 2 35	5 3 0	7 17 9	6 0 0		
9 0 0	5 1 0	6 6 8	6 0 0		
12 3 0	6 10 0	10 12 6	7 10 0		
—	—	5 0 0	4 0 0	By consent.	
87 1 35	11 6 8	30 6 5	14 10 0		
14 2 0	4 5 0	10 0 0	6 10 0	do.	
30 3 11	18 0 0	19 15 8	15 0 0	do.	
57 1 0	5 5 0	5 14 0	1 10 0	do.	
8 1 0	3 15 0	6 10 0	6 5 0	do	
9 2 10	3 10 0	6 0 0	1 5 0	do.	
11 2 25	8 10 0	8 0 0	5 0 0	do	
34 3 10	7 0 0	18 5 0	9 15 0	do	
35 0 30	6 5 0	10 15 0	7 5 0	do.	
30 1 38	6 15 0	10 7 8	1 6 0	do.	
17 3 0	6 15 0	12 1 0	8 15 0	do.	
31 3 6	5 15 0	8 10 0	6 10 0		

5313	John McNicholas, ...	James Tuohy, ...	Aillbeam, ...
5314	James Byrne, ...	do.	Tonaghmore, ...
5315	Barny McDonagh, ...	Anthony Kelly, ...	Fromlogy, ...
5316	Patrick Loftus, ...	do.	do. ...
5317	Charles Dunleavy, ...	Anne Griffin, ...	Carrowbeg, ...
5318	John Hannigan, ...	do	do. ...
5319	Thomas Fox, ...	do.	do. ...
5320	James Durkan, ...	do.	do. ...
5321	Mary Devitt (Widow),	do.	do. ...
5322	John Ginty, ...	do.	do. ...
5323	Anne Ginty, Rep. of Michael Ginty,	do.	do. ...
5324	Anthony Conway, ...	do.	do. ...
5325	William Marren, ...	William Robert Ormsby, ...	Carrowkeam, Mass,
5326	James Ginty, ...	do.	do. ...
5327	James Haran, ...	do.	do. ...
5328	Thomas Brett, ...	Lord Harlech.	Drumagh, ...
5329	Michael Durkan, ...	N. P. R. Graham, a Minor, ...	Gallagh, ...
5330	Anthony Durkan, ...	do.	do. ...
5331	Bridget Lyons, ...	John Ervin, ...	Esker (Moyfield),
5332	Francis Hanigan, ...	Hugh McNulty, ...	Coolcastle, ...
5333	Patrick Huddy, ...	do.	do. ...
5334	John Dempsey, ...	do.	do. ...
5335	Patrick McAndrew, ...	do.	do. ...
5336	Michael Cawley, ...	Joseph McDonnell D'Arcy, ...	Dunrevile, ...
5337	Henry Price, ...	William G. Dunville, ...	Drimacanan, Tonaneack.
5338	Bridget Walsh, ...	Miss Fanny Bourke, a lunatic,	Carrick, ...
5339	Terence Carroll, ...	do.	Carrakeen, ...
5340	Owen Roughneen, ...	do	Carrick, ...
5341	Thomas McLoughlin, ...	do.	Carrick, West, ...
5342	Thomas O'Brien, ...	do.	Carrick, ...
5343	Mark O'Brien, ...	do.	do. ...
5344	James M. Roughneen, ...	do.	do. ...
5345	Michael Brennan, ...	do.	do. ...
5346	Michael O'Brien, ...	do.	do. ...

MAYO—*continued.*

Content of Holding—Statute.	Poor Law Valuation.	Former Rent.	Judicial Rent.	Observations.	Value of Tenancy.
A. R. P.	£ s. d.	£ s. d.	£ s. d.		£ s. d.
[illegible] 3 [illegible]	12 10 0	27 16 6	16 0 0		
4 0 [illegible]	7 0 8	9 13 0	8 2 6		
23 3 27	18 18 0	16 9 10	15 5 0		
—	2 18 0	3 10 6	3 10 6		
—	8 12 6	6 11 0	8 10 0		
10 3 14	5 10 0	8 4 9	6 10 7	By consent.	
10 3 10	3 5 0	5 0 0	5 18 0	do.	
15 1 26	1 10 0	6 15 6	5 4 0	do.	
7 3 35	2 15 0	5 11 0	4 10 0	do.	
19 3 22	6 0 0	7 5 0	5 0 0	do.	
17 0 22	6 10 0	8 8 6	7 18 0	do.	
10 1 7	4 16 0	7 7 0	5 14 0	do.	
10 1 7	4 15 0	7 7 6	5 14 6	do.	
8 2 0	4 5 0	4 18 0	4 15 0		
16 0 0	8 15 6	9 10 0	8 10 0		
14 3 0	8 4 0	10 10 0	11 0 0		
27 2 25	12 10 0	13 0 0	11 10 0		
18 0 0	10 0 0	12 17 6	11 0 0		
18 0 0	10 0 0	13 18 6	11 0 0		
7 1 30	3 5 0	6 0 0	6 0 0		
11 3 13	5 8 0	5 16 0	4 13 6		
11 3 26	3 11 0	5 10 0	4 10 0		
10 3 5	3 14 0	5 17 6	4 17 6		
11 3 0	4 5 6	6 14 0	5 10 6		
6 0 31	2 8 6	7 6 0	4 5 0	By consent.	
19 3 6	6 5 0	16 10 0	13 10 0		
20 0 10	3 15 0	5 5 0	3 15 0		
18 0 0	7 18 0	10 3 10	8 0 0		
11 0 10	3 2 0	5 15 0	4 15 0		
15 1 10	4 15 0	8 0 0	6 0 0		
17 1 0	5 4 0	8 15 0	8 10 0		
16 3 20	8 0 0	8 0 0	4 5 0		
16 3 25	8 3 0	6 1 0	6 10 0		
24 1 6	5 15 0	7 10 6	6 15 0		
16 2 17	8 0 0	5 0 6	8 5 0		

Names of Assistant Commissioners by whom Cases were decided.	No.	Name of Tenant.	Name of Landlord.	Townland.
Assistant Commissioners—				
Charles Hamilton (Legal). J. Rice. A. Currie. E. Kelly. W. C. Coffey.	5347	James W. Walsh,	Miss Fanny Bourke, a lunatic,	Carrick,
	5348	John O'Brien,	do.	Carrokeel,
	5349	Luke Lavan,	do.	Carrick,
	5350	John Kelly,	do.	Carrokeel,
	5351	Richard Brennan,	do.	do.
	5352	Thos. & Michael Walsh,	do.	Carrick,
	5353	Walter and Catherine Walsh,	do.	Carrick, West,
	5354	James Loughnan,	do.	Carrick,
	5355	Patrick Ivers,	do.	Carrokeel,
	5356	Honor Lavan,	do.	Carrick,
	5357	Michael Lavan,	do.	Carrokeel,
	5358	John & Michael Feeley,	do.	Carrick,
	5359	David Fenrick,	do.	Carrick and Carrokeel,
	5360	Thomas Brennan,	do.	Carrick,
	5361	Michael Murray,	Colonel Devereux and Mrs. Charlotte Walker,	Knockatinny,
	5362	Bernard O'Donnell,	John Nolan Farrell,	—
	5363	Patrick Murphy,	John Birmingham,	Ballard,
	5364	Edward McLoughlin,	Major Thomas Lambert,	Crinalla,
	5365	Anthony Durkan,	Robert Evans,	Inmoore,
	5366	Thomas Fitzstephens,	Owen O'Malley,	Lecarrow,
	5367	James Greaick,	do.	do.
	5368	John Higgins,	do.	do.
	5369	Mathew Higgins,	do.	do.
	5370	Hugh McGrail,	Sir Charles James Knox Gore, Bart.	Rinnany,
	5371	Edward P. McGoff,	do.	do.
	5372	Edward Rourke, Rep. of Pat Mulloway,	do.	do.
	5373	Anthony Rourke, Rep. of Garret Rourke,	do.	do.
	5374	Jas. & Michael McGrail,	do.	do.
	5375	Sabina Deasy and John Noon,	do.	do.
	5376	Thomas Byrne,	do.	Bohola,
	5377	James Jordan,	do.	do.
	5378	John Scally,	do.	do.
	5379	Margaret McGowan,	do.	do.
	5380	Patrick McGowan,	do.	do.
	5381	John and Pat Rourke,	do.	Rinnany.

MAYO—*continued.*

Extent of Holding (Statute).			Poor Law Valuation.			Present Rent.			Judicial Rent.			Observations.
A.	R.	P.	£	s.	d.	£	s.	d.	£	s.	d.	
13	3	0	1	5	0	6	15	0	5	0	0	
21	1	0	6	10	0	10	0	0	7	10	0	
15	2	20	5	10	0	7	0	0	5	5	0	
8	0	16	3	5	0	4	0	0	3	0	0	
3	0	0	3	15	0	5	0	0	4	0	0	
15	3	0	4	0	0	5	0	0	4	0	0	
37	3	20	9	0	0	18	10	0	10	5	0	
18	3	20	4	16	0	6	15	0	5	5	0	
10	0	0	3	10	0	5	0	0	3	15	0	
7	0	0	4	10	0	7	0	0	5	0	0	
5	0	16	4	0	0	5	0	0	4	0	0	
16	1	10	6	0	0	7	5	0	5	5	0	
17	2	25	3	15	0	4	10	0	3	0	0	
11	3	0	1	15	0	4	10	0	2	15	0	
11	1	35	3	0	0	6	10	0	4	0	0	
9	2	0	5	10	0	8	11	10	5	0	0	By consent.
20	1	8	13	0	0	21	5	7	17	15	0	do.
13	1	5	5	0	0	6	7	4	5	15	0	
5	2	4	1	17	0	3	15	0	2	0	0	
16	0	0	7	5	0	9	4	10	7	15	0	
15	0	0	7	5	0	9	4	10	7	15	0	
15	0	0	7	5	0	9	4	10	7	15	0	
15	0	0	7	5	0	9	4	10	7	15	0	
8	1	27	2	18	0	4	12	4	3	12	6	
5	2	20	2	10	0	3	15	4	3	0	0	
7	3	0	2	10	0	4	5	4	3	7	6	
5	2	20	2	10	0	3	15	4	3	0	0	
7	1	0	2	10	0	3	18	0	3	0	0	
7	1	0	3	6	0	4	3	8	3	2	6	
6	0	20	2	15	0	5	0	0	3	15	0	
11	1	20	4	15	0	6	0	0	5	0	0	
5	3	0	3	0	0	4	0	0	3	2	6	
7	1	0	4	5	0	5	15	0	4	10	0	
11	2	10	4	16	0	6	0	0	4	15	0	
7	1	0	3	0	0	4	18	0	3	10	0	

COUNTY OF

Names of Assistant Commissioners by whom Cases were decided.	No.	Name of Tenant.	Name of Landlord.	Townland.
Assistant Commissioners—				
Charles Hamilton (Legal). J. Rice. A. Conty. E. Kelly. W. C. Connell.	5382	Alice McGuiff (widow),	Sir Charles James Knox-Gore, Bart.	Rinney,
	5383	William Rogers (William) Rep. of William Rogers.	do.	do.
	5384	James, Thomas Rogers, Reps. of Michl. Rogers.	do.	do.
	5385	Anthony McHugh, ...	do.	do.
	5386	Thomas & John McHugh,	do.	do.
	5387	Denis Rogers, Rep. of Bridget Rogers.	do.	do.
	5388	Pat Reddy, ...	Henry Lyons, ...	Cavanacalla,
	5389	Ellen McLoughlin, Rep. of Thomas McLoughlin	Lord Dillon, ...	Clooncan,
	5390	John Morley (Neil), ...	do.	Carrowmore,
	5391	Patrick Walsh, senior,	do.	Drumacrahy,
	5392	Patrick Malley, ...	Daniel Nally, ...	Ballyduff,
	5393	Pat Hughes, ...	Sir Charles James Knox-Gore, Bart.	Rinney,
				Total,

COUNTY OF

Names of Assistant Commissioners by whom Cases were decided.	No.	Name of Tenant.	Name of Landlord.	Townland.
Assistant Commissioners—	1273	Mary Duffy, ...	Michael Keogh, Brothers and others.	Leggs,
Cecil Roche (Legal). M. P. Lynch. H. R. Mollarney. R. B. Hickson. Redmond Roche.	1274	William Kenny, ...	Robert Cuddell, ...	Ardeela,
	1275	John Flynn, ...	Arthur O'Connor and others,	Culliard,
	1276	Mathew Flynn, ...	do. ...	do.
	1277	Farrell Lee, ...	do.	Strahreaghan,
	1278	Anne McLoughlin, ...	do.	Aghadin,
	1279	Thomas McIlrath, ...	do.	Bawnboy,
	1280	Patrick Gaffney, ...	do.	Aghaboy,
	1281	Bernard Conway, ...	do.	Derryarnadoy,
	1282	Jane McNamara, ...	do.	Balaney,

MAYO—*continued.*

Extent of Holding. Statute.	Poor Law Valuation.	Former Rent.	Judicial Rent.	Observations.	Value of Tenancy.
A. R. P.	£ s. d.	£ s. d.	£ s. d.		£ s. d.
7 1 0	2 10 0	8 14 4	8 17 6		
7 1 0	3 7 0	1 18 3	4 0 0		
6 1 37	2 5 0	8 16 0	8 0 0		
4 1 07	2 5 0	8 18 0	2 13 6		
10 0 0	2 15 0	6 5 0	2 18 0		
6 1 37	8 5 0	5 19 0	6 0 0		
60 0 30	16 10 0	26 9 7	23 9 6	By consent.	
14 1 24	4 18 0	5 19 0	5 0 0		
28 2 10	6 0 0	11 7 3	9 0 0		
9 1 37	3 8 0	4 4 8	3 8 0		
25 0 0	12 15 0	25 0 0	17 7 6		
3 1 0	1 10 0	8 7 3	2 2 6		
6,713 1 9½	2,979 14 0	3,600 3 2	3,163 18 11½		

ROSCOMMON.

Extent of Holding. Statute.	Poor Law Valuation.	Former Rent.	Judicial Rent.	Observations.	Value of Tenancy.
19 2 5	12 0 0	14 11 8	12 10 0		
26 0 35	11 5 6	14 12 3	10 10 0		
13 1 25	4 0 0	6 13 1	5 10 0		
11 3 6	3 10 0	4 13 8	5 0 0		
84 1 0	16 0 0	23 0 0	16 0 0	Rent changed in 1856 from . . . £13 5s. 8d.	
12 0 0	5 10 0	8 10 3	6 10 0	do. 5 6 0	
37 1 8	7 18 0	9 0 0	7 6 0	1863 6 10 0	
10 2 08	5 10 0	7 0 0	8 10 0	1868 3 18 0	
46 3 24	27 0 0	30 10 0	24 0 0		
34 3 20	8 15 0	14 0 0	10 0 0		
325 1 3	122 5 0	186 10 1	105 15 0		

SLIGO.

Extent of Holding. Statute.	Poor Law Valuation.	Former Rent.	Judicial Rent.	Observations.	Value of Tenancy.
43 3 30	6 15 0	7 8 2	6 15 0		
16 2 26	7 10 0	18 0 0	9 0 0		
49 0 18	16 0 0	17 16 0	14 10 0		
26 2 0	4 10 0	13 16 0	8 0 0		
43 2 16	14 5 0	23 0 0	19 5 0	Rent changed in 1871 from . . . 20 3 6	

COUNTY OF

Names of Assistant Commissioners by whom Cases were decided.	No.	Name of Tenant.	Name of Landlord.	Townland.
Assistant Commissioners—				
Cecil Roche (Legal). M. P. Lynch. H. B. Montgomery. R. S. Hickson. Redmond Roche.	1615	Anthony Weir, ...	J. J. Vernon & anor., Trustees of A. B. Vernon,	[illegible],
	1616	Francis Gurney, ...	do.	[illegible] & [illegible],
	1617	Mary Doherty, ...	do.	[illegible],
	1618	William Murray, ...	do.	[illegible] and [illegible],
	1619	John Mullen, ...	do.	do.
	1620	Roger O'Connor, ...	Meredith Thompson and anor., by F. A. Thompson and anor.,	Kilmacrinan?, ...
	1621	John Flanagan, ...	do.	do. ...
	1622	Thomas Durcan, ...	Moses Morris, ...	Kinnalion?, ...
	1623	Michael Rowley, ...	do.	do. ...
	1624	John O'Hara, ...	do.	do. ...
	1625	John Rowley, ...	do.	do. ...
	1626	Mathew Cryan, ...	Captain George Phibbs, ...	Derrinacartagh?, ...
	1627	John Durkan (Darby), ...	Henry A. Knox and others,	Ballincurry, ...
	1628	Patrick Hunt, ...	Alexander Sim, ...	Oughtam, ...
	1629	Henry McGowan, ...	do.	do. ...
	1630	Patrick Meehan, ...	do.	do. ...
	1631	Bridget Fahey, ...	Charles W. O'Hara, ...	Cloonacurra?, ...
	1632	Patrick McGetrick, ...	Captain Fitzgerald, ...	[illegible], ...
	1633	Edward Clarke, ...	John Irwin, ...	Castlerock?, ...
	1634	Thomas Henry, ...	Michael Judge, ...	[illegible], ...
	1635	John W. Curran?, ...	Richard H. Phibbs, ...	Tubbercurry, ...
	1636	John Craven, ...	do.	do. ...
	1637	Robert Craven, ...	do.	do. ...
	1638	John McLoughlin, ...	Alexander Percival, ...	Rinbane?, ...
	1639	Thomas McGarrick, ...	do.	do. ...
	1640	Thomas Hunter?, ...	do.	Ballinarrow, 6th,
	1641	James McGetrick, senior,	do.	Lackarrow, ...
	1642	Callaghan Connell, ...	do.	Rinbane, ...
	1643	James McGetrick, junior,	do.	Lackarrow, ...
	1644	Patrick Gallagher, ...	do.	Ballinarrow, 8th,
	1645	John Friell, ...	do.	Rinbane, ...
	1646	Pat Berreen?, ...	do.	Ballinarrow, 8th,
	1647	Mary Spelman, ...	do.	Ballinarrow and another.
	1648	Patrick McIntyre, ...	Colonel Richard Phibbs, ...	Curry, ...
	1649	Patrick Walsh, ...	do.	do. ...

SLIGO—*continued.*

Extent of Holding. Statute.	Poor Law Valuation	Former Rent	Judicial Rent.	Observations.	Value of Tenancy.
A. R. P.	£ s. d.	£ s. d.	£ s. d.		£ s. d.
17 2 30	6 19 0	11 0 0	8 10 0	By consent.	
[illegible] 3 [illegible]	14 0 0	16 0 0	12 15 0	do.	
16 2 [illegible]	10 10 0	13 1 0	10 6 0	do.	
60 0 0	[illegible] 10 0	[illegible] 0 0	27 15 0	do.	
19 3 20	5 18 0	6 12 0	6 0 0	do.	
19 2 [illegible]	5 10 0	7 10 0	9 0 0	do.	
34 0 19	19 5 0	31 0 0	[illegible] 2 6	do.	
13 [illegible] 5	3 14 0	4 15 0	3 15 0	do.	
19 0 9	6 13 0	7 17 0	6 13 0	do.	
6 1 [illegible]	3 15 0	4 5 0	3 15 0	do.	
10 2 0	1 15 0	6 5 0	1 15 0	do.	
14 3 5	3 10 0	10 1 0	8 0 0		
8 3 0	3 15 0	4 18 8	3 10 0		
10 0 10	6 0 0	7 0 0	6 5 0		
9 0 31	5 15 0	8 0 0	6 10 0		
19 1 37	8 15 0	13 0 0	10 10 0		
25 3 18	15 0 0	20 10 0	17 0 0	do.	
79 1 20	31 10 0	48 0 0	[illegible] 10 0	do.	
33 1 8	5 15 0	6 10 0	5 10 0	do.	
8 0 0	0 5 0	1 0 0	8 0 0		
21 0 [illegible]	12 5 0	18 15 0	17 0 0		
9 1 11	1 15 0	2 0 0	1 15 0		
[illegible] 0 31½	14 7 0	16 8 0	15 0 0		
27 2 30	11 10 0	16 0 0	13 0 0	do.	
30 3 [illegible]	7 0 0	8 0 0	8 0 0	do.	
16 2 25	18 0 0	16 18 0	13 0 0		
15 1 21	11 5 0	14 5 0	13 0 0		
9 5 0	5 10 0	6 15 0	5 10 0		
25 3 [illegible]	19 0 0	[illegible] 0 0	[illegible] 0 0		
16 0 15	11 15 0	14 10 0	12 10 0		
9 0 0	6 5 0	7 0 0	6 8 0		
10 0 26	13 15 0	17 16 0	16 0 0		
18 0 38	13 5 0	15 10 0	13 10 0		
15 1 38	4 10 0	8 10 0	4 10 0	do.	
6 2 16	1 5 0	1 0 0	1 0 0	do.	

Cecil Roche (Legal).
M. P. Lynch.
H. R. Morrison.
B. B. Hayward.
Raymond Roche.

No.	Tenant	Landlord
1650	Michael Brehany and another.	Col. Richard Phibbs,
1651	Patrick Kennedy and another.	do.
1652	Thomas Kilroy,	do.
1653	Thomas Walsh,	do.
1654	Patrick Gilligan,	do.
1655	Patrick McGuinn,	do.
1656	John Gilligan,	do.
1657	Michael Walsh,	do.
1658	John Henry,	do.
1659	Winifred Kilmore,	do.
1660	Widow Michael Kilroy,	do.
1661	Margaret Henry and another.	do.
1662	Philip Cunnane,	do.
1663	Michael Phillips,	do.
1664	Pat O'Brien,	do.
1665	Malachi Duddy,	do.
1666	Honor Gormley,	do.
1667	James Kerrane,	Roger McGarrick,
1668	John Higgins,	do.
1669	James Feely,	do.
1670	Michael Kearney,	do.
1671	John Rogers,	do.
1672	John Kennedy,	do.
1673	Martin Quinn,	do.
1674	James Brennan,	do.
1675	Pat Kerrane,	do.
1676	Thomas Coleman,	Mrs. Harriett Molloy and another.
1677	Patrick Ross,	do.
1678	Owen Dempsey,	do.
1679	James Lee,	do.
1680	Catherine Frizzell,	do.
1681	Michael Coleman,	do.
1682	John Ramsey,	do.
1683	Patrick Carey,	do.
1684	Michael Davy,	do.

SLIGO—*continued.*

Extent of Holding. Statute.	Poor Law Valuation.	Former Rent.	Judicial Rent.	Observations.	Value of Tenancy.
a. r. p.	£ s. d.	£ s. d.	£ s. d.		£ s. d.
15 1 10	6 1 0	6 10 0	6 3 0	By consent.	
16 2 0	6 10 0	7 10 0	6 18 0	do.	
14 8 18	8 5 0	8 10 0	3 10 6	do.	
14 0 0	5 0 0	6 14 0	5 0 0	do.	
31 3 19	4 0 0	4 10 0	5 10 0	do.	
6 3 [illegible]	1 5 0	3 0 0	2 0 0	do.	
61 1 [illegible]	3 10 0	4 0 0	8 10 0	do.	
10 0 18	6 0 0	7 0 0	6 0 0	do.	
16 3 27	4 15 0	6 0 0	5 0 0	do.	
14 0 8	4 10 0	6 5 0	4 14 0	do.	
8 8 23	4 0 0	5 0 0	4 5 0	do.	
14 0 10	6 0 0	4 17 6	6 0 0	do.	
10 0 4	6 0 0	6 18 0	5 16 0	do.	
18 0 0	4 0 0	6 0 0	4 6 0	do.	
34 5 6	16 18 0	17 7 0	14 10 0		
[illegible] 0 [illegible]	18 10 0	17 7 0	14 15 0		
[illegible] 0 13	16 15 0	17 7 0	15 0 0		
7 1 30	2 5 0	1 0 0	8 15 0		
22 5 25	8 5 0	10 0 0	7 0 0		
13 0 27	3 5 0	5 8 0	3 10 0		
11 0 [illegible]	4 5 0	6 0 0	6 0 0		
16 6 25	4 5 0	7 0 0	8 0 0		
19 1 30	11 11 0	16 10 0	13 5 0		
14 1 19	7 5 0	8 10 0	7 15 0		
16 8 [illegible]	4 10 0	6 10 0	6 10 0		
15 0 10	1 5 0	7 10 0	6 0 0		
13 3 0	9 10 0	13 0 0	10 0 0	do.	
16 0 30	11 8 0	13 10 0	11 5 0	do.	
45 0 26	[illegible] 10 0	[illegible] 7 0	[illegible] 10 0	do.	
40 2 30	[illegible] 0 0	64 0 0	[illegible] 0 0	do.	
[illegible] 6 0	18 0 0	21 0 0	16 0 0		
51 0 5	[illegible] 0 0	48 10 0	38 0 0	do.	
17 5 [illegible]	8 0 0	10 10 0	8 0 0	do.	
10 1 20	18 10 0	14 0 0	15 10 0	do.	
[illegible] 8 [illegible]	15 10 0	19 10 0	16 10 0	do.	

Names of Assistant Commissioners by whom Cases were decided.	No.	Name of Tenant.	Name of Landlord.	Townland.
Assistant Commissioners—				
Cecil Roche (Legal). M. P. Lynch. H. B. Morrison. R. R. Hamilton. Edmond Roche.	1685	Patrick Tuslin, ...	Mrs. Harriett Molloy & anor.	Lisnalough, ...
	1686	Patrick Henry, Rep. of Margaret Ross	do.	do. ...
	1687	James Callery, ...	do.	Carrowngarragh,
	1688	Jane McDonagh (widow),	do.	Lisnalough, ...
	1689	Bridget Meehan, Rep. of John Meehan.	do.	Rathmoulagan,
	1690	[illegible], ...	do.	Carrowkeane, ...
	1691	Bartley McGuinness, ...	R. W. Meredith, ...	Sutton Common,
	1692	John Brennan, ...	do.	do.
	1693	Michael Doyle, ...	do.	do. ...
	1694	Thomas Dwyer, ...	do.	do.
	1695	John Madden, ...	do.	do. ...
	1696	John O'Hara, ...	do.	do. ...
	1697	Edward McHugh, ...	do.	do. ...
	1698	John Gallagher, ...	do.	do. ...
	1699	John Colvey, ...	do.	do. ...
	1700	Michael Conlon, ...	do.	do. ...
	1701	Moses Gethins, ...	Col. E. H. Cooper, ...	Kilmacannie, ...
	1702	Michael Gethins, ...	do.	do. ...
	1703	John Leonard, ...	do.	do. ...
	1704	Bridget McLoughlin, ...	do.	do. ...
	1705	Bridget Cunningham, ...	do.	do. ...
	1706	Thomas Scurry, ...	do.	do. ...
	1707	Michael Durcan, ...	John W. Stratford, ...	Coolrawnill,
	1708	Patrick Harte, ...	do.	do. ...
	1709	James Durcan, ...	do.	do. ...
	1710	William J. Christy, ...	do.	do. ...
	1711	Edward Durcan, ...	do.	do. ...
	1712	Bridget Nolan,	do.	do. ...
	1713	John Lundy (Ros), ...	do.	do. ...
	1714	Anthony Cook, ...	do.	do. ...
	1715	Patrick Hyland, ...	do.	do. ...
	1716	Daniel Hyland, ...	do.	do. ...
	1717	Thomas Walken, ...	do.	do. ...
	1718	Arthur O'Hara, ...	do.	do. ...
	1719	Martin Mayo, ...	do.	do. ...

SLIGO—*continued.*

Extent of Holding. Statute.			Poor Law Valuation.			Former Rent.			Judicial Rent.			Observations.
A.	R.	P.	£	s.	d.	£	s.	d.	£	s.	d.	
17	2	0	11	0	0	14	10	0	11	0	0	By consent.
2	3	13	2	10	0	3	0	0	2	10	0	do.
61	3	18	31	0	0	63	10	0	51	0	0	do.
8	0	5	5	0	0	6	0	0	6	0	0	do.
23	1	0	18	15	0	20	0	0	16	15	0	do.
30	2	0	18	0	0	24	0	0	19	0	0	do.
31	2	18	14	5	0	23	10	0	13	15	0	do.
25	1	17	9	5	0	10	12	5	8	5	0	do.
11	3	31	6	6	0	7	14	6	6	0	0	do.
109	1	14	7	0	0	12	0	0	7	0	0	do.
25	0	8	10	5	0	14	0	0	10	5	0	do.
41	1	16	9	5	0	12	6	1	9	5	0	do.
61	0	18	31	0	0	53	10	0	30	0	0	do.
38	3	25	8	0	0	11	0	10	8	15	0	
27	1	13	9	5	0	9	10	0	7	10	0	
25	1	17	6	5	0	6	0	0	5	0	0	
12	2	25	2	10	0	2	12	0	2	12	0	
11	0	32	2	15	0	3	0	0	3	0	0	
64	3	10	25	0	0	25	0	0	23	0	0	
15	0	25	6	7	0	5	0	0	5	0	0	
14	1	33	5	0	0	6	0	0	4	5	0	
21	0	28	7	0	0	7	0	0	6	6	0	
15	0	5	5	10	0	7	0	0	6	0	0	do.
19	2	10	6	15	0	10	0	0	7	0	0	do.
15	1	15	7	5	0	8	4	0	6	15	0	do.
16	2	35	7	0	0	9	10	0	7	0	0	do.
13	0	15	6	0	0	7	7	9	6	18	0	do.
26	3	30	4	5	0	6	12	0	5	0	0	do.
18	2	20	6	10	0	6	18	0	6	7	0	do.
6	1	10	1	10	0	2	0	0	2	0	0	do.
13	0	20	5	15	0	6	16	0	5	5	0	do.
21	1	0	9	15	0	18	0	0	8	11	0	do.
12	0	5	3	5	0	3	12	0	2	5	0	do.
8	0	10	7	0	0	5	0	0	6	18	0	do.
16	1	[illegible]	6	0	0	7	0	0	5	16	0	do.

COUNTY OF

Names of Assistant Commissioners by whom Cases were decided.	No.	Name of Tenant.	Name of Landlord.	Townland.
Assistant Commissioners—				
Cecil Roche (Legal). M. P. Lynch. H. B. Meredith. R. B. Hamilton. Redmond Roche.	1780	Mary Reynolds (Pat), ...	John W. Stratford, ...	Coolrevall, ...
	1781	Bryan Mays, ...	do.	do. ...
	1782	Martin Landy, ...	do.	do. ...
	1783	James Landy, ...	do.	do. ...
	1784	James Gallagher, ...	do.	do. ...
	1785	James Christy, ...	do.	do. ...
				Total.

PROVINCE OF

COUNTY OF

Names of Assistant Commissioners by whom Cases were decided.	No.	Name of Tenant.	Name of Landlord.	Townland.
Assistant Commissioners—	2102	Richard Stacpoole, ...	Richard Bishop and another,	Kilmurry, ...
R. Reeves, Q.C. (Legal). C. O'Keeffe. E. M'Causland. H. C. Nash. E. G. Fahy.	2103	Patrick Barry, ...	Rev. George Stoddart, ...	Cloggrove, ...
	2104	Do.	do.	do. ...
	2105	John Arkins, ...	William H. W. Fitzgerald, ...	Knockroe, ...
	2106	Thomas Hanbury, ...	V. W. Russell, ...	Castlequarter, ...
	2107	James Rochford, ...	Captain E. B. Pocklington, ...	Fortanemore, ...
	2108	Richard O'Gorman, ...	Thomas G. S. Mahon, ...	Shrubeen, ...
	2109	Michael Dolaughty, ...	do.	do. ...
	2110	James Whelan, ...	do.	do. ...
	2111	Martin Cosgrove, ...	Augustine Arthur, Committee of Thomas Arthur, a lunatic.	Cloone, ...
	2112	Michael Moriarty & anor.,	Patrick Scanlan and others, ...	Drumsheragh, ...
	2113	Patrick Burke, ...	Patrick M. Cullinan, M.D., ...	Coolready, ...
	2114	Morgan Clohessy, ...	do.	do. ...
	2115	John O'Connor, ...	Captain C. G. O'Callaghan, ...	Castletown, ...
	2116	Mrs. Ellen Digan, Rep. of Michael Digan.	George Westropp and another,	Ross, ...
	2117	Patrick Corbett, ...	Captain John Finch, ...	Cragg[illegible], ...
	2118	Anne Carmody, ...	R. H. Bailey, ...	Drumullagh, ...
	2119	John Hoey, ...	Miss Olivia Gough & another,	Garthera, ...
	2120	Catherine Littleton, Rep. of Stephen Littleton.	do.	Cragboy & anr.
	2121	Patrick Marx, ...	Wyndham Q. Going, ...	Claremount and another.
	2122	Patrick Hanrahan, ...	Captain John Finch, ...	Cragg[illegible], ...

SLIGO—*continued.*

Extent of Holding, Statute.	Poor Law Valuation.	Former Rent.	Judicial Rent.	Observations.	Value of Tenancy.
A. R. P.	£ s. d.	£ s. d.	£ s. d.		£ s. d.
64 1 15	5 15 0	6 0 0	4 0 0	By consent.	
20 3 25	13 10 0	17 6 0	14 0 0	do.	
17 1 10	5 0 0	6 10 0	5 5 0	do.	
12 3 30	6 10 0	6 5 0	5 5 6	do.	
31 1 10	12 5 0	20 0 0	12 10 0		
13 0 16	5 5 0	6 10 0	5 5 0		
2,673 0 11½	1,066 17 0	1,386 17 0	1,119 0 0		

MUNSTER.

CLARE.

Extent of Holding, Statute.	Poor Law Valuation.	Former Rent.	Judicial Rent.	Observations.	Value of Tenancy.
10 1 30	6 15 0	13 3 0	10 0 0		50 0 0
23 3 7	8 10 0	11 17 0	8 10 0		90 0 0
18 0 0	15 0 0	20 12 6	17 10 0		
45 0 0	33 0 0	35 0 0	31 10 0		160 0 0
25 1 18	11 0 0	15 0 0	11 0 0		
64 3 16	30 0 0	61 18 0	40 10 0		200 0 0
62 0 18	12 10 0	60 5 0	60 5 0	Provision has been made in this case as regards a labourer.	300 0 0
30 0 0	16 10 0	31 5 0	16 10 0		100 0 0
30 3 0	23 10 0	27 17 6	25 0 0		150 0 0
35 0 0	7 10 0	15 1 10	10 0 0		110 0 0
30 0 25	24 10 0	45 6 5	35 10 0		
3 0 20	3 10 0	5 0 0	3 10 0		
39 3 18	34 0 0	70 0 0	47 10 0		
29 1 0	11 15 0	20 16 0	16 0 0		50 0 0
174 2 36	126 0 0	178 2 10	145 0 0		145 0 0
9 2 16	4 0 0	7 15 6	6 0 0		70 0 0
20 0 17	4 5 0	6 15 0	4 16 0		
90 0 31	26 0 0	40 5 0	34 10 0		200 0 0
49 0 32	30 0 0	30 17 9	31 10 0		150 0 0
17 3 0	10 5 0	16 7 0	12 10 0		
17 3 30	23 5 0	27 14 3	24 0 0		160 0 0

Names of Assistant Commissioners by whom Cases were decided.	No.	Name of Tenant	Name of Landlord	Townland.
Assistant Commissioners—				
R. Reeves, Q.C. (Legal.) C. O'Keeffe. E. McCausland. H. G. Nash. E. G. Pery.	2123	John McNamara, ...	A. F. Butler and others, ...	Ballyvergin, ...
	2124	Michael Lane, ...	Thomas Meldon, ...	Gortatober, ...
	2125	James Connell, ...	Sophia Graham, ...	[illegible]
	2126	Michael Moloney, ...	do.	do. ...
	2127	John Moloney (James),	do.	do. ...
	2128	Roger Maloy, ...	Anne F. Butler and others,...	Ballyvergin, ...
	2129	John McMahon, ...	do.	do ...
	2130	Roger Moloney, ...	Colonel Paterson, ...	Ardskeagh, ...
	2131	Michael McDonnell, ...	Mary H. Maxwell & another,	Moanmore & another.
	2132	Michael Crowe, ...	Robert L. Browne, ...	Fairybog, ...
	2133	Patrick Liddy, ...	Col. Thomas M. Keany, ...	Lisnalinna, ...
	2134	Anne Moloney, ...	Michael Casey and another,	Lifford, ...
	2135	Pat McNamara, ...	Mrs. Mary J. Phelps, ...	Cloontaragh, ...
	2136	Michael Doyle, ...	do.	do. ...
	2137	Michael Hogan, ...	do.	do. ...
	2138	Patrick Harrison, ...	Hon. C. L. Butler & another,	Knappogue, ...
	2139	Thomas Scanlan, ...	do.	do. ...
	2140	Daniel Murphy, ...	John Frost, ...	Derrymore, ...
	2141	Pat McInerney, ...	do.	do. ...
	2142	Thomas Murphy, ...	do.	Derrymore, East,
	2143	Thomas Hanley, ...	do.	do. ...
	2144	William Frost, ...	Marquis Conyngham, ...	Moolick, ...
	2145	Do.	do.	[illegible]
	2146	Do.	do.	Punchbowl, ...
	2147	James Frost, ...	do.	Moolick Villa, ...
	2148	Patrick Frost, ...	do.	do. ...
	2149	Stephen Kelly, ...	Colonel Paterson, ...	Ardskeagh, ...
	2150	William Scanlan, ...	Timothy Barton, Trustee of William Scanlan, decd.	Ballyvannigan, ...
	2151	Patrick Duggan, ...	Patrick Scanlan and others,	Drewsborough ...
	2152	Dominick Hogan, ...	Timothy Barton, Trustee of William Scanlan, decd.	do. ...
	2153	James Moynihan, ...	Patrick T. Law, ...	[illegible]
	2154	Mrs. Anne Cunningham, ...	Lord Leconfield, ...	Cloontoon and another,
	2155	Martin Moloney, ...	Anne F. Banks and others,	Uggoon, Upper,
	2156	William Scanlan, ...	William H. W. Fitzgerald, ...	Ballyvannigan,
	2157	Edmund Houghton, ...	Robt. W. H. Moreland, another,	Corbehagh, ...

CLARE—*continued.*

Extent of Holding. Statute Measure.	Poor Law Valuation.	Former Rent.	Judicial Rent.	Observations.	Value of Tenancy.
A. R. P.	£ s. d.	£ s. d.	£ s. d.		£ s. d.
56 0 0	9 15 0	17 0 0	8 14 0	By consent.	
45 2 0	[illegible] 15 0	102 0 0	80 0 0	do.	
14 0 0	4 10 0	5 15 6	4 15 0	do.	
[illegible] 0 0	[illegible]	14 5 0	31 0 0	do.	
36 0 0	7 0 0	13 0 0	9 0 0	do.	
37 0 0	5 0 0	6 10 0	5 0 0	do.	
63 1 3	8 10 0	14 0 0	9 10 0	do.	
72 1 34	30 0 0	77 17 6	66 15 0	do.	
32 0 17	14 0 0	51 3 5	36 0 0	do.	
65 2 1	12 15 0	29 10 0	23 10 0		
31 1 36	23 15 0	33 6 6	30 15 0		
18 2 0	10 15 0	15 0 0	15 0 0		120 0 0
16 0 0	8 16 0	12 6 6	8 15 0		80 0 0
16 0 0	5 10 0	7 5 0	5 10 0		30 0 0
35 3 25	11 5 0	18 0 0	13 0 0	Provision has been made in this case as regards a labourer.	65 0 0
31 2 12	10 10 0	11 16 8	13 10 0		110 0 0
16 1 7	10 0 0	21 0 0	15 0 0		100 0 0
23 3 0	13 15 0	22 10 0	16 16 0		110 0 0
21 0 0	10 15 0	16 0 0	18 0 0		130 0 0
[illegible] 2 6	11 0 9	22 10 0	17 10 0		120 0 0
120 0 0	60 10 0	110 0 0	80 0 0		450 0 0
5 0 17	6 10 0	10 0 0	8 0 0		60 0 0
60 3 26	23 0 0	36 0 0	26 0 0		320 0 0
66 2 10	42 0 0	65 0 0	45 0 0		280 0 0
93 2 [illegible]	77 10 0	124 0 0	[illegible] 10 0		400 0 0
50 0 31	45 15 0	70 0 0	63 0 0		300 0 0
30 2 16	23 10 0	35 10 0	31 10 0		200 0 0
30 0 26	34 10 0	63 0 0	15 10 0		250 0 0
83 0 [illegible]	20 5 0	87 10 0	80 0 0		
55 0 11	42 10 0	63 10 5	34 0 0		
11 0 [illegible]	6 5 0	8 16 0	8 0 0		65 0 0
140 0 0	36 10 0	60 0 0	42 0 0		150 0 0
149 1 0	18 10 0	17 16 0	17 16 0		
[illegible] 0 21	15 0 0	21 6 0	14 0 0		60 0 0
13 1 [illegible]	6 5 0	10 0 0	7 10 0		40 0 0

Names of Assistant Commissioners by whom Cases were decided.	No.	Name of Tenant.	Name of Landlord.	Townland.
Assistant Commissioners—				
R. Reeves, Q.C. (Legal).	2158	Denis Collins, ...	Earl of Norbury, ...	Clooneskar, ...
C. O'Keeffe.	2159	Michael Molony (Pat),	Mrs. Anne Hall, ...	Knockanegabe, ...
E. McCausland.	2160	Patrick Curtin, ...	Francis Coffee, ...	Killeen, ...
H. G. Nash.	2161	Michael O'Loughlin, ...	do.	do. ...
F. G. Penn.	2162	Patrick Burke, ...	Major William M. Molony, ...	Gortcreganpage,
	2163	Myles Burke, ...	do.	Derrak, ...
	2164	James Canny, ...	do.	Derryulk, Upper,
	2165	John Foley, ...	do.	Loughane, ...
	2166	Thady Walsh, ...	do.	Kildeaf, Upper,
	2167	Michael Rogers, ...	Robert R. Kane and Wife, ...	Clanabee, ...
	2168	John McInerny, ...	do.	do. ...
	2169	Patrick McNamara, ...	do.	do. ...
	2170	Pat McGrath (Miles),	do.	do. ...
	2171	James O'Hara, ...	do.	do. ...
	2172	John McIlwaith, senior,	do.	do. ...
	2173	Denis Cantey,	do.	do. ...
	2174	Andrew McNamara, ...	do.	do. ...
	2175	Michael McNamara, ...	do.	do. ...
	2176	John Ryan, ...	Augustus Arthur, Committee of Thomas Arthur, a lunatic.	Cloonbrack, ...
	2177	Pat Crowe, ...	do.	Cloonagh,
	2178	John Crowe, ...	do.	do. ...
	2179	Pat Crowe, ...	do.	Cloonbrack, ...
	2180	John Smith, ...	do.	do. ...
	2181	Michael Brett, ...	do.	Carrowkeel Arthur,
	2182	Michael Cunning, ...	do.	Killeenan, ...
	2183	James Smith, ...	do.	Cloonbrack, ...
	2184	John Ryan, ...	do.	Lackareighmore,
	2185	John Speight, ...	do.	Cloonmurrymore,
	2186	James Bourke, ...	do.	Lackareaghbeg, ...
	2187	Patrick [illegible], ...	do.	Lahinch,
	2188	James Bourke, ...	do.	Knock-down, ...
	2189	Patrick Larkin, ...	do.	Lahinch, ...
	2190	Patrick O'Neill, ...	do.	Killinane, ...
	2191	Biddy Hayes, ...	do.	Killinane, Upper,
	2192	Bridget Smith, ...	do.	Lackareagh, ...

CLARE—*continued.*

Extent of Holding. Statute.	Poor Law Valuation.	Former Rent.	Judicial Rent.	Observations.	Value of Tenancy.
A. R. P.	£ s. d.	£ s. d.	£ s. d.		£ s. d.
18 2 29	4 18 0	8 10 6	1 18 0		
18 0 0	6 0 0	6 10 0	5 5 0		
18 1 23	9 15 0	13 12 10	11 0 0		100 0 0
14 3 4	8 10 0	12 0 0	10 5 0		90 0 0
31 0 0	17 0 0	20 5 0	15 10 0		115 0 0
78 1 32	9 15 0	16 0 0	12 0 0		130 0 0
180 0 0	9 15 0	12 10 0	11 10 0		120 0 0
[illegible]80 0 0	9 0 0	19 0 0	13 0 0		110 0 0
80 0 17	14 10 0	18 2 8	15 0 0		120 0 0
22 0 31	8 10 0	11 0 0	9 10 0		90 0 0
24 2 8	6 10 0	11 0 0	8 10 0		40 0 0
20 2 30	7 10 0	9 0 0	7 10 0		60 0 0
70 0 35	10 10 0	13 0 0	10 0 0		80 0 0
19 3 21	8 15 0	7 0 0	6 0 0		80 0 0
40 0 31	8 1 0	6 0 0	5 5 0		80 0 0
21 2 37	9 0 0	9 15 0	9 0 0		90 0 0
23 1 30	11 15 0	12 0 0	18 10 0		120 0 0
70 0 14	22 0 0	22 0 0	19 10 0		180 0 0
28 3 [illegible]	9 10 0	12 5 6	10 0 0		90 0 0
23 3 18	10 10 0	14 5 0	12 0 0		110 0 0
35 0 18	12 6 0	22 0 10	18 0 0		160 0 0
31 1 14	10 0 0	13 8 9	11 5 0		100 5 0
30 3 1	19 0 0	21 11 0	20 10 0		150 0 0
79 1 25	5 5 0	10 1 8	8 10 0		
33 3 35	14 5 0	16 15 8	12 10 0		120 0 0
70 1 7	24 0 0	29 11 2	25 0 0		180 0 0
18 1 37	11 0 0	13 9 7	11 15 0		100 0 0
18 0 10	5 5 0	9 16 7	9 0 0		60 0 0
[illegible]2 3 22	10 5 0	15 0 0	15 0 0		100 0 0
24 1 4	6 15 0	13 3 5	10 0 0		100 0 0
20 3 35	4 10 0	6 16 11	8 16 0		90 0 0
22 1 22	5 5 0	16 15 4	18 10 0		170 0 0
18 1 10	6 10 0	6 1 4	5 10 0		60 0 0
26 1 26	13 0 0	15 10 4	13 10 0		110 0 0
9 0 23	8 0 0	5 0 0	4 0 0		70 0 0

Names of Assistant Commissioners by whom Cases were decided.	No.	Name of Tenant.	Name of Landlord.	Townland.
Assistant Commissioners—				
R. Reeves Q.C. (Legal). G. O'Keeffe. E. McCausland. W. O. Nash. E. G. Pery.	2193	John Hogan, ...	Augustus Arthur, Committee of Thomas Arthur, a lunatic.	Kilbane, ...
	2194	John Hayes, ...	do.	do. ...
	2195	Patt Crowe, ...	do.	Lackareagh, ...
	2196	Cornelius Hayes, ...	do.	Lackareaghbeg,
	2197	Cornelius Crowe, ...	do.	Cloon, ...
	2198	Thomas Hayes, ...	do.	Cummeenduff, ...
	2199	Patt Rogers, ...	William Butler, a minor, and Mrs. Margaret Butler.	Maghera, ...
	2200	Thomas Rogers, ...	do.	do. ...
	2201	John Hayes, ...	do.	do. ...
	2202	John Rodgers, ...	do.	do. ...
	2203	John Hayes (James), ...	Augustus Arthur, Committee of Thomas Arthur, a lunatic	Lackareagh, ...
	2204	Thomas Cosgrove, ...	do.	Clooncurrybeg, ...
	2205	John Hayes, ...	do.	Magherareagh, ...
	2206	Patrick Moroney, ...	do.	Clooncurrybeg, ...
	2207	Patrick Walsh, ...	do.	Lackareagh & anor.,
	2208	James McNamara (Sheedy).	do.	Ballymulcashel, ...
	2209	James Moroney (John),	do.	Fermoylebeg, ...
	2210	Do.	do.	Springmount, ...
	2211	John O'Halloran, ...	do.	Leitrim, ...
	2212	John Hayes (James), ...	do.	Inishgrave, ...
	2213	James Moroney (John),	do.	Cappanaslish, ...
	2214	Daniel O'Connell, ...	do.	Dunmore, ...
	2215	Owen Moroney and anor.,	do.	Springmount, ...
	2216	James Hayes, ...	do.	Lackareagh, ...
	2217	Cornelius Hayes, ...	do.	Mahareagh, ...
	2218	Patt Carmody, Rep. of James Carmody.	do.	Kilbane, Upper,
	2219	William O'Donnell and another.	do.	Kilbane, ...
	2220	John Hayes (John), ...	do.	Mahareagh and another.
	2221	John Hayes (Gunner), ...	do.	do. ...
	2222	Patt O'Brien, ...	do.	do. ...
	2223	Owen Hayes, ...	do.	Cappanaslish, ...
	2224	Cornelius Moroney and another.	do.	Ballyguanabeg, ...
	2225	John Moroney, ...	do.	do. ...
	2226	Do.	do.	Cappanaslish, ...
	2227	Cornelius Moroney, ...	do.	Springmount, ...

CLARE—*continued.*

Extent of Holding. Statute.			Poor Law Valuation.			Former Rent.			Judicial Rent.			Observations.
A.	R.	P.	£	s.	d.	£	s.	d.	£	s.	d.	
20	3	7	8	0	0	11	9	11	10	0	0	
13	2	16	5	0	0	5	2	5	4	10	0	
27	0	[illegible]	7	0	0	10	0	0	6	5	0	
10	3	37	3	0	0	6	0	0	4	1	0	
25	2	21	9	15	0	14	0	0	12	15	0	
24	3	30	11	5	0	17	12	6	16	10	0	
6	0	0	4	5	0	6	0	0	2	11	0	
6	0	0	3	5	0	6	0	0	3	15	0	
4	3	0	1	0	0	3	3	0	1	12	0	
21	1	39	15	0	0	23	6	3	17	0	0	
23	0	21	14	15	0	15	14	3	15	10	0	By consent.
40	3	24	16	10	0	21	0	8	18	10	0	do.
34	0	3	15	0	0	17	14	10	16	10	0	do.
37	3	1	16	15	0	18	11	2	18	11	2	do.
19	2	24	13	0	0	15	12	0	14	0	0	do.
11	1	11	6	10	0	8	13	2	6	10	0	do.
9	3	35	4	0	0	4	5	6	3	15	0	do.
16	0	37	8	15	0	10	19	4	9	15	0	do.
34	1	6	10	0	0	13	17	6	12	10	0	do.
14	2	16	5	10	0	7	0	6	6	5	0	do.
27	3	4	4	15	0	6	3	8	5	10	0	do.
44	2	30	43	5	0	70	0	0	63	0	0	do.
24	1	10	8	0	0	13	11	2	13	10	0	do.
23	0	1	21	5	0	23	16	10	22	10	0	do.
27	1	22	15	10	0	17	17	1	15	10	0	do.
11	1	14	4	10	0	5	16	6½	5	5	0	do.
64	0	2	14	10	0	15	0	0	14	0	0	do.
[illegible]	[illegible]	[illegible]	20	0	0	17	0	8	16	10	0	do.
34	0	3	14	15	0	17	3	10	15	10	0	do.
34	0	8	15	0	0	17	9	7	16	10	0	do.
19	3	6	1	0	0	5	5	8	5	0	0	do.
27	1	0	15	10	0	21	8	11	19	0	0	do.
23	0	29	10	0	0	18	19	4	12	10	0	do.
27	1	20	5	15	0	6	14	5	4	0	0	do.
14	0	0	19	15	0	23	10	8	18	10	0	do.

COUNTY OF

Names of Assistant Commissioners by whom Cases were decided	No.	Name of Tenant.	Name of Landlord.	Townland.
Assistant Commissioners—				
R. Reeves, Q.C. (Legal). C. O'Keeffe. E. McIlhagga. H. G. Nash. E G. Prest.	2228	Mary Gleeson, ...	Augustus Arthur, Committee of Thomas Arthur, a lunatic.	Ballyrashane, ...
	2229	Patrick Walsh, ...	do.	Kildrehill, ...
	2230	Jasper Dillon, ...	Robert Dundas, ...	Glenbrick, ...
				Total, ...

COUNTY OF

Names of Assistant Commissioners by whom Cases were decided	No.	Name of Tenant.	Name of Landlord.	Townland.
Assistant Commissioners—	2576	William Bowler, ...	Miss Frederica H. Bunbury,	Ballykeary, ...
E. G. MacDevitt (Legal). T. Walpole. F. Massey. P. G. Griffith. F. M. Garrick.	2577	Thomas Kirby, ...	do.	Ballykeary and Haggars, ...
	2578	Catherine Burke, ...	do.	Ballykeary, ...
	2579	John Gorman, ...	do.	do.
	2580	James Riordan, ...	do.	do. ...
	2581	James Harrington, ...	Patrick McCarthy, ...	Reavoleen, ...
	2582	John Daly, ...	do.	do. ...
	2583	Jeremiah Driscoll, ...	Henry B. Beamish, ...	Dunmore, ...
	2584	Michael Mullane, ...	W. H. Penrose, ...	Laughane, East,
	2585	Thomas Shea, ...	James S. Hunt, ...	Garrandonoghmore,
	2586	Catherine Anderson, ...	do.	Garth, ...
	2587	Julia Donovan. ...	Rev. James Freke and another,	Unterbeg.
	2588	Michael Sweeny, ...	do.	Castletadane, ...
	2589	Mrs. Mary Donovan, ...	Miss Hungerford and others,	Derreeven, ...
	2590	Michael Whelton, ...	do.	do. ...
	2591	Daniel Connor, ...	William J. Glasgow, ...	Rathmacown, ...
	2592	John Murphy, ...	do.	do. ...
	2593	Michael McNamara, ...	do.	do. ...
	2594	William Murphy, ...	do.	do. ...
	2595	Daniel Coughlan, ...	William S. Limerick and anr.,	Clashmarville, ...
	2596	John Hill and Michael Carbery,	Randal T. Webb, ...	Commons, ...
	2597	Patrick Connolly, ...	Henry Trench, ...	Derrintaggart, ...

CORK.

25	1	10	[illegible]	0	0	35	17	8	37	0	0
[illegible]	3	11	123	10	0	164	10	0	150	0	0
29	3	7	31	0	0	54	16	8	80	0	0
20	0	23	20	5	0	37	10	10	23	10	0
15	0	20	18	0	0	28	0	0	23	10	0
46	2	0	8	5	0	17	10	0	14	0	0
19	1	26	6	12	0	8	10	6	9	10	6
6	0	15	4	0	0	7	19	1	8	10	0
75	0	21	55	0	0	63	12	0	60	0	0
68	0	0	20	5	0	[illegible]	0	0	24	0	0
31	2	0	14	15	0	23	10	0	19	0	0
33	3	6	12	5	0	18	0	0	16	0	0
34	0	5	17	10	0	28	0	0	21	0	0
17	0	11	13	10	0	31	0	0	17	0	0
16	0	0	11	5	0	16	10	0	19	10	0
5	0	27	5	10	0	8	4	0	7	0	0
5	0	0	3	8	0	5	0	0	4	0	0
[illegible]	0	31	18	0	0	21	10	0	37	0	0
11	0	23	8	10	0	13	16	11	19	0	0
48	0	31	23	10	0	33	0	0	30	0	0
84	0	0	72	0	0	130	0	0	110	0	0
45	5	20	8	15	0	18	16	3	10	0	0
28	1	19	6	5	0	8	13	4	7	0	0
68	3	10	13	10	0	35	0	0	80	0	0
85	0	0	18	10	0	38	0	0	28	0	0
39	8	0	6	0	0	11	10	0	10	0	0
20	1	0	4	0	0	7	8	8	6	0	0
64	3	83	81	0	0	48	13	6	40	0	0

Assistant Commissioners—

R. O. MacDermott (Legal),
T. Walpole,
P. Mahony,
F. O. Griffin,
F. M. Carroll.

2604	Maurice Brown, ...	William H. Townsend, ...	Clonakilty, North,
2605	Richard W. Long, ...	Rev. John Lamb, ...	Castletown and Paddock
2606	Michael Driscoll, ...	Mrs. Margaret Fitzpatrick, ...	Kilbrogan, ...
2607	Patrick Burke, ...	Herbert B. O'Sullivan, ...	Ballymakeera, ...
2608	James Quill, ...	Sir George Colthurst, Bart., ...	[illegible], ...
2609	John Healy, ...	Robert H. S. White, ...	Farranfield, ...
2610	Florence Driscoll, ...	Richard Beamish, ...	Lahanaght, ...
2611	James Donovan, ...	do	Kilmacabea, ...
2612	Catherine Coughlan, ...	Robert Long, ...	Cloher, ...
2613	Patrick Sullivan, ...	Earl of Bantry, ...	[illegible], ...
2614	Thomas Kingston, ...	Adam Newman, ...	Clohane, ...
2615	Simon Lewis, ...	Daniel McSwiney, ...	Shanagarry, West,
2616	Timothy Sullivan, ...	John A. Jagoe, ...	Reenavanagh Big, ...
2617	Robert Swanton, ...	Robert Swanton, ...	—
2618	Jeremiah Mahony, ...	do.	—
2619	John Carey, ...	John Morris, ...	Gurteenaduige, ...
2620	John McCarthy, ...	William Wolfe, ...	Cashel, ...
2621	Daniel Brien & another,	Mrs Power, ...	Curraun, ...
2622	Timothy Brien, ...	Captain Beamish, ...	Coolmacee, ...
2623	Jeremiah Sullivan, ...	John H. H. de Burgh, ...	Kilfinnan, ...
2624	Peter Hennessy, ...	James P. Welply, ...	Cahergal, ...
2625	Timothy Crowley, ...	Joseph Whitehorne, ...	Kilmalight, ...
2626	John Brien, ...	Wm. R. F. Barry and others, minors, by F. Barry, their guardian	Garryowen, ...
2627	Francis Lewis, ...	Mrs. Lucinda Hull, ...	Lowertown, ...
2628	John Keohane, ...	John H. H. de Burgh, ...	Kilmona, ...
2629	Michael Donovan, ...	George Long and another, ...	Loughlintown, ...
2630	Peter Dineen, ...	Samuel Hawkes, ...	Maulbrack, ...
2631	James Keohane, ...	William R. Beattie, ...	[illegible], ...
2632	Francis Hayes, ...	Mathew O'Hea and others, ...	Ahagilla, ...
2633	Michael Murphy, ...	James Wheeler, ...	Ballinroughter, ...
2634	Do.	do.	do. ...
2635	William Perrott, ...	The Misses Harris, Reps. of George C. Harris	Ballinglanna, ...
2636	Joseph Hayes, ...	Mrs. Ellen Wright, ...	Lower Tureen, ...
2637	John Bennett, ...	A. H. S. Barry, ...	Durrus, ...
2638	Michael Scully, ...	Richard Wilmot and others,	Dunowen, ...

CORK—*continued.*

Extent of Holding Statute.	Poor Law Valuation.	Former Rent.	Judicial Rent.	Observations.	Value of Tenancy.
A. R. P.	£ s. d.	£ s. d.	£ s. d.		£ s. d.
18 0 0	4 0 0	5 12 0	5 13 0		
[illegible] 0 0	67 10 0	125 0 0	105 0 0		
34 0 11	18 0 0	30 0 0	18 0 0		
50 1 12	11 0 0	22 15 0	20 0 0		
75 2 7	7 0 0	14 5 0	12 0 0		
11 2 23	7 5 0	10 0 0	8 0 0		
25 0 0	9 2 0	26 0 0	20 0 0		
20 0 0	11 0 0	16 0 0	16 0 0		
33 [illegible] 4	18 0 0	22 0 0	17 0 0		
[illegible] 2 15	18 10 0	11 0 0	11 0 0		
44 3 30	13 10 0	20 0 0	17 0 0		
13 0 24	8 0 0	11 0 0	7 10 0		
16 0 36	3 5 0	7 0 0	5 10 0		
35 0 0	9 15 0	19 0 0	17 0 0		
15 3 11	6 15 0	16 0 0	13 0 0		
31 3 23	9 18 0	16 10 0	14 0 0		
4 0 0	1 13 0	4 0 0	3 0 0		
29 2 12	11 19 0	25 0 0	18 10 0		
15 0 0	2 16 0	5 0 0	5 10 0		
36 2 4	37 0 0	60 0 0	53 0 0		
25 0 0	15 15 0	26 0 0	21 0 0		
19 3 1	10 18 0	20 0 0	18 0 0		
13 0 0	6 5 0	14 0 0	11 0 0		
88 1 3	13 10 0	34 14 8	28 10 0		
60 0 0	20 5 0	30 0 0	28 0 0		
80 0 0	9 13 0	34 0 0	18 10 0	By consent.	
67 0 0	38 15 0	65 0 0	50 0 0		
14 3 20	13 10 0	20 11 8	18 10 0		
56 0 0	23 10 0	31 13 8	31 18 3		
4 2 0	2 10 0	3 11 0	3 11 0		
6 2 18	6 10 0	8 3 3	6 10 0		
80 3 15	19 18 0	33 0 0	25 0 0		
80 1 13	24 0 0	45 10 0	39 0 0	Provision has been made in this case as regards a labourer.	
356 1 30	176 0 0	260 0 0	215 0 0	Rent changed in 1865 from - - - £300 0 0	
34 0 0	31 5 0	62 0 0	39 0 0	1876 £84 0 0	

COUNTY OF

Names of Assistant Commissioners by whom Cases were decided.	No.	Name of Tenant.	Name of Landlord.	Townland.
Assistant Commissioners—				
E. O. MacDevitt (Legal). T. Waller. F. Massey. P. O. Griffin. F. M. Gardner.	2639	Edward Finn, ...	George Ronaldson, ...	Pallas,
	2640	James Calnane, ...	Henry O'Hea and others, ...	Carrakeale,
	2641	Michael Driscoll, ...	do.	Carline,
	2642	James Donovan, ...	William Shaw, M.P. ...	Cloonafree,
	2643	Denis Daly and another,	Anne O'Sullivan and others, ...	Inchanoska,
	2644	Cornelius Reardan, ...	Herbert O'Sullivan, ...	Farranhenry,
	2645	Edmund Sweeny, ...	Michael A. H. Becher, ...	Inchincurky,
	2646	Owen Hayes, ...	William Thornton, ...	Edencurra,
	2647	Honora Regan, ...	R. W. Chenevix, ...	Lisgoolda,
	2648	William Perrott, ...	W. F. Bence Jones, ...	Mountain,
	2649	John Sullivan, ...	Pascoe F. French, ...	Lisladeen,
	2650	Timothy McCarthy, ...	W. H. Dobson, ...	Ballyvaloon,
	2651	Edmond Fitzgerald, ...	do.	do.
	2652	Thomas and M. Forrest,	Sir George Colthurst, Bart. ...	Garrane,
	2653	Honora Barrett, ...	John W. Spread, ...	Loughane,
	2654	John Donohy, ...	Thomas W. Browning, ...	Ballinaspig Beg,
	2655	Jeremiah Cronin, ...	W. H. Pearson, ...	Loughane, ...
	2656	Ellen Buckley, ...	Thomas W. Browning, ...	Bishopstown,
	2657	Nicholas Fitzgerald, ...	George S. Nason, ...	Rosevear,
	2658	Jeremiah Kidney, ...	Daniel Humphreys, ...	Onganabe,
	2659	Patrick Kearney, ...	Earl of Shannon, ...	Ballyrussell,
	2660	Timothy Ring, ...	Henry P. Garde, ...	Kilrush,
	2661	Edward French, ...	N. E. Orpen and others, Executors of P. Gould.	Dean Rock,
	2662	Timothy Halliban, ...	Michael A. H. Becher, ...	Inchinerack,
	2663	Patrick Donoghue, ...	Earl of Bandon, ...	Breaked,
	2664	William Murphy, ...	do.	Ardcahig,
	2665	Florence McCarthy, ...	do.	Benlad,
	2666	John Buttimer, junior, ...	do.	Raharoe,
	2667	Abraham Buttimer, ...	do.	Derryvreen,
	2668	Patrick Keohane, ...	Rev. James Fitche & another, Trustees of Lord Carbery.	Mual,
	2669	John T. Sullivan, ...	Earl of Bandon, ...	—
	2670	John Shea, ...	Sir H. W. Becher, Bart., ...	Glandarta,
	2671	Patrick Connolly, ...	do.	Garrane,
	2672	James Cronin, ...	Earl of Kenmare, ...	Lahaghdrum,
	2673	John Duggan, ...	James H. Swanton, ...	Cappaghmore,

[illegible] Statute			Poor Law Valuation.			Present Rent.			Judicial Rent.			Observations.				Value of Tenancy.		
A.	R.	P.	£	s.	d.	£	s.	d.	£	s.	d.		£	s.	d.	£	s.	d.
9	0	0	4	15	0	11	0	0	9	0	0	Rent changed in 1856 from . . .	8	0	0			
60	3	0	21	5	0	31	10	0	31	10	0							
33	0	13	16	5	0	25	0	7	23	0	0							
43	3	0	31	15	0	30	14	4	30	11	4							
91	3	28	22	5	0	28	0	0	23	0	0							
42	2	30	11	15	0	17	0	0	13	10	0							
44	0	0	21	15	0	33	0	0	30	0	0							
30	0	38	15	15	0	21	13	8	15	15	0							
72	0	0	42	10	0	36	0	0	45	0	0	By [illegible].						
21	2	0	11	5	0	28	10	5	16	10	0	do.						
213	0	0	36	6	0	106	0	0	102	0	0							
78	1	18	28	10	0	44	0	0	33	15	0							
104	0	0	30	15	0	40	0	0	33	0	0							
155	0	0	114	10	0	108	12	0	103	12	0							
4	3	0	8	16	0	6	0	0	1	8	0	Rent changed in 1857 from . . .	3	0	0			
96	2	12	204	0	0	294	0	0	268	10	0							
40	0	16	42	0	0	63	1	6	46	0	0							
34	2	14	67	0	0	84	13	0	84	15	0							
53	2	3	14	15	0	22	0	0	19	0	0							
2	2	16	4	0	0	5	0	0	5	0	0							
16	3	37	17	0	0	22	0	0	18	10	0							
67	1	25	52	0	0	46	10	0	42	0	0							
4	0	0	17	15	0	18	0	0	16	0	0							
31	3	9	9	5	0	10	0	0	8	8	0	By [illegible].						
74	0	0	25	5	0	34	19	6	30	0	0							
110	0	0	70	10	0	87	0	0	67	0	0							
39	0	0	22	0	0	14	6	0	14	0	0							
36	1	20	16	8	0	21	13	4	21	13	4							
37	0	0	36	5	0	41	16	10	41	16	10							
5	0	0	2	5	0	6	0	0	5	0	0							
10	0	0	26	15	0	35	18	8	30	10	0							
160	0	0	18	10	0	79	18	5	79	12	6							
60	2	0	5	0	0	16	0	0	15	0	0							
47	0	1	15	13	0	20	0	0	15	0	0							
5	1	16	2	0	0	2	15	0	2	15	0							

Names of Assistant Commissioners by whom Cases were decided.	No.	Name of Tenant.	Name of Landlord.	Townland.
Assistant Commissioners—				
E. G. MacDevitt (Legal). T. Walpole. P. Mahony. P. G. Griffith. F. M. Carroll.	2674	Denis McCarthy,	Thomas Donovan,	Knocknagree,
	2675	Cornelius Ahern,	Susanna Stawell, Committee of George Stawell, a lunatic.	Liscahane,
	2676	John Donovan,	do.	Roskill,
	2677	James Long,	Misses McCarthy & ors., Reps. of McCarthy Downing.	Derreeragh,
	2678	John Walsh,	do.	do.
	2679	Cornelius Harrington,	Mrs. S. M. Taylor,	Gortnascreeny,
	2680	Daniel McSweeny,	do.	do.
	2681	Ellen Mahony,	William Clarke,	Lyre,
	2682	Timothy Donoghue,	do.	do.
	2683	Ellen Cronin, Committee of Con Cronin.	do.	do.
	2684	John Barry,	do.	Templemichael,
	2685	Michael Scanlon,	A. H. S. Barry,	Barnafishane,
	2686	Thomas Scanlon,	do.	do.
	2687	John Regan,	do.	Barnahone,
	2688	Michael Regan,	do.	do.
	2689	Daniel T. Kelleher,	Robert N. F. Uniacke,	Kilcanway,
	2690	Patrick Hegarty,	do.	Castletown and ...
	2691	William Kelleher,	do.	Kilcanway.
	2692	Michael Kelly,	Earl of Bantry,	Cronin, West.
	2693	Timothy Kelly,	do.	do.
	2694	Bartholomew Reilly,	do.	Ardgroom (Inward).
	2695	John Lynch,	do.	do.
	2696	Jeremiah Shea,	do.	do.
	2697	Michael Sheehan,	do.	Canfie Ardgroom,
	2698	Jeremiah Reilly,	do.	Ardgroom (Inward).
	2699	Edward Sullivan,	do.	Ardgroom,
	2700	Michael Crowley,	do.	Kanuckeen,
	2701	John Sheehan,	do.	Canfie Ardgroom,
	2702	Ellen Crowley, Rep. of Jeremiah Crowley.	do.	Teraliffan,
	2703	Richard Dwyer,	do.	Tooreennamona, East,
	2704	John Dwyer,	do.	do.
	2705	Jeremiah Regan,	do.	do.
	2706	Rep. of Julia Cronin,	do.	Coulagh,
	2707	William Kennedy,	Robert Swanton,	Toorard,
	2708	Jeremiah Keohane,	Earl of Kenmare,	Maughin,

CORK—*continued.*

Extent of Holding (Statute).	Poor Law Valuation.	Former Rent.	Judicial Rent.	Observations.	Value of Tenancy.
A. R. P.	£ s. d.	£ s. d.	£ s. d.		£ s. d.
25 2 0	19 5 0	28 0 0	22 0 0		
34 0 18	12 5 0	18 17 9	19 10 0	By consent.	
40 0 0	19 0 0	24 14 11	25 10 0	do.	
86 0 31	15 10 0	31 0 0	18 0 0		
65 2 25	[illegible] 10 0	51 0 0	45 0 0		
22 0 0	8 10 0	15 15 0	13 10 0		
30 2 0	10 10 0	20 0 0	15 0 0		
54 0 0	11 15 0	26 0 0	20 0 0		
58 0 0	21 16 0	37 10 0	30 0 0		
51 0 15	24 5 0	39 0 0	34 0 0		
37 2 20	10 5 0	16 0 0	16 0 0	Rent changed in 1863 from £11 0 0	
97 0 0	51 5 0	64 16 0	40 0 0		
101 2 0	76 5 0	69 0 3	63 0 3		
96 3 0	36 0 0	44 16 0	41 11 0		
131 0 30	64 0 0	102 16 0	85 0 0		
81 1 33	[illegible] 5 0	35 0 0	32 0 0		
84 0 20	46 10 0	65 0 0	55 0 0		
61 0 0	30 5 0	32 0 0	30 0 0		
16 3 16	5 0 0	8 0 0	6 5 0	By consent.	
18 3 16	5 0 0	8 0 0	6 5 0	do.	
34 0 30	8 15 0	11 10 0	8 15 0	do.	
9 3 20	4 0 0	5 15 0	5 0 0	do.	
22 0 20	5 15 0	7 0 0	6 0 0	do.	
6 0 0	1 10 0	7 10 0	6 10 0		
11 3 10	8 0 0	13 0 0	8 0 0		
80 1 33	3 0 0	4 0 0	4 15 0		
70 0 0	18 10 0	18 18 0	14 0 0		
7 2 20	4 0 0	6 5 0	5 5 0		
25 0 0	7 0 0	9 10 0	7 15 0		
61 0 1	18 10 0	27 0 0	15 0 0		
61 0 1	13 5 0	17 0 0	16 0 0		
56 1 20	11 15 0	17 0 0	14 0 0		
73 2 5	23 5 0	50 18 0	44 0 0		
114 0 0	55 0 0	63 0 0	45 0 0	Provision as regards labourer has been made in this case.	
135 2 18	4 15 0	4 0 0	9 0 0		

2716	Jas and Philip Murphy,	Gustavus W. Herbert,
2717	Margaret Murphy, ...	do. ...
2718	Michl. Sullivan (Bowrig),	do. ..
2719	Do.	do. ...
2720	Timothy Leary, ...	do. ...
2721	Denis D. Sheehan, jun.,	do. ...
2722	Robert Spencer, ...	Lord C. P. P. Clinton.
2723	John Neile, ...	do. ...
2724	Batt Barry, ...	do. ...
2725	Mortimer Sullivan, ...	do. ...
2726	Patrick Barry, ...	do. ...
2727	Daniel Barry, ...	do. ...
2728	John T. Harrington, ...	do. ...
2729	Johanna Sullivan, ...	do. ...
2730	Catherine McGrath, ...	do. ...
2731	Michael Sheehan, ...	do. ...
2732	John Lowney, ..	do. ...
2733	Timothy O'Sullivan, ...	do. ...
2734	Patrick Shea, ...	do. ...
2735	John Fitzgerald, ...	do. ...
2736	James Cogan and Thomas Kirby, Exors. of John Cogan, deceased.	Robert St. Leger Atkins,
2737	William Cogan, ...	do. ...
2738	William Kenny, ...	William H. Dutton,
2739	Hannah Owens, ...	do. ...
2740	Thomas Barry, ...	James Hamilton, ...

CORK—*continued.*

Extent of Holding Statute	Poor Law Valuation	Former Rent	Judicial Rent	Observations	Value of Tenancy
A. R. P.	£ s. d.	£ s. d.	£ s. d.		£ s. d.
275 0 22	11 0 6	6 0 0	18 0 0		
80 2 17	67 18 0	120 0 0	110 0 0		
49 3 16	14 10 0	32 0 0	21 0 0	By consent.	
31 2 19	5 0 0	10 0 0	7 10 0		
78 0 3	4 15 0	8 10 0	7 0 0		70 0 0
111 3 15	53 5 0	45 2 8	67 0 0		
110 2 34	83 15 0	116 14 4	100 0 0		
164 1 30	90 18 0	64 0 0	46 0 0		
58 0 0	23 10 0	34 0 0	30 0 0		
36 0 0	12 5 0	38 0 0	16 0 0		
22 0 0	9 10 0	18 0 0	12 0 0		
17 0 0	6 5 0	18 0 0	11 0 0	Rent changed in 1875 from . . . £15 4 0 to . . . do. 21 18 0	
38 1 0	18 10 0	34 0 0	21 10 0		
8 0 4	4 15 0	8 3 0	6 10 0		
27 0 0	5 5 0	8 0 0	8 0 0		
16 0 8	3 8 0	7 5 0	8 0 0		
21 0 30	3 14 0	6 8 0	5 0 0		
6 0 28	4 4 1	7 5 0	4 10 0		
15 0 15	3 9 0	7 5 0	5 0 0		
16 1 0	7 5 0	12 12 0	6 0 0		
18 3 31	5 3 0	7 14 0	6 0 0		
6 3 14	4 5 0	7 4 0	1 0 0		
21 3 6	6 0 0	11 6 0	9 15 0		
30 3 33	6 5 0	11 10 0	10 0 0		
10 0 16	3 15 0	4 10 0	4 10 0		
8 3 26	6 9 1	7 5 1	5 0 0		
6 1 37	1 7 0	3 13 6	3 0 0		
71 0 39	106 10 0	80 10 0	108 10 0		
75 3 34	13 0 0	60 0 0	40 0 0		
147 0 0	30 15 0	36 0 0	34 15 0		
49 3 30	16 15 0	25 0 0	23 7 0		
116 1 3	57 0 0	65 0 0	60 0 0		
64 0 0	18 0 0	20 16 0	16 0 0		
100 0 0	53 15 0	88 0 0	80 0 0		
77 0 0	17 0 0	23 0 0	21 0 0		

COUNTY OF

Names of Assistant Commissioners by whom Cases were decided.	No.	Name of Tenant.	Name of Landlord.	Townland.
Assistant Commissioners—				
E. O. MacDevitt (Legal). T. Waldron. P. Mahony. P. O. Griffin. P. M. Cahill.	2744	John J. Sheehy, ...	P. H. Spragge, ...	Ballinard, ...
	2745	Patrick Sheehy, ...	do. ...	do. ...
	2746	John Edward Sheehy, ...	do. ...	do. ...
	2747	Johnson Sweeney, ...	Rev. James Freke and Hon. William Evans Freke.	[illegible], W[illegible]
	2748	Daniel Sweeney, ...	do. ...	do. ...
	2749	John Sheehan, ...	do. ...	do. ...
	2750	Dennis Minihane, ...	do. ...	Ballym[illegible], E[illegible]
	2751	Cornelius Collins, ...	do. ...	do.
	2752	John Fitzgerald, ...	do. ...	Ballym[illegible] ...
	2753	Florence Driscoll, ...	do. ...	Rath[illegible], ...
	2754	Patrick Driscoll, ...	do. ...	do.
	2755	John Baker, ...	do. ...	do. ...
	2756	Daniel Cadogan, ...	do. ...	do.
	2757	Patrick Collins, ...	do. ...	do. ...
	2758	Daniel Driscoll, ...	do. ...	do. ...
	2759	John Donovan, ...	do. ...	[illegible], ...
	2760	Daniel Bohane, ...	do. ...	do. ...
	2761	Mary Minihane (widow),	do. ...	do.
	2762	John McCarthy, ...	do. ...	Rath, ...
	2763	Samuel Taylor, ...	do. ...	Ballym[illegible], ...
	2764	Patrick Regan, ...	George and Richard Long,	Leightown, ...
	2765	Daniel McCarthy, ...	do. ...	do. ...
	2766	Daniel Corbett, ...	Mrs. M. O'Callaghan, ...	Lahan,
	2767	James Ryan, ...	John B. Gough, ...	Ballyandrew,
	2768	Michael Nyhan, ...	John Gilman and James Raymond.	Carragh[illegible],
	2769	Hannah Driscoll, ...	Woulfe v. Gilman (in Chancery).	Carragh[illegible]
				Total, ...

CORK—*continued.*

Extent of Holding (Statute).	Poor Law Valuation.	Former Rent.	Judicial Rent.	Observations.	Value of Tenancy.
A. R. P.	£ s. d.	£ s. d.	£ s. d.	£ s. d.	£ s. d.
10 1 15	11 15 0	18 10 0	15 0 0		
12 0 20	6 5 0	10 0 0	8 0 0		
35 1 8	18 10 0	20 10 0	17 0 0		
65 2 31	11 15 0	18 0 0	15 10 0		
29 0 35	7 10 0	10 10 0	10 0 0		
21 3 20	9 0 0	10 10 0	10 0 0		
16 3 20	6 15 0	8 10 0	6 5 0		
22 2 0	7 15 0	10 10 0	10 10 0		
23 3 0	4 10 0	6 0 0	5 15 0		
7 3 8	1 15 0	4 10 0	3 0 0		
7 2 13	3 15 0	6 12 0	5 0 0		
31 1 19	16 15 0	25 16 0	22 0 0		
11 0 21	5 10 0	6 10 0	6 0 0		
25 0 36	10 0 0	14 18 0	13 0 0		
10 3 5	2 5 0	3 14 0	3 0 0		
14 2 8	6 10 0	10 5 0	7 15 0		
25 0 4	5 0 0	10 0 0	10 0 0		
18 2 10	6 0 0	9 0 0	8 0 0		
4 0 16	2 5 0	8 6 0	7 0 0		
0 1 10	1 15 0	3 10 0	2 5 0		
15 0 0	7 10 0	17 0 0	11 15 0	By consent.	
7 0 0	3 5 0	7 10 0	4 10 0	do.	
16 1 30	6 15 0	7 10 0	7 0 0	do.	
18 0 0	11 10 0	16 16 10	15 0 0	do.	
35 0 0	17 5 0	24 0 0	20 0 0	do	
38 0 7	17 15 0	30 0 0	23 10 0	do.	

Names of Assistant Commissioners by whom Cases were decided.	No.	Name of Tenant.	Name of Landlord.	Townland.
Assistant Commissioners—				
J. G. MacCarthy (Legal).	1843	Patrick Kennedy, ...	George Sandes, ...	[illegible],
J. [illegible].	1844	William Walsh, ...	Edward Nash, ...	[illegible], ...
J. J. O'Shaughnessy.	1845	James Barry, ...	[illegible] C. [illegible], ...	Ballyegan,
P. Newton.	1846	William Hannigan, ...	Edward G. Stokes, ...	[illegible], ...
G. [illegible].	1847	James Quinlan, ...	John Sandes, ...	[illegible], ...
	1848	Michael Crowley, ...	Patrick Connor, ...	[illegible], ...
	1849	Patrick Barrett, ...	Stephen Huggard, ...	Ardagh, ...
	1850	John Hayes, ...	Justice D. [illegible], ...	[illegible], ...
	1851	Laurence White, ...	John Bateman, a lunatic, by F. R. Bateman, his Committee.	[illegible] and [illegible],
	1852	Mary Mulvihill, ...	Colonel James Crosbie,	[illegible], ...
	1853	John Cox, ...	do.	[illegible], ...
	1854	Thomas Moloney, ...	Deborah Fitzmaurice, ...	[illegible],
	1855	Thomas Corridan, ...	do.	do. ...
	1856	Johanna Collins, ...	Rev. George Brown, ...	[illegible], ...
	1857	John Walsh, ...	Georgina M. H. Julian, ...	[illegible], ...
	1858	Timothy Horgan, ...	do.	[illegible].
	1859	Mary O'Connor, ...	Thomas W. Sandes, ...	[illegible],
	1860	Michael McEnery, ...	do.	[illegible], ...
	1861	Jeremiah Connor, ...	Lord Ormathwaite, ...	[illegible], ...
	1862	Mary Connor, Admix. of Cornelius Connor.	do.	[illegible], ...
	1863	Jeremiah Reardon, ...	do	Tullamore, ...
	1864	Robert Parker and another, Admors. of John McCarthy	John C. D. Hurly, a minor, by Lucy A. Thompson.	[illegible], ...
	1865	Mary Connell, Admix. of Michael Connell.	John C. D. Hurly, ...	[illegible],
	1866	David Nolan, ...	do.	[illegible], ...
	1867	Edmond Carey, ...	do.	do. ...
	1868	[illegible] Sheehy, ...	do.	do. ...
	1869	Daniel Moloney, ...	do.	[illegible], ...
	1870	John Moloney, ...	do.	do. ...
	1871	John Nolan and another,	do.	[illegible], ...
	1872	Margaret Molyneux, Admix. of John Molyneux.	do.	do. ...
	1873	John [illegible], ...	Jane Kennedy, ...	[illegible], ...
	1874	Peter Connor, ...	do	do ...
	1875	Timothy [illegible], ...	do.	do. ...
	1876	[illegible] Nolan, ...	do	do. ...

KERRY—*continued.*

Extent of Holding. Statute.	Poor Law Valuation.	Former Rent.	Judicial Rent.	Observations.	Value of Tenancy.
A. R. P.	£ s. d.	£ s. d.	£ s. d.	£ s. d.	£ s. d.
70 8 25	8 0 0	35 0 0	25 10 0		150 0 0
127 8 8	18 10 0	30 0 0	21 10 0	Rent changed in 1865 from . . 16 0 0	180 0 0
17 3 0	6 15 0	11 4 0	6 10 0	1858 6 4 0	55 0 0
77 1 18	33 5 0	60 4 6	50 0 0	Provision has been made in this case as regards a "labourer".	250 0 0
37 1 10	8 15 0	20 0 0	15 0 0		
0 3 8	—	2 10 0	1 10 0		
45 3 11	15 10 0	40 0 0	28 10 0		150 0 0
14 3 23	5 15 0	10 5 0	8 5 0		
41 3 10	8 5 0	14 0 0	11 0 0		170 0 0
33 3 10	17 0 0	27 12 0	20 0 0	£ s. d. Rent changed in 1878 from . . 25 0 0	160 0 0
47 3 11	18 0 0	37 18 0	28 0 0	do. 24 0 0	170 0 0
88 3 10	17 10 0	40 0 0	34 0 0	1871 30 8 7	280 0 0
40 0 8	30 5 0	45 0 0	36 15 0	1876 31 0 0	280 0 0
12 0 0	4 10 0	8 0 0	5 0 0	By consent.	
227 3 30	77 15 0	45 0 0	37 0 0		
274 1 23	14 0 0	30 0 0	24 0 0	Rent changed in 1880 from . . 23 0 0	
38 3 7	15 10 0	33 0 0	25 15 0	1869 28 0 0	200 0 0
—	58 10 0	104 0 0	80 15 0		500 0 0
81 0 0	23 10 0	37 0 0	32 15 0	1880 34 10 0	160 0 0
114 0 33	50 10 0	130 0 0	99 0 0	do. 58 0 0	450 0 0
74 0 20	33 10 0	56 0 0	44 0 0		
46 1 17	43 10 0	78 10 0	17 0 0		300 0 0
83 3 18	5 0 0	19 0 0	14 0 0	By consent.	
106 3 31	13 7 0	45 0 0	37 0 0		
87 2 0	8 12 5	35 0 0	18 10 0		
18 0 0	1 0 0	14 0 0	8 0 0		
—	7 0 0	23 10 0	15 5 0		
—	7 0 0	27 10 0	15 5 0		
40 0 35	9 5 0	23 0 0	16 5 0		
18 0 0	6 5 0	16 5 0	6 10 0		
4 3 33	—	3 17 6	2 10 0		
1 3 14	—	1 5 0	0 15 0		
1 3 24	—	1 8 6	1 4 0		
4 3 14	—	5 0 0	1 17 0		

COUNTY OF

Names of Assistant Commissioners by whom Cases were decided	No.	Name of Tenant.	Name of Landlord.	Townland.
Assistant Commissioners—				
J. G. MacCarthy (Legal). J. Harrington. J. J. O'Shaughnessy. P. Newton. G. Adamson.	1877	Edmund Scanlon, ...	Jane Kennedy, ...	Dromada,
	1878	Bridget Shanahan, ...	do.	do. ...
	1879	Timothy Enright, ...	do.	do. ...
	1880	Margaret Leigh, ...	do.	do. ...
	1881	Timothy Mahony, ...	Sophia P. Chambers, ...	Tarmons, East, ...
	1882	John O'Grady, ...	do.	Tarmons, West, ...
	1883	Edmund Brandon and another,	do.	do. ...
	1884	John Colbane, ...	do.	do.
	1885	Timothy Kennelly, ...	do.	do. ...
	1886	Jeremiah Mulvihill, ...	do.	do. ...
	1887	Johanna Flynn, ...	Samuel M. Hussey, ...	Kinsknowel and another.
	1888	Maurice Walsh, ...	do.	Aghaloy, East ...
	1889	Patrick O'Connell, ...	do.	do. ...
	1890	Patrick Dunnan, ...	Charles William Stoughton, ...	Glenderiva, ...
	1891	Stephen Dunnan, ...	do.	do. ...
	1892	John J. Dunnan, ...	do.	do. ...
	1893	Patrick Cavan, ...	do.	do. ...
	1894	John M. Dunnan, Admnr. of Marion Dunnan,	do.	do. ...
	1895	Timothy Driscoll,	do. ...	do. ...
	1896	Michael Halloran, ...	do.	do. ...
	1897	Pierce Creagh, ...	do.	Ballinaclogher, ...
	1898	Michael J. Conway, ...	do.	do. ...
	1899	James Conway, ...	do.	do.
	1900	Michael T. Conway, ...	do.	do. ...
	1901	Thomas Dowling, ...	do.	do. ...
	1902	John Sullivan, ...	Thomas A. Stoughton, ...	Knappogue & c.,
	1903	Timothy Fitzmaurice, ...	do.	Lough, ...
	1904	Daniel Tracy, ...	do.	Leaha, East, and another
	1905	John McEnery, ...	do.	Knappogue,
	1906	Patrick Conroy, ...	do.	Beaumore, ...
	1907	Bridget Conway, ...	do.	Lough, ...
	1908	Francis Griffin,	do. ...	Leaha, East, ...
	1909	Denis Ryle, ...	do.	Lough Marsh,
	1910	Cornelius McCarthy, ...	do.	Knappogue, ...
	1911	Thomas Callaghan, ...	do.	do. ...

KERRY—*continued.*

Extent of Holding. Statute.	Poor Law Valuation.	Former Rent.	Adjusted Rent.	Observations.		Value of Tenancy.
A. R. P.	£ s. d.	£ s. d.	£ s. d.		£ s. d.	£ s. d.
5 3 17	—	2 1 6	2 0 0			
4 3 10	—	3 18 9	1 2 0			
3 2 15	—	3 2 8	1 11 0			
1 2 35	—	1 1 5	0 16 0			
11 0 37	6 5 0	5 5 0	5 0 0			
11 0 4	6 5 0	5 13 0	5 15 0			
25 3 34	7 10 0	13 0 0	9 0 0			
16 1 6	5 10 0	10 0 0	8 0 0	Rent changed in 1858 from	8 18 6	
30 2 8	4 5 0	8 10 0	7 10 0			
18 3 34	8 10 0	6 15 0	5 0 0			
63 1 13	18 15 0	28 18 1	25 10 0			200 0 0
2 2 21	—	1 10 0	1 10 0	1876	0 12 0	15 0 0
20 1 0	4 5 0	5 5 0	6 0 0			30 0 0
19 2 10	3 0 0	7 10 0	6 10 0			60 0 0
18 0 35	4 10 0	6 10 0	6 0 0			60 0 0
13 1 14	3 15 0	5 0 0	5 0 0			50 0 0
1 2 25	1 10 0	3 15 0	3 0 0			30 0 0
70 3 14	33 5 0	39 0 0	35 10 0	1859	29 0 0	240 0 0
12 0 6	23 0 0	35 10 0	31 10 0			200 0 0
26 1 34	6 5 0	16 0 0	11 10 0	1875	11 0 0	100 0 0
58 1 21	17 15 0	33 7 0	29 0 0	1877	24 0 0	200 0 0
76 3 2	19 15 0	37 0 0	31 0 0	do.	31 1 6	180 0 0
60 1 29	31 10 0	64 15 0	56 0 0	do.	65 0 0	350 0 0
61 0 0	18 10 0	36 10 0	29 0 0	do.	73 0 0	300 0 0
53 3 23	18 10 0	34 0 0	27 10 0	do.	25 10 0	230 0 0

COUNTY OF

Names of Assistant Commissioners by whom Cases were decided	No.	Name of Tenant.	Name of Landlord.	Townland.
Assistant Commissioners—				
J. G. MacCarthy (Legal). J. Haughton. J. J. O'Shaughnessy. P. Newton. G. Adamson.	1912	John William O'Connor,	Thomas A. Stoughton, ...	[illegible] Court and another,
	1913	Charles Pickford, ...	do.	Knoppogue,
	1914	John Harrington, ...	do.	Rossmore, ...
	1915	John Costello, ...	do.	Knoppogue, ...
	1916	John Barrett, ...	Sir John T. B. Douglas, ...	[illegible] and another,
	1917	John Keane, ...	do.	[illegible], ...
	1918	William O'Donnell, ...	do.	Kilgarvan, ...
	1919	Catherine Lynch, ...	do.	do. ...
	1920	Daniel Madden, ...	do.	do. ...
	1921	Thomas Madden, ...	do.	do. ...
	1922	Maurice Murphy, ...	George P. G. Mahony, ...	[illegible],
	1923	John Kinsella, ...	do.	Glenrea, ...
	1924	John Francis, ...	Wilson Gunn, ...	[illegible], ...
				Total, ...

COUNTY OF

Names of Assistant Commissioners by whom Cases were decided	No.	Name of Tenant.	Name of Landlord.	Townland.
Assistant Commissioners—	1195	Michael Blackwell, ...	Wm. J. J. White and others, minors.	Drumbane, ...
T. D. Brabazon (Legal). J. Gardiner. T. Baldwin. W. C. Horsfall. William Evans.	1196	Ellen Meade, ...	Col. F. G. T. Gennaign and another.	Ballinacloher, ...
	1197	Michael Sheehy, Admor. of Henry Sheehy,	Goodrich T. Pasmole, ...	Rylane & others,
	1198	Thomas Fitzgerald, ...	Marchese Della Rovella, ...	Kinkyardrine, ...
	1199	James Hayes, ...	Walter M. O'Grady, ...	Cragbirlane, ...
	1200	Terence Deere, ...	do.	do. ...
	1201	Cornelius Hayes, ...	do.	do. ...
	1202	William Ryan, ...	do.	Graham, ...
	1203	Denis Murray, ...	Edward L. Griffin, ...	Castle Mungret,
	1204	John McKnight, ...	do.	do. ...
	1205	Richard Laffan, ...	Rev. Joseph Gabbett, ...	[illegible],

KERRY—*continued.*

Extent of Holding (statute).	Poor Law Valuation.	Former Rent.	Judicial Rent.	Observations.		Value of Tenancy.
A. R. P.	£ s. d.	£ s. d.	£ s. d.		£ s. d.	£ s. d.
71 3 30	55 15 0	70 0 0	70 0 0	Rent changed in 1870 from	64 0 0	550 0 0
19 1 8	6 15 0	14 0 0	11 10 0	1873	9 15 6	90 0 0
23 3 23	9 15 0	20 0 0	20 0 0	1875	15 0 0	100 0 0
83 2 10	16 5 0	24 0 0	16 10 0			180 0 0
264 0 23	51 10 0	65 18 0	71 0 0	By consent.		
93 0 0	23 0 0	44 0 0	64 0 0	do.		
90 1 32	11 5 0	32 0 0	15 10 0	do.		
52 3 6	10 0 0	27 0 0	16 0 0	do.		
41 2 17	12 10 0	26 0 0	19 0 0	do.		
58 3 1	10 0 0	22 0 0	18 0 0	do.		
69 2 30	21 15 0	60 0 0	45 0 0			225 0 0
76 1 16	39 10 0	65 0 0	48 10 0			250 0 0
91 3 35	38 15 0	75 0 0	40 0 0	Rent changed in 1871 from	50 0 0	500 0 0
1,030 1 29	1,191 10 6	2,118 8 4	1,011 15 6			

LIMERICK.

Extent of Holding (statute).	Poor Law Valuation.	Former Rent.	Judicial Rent.	Observations.	Value of Tenancy.
15 3 8	54 15 0	49 14 6	49 14 6		
135 2 37	81 10 0	65 0 0	87 0 0		
137 0 0	118 0 0	170 11 0	160 0 0		
18 0 35	18 10 0	37 5 0	23 0 0		
59 1 25	6 15 0	10 0 0	8 15 0	By consent.	
76 0 0	6 10 0	8 11 6	7 5 0	do.	
41 2 14	6 15 0	10 0 0	9 5 0	do.	
11 3 18	3 15 0	5 15 0	5 10 0	do.	
1 1 34	2 10 0	5 10 10	3 5 0	do.	
1 3 9	2 10 0	5 10 10	2 10 0	do.	
78 1 15	31 5 0	45 12 0	40 0 0	do.	
563 3 23	347 15 0	383 11 0	515 4 8		

COUNTY OF

Names of Assistant Commissioners by whom Cases were decided.	No.	Name of Tenant.	Name of Landlord.	Townland.
Assistant Commissioners— T. D. Reardon (Legal). J. Gordon. T. Baldwin. W. G. Horsfall. William Evans.	1616	John O'Neill, ...	Rev. H. L. Baker, ...	Mountshannon, ...
	1617	John Hanrahan, ...	Thomas J. Ryan, ...	Munnum, ...
	1618	James Hassett, ...	Robert R. Stannard, ...	Park, ...
	1619	Thomas Troy, ...	do.	do. ...
	1620	Hannah Shannon, ...	Henry Eustace, ...	Graiguenamanagh, ...
	1621	Patrick Cormack, ...	do.	do. ...
	1622	Ellen Ryan, ...	James W. Wellington, ...	Killinafinch, ...
	1623	Mary Haugh, ...	John P. Hare, ...	Killamoyne, ...
	1624	George M. Finch, ...	Sir Edmund A. Waller, Bart.,	Newport, ...
	1625	James Hogan, ...	Patrick Harty, ...	Ballyvenny, ...
	1626	James Cleary, ...	John Dugg, ...	Moneytown, ...
	1627	Joseph Ryan, Admor. of Ellen Ryan,	John S. Wolfe, ...	Ballymany, ...
	1628	James Ryan (Tom), ...	Frederick C. Henry, ...	Ballyvarlandmore,
	1629	John Coghlan, ...	Godfrey L. Taylor and others, Trustees of F. Hare,	Ballyhane, ...
	1630	Thomas Dundy, ...	Ernina Scully, ...	Mallough, ...
	1631	Patrick O'Brien, ...	Major Tanner, ...	Gortdrehall, ...
	1632	Mary Egan and others,	Elizabeth J. Guinness, ...	Affoley, ...
	1633	Edmond Gardiner, ...	do.	Toolantapple, ...
	1634	Michael O'Donnell, ...	Thomas O'Brien, ...	Ballyhanigan, ...
	1635	John Bussey, ...	Frederick Hamilton, ...	Castlewaller (Lot 3),
	1636	William O'Brien, ...	Frederick Hamilton & anor.,	do. ...
	1637	Michael Hogan, ...	Richard Gason, ...	Coolnaclogh, ...
	1638	Patrick Brien, ...	Daniel Maxwell, ...	Bober, ...
	1639	Cornelius Cleary, ...	Elizabeth Young and others,	Shesheraghkeale and another.
	1640	Patrick Hayes, ...	Cecil Leslie, ...	Millbrook, ...
	1641	Stephen Howard, ...	David Clarke, ...	Brook, ...
	1642	Margaret Cahalan, Admix. of Morgan Cahalan.	do.	Feigh, ...
	1643	Bridget Slevin, ...	do.	Shesheraghmore, ...
	1644	Patrick Gleeson, ...	William Tuthill and another.	Gortmore, ...
	1645	Jeremiah McMahon, ...	Robert de Ros Rose, ...	Cleanbaley, ...
	1646	Dennis Ryan, ...	do.	Killeen, ...
	1647	Mathew Ryan, ...	do.	Foxhall, ...
	1648	Michael Quinlan, ...	do.	Cleanbaley, ...
	1649	Margaret Coffey, ...	do.	Killeen, ...
	1650	Margaret Brien, ...	Miss Susannah Hamilton, ...	do. ...

TIPPERARY.

Extent of Holding. Statute.	Poor Law Valuation.	Former Rent.	Judicial Rent.	Observations.	Value of Tenancy.
a. r. p.	£ s. d.	£ s. d.	£ s. d.		£ s. d.
7 2 11	7 0 0	18 5 0	7 10 0	By consent.	
[illegible] 3 34	16 5 0	19 0 0	19 0 0		
[illegible] 1 [illegible]	16 0 0	24 0 0	18 10 0		
75 1 10	[illegible] 0 0	41 10 6	44 0 0		
7 2 34	6 0 0	8 17 0	8 0 0		
[illegible] 0 24	17 10 0	26 1 8	20 0 0		
13 3 15	6 0 0	9 6 0	8 0 0		
62 0 16	21 10 0	30 15 1	28 0 0		
71 1 16	20 15 0	29 15 0	24 0 0		
5 1 16	8 15 0	6 0 0	4 10 0		
4 3 26	4 15 0	6 0 0	5 5 0		
21 0 4	11 0 0	13 16 0	12 15 6		
14 2 0	6 10 0	13 0 0	10 0 0		
31 1 14	16 5 0	[illegible] 8 0	21 0 0		
61 2 6	45 0 0	59 18 6	48 0 0		
16 0 31	13 5 0	18 14 0	15 0 0		
71 1 2	33 0 0	45 10 6	34 0 0		
37 1 0	23 0 0	33 0 0	26 0 0		
18 1 23	18 16 0	16 14 3	13 0 0		
6 3 37	3 10 0	6 0 0	8 10 0	do.	
65 3 24	34 0 0	30 0 0	21 0 0		
[illegible] 1 37	67 0 0	31 10 6	[illegible] 0 0		
37 1 23	78 15 0	83 16 8	35 16 6		
19 1 30	55 15 0	55 10 0	45 0 0		
[illegible] 1 24	91 0 0	[illegible] 0 0	71 0 0		
18 2 20	8 10 0	10 10 0	8 10 0		
15 1 16	16 0 0	18 15 0	17 10 0		
35 1 23	[illegible] 5 0	40 0 0	40 0 0		
67 2 0	17 0 0	25 16 11	20 10 0		
31 2 37	20 13 0	30 0 0	24 0 0		
80 3 33	46 10 0	81 0 0	72 0 0		
60 0 0	56 5 0	68 0 0	57 0 0		
13 0 0	8 10 0	18 9 11	18 10 0		
204 3 26	164 5 0	276 0 0	200 0 0		
25 2 30	14 0 0	18 9 6	15 15 0		

Names of Assistant Commissioners by whom Cases were decided.	No.	Name of Tenant.	Name of Landlord.	Townland.
Assistant Commissioners—				
T. D. Reardon (Legal).	1651	Patrick Hayes, ...	Miss Susannah Hamilton, ...	Killeen, ...
J. Gorman.	1652	Bridget Hayes, ...	do.	do. ...
T. Baldwin.	1653	Patrick Hartigan, ...	do.	Lessamore, ...
W. C. Horsfall.	1654	John Delaney, ...	Hon. Otway Toler, ...	Lisgarre, ...
William Evans.	1655	David Burke, ...	do.	Killeedangan, ...
	1656	Richard Galway, ...	do.	Keigh, ...
	1657	Do.	do.	Keigh (part of),
	1658	John Dwyer, ...	Mrs. Eliza Studdert, ...	Prospect, West,
	1659	Thomas Fitzgerald, ...	do.	Lodge, ...
	1660	John Gavin, ...	do.	do. ...
	1661	John Dwyer, ...	do.	Prospect, West,
	1662	Charles Lynch, ...	do.	do. ...
	1663	Patrick Cahill, ...	Lt.-Col. Charles Fitzgerald, ...	Glenahilty, ...
	1664	James Kennedy, ...	do.	do. ...
	1665	John Nowlan, ...	T. W. Von Tunzelmann, ...	Gortsmakills, ...
	1666	Patrick Woods, ...	do.	do. ...
	1667	Mary Slattery, Rep. of Michl. Slattery & anor.	do.	do. ...
	1668	George Clarke, ...	Richard S. Fox, ...	Shanacashel and ampliary,
	1669	Daniel Kennedy, ...	do.	Killeen, ...
	1670	Joshua Fletcher, ...	do.	Garrynacolpa, ...
	1671	Edmond McGrath, junior,	do.	Drumlamar, ...
	1672	Do.	do.	Garryduff, ...
	1673	Henry Fletcher, ...	do.	Curtygrain, ...
	1674	Mathew Green, ...	do.	Carrig, ...
	1675	James Hogan, ...	do.	Cunlahanda, ...
	1676	John Clarke, ...	do.	Garranacolda, ...
	1677	Michael Hogan, ...	do.	do. ...
	1678	Do.	do.	do. ...
	1679	John McGrath, jun., Rep. of Mary McGrath.	do.	Ballydrinan, ...
	1680	Denis McGrath (Melvin),	do.	Dromlamar, ...
	1681	William O'Brien, ...	William Abbott and others, ...	Clarrigtaher, Abbott,
	1682	Thomas Green, ...	do.	do. ...
	1683	Patrick Slattery, ...	R. A. Mangan, ...	Ballyvasey, ...
	1684	Do.	do.	Upper Grange, ...
	1685	William Fitzgerald, ...	William H. White, ...	Ballydaggan, ...

TIPPERARY—*continued.*

Extent of Holding. Statute.	Poor Law Valuation.	Former Rent.	Judicial Rent.	Observations.	Value of Tenancy.
A. R. P.	£ s. d.	£ s. d.	£ s. d.		£ s. d.
77 1 18	10 0 0	13 10 8	11 15 0		
13 1 39	5 10 0	6 0 0	5 0 0		
30 0 0	8 5 0	14 19 8	18 10 0		
[illegible] 1 0	41 0 0	60 4 2	51 0 0		
9 1 [illegible]	4 13 0	6 8 8	6 2 4		
111 0 [illegible]	38 0 0	50 0 0	50 0 0		
28 0 10	8 5 0	11 5 3	11 5 9		
1 2 8	8 5 0	1 0 0	1 10 0	By consent.	
16 1 1	8 0 0	10 0 0	10 0 0		
16 2 [illegible]	16 5 0	30 0 0	25 0 0		
25 3 28	13 10 0	20 0 0	18 0 0		
30 3 0	14 3 0	18 0 0	17 0 0	Provision has been made in this case as regards a labourer.	
43 3 8	14 18 0	17 8 0	17 8 0		
18 0 8	7 0 0	11 11 6	10 10 0		
4 3 17	2 15 0	4 7 5	2 15 0		
9 2 33	4 10 0	7 1 4	6 5 0		
8 0 15	4 15 0	7 11 11	5 10 0		
105 1 28	49 10 0	79 13 8	70 0 0		
40 0 5	26 15 0	30 7 8	27 0 0		
[illegible] 3 34	41 13 0	49 12 4	44 10 0		
58 2 18	40 0 0	45 4 6	45 1 6		
88 0 39	23 10 0	28 4 0	29 0 0		
95 0 30	55 0 0	62 6 0	58 0 0		
111 2 33	61 10 0	70 11 8	68 0 0		
59 3 25	21 0 0	31 6 0	28 0 0		
64 0 37	36 15 0	37 0 0	34 0 0		
18 1 31	--	9 15 5	8 10 0		
20 3 38	8 15 0	9 13 7	8 0 0		
43 2 16	19 0 0	20 8 0	20 8 0		
23 0 18	14 0 0	13 15 7	13 10 0		
9 3 25	8 5 0	10 0 0	9 0 0		
39 0 0	48 5 0	60 0 0	61 10 0		
4 0 17	1 5 0	6 4 0	3 8 0		
31 1 11	18 15 0	25 13 2	19 10 0		
49 1 1	27 0 0	32 11 1	27 10 0		

Names of Assistant Commissioners by whom Cases were decided.	No.	Name of Tenant.	Name of Landlord.
Assistant Commissioners—			
T. D. Reardon (Legal). J. Gollock. T. Baldwin. W. C. Hemphill. William Evans.	1686	Nicholas Neill, ...	William H. White,
	1687	Edward Gardiner, ...	do. ...
	1688	Robert Moore, ...	Lord Dunalley, ...
	1689	James Oakley, ...	do. ...
	1690	Thomas Armitage, ...	do. ...
	1691	Denis Quirke, ...	William D. Farrer,
	1692	Michael Fitzpatrick, ...	do. ...
	1693	Thomas Cormack, ...	do. ...
	1694	Patrick Maher, ...	do. ...
	1695	John Carew, ...	do. ...
	1696	Terence Dunne, ...	do. ...
	1697	William Armitage, ...	do. ...
	1698	John Burns, ...	do. ...
	1699	Margaret Hogan, ...	do. ...
	1700	Bridget Nolan, ...	do. ...
	1701	Edward White, ...	do. ...
	1702	William Quirke, ...	Lady Margaret Charteris,
	1703	Ellen Wilkinson, ...	do. ...
	1704	Marga. M'Carthy, Admix. of Denis M'Carthy.	do. ...
	1705	Richard Heffernan, ...	do. ...
	1706	Morgan Sheehan, ...	do. ...

TIPPERARY—*continued.*

Extent of Holding. Statute.	Poor Law Valuation.	Former Rent.	Judicial Rent.	Observations.	Value of Tenancy.
A. R. P.	£ s. d.	£ s. d.	£ s. d.		£ s. d.
31 0 0	13 10 0	17 17 6	18 10 0		
9 0 15	6 0 0	7 10 0	4 14 0		
15 2 30	7 0 0	8 5 0	8 5 0		
43 0 15	13 15 0	11 14 0	14 10 0		
20 3 1	11 0 0	10 5 10	10 5 10		
43 2 37	26 0 0	33 16 3	28 0 0		
52 2 20	31 13 0	31 10 0	26 0 0		
60 1 31	23 0 0	33 14 6	33 0 0		
47 0 0	21 1 0	21 15 3	19 0 0		
90 2 5	13 5 0	16 11 10	15 11 10		
43 3 27	13 5 0	14 6 0	13 10 0		
44 2 14	16 0 0	23 0 0	20 0 0		
29 3 16	16 0 0	16 15 6	17 0 0		
21 1 16	10 10 0	12 5 5	12 5 5		
17 2 11	8 10 0	10 0 0	9 0 0		
33 3 34	16 15 0	19 16 0	17 0 0		
150 3 15	131 0 0	143 0 0	120 0 0		
49 3 16	45 0 0	55 0 0	48 10 0		
43 1 31	52 0 0	45 0 0	46 0 0		
97 0 30	70 0 0	84 0 0	66 0 0	Provision has been made in this case as regards a labourer.	
36 0 25	23 0 0	26 0 0	23 5 0		
27 1 17	16 17 0	24 0 6	16 0 0		
25 0 38	15 15 0	22 0 0	18 10 0		
53 2 21	35 10 0	60 0 0	57 0 0		
22 1 10	10 5 0	20 0 0	17 0 0		
61 1 0	15 0 0	33 10 5	41 10 0		
0 3 20	6 10 0	6 15 4	6 15 4		
1,834 0 5	1,216 15 0	1,331 2 6	1,183 19 7		

WATERFORD.

727	Michael Keane, ...	do.	Carrigeen, ...
728	Patrick Terry, ...	do.	Knockinpower, Lr.
729	Patrick Griffin, ...	do.	do. ...
730	Maurice Griffin, ...	do.	do. ...
731	Thomas Morrissey, ...	do.	Knockinpower, Up.
732	John Flynn, ...	H. P. Chearnley, ...	Scartadrum, ...
733	John Hellihan, ...	do.	do. ...
734	Patrick Grady, ...	do.	do. ...
735	James Grady, Rep. of Thomas Grady.	do.	do. ...
736	William Keever, ...	do.	Killeenan, ...
737	Thomas Keever, ...	do.	do. ...
738	James Hickey, ...	do.	do. ...
739	Patrick Murray, ...	do.	Mountain Castle,
740	Johanna McGrath, ...	do.	do. ...
741	Edmund Healy, ...	John D. Hargreaves and others,	Drumore, ...
742	Michael Daly, ...	do.	do. ...
743	John Flynn, ...	do.	do. ...
744	Maurice Hickey, ...	do.	do. ...
745	William Duggan, ...	do.	do. ...
746	Michael Keating, ...	do.	do. ...
747	John Carey, ...	do.	do. ...
748	Jeremiah McGrath, ...	Hon. James B. B. Roche and others.	Garteenakilla, Upper
749	Patrick Curran (Pat), ...	do.	Ballynamorty, 5th
750	Lawrence Walsh. ...	do.	Garteenakilla, ...
751	William Harty, ...	do.	Ballinamorty, 5th
752	James Curran (John), ...	do.	do. ...
753	Edmond P. Curran, ...	do.	Ballinamorty, 5th
754	Thomas Kelly, ...	do.	Garteenakilla, Upper
			Total, ...

WATERFORD—*continued.*

Extent of Holding. Statute.	Poor Law Valuation.	Former Rent.	Judicial Rent.	Observations.	Value of Tenancy.
A. R. P.	£ s. d.	£ s. d.	£ s. d.		£ s. d.
80 0 38	92 0 0	111 19 7	90 0 0		
139 0 30	185 15 0	189 1 8	164 0 0		
43 0 0	18 18 0	18 9 0	16 10 0		
99 0 5	75 0 0	94 10 0	84 10 0		
7 0 4	5 10 0	6 7 2	5 5 0		
6 2 10	5 15 0	7 11 2	5 15 0		
7 3 0	7 6 0	11 15 0	7 10 0		
4 1 0	4 5 0	6 7 8	4 10 0		
10 1 0	6 10 0	8 8 4	7 0 0	By consent.	
105 0 0	25 3 0	35 0 0	30 0 0	do.	
80 1 0	20 0 0	30 0 0	25 10 0	do.	
112 0 0	31 0 0	33 0 0	26 10 0	do.	
130 0 0	17 0 0	25 0 0	21 0 0	do.	
39 0 0	11 17 0	22 0 0	17 0 0	do.	
34 0 0	19 10 0	31 0 0	26 0 0	do.	
64 3 1	23 0 0	33 0 0	27 10 0	do.	
46 1 17	39 0 0	52 0 0	45 0 0	do.	
53 0 5	41 0 0	60 0 0	53 0 0	do.	
110 0 38	59 15 0	95 14 6	80 0 0		
36 0 6	12 5 0	19 6 8	16 0 0		
29 1 39	21 0 0	30 17 8	25 0 0		
33 1 9	26 0 0	34 9 8	29 10 0		
40 2 35	38 0 0	51 6 2	41 8 8		
67 0 25	45 0 0	42 0 0	17 0 0		
81 3 9	21 10 0	31 16 4	22 0 0		
1 3 15	1 5 0	2 0 0	1 10 0		
57 2 18	84 0 0	48 1 1	41 0 0		
7 0 14	4 5 0	6 11 0	5 10 0		
6 1 6	4 10 0	7 6 8	6 5 0		
51 2 0	37 0 0	12 4 0	35 0 0		
76 1 36	43 10 0	84 10 8	67 0 0		
80 3 24	55 0 0	49 16 8	30 10 0		
1,863 0 19	1,010 5 0	1,436 1 10	1,239 8 8		

CIVIL BILL COURT.

SUMMARY.

Of Cases in which Judicial Rents have been Fixed by the Civil Bill Courts and notified to the Irish Land Commission during the month of December, 1883.

	Number of Cases in which Judicial Rents have been fixed.	Acreage.	Tenement Valuation.	Former Rent.	Judicial Rent.
		Statute Acres.	£ s. d.	£ s. d.	£ s. d.
LEINSTER—					
Longford, ...	72	1,766 0 37¼	1,065 1 0	1,449 12 5½	1,145 9 4
MUNSTER—					
Cork, ...	1	55 1 32	35 0 0	45 3 3	35 0 0

IRELAND.

LEINSTER, ...	72	1,766 0 37¼	1,065 1 0	1,449 12 5½	1,145 9 4
MUNSTER, ...	1	55 1 32	35 0 0	45 3 3	35 0 0
TOTAL, ...	73	1,821 2 29¼	1,100 1 0	1,494 15 7½	1,180 9 4

PROVINCE OF

COUNTY OF

County Court Judge.	No.	Name of Tenant.	Name of Landlord.	Townland.
John Adye Curran.	64	Anne Kirk,	A. W. B. Greville,	Granard Hill,
	65	Thomas Reilly,	do.	Kinkillew,
	66	Margaret Ceaskey,	do.	Cartron,
	67	Michael Lee,	do.	Ballinacross,
	68	Michael O'Reilly,	do.	Part of Tonnel,
	69	Mary Bermingham,	do.	Clongowes,
	70	Richard Gilpin,	do.	Ballybrien,
	71	Honor S. Baron,	do.	Gaول,
	72	Peter Reilly,	do.	Ballyglichrist,
	73	Patrick McCabe,	do.	Carlow,
	74	George Strong,	do.	Cartron,
	75	Owen Mallon,	Mrs. Mary Adelaide Archdall,	Geldin,
	76	Michael Donoghue,	do.	Carrickmaquirk,
	77	Thomas Connolly,	do.	do.
	78	Peter Murphy,	do.	do.
	79	James Morrow,	Antonio E. Edgeworth,	Drumlary,
	80	William Griffith,	do.	Kraiganaamne,
	81	Do.	do.	Edgeworthstown,
	82	John Duffy, deceased, per Thomas Duffy,	George Mannsely,	Legga,
	83	Mary Duffy,	do.	Moyne,
	84	Margaret Mulligan,	do.	Derragh,
	85	Daniel Mulvey,	Lord Annaly,	Finnilick,
	86	John Casey,	do.	Cornacrow,
	87	Francis Farrell,	do.	Knock,
	88	Do.	do.	Cartoonagar and Commons, North
	89	John Casey,	do.	Tullavrane,
	90	James Cassender,	do.	Kilcurry,
	91	John McCormick,	do.	do.
	92	John Casey,	do.	Aughnacarr,
	93	Do.	do.	Knock,

LEINSTER.

LONGFORD.

Extent of Holding, Statute.			Poor Law Valuation.			Former Rent.			Judicial Rent.			Observations.
A.	R.	P.	£	s.	d.	£	s.	d.	£	s.	d.	
16	0	3½	—			20	9	0	21	10	0	
7	2	30	5	0	0	5	11	0	4	18	0	
[illegible]	1	4	15	15	0	20	6	6	16	16	0	
63	1	16	64	0	0	86	15	6	59	12	6	
25	3	7	28	10	0	39	10	0	26	0	0	
16	3	1	16	0	0	21	2	6	15	5	0	
13	3	11	11	10	0	15	4	1	12	0	0	
27	1	0	28	10	0	50	0	0	41	0	0	
13	3	0	34	0	0	45	0	0	35	0	0	
17	1	2	12	15	0	16	8	2	13	10	0	
30	0	34	35	0	0	45	0	0	35	0	0	
6	2	28	6	5	0	5	10	2	4	10	0	
20	2	16	9	5	0	9	2	0	8	0	0	
6	2	25	3	16	0	3	14	0	2	0	0	
9	0	19	8	15	0	3	11	0	3	14	0	
[illegible]	0	31	10	15	0	15	0	0	11	16	6	
61	0	5	34	10	0	30	0	5	30	0	0	
6	1	20	6	0	0	9	0	0	6	8	0	
61	3	6	19	0	0	22	0	0	16	16	0	
27	1	13	14	0	0	17	0	0	14	0	0	
26	2	23	16	10	0	17	0	0	14	0	0	
51	0	11	47	10	0	65	0	0	38	0	0	
25	2	0	15	16	0	14	0	0	17	0	0	
6	1	10	5	10	0	9	0	0	7	18	0	
[illegible]	0	19	30	5	0	30	0	0	24	0	0	
19	2	5	12	0	0	18	0	0	12	0	0	
30	2	26	15	5	0	30	0	0	16	10	0	
37	2	38	19	18	0	25	0	0	18	0	0	
5	0	0	5	0	0	8	0	0	5	8	0	
7	3	7	5	10	0	12	0	0	6	0	0	

COUNTY OF

County Court Judge.	No.	Name of Tenant.	Name of Landlord.	Townland.
JOHN ADYE CURRAN.	94	John Casey, ...	Lord Annaly, ...	Aughinamy,
	95	James Rhatigan, ...	do.	[illegible],
	96	Thomas Kenny, ...	do.	Ballyglassan,
	97	Owen Gill, ...	do.	Tuckleary,
	98	Francis Farrell, ...	do.	Kainch,
	99	Do.	do.	Aghamore,
	100	Hugh Whitney, ...	John H. Jessop, ...	Bohee, North,
	101	Lawrence Egan, Repr. James Egan, decd.	Messrs. Stewart and Kincaid,	Morain,
	102	Pat Deere, ...	Christopher Reynolds, ...	Kelleter,
	103	Bridget Cunningham, ...	Michael Murry, ...	Lightfield,
	104	James Farrell, .	Messrs. Richard and Maurice Fitzgerald.	Loughan,
	105	James Creally, ..	do.	do.
	106	Patrick Dalton, ...	Luke White, ...	Aughmagarron,
	107	Anne Reilly, ...	do.	Mulbarra,
	108	Thomas Mulligan, ...	Rev. Francis Dopping. ...	Culray,
	109	[illegible]	Mrs. J. A. Motherwell, ...	[illegible],
	110	Mark Rourke, ...	Robert O'Brien and Messrs. Carey and Clay.	Corrakelly,
	111	Charles Rourke, ...	do.	do.
	112	Mary Murtagh, ...	Arthur O'Beirne, ...	Trillickwarry,
	113	Alexander Wilson, ...	The Ven. Henry Stewart, ...	Duroga,
	114	Francis Cosgrove, ...	John Galbraith, ...	Derrymanie,
	115	Philip Brady, ...	Edward Fitzgerald, ...	Fallasboy,
	116	Thomas Shaw, ...	Mrs. Margaret Magan, ...	Lisdanagh,
	117	Ellen Shaw, ...	do.	do.
	118	Luke Killian, ...	do.	do.
	119	Pat Commerton, ...	do	do.
	120	Michael Killian, ...	do.	do.
	121	Patrick Cosgrave, ...	Mrs. Margt. Howell, Mrs. M. E. Beatty and Mrs. M. J. Beatty,	Rathane,
	122	Philip Reilly, ...	do.	do.
	123	James Reilly, ...	do.	do.
	124	Thomas Clarke, ...	William Bond, ...	Glenaugh,
	125	Mary O'Hara, ...	Henry Sholto Douglas, ...	Bawn,
	126	James Conway, ...	Patrick Rhatigan, ...	Lisnamore,
	127	Robert Wright, ...	John H. Jessop, ...	Corragh,
	128	Thomas Mills, ...	William Shaw, Maria Shaw and others.	Clonara,

25	8	16	30	10	0	30	0	0	23	0	0
5	8	1	5	0	8	8	0	0	8	0	0
17	1	18	7	5	0	14	0	0	8	0	0
57	0	[illegible]	16	15	0	33	13	4	21	10	0
43	2	24	13	10	0	17	14	8	16	10	0
11	1	[illegible]	6	5	0	9	11	2	7	15	0
5	1	0	1	18	0	4	8	4	5	8	4
23	0	0	7	10	0	30	0	0	11	0	0
23	0	0	7	15	0	20	0	0	11	0	0
27	2	13	19	0	0	25	6	0	18	0	0
18	0	0	18	0	0	13	1	0	13	0	0
16	1	13	7	18	0	10	10	8	9	0	0
10	3	6	5	15	0	8	8	0	6	18	0
88	0	30	8	15	0	13	0	0	9	10	0
25	0	23	8	15	0	18	0	0	9	10	0
26	8	10	19	18	0	18	0	0	10	10	0
46	0	31	11	18	0	37	0	0	83	0	0
20	1	34	6	15	0	7	10	0	6	13	6
19	8	31	19	10	0	13	13	0	11	11	0
6	1	18	5	18	0	3	6	8	1	18	6
11	1	7	10	11	0	10	13	4	5	0	0
18	1	0	15	10	0	16	0	0	13	0	0
11	0	0	11	11	0	10	13	4	6	0	0
5	3	8	5	12	0	5	8	8	4	8	0
15	3	37	18	10	0	14	0	0	18	0	0
80	0	0	28	10	0	36	5	0	31	0	0
51	1	34	35	10	0	58	5	0	30	10	0
51	0	20	35	0	0	45	5	0	26	10	0
33	1	26	11	0	0	16	15	0	13	0	0
61	5	31	72	0	0	25	14	6	18	0	0
35	1	18	17	0	0	22	0	0	17	0	0
9	0	0	1	5	0	8	8	0	5	5	0

COUNTY OF

County Court Judge.	No.	Name of Tenant.	Name of Landlord.	Townland.
John Adye Curran,	129	Bernard Brady, ...	John Whelan, ...	Rathbrackan, part of,
	130	Timothy Sullivan, ...	Dacre Hamilton, Robert H. Stubber, and others,	Fernhill, part of,
	131	Charles O'Reilly, Rep. of Rev. B. O'Reilly,	Thomas Gregory, ...	Kilteelan, ...
	132	Patrick Horan, ...	Patrick Shaughnessy, ...	Glencoughill, ...
	133	Patt Beason, ...	Colonel E. R. King-Harman,	Feyglin, ...
	134	John Smith, ...	Francis Edward Grier, ...	Roano, ...
	135	Amelia Job, ...	Colonel E. R. King-Harman,	Gunary, ...
				Total, ...

PROVINCE OF

LONGFORD—*continued.*

Extent of Holding Statute.	Poor Law Valuation.	Former Rent.	Judicial Rent.	Observations.	Value of Tenancy
A. R. P.	£ s. d.	£ s. d.	£ s. d.		£
37 2 [illegible]	35 10 0	36 11 0	[illegible] 10 0		
73 0 18	45 15 0	56 1 8	45 0 0		
[illegible] 0 [illegible]	[illegible] 15 6	[illegible] 14 8	80 0 0	By consent.	
[illegible] 3 [illegible]	17 0 0	20 0 0	18 0 0	do.	
27 2 26	18 15 0	19 8 0	15 0 0		
18 0 35	--	10 5 8½	11 0 0		
23 1 20	15 15 0	19 3 0	14 0 0		
1,756 0 37½	1,085 1 0	1,419 12 5½	1,165 9 4		

MUNSTER.

CORK.

58 1 22	26 0 0	35 5 2	25 0 0		210 0 0

SUMMARY.

Showing, according to Counties and Provinces, the Number of Cases in which Judicial Rents have been Fixed, upon the Reports of Valuers appointed by the Irish Land Commission, on the Joint Applications of Landlords and Tenants.

	Number of Cases in which Judicial Rents have been Fixed.	Acreage.	Tenement Valuation.	Former Rent.	Judicial Rent.
		Statute Acres.	£ s. d.	£ s. d.	£ s. d.
ULSTER—					
Donegal, ...	18	284 1 20	97 7 0	131 10 2	89 5 0
LEINSTER—					
Kilkenny, ...	1	33 1 25	19 0 0	25 0 0	22 0 0

IRELAND.

ULSTER, ...	18	284 1 20	97 7 0	131 10 2	89 5 0
LEINSTER, ...	1	33 1 25	19 0 0	25 0 0	22 0 0
TOTAL, ...	19	317 3 5	116 7 0	156 10 2	111 5 0

Rents fixed upon the Reports of Valuers appointed by the Irish Land

PROVINCE OF

COUNTY OF

Number.	Name of Tenant.	Name of Landlord.	Townland.
1	Neil Farren, ...	John Loughrey,	Trumaly,
2	James Farren,	do.	do.
3	John Brisson,	do.	do.
4	Margaret Harrigan,	do.	do.
5	Kate Reddy,	do.	do.
6	Neil Logan, ...	do.	do.
7	John Logan, senior,	do.	do.
8	Bernard McLaughlin,	do.	do.
9	Hannah Margay,	do.	do.
10	Mary Greamy,	do.	do.
11	Margery Doherty,	do.	do.
12	James Harley,	do.	do.
13	Ellen Coyle, ...	do.	do.
14	John Bradley,	do.	do.
15	Daniel McLaughlin,	do.	do.
16	Patrick Doherty,	do.	do.
17	John Harley,	do.	do.
18	James Quigley,	do.	do.
			Total,

PROVINCE OF

Commission on the Joint Applications of Landlords and Tenants.

ULSTER.

DONEGAL.

Extent of Holding, Statute measure.	Poor Law Valuation.	Former Rent.	Judicial Rent.	Observations.
A. R. P.	£ s. d.	£ s. d.	£ s. d.	
14 0 15	4 15 0	6 7 9	5 0 0	
14 0 15	4 15 0	6 7 9	5 0 0	
27 3 20	8 0 0	11 7 0	7 6 0	
7 1 12	1 15 0	2 15 6	2 0 0	
4 1 0	1 15 0	4 0 0	2 0 0	
24 3 10	5 0 0	9 6 0	4 8 0	
11 1 20	2 15 0	4 6 0	3 0 0	
16 3 20	1 15 0	6 1 0	3 14 0	
32 3 30	10 15 0	16 16 0	10 10 0	
11 1 20	3 5 0	5 16 0	3 7 0	
10 3 5	3 10 0	4 7 3	2 10 0	
7 0 9	4 2 6	6 6 6	3 15 0	
21 1 30	7 10 0	10 14 0	6 18 0	
10 0 26	5 15 0	6 6 0	4 10 0	
7 0 35	2 7 0	2 16 0	2 5 0	
35 1 25	15 5 0	17 0 0	12 10 0	
7 0 9	4 3 6	5 5 6	2 15 0	
22 1 19	5 5 0	7 8 6	7 0 0	
304 1 20	97 7 0	181 10 2	89 5 0	

LEINSTER.

KILKENNY.

www.ingramcontent.com/pod-product-compliance
Lightning Source LLC
Chambersburg PA
CBHW031109020726
47495CB00007B/2116